Lois Crockett

Tough Luck Lane

ALL RIGHTS RESERVED

Publisher's Note:
This is a work of fiction. All names, characters, places, and
events are the work of the author's imagination.
Any resemblance to real persons, places, or events is
coincidental.

Solstice Publishing - www.solsticepublishing.com

Tough Luck Lane

Lois Crockett

Dedication

For John and Ellen
With Love

Chapter One

I was born in a trailer off Tough Luck Lane in Lake Okeechobee, Florida. Thirty years later, I'm heading out. After packing up my recently deceased mother's belongings and the legacy of booze she left me, I decided to change my life for the better and head to Fort Lauderdale. It was interesting telling people I lived on "Tough Luck Lane" when they asked. It's almost as if I was *asking* for trouble. Hell, a lot of times they just didn't *believe* me! As if I could make up something like that. You learn real quick and early how to keep your mouth shut on Tough Luck Lane. So, I lied and said I lived on Main Street. That always worked for me, but there is no Main Street in Lake Okeechobee.

This legacy of booze was all that was left after my no-account brother Ed made off with the bankbook, which held the family nest egg of about $10,000. He'd *said* he'd come to see Mom. Yeah, Mom and her bankbook. Well, she never could refuse him; maybe out of pity, seeing as how he's been in jail more than out in his forty years.

The trailer had been paid off years ago and sold through the DMV to a new owner. The land got me about $1,700. Screw Ed—he got his. I'd been able to stash a couple bucks off Mom's social security and collect some more coin working part-time at the local bar, The Swamp, when I wasn't taking care of Mom at the end of her days. I figured a move would do me some good.

All this high finance was giving me an ache in my fingers as I pressed the miniscule buttons of my tiny pocketbook calculator, running up a tally to see where I stood: about $2,800. I became aware of the trailer, its faded curtains, scarred paneling and musty carpet. The place needed a real dusting and a cleaning, the pink paint on the outside had been peeling real bad for years; the little rose garden out front was all dried up and I had to go. Mom had entertained a lot, mostly herself and me, since Dad ran off about fifteen years ago. When the cancer came, she quit smoking and drinking and cleaning, as well. All that was left was a mailbox full of bills and about eight bottles of industrial size liquor. You know, the big, expensive multi-gallon bottles that'll break your arm trying to pour a shot–God forbid you drop the bottle. Don't ask, I've done it, and it's not hard to do.

Looking at piles of bills that weren't mine, and even if they were, I couldn't pay them anyway, was too damned depressing. I packed up anything worth something and tried to cram it all with the booze and a world-class shoe collection, into my '87 White T-Bird, "The Mir." I felt a small twinge of sadness and more than a pang of guilt as I locked the trailer door for the last time, slipping the key under the step mat as I'd promised for the new tenant. The faded pink roses seemed to wave goodbye to me as a zephyr ruffled their petals.

Hell, I was happy to be leaving, no longer a slave to the clock for Mom's meds schedule, chemo sessions, wheelchairs and oxygen; all the trappings of the old and sick. I missed her. Sort of. I looked down at my watch; it was nine o'clock in the morning, time to get moving. It was hot, sticky and sunny, a typical day on Lake Okeechobee in mid-February. A fat local mosquito decided I'd make a fine breakfast. I swatted uselessly at the bite welt, but it was a done deal. I headed straight for The Mir.

Named after the Russian Space Station launched the same year, The Mir was just as old and certainly just as decrepit. I figured it probably cost about the same to keep running. But it was a real pretty white T-Bird with a soft blue velveteen interior and Big-8 under the hood. It got me where I had to go, most times. I bought it off one of Ed's friends who needed bail money awhile back. I'd promised to keep the car in good running condition for when he got out but he skipped on the bail so The Mir was mine, free and clear.

I figured I got the better part of the family estate. You can meet a lot more people and close a lot more deals with a couple of well-liquored-up acquaintances than you can with $10,000. About all ten grand will get you is three months' rent and living expenses and that's not even living in the fast lane. Hell, that would last a week, maybe, livin' high. I thought about my brother and wished him luck with his choice as I started up The Mir and felt the powerful rumble of the engine spring to life.

My name is Stacey. Stacey Jennifer Longacre, a fine Southern name, I've been told. I'm sure as hell there's some rich southern Longacres someplace, but we're not them and I'm not about to look them up, either. I'd probably find another bunch of sick old relatives I'd wind up emptying bedpans for. Even though I was sorry Mom passed, I'm out of that game and on to greener pastures, or bluer waters, hell, whatever.

So, I took the long drive down 441 looking at Big Sugar's fields, past Pahokee. Now *that's* a trip for a nice girl like me driving a beat up old car, which breaks down more than it runs. I got through all the crack boys buzzing around me wanting to play "Let's Make A Deal!" I think, maybe, they recognized the car, but not the current driver. With ponderous grace, The Mir kept rolling right on through to more endless cane fields and into Palm Beach County.

I passed on the crack, it's shit, anyway. "Pahokee Poof" we used to call it in the good old days. The real deal comes out of Miami or North Lauderdale. But I'd given it up years ago and, since I'd retired from partying, didn't know where you'd go for it now, certainly not Pahokee.

I stopped at a tumbledown drive-thru

convenience/beauty-supply store and grabbed a Dr. Pepper with a bag of BBQ Fritos for breakfast at their drive-thru. The young, skinny black store clerk eyed me suspiciously as he handed me my soda and chips. I paid with exact change. As I exited the drive-thu, I mused I was happy not to have parked The Mir while the safety of the T-bird's fast 8-cylinder engine purred beneath my feet on the pedal.

Now, few grand isn't enough to even breathe the air in Palm Beach County, so I turned the Mir south, straight for Broward's county seat, Fort Liquordale. With all the booze I was importing, I thought it was a good choice. I owned some really good-fitting jeans and a complete wardrobe of T-shirts begged, borrowed, and stolen from who knows where. Oh yeah, I had a dress, too, an old TV, and a radio-alarm, and my Tigger slippers: you know, the little comforts of life.

Actually, compared to Miami, Fort Lauderdale is a *dinky* city. With all that beachfront, though, who am I to say? I just hoped I could find an affordable place, something new to wear, and a new pair of shoes. I daydreamed I'd land a real job as a bartender in a place that didn't just jerk beer and run shots until you pour the patrons out the door at closing like I did in the old Swamp. I was a little worried. I'm more of a drunk-wrangler than a fancy bartender, so I was really concerned I might not cut it. I remembered the Swamp back home looked like a bog and smelled just as bad. It was located in the middle of a marsh on teetering stilts, built from weather-beaten clapboard yanked off the frames of hurricane-wrecked houses. Most of the good old boys drinking the watered-down booze and cheap, watery draught beer were teetering as well. I even invented a drink, one time, of ginger ale and Dunk's draught, calling it Swamp Water for serving to the more inebriated patrons in order to give them "something." Drunks always like to keep their mouths moist; it doesn't make no nevermind with what. The customers either looked like they needed to be buried in the swamp, especially after closing, or like somebody had forgotten to bury them a few weeks out the morning after.

Cosmos, chocolatinis, Christ. I didn't want to jerk beer anymore, but I sure as hell didn't want to make sissy drinks with flowers and umbrellas in them either. I wanted to get something regular–maybe a nice sports bar where the guys are cute and nobody orders pink drinks! Well, maybe a rumrunner with a good stiff 151 float. I'd do that.

The first order of the day was to find a place to park my shoe collection and stash all that liquor. Hell, maybe I could have opened my own bar.

I had no idea where to begin, so I decided to start with a cup of coffee and a piece of pie at some local diner and talk up the waitress to help me figure out what's what. Usually, some good conversation, covered by a very generous tip, of course, greases the wheels of commerce towards turning in my direction. I was amazed at the selection of eateries in that town. I could most likely eat my way from one end to the other and never have to bother looking for a place to live as long as I had money and appetite and didn't need a whole lot of sleep, either. I figured I could go about a week. Pity I'd passed on the "Pahokee Poof"; I could have kept going for two weeks. Of course, I wouldn't have eaten very much.

I finally settled on this little diner by the beach, which wasn't, as it turned out, even in Fort Lauderdale. Begging your pardon, it was Lauderdale-by-the-Sea, *with* dashes, if you please. Now, I know any time they put an "e" on the end of a word, such as Foxe Chase (a toney RV park up by Lake Placid), or they hyphenate a couple of words together, such as Boca-Pointe, the price goes up. Never mind neighborhoods where they *name* the houses like people. So, Lauderdale-by-the-Sea was double trouble with four words hooked up together instead of just two. The Rule is: if it sounds more expensive and looks more expensive, it *is* more expensive. It's no better or worse, judging from the lukewarm coffee and cold apple pie I was served. It's just pricier and snottier. Even the waitress was snotty and looked at me like I was road kill. I think if I ever have a house big enough, I can name it like a kid or dog or something, I'll call it "Fred" so people don't think I'm the kind of person who puts on airs. Imagine making the butler say, "Welcome to Fred", to guests with a straight face.

I had my coffee and pie, paid the bitch—yeah, I tipped her—a *little*, okay? I'm not that much of a bitch, nor am I road kill. It was barely a tip. The clock on the counter showed high noon, and instead of a showdown with a snotty waitress over a crappy tip, I walked briskly out of the diner into the first day of my new life to think things over.

Having had no luck at the diner in Lauderdale-dash-by-dash-the-dash-Sea, I headed north, up the A-1-A to Pompano. Pompano is a little smaller and more relaxed than Fort Lah-dee-dah, where, I hear, you have to wear high heels to the pool at some of the fancy resorts and condos. In some places, even the men as well. In spite of my sufficient supply of heels, high and otherwise, I decided that was not for me. Nor were the fancy rents advertised in some of the roach motels I'd seen while driving around the Fort proper.

I found a side street just south of Atlantic Boulevard. Since noon on Tuesday wasn't usually prime time for the beach in a lower-middle-class neighborhood, I figured I'd have pretty good parking luck. The Mir was loaded with my all and only shit and I would just curl up and die if it got stolen. My Tigger slippers are irreplaceable, not to mention the rest of my shoe collection gleaned from consignment shops from Boca to the Palm Beaches. The collection included a particularly lucky find, an ancient pair of black Jimmy Choos. The Choo high-heeled sandals didn't even look worn when I bought them—

those rich old ladies just get tired of shit and give it away for a price, of course. I turned into an empty lot and felt the soft scrunch of gravel under my tires. Shit. Usually, that soft gravel harbors a nail or two just waiting to jump out and bite a tire. But here I was, let the fates decide their will.

Getting out of the car, I stood with the door open and took a good hard look around the neighborhood. It seemed okay. Directly in front of me was a two-story building with chipped white paint surrounded by several ramshackle bungalows with the same chipped-paint look, but in washed-out salmon pink. They were partially hidden by coconut palms, large ferns and other standard SoFla flora. It doesn't matter if you have a green thumb, a brown thumb, a black thumb, a white thumb, or even no thumbs at all. Everything grows here: a lot. It's a constant battle keeping the plant life at bay, and I've often wondered if some of it might even be carnivorous if left to grow on its own for very long.

I spotted an old guy with a dingy white commodore's cap tipped over his eyes, sleeping on a ratty chaise lounge. An ancient mango tree shaded what passed for a courtyard. Bare brown dirt bordered by scraggly yellow monkey grass sported some old, ratty PVC pipe patio furniture topped by moldy cushions. I figured I'd just ask if it was okay to park where I was for about an hour or so, and maybe pay out a buck or two for the privilege.

Walking up to him, I gently tapped him on the shoulder and said, "Hey, captain," very softly.

He stirred, snuffled a couple times and, wiping his nose on his hand and then wiping his hand on his shorts, mumbled incoherently before rising. I was sorry I touched him.

"Ugh, whaaa…" he sputtered, gradually waking up from what must have been a King Kong-sized hangover judging from the reek of beer and God-knows-what-else issued thickly from his pores. "Uh, you…oh! Miss!" he started, "Yeah, yeah, what? Can I help you?" he asked blearily, slurred and slow. He reached down and knocked over an empty beer can next to his chaise.

"Um, yeah, maybe you can, man," I replied. Years of drunk wrangling had taught me that no one wakes up from a hangover fast or easy. It takes time to get to the point, have it understood, and get a response. It's kind of like talking with a bottle; all liquid and no response, whatsoever. So, I stood there and waited for The Captain to get the cotton out of his mouth with a couple of good hacks. He swept the cobwebs out of his head by slowly wiping his palm over his sweaty face.

"I'm just parked over here for a few and want to know if it's okay," I finished, when I felt he was ready for it. I didn't mention whether it would be a few minutes, a few hours, or a few days—not that it mattered within his current reality and realm of understanding.

"Oh, yeah, sure. Danny'll be back at five or six. Come back then," he answered and artfully placed the cap over his face again, settled back on the ratty chaise and, immediately, was deep in drunken dreamland once again.

"Sweet dreams, Cap'n," I said, walking back towards The Mir to double check the locks and get my bearings. Sure as shit, The Mir had a flat left front tire.

Deciding I could worry about that later, I walked north up A-1-A towards Atlantic. The traffic was sparse and the tourists were somewhere, but not here. I got to the corner and spotted a little outdoor coffee shop on the southeast corner and thought I might try my luck there. Hell, who knew who'd pass by? In Pompano. Right. I found a small bistro table on the sidewalk and sat down. The cheesy vinyl umbrella overhead did nothing but block the breeze, which made the air beneath it humid and still. The last thing I needed was a cup of hot coffee, so I decided this wasn't for me, picked up my pocketbook and left before a waiter pounced on me.

Heading west on Atlantic, I saw another coffee shop across the street: Dana's Diner. Almost next to Dana's was an old, well-worn strip mall with a shoe store not a spit from where I was standing after jaywalking across the street. Having about $2,794 in my pocketbook and a shoe store within spending distance, I defined my priorities. I had no plan where I was going to go, or live, or work, but there were new s*hoes* in close proximity. I ambled over to the shoe store, trying to look as if I shopped there all the time, knew exactly what they had and was rather choosy, to boot. I sniffed with disdain at the goodies in the window, more of an act, actually, they had some hotties in there! And, not thirty minutes later, I was walking out wearing a pair of high platform wedge espadrille ankle-tie sandals in a pretty beige tone that almost matched my walk-around tan. Boxed up along with my old consignment sandals, a new pair of cutesy red leather and cork thong wedgies so comfy I could probably sleep standing up, and why not? …an adorable pair of surfer-girl flip-flop sandals that made me hear the ocean just standing in them. I'm a shoe freak, when in doubt, take 'em all. I was also about $150 lighter. We do define our priorities, don't we?

Delighted with and bolstered by the utter satisfaction of my purchases, after the disaster in Lauderdale-by-the-Sea, I needed that little boost and headed off to Dana's Diner, shoe bags in tow, and a *big* smile on my face. That was something I hadn't felt like doing for a while. There's something about a woman with three new pairs of shoes, (four pairs are definitely overkill: Imelda territory), in pretty boutique bags that not only makes her *feel* good, but look terrific as well. Maybe it's just that afterglow from spending a pile of money she absolutely doesn't have on something she absolutely doesn't need, but what the hell?

The cold blast of AC in Dana's woke me out of my shoe-phoria and back into the real world. The steaming hot coffee smelled fantastic and I spotted some freshly baked blueberry muffins in a cake stand on the counter. This was my kind of place. The waitress at the counter smiled at me and I sidled on over to her, smiling back, shoeboxes gently rustling in boutique tissue paper in their bags.

"Hi! See you've been over to Pizzzazzz," she smiled openly, indicating the bags. There's nothing like one shoe freak recognizing another in the wilds of sensible-shoe-wearing Birkenstock folk, which probably means the rest of the planet.

"Yeah," I sighed. "I think I'm in love," as I took a seat.

"Coffee, honey?" she asked as I tenderly set down the Pizzzazzz bags. I noticed her name was "Tracey" by the name badge on her pink uniform. Stacey–Tracey; I was certain the connection was destiny.

"Yeah, great, with cream, please. Thank you," and ordered a blueberry muffin.

"Cool. They were made fresh this morning and they're good. Just had one myself before you walked in." I felt the first bud of friendship starting to bloom and quickly put my guard up behind a quasi-façade of humor.

"Good thing I was shopping, I wouldn't have wanted to interrupt your brunch."

"You woulda waited, honey. That muffin was good," Tracey parried back.

I took my coffee and looked over the soothing blue theme of the diner's décor-blue walls, blue leatherette booths and counter seats, a blue and white tile floor. The place was a cool, soothing oasis. I looked over at the cashier's glass display case which held yet more muffins to go and got back to business, setting my coffee mug down on the clean white counter, savoring the contemplation of my own blueberry muffin.

"You're new?" Tracey asked.

"Yeah, just came in from Okeechobee."

"Some treat, huh? Okeechobee to Pompano," she kidded.

"Well," I answered, "I'm really thinking of moving to this area."

Tracey nodded and the conversation continued. The place was slow; the lunch rush had finished early. She busied herself cleaning and talking, explaining she was pretty new to the area as well, from New Jersey. The top subject for discussion was Pizzzazzz, the shoe boutique, a close second to her favorite shoe store in Paramus, Shopping Mecca of the World. "Pretty new" in South Florida means about five years or less. If you can tough out the first five years, you'll be okay. We are The South, after all, not The Shore–that's The Keys. We played twenty questions and at the end of the session, while I hadn't found a place or a job, the muffin was scrumptious, and I'd found a friend. That was okay, too.

"Here's my number, Stacey," Tracey offered, handing me a matchbook with her phone number neatly written on the inside cover. "Call me when you get yours."

"Will do," I said, laying a ten and a five on the counter. "Keep the change."

"Keep comin' back like that and we'll both be able to go to Pizzzazzz," she said, grinning.

"It's a date!" I promised and headed out the door to The Mir, stuck in the parking lot.

It wasn't a nail that murdered my left front tire, but some sort of hard metal cable wire, placed on this earth for the sole purpose of flattening innocent unsuspecting rubber. The only thing to do was offload the booze and shit out of the trunk and go through the pain-in-the-ass process of putting on the spare. Just as I'd gotten the trunk open, The Captain came shuffling by just in time to see all the booze inside. And the flat.

"Need help with that, lady?" The Captain drawled. I wondered when, in the sobriety process, I had gained several years in The Captain's eyes and had gone from "miss" to "lady." I also wondered if he was asking whether I needed help with the booze or the flat. I took a chance.

"Yeah, jack's in the back. Give me a hand and I'll get you a drink when we're all done."

"Good enough," he said, proceeding to remove the jack, crowbar, and spare tire out of the trunk after helping with the booze. "Lotta good stuff here, lady."

Damn! There was that lady shit again. "Look, Captain, my name is Stacey." I tried to sound nice, but it came out flat.

"Okay, lady, uh, Stacey. Whatever. My name's Bill. But I useta be a captain," he answered.

"All rightee then, how about you call me Stacey and I call you Captain Bill, and we get this tire changed and have us a good drink?"

"You got it, lady." There was no use.

I was surprised at how wiry and coordinated The Captain was, comfortably moving from task to task. Ten minutes later, with the flat changed and the spare tightly in place, he ducked around a corner of a row of buildings facing the parking lot and, miraculously, given the circumstances, came up with a couple of clean cups for our drinks.

"You need ice, lady?" he asked.

"Stacey, please. And yes, if you have ice that would be great."

He ducked around back and retrieved some ice. There are some things in the world one is better off not knowing, so I didn't bother to ask where he got it.

"Danny'll be back at about five or six, he can tell you where to get that tire plugged," The Captain offered. We lifted our cups and toasted *whatever* with a smidgeon of "the good stuff" as the captain called it.

"Danny?" I asked curiously.

"Yeah... he's at work right now."

And you're not, I thought, but said, "And you're on a day off?" Was that polite or what?

"Honey, I'm on a *life* off." He laughed and held out his cup for a refill. I needed the flat plugged and maybe this Danny had a line on what was what around here. I figured what the hell, poured us both another tot of booze and settled in with the captain to wait for Danny.

Actually, The Captain was very nice. He used to be a *real* captain of a 100-footer until this little problem of drinking got in the way. He used to hobnob with the hoi-polloi, so I figured maybe, after all, he wasn't stupid or useless, just kind of sad.

After about an hour, I was feeling hunger pangs again. I'd had nothing but tidbits since I'd started this day, and I was in the mood for some real food.

"Hey, Cap'n," I said, "is there a store around here?"

"Yeah, down the block. I need some beer to go with this shit," he replied.

"Shit!" I raised an eyebrow. "You said it was 'good stuff.'"

"Yeah, if you drink alcohol. I like beer." So, *now* he was getting choosy.

I sighed, "Okay... show me." And off we went, around the corner and down the block to a small Mom-and-Pop convenience store tucked into a palmetto-studded parking lot. I found some cheap American *cheez* slices, but hey, what could I do? I paid Mom or Pop–I wasn't sure whom. They were of Asian extraction, small, old, grizzled, and basically interchangeable. The Captain found his beer and looked at me. I paid for it with a skyward roll of my eyes and a sigh. The Captain shrugged and took the six-pack of cheap beer as his due. We trundled back to the courtyard and settled in on the stoop to drink–The Captain; peel some convenient-paper-between-the-slices of *cheez*–me, and wait some more for this Danny person.

A big, shiny black Ford F-150 roared into one of the

parking spaces. It kicked up dust and gravel as the driver made a short stop and just barely nicked the hedges. A small wiry man with curly black hair cut the engine and looked over at The Mir. Slinging a half-case of cold beer out of the bed of the truck, Danny sauntered over towards The Captain and me.

"Hey, Captain Bill," he jibed, "you got a girl friend?" Girlfriend was said in two words, not one, with more emphasis on the friend than the girl part. *Thanks a lot,* I thought.

Danny made up for it, though, by tossing us both a cold one. He headed into the two-story building and up the stairs towards the second floor apartment.

"Thanks, Danny!" said The Captain, "but I thought she was *your* friend!"

"Hold up a sec, Danny, if you would, please," I implored, hoping he'd hear me and more so hoping he'd stop. I heard Danny's footfalls cease on the stairwell, then a thump-thump back downstairs. Standing on the third step and holding the front door to the building open, he gave me a measuring look. I couldn't tell if it was good or bad, he was that good.

"Yeah, hello," he said.

"Hi," I replied, as warmly as I could. "I'm Stacey and I got a flat here and The Captain said you could point me in the direction of a good shop to get it plugged."

"You're not from around here, are you?" Danny asked.

"No, afraid not," I said.

"You're not even a friend of The Captain?" he asked.

"Nope. Afraid not, either." I hung my head, slightly ashamed I had so brazenly used The Captain.

"Okay, then. What are you doing here?" he asked, a little harsher and flatter than his original question. He emerged from the stairway to the front stoop. I stood up to my full height of five-four and towered over him. What a surprise–and I was no longer intimidated by the tough, flat attitude.

"I told you, I got a flat and The Captain told me to talk to you about it. How do you know I'm not from here?" I was starting to get defensive.

"Because nobody who's from here is stupid enough to park in that spot where the metal cable sticks up from the ground." He looked at me and decided to continue with an explanation. "Everyone knows that's where the cable company fried their truck a couple of weeks ago. The metal cable stuck in the ground was just some residue from the explosion."

"Okay, look, I'm sorry. No, I'm not from around here. I just came down from Okeechobee..." I started to explain my circumstances to him: my Mom just died, the trailer had been sold, I was trying to start a new life and got a flat. I told him about the coffee bistro, Pizzzazzz and Dana's. Lauderdale-by-the-Sea was long forgotten. He started to soften while he listened to my troubles. For a closed-mouthed woman, a facet of my personality on which I pride myself, this little guy pried the lock on my jaw wide open with just a look.

"Yeah, my daughter likes Pizzzazzz. Can't keep her out of there and she thinks money grows on trees. Okay, so you know Tracey?"

A friendly name, but not asked after in a friendly fashion. "Well, sort of."

"Sort of, how?" he interrogated.

"I just met her when I had coffee in there just this afternoon at Dana's."

"Oh, man. You're really new down here, aren't you?" he asked, his tone growing noticeably warmer. "So, you're letting that beer go to waste?" He popped his own can open. I popped mine and sat quietly, wondering if I'd be asked to leave or, worse, to stay–with him–in an untoward way. I took a pull of the beer and contemplated how I'd gotten from Point A, Okeechobee to Point B, here and, when and where I'd get to Point C, my own place, a job, a *life*.

Drinking beer, he looked thoughtfully at the can, drained it, and as he went halfway upstairs to get another beer, "You got a job?"

Oh, boy, was *I* going to sound like a loser. "Nope." I sat very still.

"Okay, so you're here, you have no place to stay, no job, nobody down here with you..." He let it slide off into nowhere, just like I felt.

"That's about the size of it," I said quietly.

He sized me up. And down. And sideways. I could tell this was a man who was used to making quick decisions and hard judgment calls when needed.

"Fine," he said. I didn't know if it was "fine" good or "fine" bad. I held my breath. "Just a minute." He ducked over to the right side of the building, momentarily coming back with a very portly, sunburned, barefoot, bare-chested gentleman wearing shorts. I was getting invited to leave in a hurry, I was sure.

"This is Edmond. Edmond, this is..."

"Stacey." I filled in the blank with a nod towards Edmond. "Hi, Ed." Oh, no... Ed! Not my Ed, but the name still struck fear in my heart and dreams–nightmares, actually–of whatever little money I had dashing off without a sound in the night.

"It's Edmond, please," he said pleasantly. "Dhani tells me you don't have a place and might be needing one."

Dhani? I thought it was Danny! Okay, a place is a place. I wasn't about to argue semantics at this point until I knew where we were going with the conversation. "Um, well, maybe. Depends."

I stood up and at five foot four, found I saw almost eye-to-eye with Edmond while towering over Dhani. The

Captain, still parked on the stoop, watched the show. Dhani looked at Edmond who looked at me. Once again, I got the ups-n-downs, double-whammy style this time, since they *both* were doing it.

"You know, Edmond, the last tenant in the bungalow skipped and this one looks okay, maybe. Bebe's been after you for the rent for that place, no?" Dhani inquired.

Edmond put finger to cheek and thought about that for a moment. He looked like a tropical Santa considering whether I'd been naughty or nice. I held my breath. His blue eyes twinkled and he shrugged, "Okay, I guess. Stacey, you got any money?" Edmond asked.

I breathed a sigh of relief. Neither was asking me to stay with them and they weren't asking me to leave, either. "A little," I said, hedging my response. Edmond looked at me skeptically; hammy arms crossed over his barrel chest, so I continued, perhaps somewhat defensively, "Enough to get by."

"You got a car, I see." Edmond gestured towards The Mir.

"Yeah, that's paid for."

"And insured?"

"Yes, of course," standing a little straighter than just a minute ago.

"And you're legal?" Edmond continued.

"Well, yes—I mean, if you're asking if I have a driver's license, I'm legal." This was insulting. I was getting ready to start taking my chances in a bar or two after I could exit this scene, gracefully or not. I was starting not to particularly care how it went. Bars are always good to scope out the local scoop, but it's chancy at best after happy hour ends.

Edmond looked over at a little stand-alone bungalow in a back corner lot behind the main building. He looked back at me, "Okay. It's back there," thumbing towards the little pink bungalow. "Rent's three hundred a month, six hundred up front."

I looked at him incredulously.

"It's South Florida, ya know?" Edmond shrugged then grinned, "and you're at the beach."

"I'd like to see it, first, please."

Edmond was going to rent me the place and I was going to take it. However, before I got screwed, he was going to have to ask for a dance first. That's part of the game. I had to have a look at the place and play the game properly.

Dhani crossed his arms across his chest and watched our transaction in silence. Then he said, grinning, "She's picky, too."

"Thanks a lot," I shot back. Dhani looked as if he didn't know whether or not I was being facetious. I was.

Edmond took me back by the bungalow. It was a hovel. Hell, I just came off a trailer park and I know a hovel when I see one. But it was a cute hovel, and now that it was dusk, a lot of the flaws were hidden and the place looked, well, almost adorable. A little stand-alone house a block from the beach in the middle of town directly off A-1-A with cool people–maybe, and at three hundred a month, six up front–I was home. It wasn't the kind of place that involved a whole lot of paperwork, and if I hated it in two months, I'd just pack up the Mir and leave.

Edmond took a key out of his back pocket and opened the door, turning on the porch and inside lights. "This is it! Welcome to Paradise!"

I looked around inside and discovered to my sheer delight it had everything a girl could want: a small private bath and mini shower, a mini-kitchen, a mini-refrigerator, a mini-closet–the place was *little*, okay? But the place wasn't too dirty for all its shabbiness. There was a comfortable-looking brown velvety sofa bed, a little coffee table, a stand for the refrigerator and a small open storage space for pots and pans underneath the sink. Windows on three sides would give some nice cross-ventilation, since the little window-shaker AC just blew an occasional draught of lukewarm fusty air if you smacked it on the side once in a while, as Edmund showed me how to do. A TV had been left by the prior tenant who skipped and was included now as part of the property. The wallpaper was reminiscent of Ralph and Alice Kramden's place on *The Honeymooners* but, with a little paint and a smidge of cleaning, one of the perks of a small place, it doesn't take much, it would be a dandy bungalow. And it was mine. All mine.

"It looks okay, but it'll need a little work," I said, hoping to hedge the rent down even further to two-fifty. We finally agreed on two-seventy-five and Edmond would help fix the place up—gratis. Well, for some beer, anyway.

I excused myself to use the bathroom, fished for five hundred and fifty dollars in the secret zipper compartment of my pocketbook, and handed it over to Edmond when I emerged.

We shook hands on it, and Edmond said, "Had to get the cash out of the secret compartment, huh, Stacey?"

I hate to admit it, but I flushed with major embarrassment. Busted.

"My sister has one of those bags, that's how I know. Besides, your hands were dry when you came out of the bathroom," Edmond observed. *A regular Sherlock Holmes*, I thought. He chortled, "My sister likes the shoe store across the street, Piss-Ass or something like that. Maybe you would, too."

I decided I was going to get along fine here. "I already do."

I headed to the Mom-and-Pop to buy more beer and got ready to start unloading The Mir, with a little help from my newfound friends. The bottles of booze had them all twittering like the little green parrots now settling in the ancient mango tree in the center of the courtyard. The rest of the stuff was trundled into the bungalow, and I finally got a look at how much space I didn't have. I decided some stuff would have to go. The shoe collection and the new Pizzzazzz bags were a source of much good-natured teasing and fun. They stayed. When everything was mostly moved in, I broke out a bottle and we passed it around, making a substantial dent in the contents.

"Have you eaten yet, Stacey?" Edmond asked.

I shook my head, "A little lunch, maybe."

He looked at the American *Cheez* now starting to harden and curl up on the corners, sitting on the counter next to the mini-fridge. "That's not lunch. And it's not dinner, either. Look, whenever somebody new comes, it's an excuse for a party and we cook out. Are you hungry?"

I nodded. "What can I do?"

"We need paper plates and napkins. You can get that."

Every Florida household has a full stash of paper goods in case of a hurricane, and my home was no different. I searched through the boxes and came up with a good supply, which I donated for the common cause. In moments, grills were fired up, people were actively walking all over the courtyard, and preparations for a party were in progress.

I unearthed a white paper tablecloth and covered the table in the center of the courtyard. I put some beer and liquor on top to secure it and brought out some plastic cups. The smell of grilled meats, including a choice steak or two, infused the air with heavenly aromas.

"What about veggies?" someone called from the row of apartments where Edmund resided. "I can give you salad." A beautiful, bikinied Latina chick came out with a huge bowl of lettuce and salad stuff, setting it on the table and starting preparations.

"Welcome to the neighborhood!" she said, grabbing my hand in an enthusiastic handshake. "It's nice to have another woman, yes?"

"Yes! It sure is! Hi! I'm Stacey."

"Maricella."

An old woman in a blue housedress came out of Maricella's apartment and seated herself on an old metal patio chair.

"My mother," Maricella said. I waved and the mom waved back. "She speaks very little English, but she does okay. I'll come back at dinner," she said with a charming smile, and went off to give her mother a kiss and stepped back into their apartment. I found her lilting Spanish accent charming and her manner polite, yet warm. Even Mama smiled at me–a good sign, I hoped.

I went over to where Edmund was grilling, offering to help. He declined with a smile, covered the grill and took me around to meet the neighbors. There was Alex, a tall, handsome blue-eyed blond guy who lived below Dhani. In the third apartment of the central building, off to the right, were Eduardo and Amillia, two newlywed Brazilian students.

Armand lived in the row of bungalows behind the central building, next to Chet, a surfer dude, who lived next to Geo, a surfer guitarist. Geo's apartment had an elevated deck in back, and he invited me to come over to hang out anytime I heard music playing.

Across the yard was another row of apartments, the sole tenant of which was Antonio, an older Portuguese man who built out three original apartments to make one single unit. He was very proud of his handiwork and invited me inside to take a look. It was cool, clean, and nicely tiled. He also tried to slip me the tongue while inside and I pushed him away with a smart little smack on his shoulder to let him know I meant business and a firm, resounding, "No!"

Edmund was laughing as I came out of Antonio's, wiping my mouth on the back of my hand, "He does that to everybody."

"Even you?"

"Not me..." he grinned and smacked me playfully on the shoulder. "Welcome aboard."

The grilling completed, we all sat together and ate, drank, and talked. Dhani was originally from Belgium, his father having served in the diplomatic corps for Belgium in the Congo. His mother was of African aristocracy, hence his exotic, dark good looks.

Edmund was from "Noo Yawk," he, his sister, and mother all moved down here after his father died. Nobody was interested in inheriting the family business–his father had owned a funeral parlor. They sold the place and moved to Florida, Mecca of the Snowbirds.

Alex and Chet were native Floridians and very kickback, mellow guys.

Guy was from the great northwest–Washington, or Oregon.

Armando was from Puerto Rico.

Everyone was from everyplace, and everyone was here for the weather and the beaches.

After making up the sofa bed and sliding my Tigger slippers underneath, I took a shower, attended my brief evening toilette, locked the door, and took a very long, very sound, very much needed sleep.

Chapter Two

I woke up slightly disoriented, rather fuzzy, and really having to pee. While answering the call of nature, I slaked my raging thirst with brownish water drawn off the little sink in the bathroom. It finally ran clear right after I was done drinking. I sized up the shower stall and figured I'd fit–barely. Standing up from the toilet, I started running the shower. Wowee! Water pressure! And lots of it! Who'd have thought it in a little dump like this? Getting water by the beach is usually an iffy proposition at best and, for all the love and money in the world, some of the pricey condos along the shore didn't have it this good. Many times, the water just dribbles out enough to wash the body, but nothing refreshing.

I got my kit bag out of the living room-slash-bedroom-slash-dining room-slash-kitchen. I think that's what's meant by an "efficiency apartment." The rooms are very efficient, being all rolled up into one. I tossed my sleepy-tee onto the sofa bed and padded to the shower for a long, hot soak. I lathered up with my favorite soap from home and shampooed and conditioned my hair. I thought about shaving, but gave it the go-by because the shower was way too cramped. I just stood in the shower as the water washed over me, closed my eyes, and pretended it was an exotic tropical waterfall in paradise.

Duly refreshed, I dried off, stepped into the living room-slash-bedroom-slash-dining room-slash-kitchen and realized all three windows were wide open. There I was, wrapped in a skimpy, shabby towel just barely covering half my ass. Dhani and Edmund were hanging at the table in the center of the compound, watching my bungalow while they sipped from mugs that contained a beverage more potent than coffee, judging from the chortles coming from their direction. The Captain lounged on the chaise, then looked in my direction as well. I ducked down below the window, more than a bit embarrassed, and tried to find something to wear.

I located a pair of denim shorts from the move-in pile of clothing heaped on a chair and my favorite soft blue tee shirt washed a thousand times or better. I slid my feet into new surfer-girl flip-flops from Pizzzazzz and emerged from the bungalow.

"Well, gotta get to work," said Dhani, abruptly getting up and walked towards his truck, hiding a smirk.

"Yeah, me too," added Edmund. The Captain just snorted and shifted in the chaise.

"Hold up you guys!" I called. They halted. "Are there any shades for my windows, Edmond?" I asked. "Because if there are," I continued, "I want some and I want some now!" Dhani looked at Edmond who had the faint beginnings of a grin.

"Oh, and Dhani, by the way, thanks for hooking me up with this place, but that doesn't entitle you to a free show either!" I said severely.

Dhani and Edmund looked sheepishly at me, but I could see underlying half-smirks of wolves beneath the sheep's cloak. They were busted, and they knew it.

"Sorry," Dhani said softly "I was out here anyway…" the statement drifted off.

I started laughing because they looked like a couple of little boys who got caught with bullfrogs in their pockets when Mama did the wash.

"Okay, guys, y'all got a free look. Great. It's my fault as much as yours. If there's anything you haven't seen before, tell me about it and I'll see a doctor to have it removed. Otherwise, we'll just let it slide—but Edmond, I do want those shades."

Edmond ducked into his apartment, a long, squat three-unit structure next to the bungalow, and came out with some thin, yellowed, brittle parchment shades, which looked older than all of us put together. One dropped from his grasp and crumbled as it hit the dirt.

"Fine," I said. "I'll get my own and it'll come off the rent." Edmund nodded and, picking up the dropped shade, tossed all of them into a garbage can near the hedge fronting the parking lot behind my bungalow.

Edmund and Dhani then crossed the yard towards the hedgerow leading out to their vehicles. When they thought they were out of my sight, Dhani punched Edmund playfully on the bicep and they both laughed. Most likely at my expense, I sighed, ruefully shaking my head. I turned back towards the bungalow, which was now fully visible in the harsh eastern light of the beach morning.

I looked at the little bungalow square on, hands on my hips, surveying my new domicile. On the one hand– ugh! It was painted a nondescript washed-out Floridian peachy-pink. I don't know if paint stores actually stock this shade in any other state in the union, but it seemed to dominate not only the compound, but various other small, cheap rental complexes and trailer parks all over the state. Tough Luck Lane had been no exception. The only color that was worse, in my eyes, was the hideous Grey Poupon mustard yellow favored by the rich owners of Spanish Mission-style mansions in the Palm Beaches. I had seen plenty of them in my ride down from Lake Okeechobee the day before. I decided that my dream mansion, "Fred", would be white with black shutters and perhaps some ivy growing in a crisscross pattern on a white stone wall by the entrance gate.

On the other hand, the bungalow was kind of cute; a stand-alone dollhouse, just for me. There was room for a few flowerpots and plants in the front and on the left corner. A small overturned boat on cinder blocks stacked three high on the left side of the bungalow reminded me of a miniature version of the "Minnow," from the old *Gilligan's Island* TV show–after the wreck. A tall tree with a few low-hanging branches stood planted between the bungalow and Edmund's row of units. An old, rusted-out kettle-style charcoal grill sat next to the tree and I wondered if that came with the bungalow.

Next door, just outside Edmund's apartment stood the huge, fancy, state-of-the-art, multi-function, top-of-the-line, everything-but-the-kitchen-sink brushed steel propane unit, which looked as if it could have done restaurant-size meals, pressed into service the night before. Given Edmund's girth and breadth–the guy looked like he loved to eat–I assumed the smaller kettle-style grill was mine.

The right side of the bungalow boasted a walkway covered over with cheap cement and stone paving, and a long wall that was just crying out for a mural painting, when I had time and money for paint–not to mention a few friends and a few cases of beer, as well, to help fuel the creative process on a lazy weekend afternoon. Pine trees softly shaded the walkway and hummed gently in the morning breeze. Yeah, it was a hell of a lot better than Tough Luck Lane.

The boys had left for their respective jobs. From last night's moving escapade, I learned Dhani was a building contractor and Edmond, a groundskeeper for a fancy old age home. I looked around the compound to see The Captain peacefully snoozing off a major league hangover on the courtyard chaise. Giving thanks I wasn't in that position, I realized it was high time to find a job and figure out my life and fortunes from here. Here was another first day of the rest of my life. Feeling free as a bird and just about as happy, I wasn't about to squander this newfound freedom on the bottle.

I went back into the bungalow, grabbed my

handbag, and headed over to Dana's for some coffee and one of those awesome muffins. Outside there were a couple of freebie newspapers in a metal stand, one featuring hip, in-the-biz bartending ads on the front cover. I helped myself to one of each.

Dana's was as cool, refreshing and inviting as it had been yesterday afternoon. Perhaps even more so, with the warm homey smells of fresh breakfasts cooking on the griddle of the little kitchen. I breathed in deeply, savoring the aroma, and looked around to see people of all shapes, sizes, and income levels comfortably eating, quietly talking, and just generally starting their day. No one remotely like The Captain was in sight, for which I was extremely grateful.

Behind the counter, Tracey looked up and gave me a friendly wave, "Hey stranger!" she called out, and motioned me over to her section of the counter.

Being a small diner, the whole counter was her territory, so I had my pick of seats to get her service. I took the stool at the end of the counter near the coffee station. I hoped would be where she would hang out for the best part of the breakfast shift even though the place was pretty packed.

"Back for more, huh? You must be a glutton for punishment." Tracey set down a steaming cup of fresh coffee in front of me. It smelled wonderful. There's nothing like the magnificent aroma of a great cup of coffee. I added some cream, Pink Packet sweetener and took the first sip. The coffee was everything it should be, and then some: fresh, hot, aromatic, and flavorful.

I watched Tracey run her counter. Being a bartender myself, I knew a diner's counter isn't all that different. Tracey plied her trade, juggling cups, saucers, plates–full and empty–with all the aplomb of a master magician while holding a constant patter of conversation with the regulars.

Her dark brown eyes flashed mischievously as she

caught a particularly raunchy double entendre, something about a muff and a muffin. Make up your own joke, they're all pretty much the same. She came back equally fast with a few more wisecracks thrown in for good measure. Tracey was petite and her slight, wiry frame didn't look as if it could handle the weight of all the diner trappings, but she slung the tools of her trade around like they were nothing and continued her patter nonstop. Her short, dark brown hair stayed neatly in place and didn't pop a single frizz. *She* didn't sweat. She was *too* good to be just a standard-issue counter waitress. I briefly wondered what *her* story was. Everyone has one. I was mightily impressed with the show.

I opened one of the papers and started looking over the ads while enjoying my coffee.

Finally, there was a break in the action and Tracey poured me a fresh cup. I smiled.

Tracey leaned over and said, "Thought you could use another cup before we got started. What's your pleasure?"

I ordered breakfast. She took the order, handed it through to the cook like a quarterback to a running back. I could tell there was a mutual respect, albeit grudging, between Tracey and the cook. She gave out a few final checks to the guys sitting at the counter, and came back to me.

"Great sandals, by the way. Pizzzazzzz?" she asked.

"Yeah, one of three pairs I got yesterday."

"Yeah, I remember." Tracey grinned. "So, what's up, Doc?" She asked in her best Bugs Bunny imitation which, given her Jersey accent, wasn't all that bad.

"Well…" I started, only to be interrupted by a beefy guy finishing breakfast and wanting a little social peck from his favorite waitress on his way out the door. Upon receiving it, he left an extremely generous tip.

"'Scuse me, hon," Tracey said as she came back. "My uncle," she said, with a big wide-eyed wink.

"Yeah, a funny uncle, you mean," I shot back.

She looked around and, deeming all was well with her little Queendom at the counter, leaned across the counter on her elbows, and glanced back at the cook.

"Well…" I re-stated, "Do you know a Dhani and Edmond?" I asked.

Tracey rolled her eyes, flipped around to the cook, snagged my breakfast from the pass-through to the kitchen and had it in front of me like a flash, speed-poured three cups of coffee to the patrons, and was back to me.

"Yeah, eat," she said and gestured to the steaming plate of food set before me. "A little nutsy, but a nice bunch of guys, anyway. How'd you hook up there?" she asked.

I explained about the flat tire, the Captain, which resulted in another skyward roll of Tracey's eyes, the bungalow, and my little exploit with Dhani and Edmond this morning.

"You can get shades at Knott's Hardware over on Dixie Highway," Tracey advised. "They're cheaper than the big stores and they'll measure them up for you. Oh," she cautioned, "they might measure you up as well, but they get over it quick if you're firm with them."

Now, it was my turn to roll my eyes. This was a good start and what I'd been looking for, but sadly lacking at the diner in La-de-dah-by-the-Sea yesterday. I shrugged and pondered the cost of doing business for an attractive woman. You get checked out in more ways than one, but usually, you can parley an ogle into a discount and make out pretty good sometimes, figuratively speaking, of course.

"Hey," Tracey said, "Did the Captain give you that line about 'having his life off' to justify his permanent state of perpetual unemployment?"

"Yeah, he did," I nodded, "and I have to tell you, I thought it was pretty funny, given the Captain. Love that hat."

We both laughed.

"So," Tracey continued, "What are you gonna do?"

"I bartend."

"Ah, I see," Tracey said, sticking a finger up in the air as if to check the direction of the wind in the diner. "That answers the question as to why you're not schitzy so early in the morning. You're not even up yet."

I thoughtfully munched on some bacon as she poured my third cup of coffee, which turned out to be just as terrific as the first. She was right. My eyes were barely starting to open, and my brain was just starting to engage. Collecting tips and debris from the counter and wiping it clean, she headed back to me.

She stepped out from the end of the counter and eyed me up and down.

"Got a job yet?" she asked.

I shook my head no, but motioned to the paper where I'd found some promising ads. "I think I'll try Geoffrey's. Do you know it?"

Tracey nodded. "It's a slick place and you're cute and tall enough and the uniforms aren't too bad." She threw me a warning look, "But just watch your ass."

"Okay, so where is this place?"

"Off Ocean Boulevard." I looked at her questioningly. "A-1-A, in Fort Lauderdale, just after motel row," she explained. "The money should be pretty good." She stacked up my dishes and said no more.

"I'll keep that in mind," I replied, making a mental note to go there that afternoon. I also wondered to myself why she wasn't bartending and making the legendary big bucks, especially in season. "Thanks." I said, once again leaving a generous tip as I got up from the counter.

"Thanks yourself. Come back again. Really. I mean that," Tracey said as I made my way to the register. I stood at a little over two grand now, so I had to find some way to earn.

But this morning, I'd decided to take care of the bullshit: my driver's license and registration. Anyone who's tangled with any motor vehicle agency knows what a pain in the ass that can be, especially with a car like the Mir. I've heard some states even inspect the car you drive. Jeez, the Mir would never stand up to it. Oh, yeah—and the tire.

The department of motor vehicles was everything I expected it to be and more. I stood in an endless line full of shabbily dressed people and wondered if any of them were posted on the walls of the local Post Office. I paid my money, smiled at the birdie, I thought about giving the cop behind the counter the birdie, which was cause enough to smile, and—voila! About three and a half hours later, I had a new license with my new address. I filled out a form for the registration by mail. I prefer to stay as far away from courthouses as possible and that was just where registrations were issued. One does have one's limits. I was maxed out on the law already this morning.

On the way back to the bungalow from the motor vehicle mess, I spied a tire shop. How do you spell relief? Baxter Tire. The guys there were really nice to me (even threw in an oil change for the Mir without the damned thing falling apart at the seams). They didn't even try to snag me for anything extra, though heaven only knows they could have gotten me for a bundle. Under two grand now, so work was going to be a priority. I had seen an old Car & Driver magazine in the shop and was very surprised to find out The Mir had been Car of the Year in 1987. No wonder the guys were so nice about The Mir. They told me it would be a little while and asked if I had any errands I could run in the meantime.

I spotted a bank across the street and walked into the overly air conditioned First Mutual. The well done-up lady at one of the desks coolly smiled at no one in particular with a vacant stare, as I approached.

"*How* can I help you?" It was a statement, not a question. Friendly banking at its best. I don't give a hoot what they say in the ads, banks are *not* friendly places, especially if you don't have money. I wanted to say "This is a stick up" but, instead, I asked to open a savings account. After much to-do about proving who I was, where I lived, and being rewarded with a sneer over her reading glasses when asked about my employment, I finally got to stash my dough in the bank. At least I had a driver's license with the correct address on it and Thank God they didn't ask for a credit check.

I kept a few bucks out to gas up the Mir in my quest for gainful employment and stock up the mini fridge with food. I left the bank with a piece of paper in my hands stating that I was a legal and valid account holder at First Mutual Bank and, come hell or high water, my privacy would be protected to the utmost of confidentiality they could provide. What the hell was this–Switzerland? Yeah, right. I knew it was all horsepucky because I saw how easy Ed got Mom's money out once he had her bankbook. Jeez. It's as bad as the airlines saying you'll be all right if they crash. Here's a News Flash: they lie. Best of all, the paper said the funds were insured. I'd bet odds-on that if I went to the bank for *my* money and some rich dork went to the bank for *his* money and the bank had to make a choice, guess who gets what first? Bingo. So, I am a firm believer in stuffing the mattress and keeping a big dog on top for insurance. Since that wasn't an option for me, I got a bank account instead.

Across the street from the bank was a Super Duper Market, which beat the hell out of the Stop & Cop back in Okeechobee. This place didn't smell like week-old meat and unwashed floors. It was bright, cheery, and everyone went out of their way to wish me a "Top of the afternoon, Miss!" A young man stocking shelves brightly asked me if I had seen the "Super Duper Sales" going on "right now!"

They bugged me for some reason.

I took my cart, got some beer and a six of Heineken for the shop guys and a few simple food and paper supplies. My shopping done, I went back to the shop, paid the guys in cash and Heineken, loaded up the Mir and home I went.

Back at the bungalow, studiously avoiding the parking space with the metal cable, I stocked the fridge, popped open a Coke, and sliced off a good chunk of pepper jack for lunch. Measuring up the windows for shades, I decided to head over to Knott's Hardware on Dixie as Tracey suggested and then over to Geoffrey's to see about that bartender job.

Knott's Hardware and Gun Shop, complete with a rifle range in the back, smelled of new lumber, sawdust, leather tool belts and gun oil. It was a man's smell. I waited behind a couple of rough-cut guys in dirty tee shirts and wondered if they would be my potential bar customers at the end of their long hard days, once I landed my dream job at a local bar. I smiled sweetly at them, just in case.

Mr. Knott, the elder, was waiting on customers and Mr. Knott, the younger, was giving me the big-time fishy eye. Even though I'd been warned by Tracey, my skin crawled as I stood in line, uncomfortably aware of my too short shorts–when did that happen? They were okay earlier on. The soft blue tee shirt I had on may have been a wee bit too tight after all. I pretended to ignore Knott the younger and focus on the guys in front of me. I was really concentrating on the little mole on the back of the guy's neck in front of me when it was suddenly my turn, and I was confronted face to face with Mr. Knott, the elder. The apple didn't fall far from the tree in this case, as he insisted on addressing my chest instead of me. I was quickly losing patience when, pulling out the window measurement sheet, I got a leering glance at my legs as he sized up measurements other than what was I was offering to share with him.

Just then, the cheesy wooden screen door slammed shut and Dhani swaggered up to the counter.

"Howie." Dhani said to the elder Mr. Knott, proffering his hand for a shake. He moved out from behind the counter in my direction while looking at Dhani.

Looking at me, Dhani said, "Stacey, hi. Fancy seeing you here, stranger," he smirked.

Old Howie was feasting his eyes on my chest. Okay, let's be explicit–he was checking out my boobies and wondering how he could cop a free feel by bumping against me or something just as seemingly innocuous, but invasive just the same. A thumb and forefinger, coming together on Howie's hand, were aimed straight in the direction of my chest.

"Dhani," I stated sidestepping away from Howie as he pinched Dhani instead of where he was aiming to go, "how nice to see you. I'm here for new shades. I think I measured them up okay, but could you check for me, please?"

Dhani brushed off Howie's untoward advance with an admonishing look and took the sheet from me. He studied it, giving me time enough to meet elder Mr. Knott eyeball to eyeball this time with an ice-cold see-through stare on my part and then doubled back to young Mr. Knott with an equally withering glance. The peep show–real or fantasized–was over for them and they knew it.

"It looks okay to me," Dhani said. "Howie, cut these for the lady here and give me the bill."

"Friend of yours?" Howie asked Dhani.

"Client," Dhani said easily. "I'm doing a little work at her place." He winked at Howie. Jeez! Was there no end to this bullshit?

Howie shared a conspiratorial grin with Dhani and went to cut the shades for me. Mr. Knott, the younger, had cast his eyes to the floor, perhaps looking for termites, but definitely staying out of his Daddy's business. Dhani approached him with a list.

"Fill this out for me, please, Hank," Dhani requested. Hank complied, turned and went back behind the front counter, selecting hardware items displayed on pegboard hooks on the wall.

I went over to Dhani. "Thanks, pal," I said, playfully punching him lightly on his wiry bicep.

He smiled back at me, for real this time, took the shades from Howie and handed them to me.

"I'll be over to hang these tonight for you," Dhani said, gently leading me towards the cheesy door and out of the store–not quick enough but quick enough, if you catch the drift. Dhani stayed in the store, to complete his purchase.

As the screen door slammed shut behind me, I could hear Howie and Hank laughing with Dhani–something about hanging shades or being hung. Make up your own joke, they're all pretty much the same. *Men.* I looked toward the sky and then over at the Mir and couldn't get out of that parking lot fast enough. The Mir hauled ass, much to my delight, kicking up a little dust while doing a fancy fishtail on the way out.

I was back at the bungalow a few minutes later. After a cursory nod to The Captain in his chaise, now more or less upright with beer in hand, I waved to him. I decided on another shower. The hotter the better.

Ten minutes later, I emerged from my tropical waterfall, which did a marvelous job of washing away the memory of those skeevy Knotts. I dried off, blew out my hair, and selected a pair of black cigarette pants, the ancient black Jimmy Choos, and a white tube top. Finishing the look with some makeup and a silky black cardigan open to the waist and banded with a slim gold fish scale belt, just enough for the tube to peek through, I was ready to job hunt.

I stepped out of the bungalow to a wolf-whistle

from The Captain, which was good enough for me.

Into The Mir, I fired her up, revved the engine a time or two, and took off down the A-1-A for Geoffrey's off Ocean Boulevard.

Ocean Boulevard, in Fort Lauderdale, isn't really on the ocean. It's on the Intracoastal Waterway. I guess it got that name because it's *near* the ocean. On the east side of the waterway, but about two blocks west of the ocean, was Geoffrey's. Tracey was right; it was slick looking.

A sleek, wood-and-black glass structure with a large empty parking lot stood before me. The staff was setting the patio to rights from the prior night's closing and the bar crew were whirring blenders in preparation for this evening's libations.

Taking a deep breath, I opened the side door and approached a young, good-looking bartender who was prepping mixes in no less than three side-by-side blenders. It was a good sign. It was, obviously, a busy place. There were mile-high tables with soft cushions of chocolate leather on the stools inside the lounge, with a good sprinkling of roomy butterscotch leather banquettes and booths along the walls. The walls were dark green, almost the color of money, and wainscoted in cherry wood. A large dance floor stood in the middle of the room with a stage for live performances and a glass DJ booth for between sets. A mirrored ball sat dormant in the center of the black ceiling. The lighting was soft and diffused with a warm pink under-glow. I thought it could be real easy to just sit and drink here all night long, with no thought of going elsewhere. The patio was just visible from over the bar. Beyond was the Intracoastal, which sparkled in the afternoon sun. There was ample dockage for Geoffrey's as well as other restaurants and bars along this strip. The black carpet had been freshly shampooed and the place smelled stinking rich.

"We're not open just yet, miss," the bartender said.

Well, miss was definitely a step up from lady.

"I'm looking for work, there was an ad. Can I apply here?" I asked.

He nodded in the direction of the kitchen door after giving me the eye, determining I passed muster and was worthy of applying for work at Geoffrey's. Whoa. His glacial blue stare reminded me of my brother Ed, as did his chilling good looks. Although Ed had black hair and this guy was blond, there were similarities: a cut of conceit to the face, a cocky tilt of the head. However, when he faced the window with the sun on his face, there were traces of laugh lines in the outer corners of his eyes and frown lines around the mouth, which was a hard, thin-lipped slash on his face. Yes, he reminded me of Ed. There was no way I'd fuck with this dude or buy into his bullshit, either. He was strictly "hands off" for me.

"Ask for Geoffrey in the kitchen," he said.

Interesting, I thought to myself, *a Geoffrey at Geoffrey's*. Usually, the owners of these high-end places were named Joe or Spike and were "connected" to the kind of people you or I would not wish to know on an everyday basis. My brother Ed, on the other hand, would see endless opportunities for a con as soon as he could hatch a good one.

Opening the swinging door to the kitchen, I was greeted by hideously bright white light in an immaculately maintained kitchen. This is the worst kind of light to show off any kind of looks. It brings out every wrinkle, zit, tired-eye circle and flaw imaginable. If your makeup foundation is applied just a touch too much, it looks like it was troweled on and left to set in the sun like wet cement on a hot day. I was thankful there was no one in the kitchen.

A tiny door stood open in the back of the empty kitchen, which led to a tiny set of stairs going up to the second level.

"Hello?" I called, tentatively pointing my voice in

the direction of upstairs. "Geoffrey?"

"Yo! In here!" There was a muffled call from someplace in the kitchen, but definitely not upstairs.

"Where?" I called back. "I can't see anyone."

"Freezer! Walk-in box!" Another muffled cry came from the box against the far wall of the kitchen.

I walked over to a large silver door set in the center a stainless steel box. I saw a man in an expensive business suit leaning against a stack of cases. He was panting heavily, and his breath hung in white plumes on the frigid air. Frost had already formed on his lapels in glittering patches.

"I'm looking for Geoffrey," I said.

"You found him! Open the door, please!" said the popsicle-man, pounding on the door to emphasize his request.

"Okay, okay!" I slid the bolt-hinge out and opening the heavy door with all my strength. I was lucky not to have broken a high heel or–God forbid–a fingernail.

Geoffrey popped out of the freezer like a Jack-in-the-box, shook himself free of frost on his suit and in his hair. He stamped on the floor and flapped his arms across his chest. Once he restored some warmth, I averted my eyes and tried not to laugh.

"Thanks, honey," he said fervently. "Jesus! I've been calling for hours!" He shivered. His wide lapels, once stiff with frost, were now limp.

"They're all on the patio and mixing stuff in the blenders," I said.

"That's probably why they didn't hear me," Geoffrey said, and the color seeped back into his face. "Who are you?" He looked at me, thankful for the rescue, but not sure how I fit into the picture.

Not being one to pass up a good opportunity to shut up, I said nothing for a moment, and then answered slowly, "I'm here for a job." I held up the paper and pointed to the ad I'd found.

"Okay. Did anyone send you?" Geoffrey asked.

"Uh, no," I said as I looked down at the floor. "Um, yes. Tracey did. I'm here for a job."

"Tracey?" Geoffrey asked. "Do I know a Tracey?"

"Okay," I said, "I don't know if you know a Tracey because I've just met you," I said. "Tracey is a friend of mine who said this place was slick and I might find work here."

"Ah, I see. Tracey, right. She used to work here some time ago. Good kid. How's she doin'? You carded?" Geoffrey asked. He was referring to the Florida Food Handler I.D. cards Florida residents need to work in such establishments. They're not easy to get, either, because you need a card to *get* a job and you can't get a *job* without a card. Local government, in its infinite wisdom, figured it out that way. Luckily, a few places just sell the cards if you bring a note from an establishment that they're *thinking* about letting you work there.

"I am," I said, pulling my wallet out of my pocketbook and extracting my card.

Geoffrey studied the card and held it up to the light to check the hologram. It flashed visibly in the bright kitchen light. "Stacey Jennifer Longacre, huh?" He pursed his lips thoughtfully, and then looked up. "Quite a handle. Where are you from? Not from here."

It was more a rhetorical question than anything. I just kept my mouth shut and just looked levelly at the newly melted Geoffrey. He didn't smell exactly fresh, either. He had light brown eyes and light brown hair, which, at some point during the day, must have been heavily moussed and styled. His light gray suit was of Saville Row style and cut so sharp, he could have probably shaved with it in the morning. He wasn't bad looking, just expensive looking even when defrosted, but a little too pimped up for my taste. Yet, I thought, what the hell, I was just going to work for the guy, not bed him.

"Yeah, okay," he continued. "You drive?"

"White T-Bird, big eight," I replied proudly. Love that Mir.

He sized me up, down, sideways, and probably six, or more, ways to Sunday. Here we go again. He took such a hard look at me it seemed he could see right through me, like an x-ray. I felt sure he could see how my guts worked inside of me. It was damned creepy. I was so nervous, I thought by the time this ordeal was over, I'd be down a size. But I never pass on a chance to stand stock-still, shut up and see what happens next, so I did and just let him look me over.

"All right," he said, walking over to a closet at the opposite end of the kitchen where the chef's whites and uniforms were stored. "I owe you for getting me out of that freezer, I guess, and you're carded and licensed. You look okay as well." Again with the size-up and a thoughtful look. "Cocktail waitress, I think. Come in four tomorrow, fill out the forms, start at five for prep. Shift's 'til two-thirty a.m. You wear this." He tossed something black and white in my direction. "Make sure it fits–good. Oh, yeah, make sure you got a push-up bra underneath. Comfortable shoes, too. Not those. Little heels are best. Show off your legs, but don't kill the foot. Black pantyhose, too. I think the girls here like the shiny egg things, they say they're support. We'll see how you look tomorrow." He pronounced tomorrow like "tomarra"–there was New York somewhere in his background, but I wasn't asking.

I took the black-and-white something-or-other, supposing it was my "uniform", shook his hand and left him to thaw completely. Heading out of the kitchen past the bar, I encountered the good-looking bartender, still mixing his potions for the evening ahead.

"Find him?" he asked me.

I shook the flimsy little uniform at him, "Yeah, I

start tomorrow."

He looked at me, sighed, and shrugged, "Another victim."

I laughed, "Yeah, but a willing one!" He looked at me with a cold eye and, as handsome as he was, it was like the beauty of ice, the iceberg that sank the Titanic–lovely to look at but lethal. "See you tomorrow!" I said flippantly to him over my shoulder and heading out the door. I'd snagged a job and how lucky was *that?*

Back at the bungalow I changed out of my job-huntress duds and into some black bicycle shorts, a tie-dye floppy tee and the surfer-girl flip flops, ready to hang out. I popped a beer with The Captain and broke out some of the "good stuff" to celebrate the new job. We toasted to working, to not working, to wanting to work or not, to easy jobs, to tough jobs, to weekends, and to vacations, lifelong or not. Somewhere along the way, I lost count. Eventually, Dhani and Edmond came home from work and we all toasted the new job. I was going to have to buy more beer. Oh, well, at least I didn't have to pay for the shades.

Dhani and Edmond were as good as their word and hung the shades for me that evening. Not only that, they grilled burgers and dogs for the whole Compound and I was more than happy to partake of the feast after all that drinking!

I took a stroll on the beach, going over the last couple of days in my head. Sitting down in the sand, I looked over at a couple in the throes of passion, completely oblivious to my presence. A little further down the beach, a Native American gathering formed a circle and chanted while pounding a tom-tom as the couple pounded each other and the surf pounded the sand. I focused on the different beats for a while, zoning in on the tom-tom, then lifted my ass off the sand to get back to the bungalow.

The Compound was silent as I arrived with that damned beat stuck in my head. I popped another beer and sat quietly on my stoop waiting for the beat to subside. It finally did and, with Tigger slippers softly placed under the sofa bed, I settled in for a long, dreamless sleep with the new shades pulled down on the windows.

Chapter Three

The shades worked so well, I slept in until eleven, when the Captain gently tapped on my window to make sure I was all right.

"Hey, missy," he called softly. Ah, the pleasure of friendship–back to "missy" from "lady." "You okay in there? Hello!"

I lifted the shade on the window by my bed just a wee bit and got an eyeful of the well worn, unshaven Captain peering in at the side of my window. Not the most beautiful sight when you're somewhat hung over. On the other hand, somebody actually cared about whether or not I made it through the night.

Rolling out of bed, shaking my hair loose from the knotted tangle of a good night's sleep, I padded over to the door, opened it a crack and said, "Mornin' Cap," as cheerily as I could muster. The sun in my eyes caused a Draculean response as I withered away from the sunbeam.

The Captain winked at me, then turned and shuffled off to his chaise. He must have thought he got a free peep, but there was nothing to see other than my oversized sleepy tee and less-than-perfect hair.

I closed the door and made sure the shades were securely drawn. I didn't want them to suddenly pop open and douse me with a blast of blazing sunshine. I pulled an almost-cool Coke from the mini-fridge and contemplated breakfast-pepperjack cheese or Dana's. I figured if I had a nice hot shower, downed the Coke, and found a couple of aspirin, I'd be all right for a plate of eggs and home fries with Tracey. I've always found that as hung over as I've ever been, some eggs and greasy potatoes set you back on the road to righteousness, especially if they're jazzed up with a little hot sauce to spark your engine.

I sauntered out the door at eleven forty-five, in much better shape than my awakening, as a wolf-whistle emanating from the Captain indicated on my way to Dana's.

I went over to the Captain on his chaise and sat down on the end. "Need a beer, sir?" I asked politely, thinking it was a tangible way to thank him for his wolf-whistle compliment. He nodded yes and seemed to perk up a little from his permanent state of stupor.

Fetching him a beer and none for me, I popped the top and sat back down on the end of his chaise. "You don't mind, do you?"

Taking a long swig of the cold beer, then shaking his head as if he'd just taken a plunge into an ice-cold pool, he motioned no and indicated it was all right for me to stay seated.

"Only got a minute, Cap'n," I said, "stuff to do."

"So, you got a job, Miss Stacey. Congratulations!"

"Yeah, starting tonight. Geoffrey's."

The Captain frowned and looked thoughtful. "I know the place. That's all I'm sayin'."

"Cap–you can't leave me hanging with just that," I said. "What's the scoop?"

The Captain sighed, "Well, sooner or later, you'll find out. The people who run the place aren't very nice and the people who own it aren't much nicer. In fact, the people who own the place own the people who run the place."

"Really," I said. "I thought slavery was abolished."

"Officially, yeah. But it still goes on. You'll find out. Just keep your nose clean, Miss Stacey, and you'll do all right. You don't gamble, do you?"

"Hell, no," I answered, thinking I'd just as soon flush a dollar bill down the toilet than buy a lottery ticket.

Casinos were way out of my league and I tended to shy away from them whenever possible. They were Indian Games and I'm not an Indian. As far as I knew, anyway.

"Before the gover'mint and the Indians got involved," The Captain said, almost mirroring my thoughts, "there were numbers games. There still are numbers games but they're way down low with the casinos now. People who gamble will bet a number soon as they'll go to a casino–it's just a fix for them, any port in a storm." He took another long swallow of cold beer.

An inkling occurred to me. "Did you gamble, Cap'n?" I wondered if he'd gambled boats, lost a fortune in money, run drugs, and all kinds of crazy shit went through my head.

"Nope," he shook his head, "I drink." That put the kibosh on my fantasies. I wondered why he drank so much but was too polite to ask just yet.

"So, how do you know Geoffrey's and why do you care if I gamble or not?"

"I knew the owners, years ago. Skippered a boat for them when they were young and mixed up in other places. Geoffrey's has a boat, too, the "Golden Girl". From what I hear, Geoffrey gambles. Almost lost that boat a few years back." He finished his beer, so I got him another and jaywalked across the street to Dana's Diner.

I waved at Tracey as I entered the diner. Tracey was plying her usual prestidigitation with the counter customers, the cook, and others in the diner. Though I was just one more person for her to serve, she made me feel like an especially welcome friend–a trick in and of itself, given that we knew each other so little.

"You're late!" Tracey cracked with hands on hips and an imperious stare down her nose in my direction. Being that I had her by about half a foot, that was a neat trick.

"I've got a note," I parried back smartly.

"Forged, I'm sure," Tracey replied. "Just take your seat, young lady, and behave in class," she jibed. "Now, what'll it be?" she asked, looking over at me as I sat down at the end of the counter. "Oh," she stated, observing me as if I were a bug under a microscope, "a bit under the weather, huh?" Cocking her head, snapping her fingers, and thumbing the way to the kitchen, she said, "Just a sec, I've got just the thing to fix you up," and she ducked behind the door to have a word with the cook.

"Hey, Louie, lemme have a La-La-Land special for one, 'K?" Tracey said.

"Who's da victim dis time?" Louie asked, another New Yorker.

"My cousin, 'K? So, make it nice." Tracey answered.

"Cousins, uncles, aunts, grandmothers," Louie grumbled. "Christ, Tracey, you got more family than Adam and Eve–and I thought *they* were related to everybody."

Blowing Chef Louie a kiss, Tracey nipped out the kitchen door and poured me a steaming hot cup of Joe and served five other customers at the counter.

"Black only this morning, sweetie," she said, tossing her head of short black curls in my direction. "You agree?"

Looking up I nodded assent, and asked, "Maybe a little sweet?"

Sliding the glass sugar container within easy reach perfectly, Tracey advised, "Yeah, cool. Do sweet, but no milk, it'll curdle your tum." I took three spoonfuls of sugar and sipped at the hot coffee.

Leaving me to my black-only-this-morning coffee, Tracey nipped and tucked all over the diner as happy customers everywhere munched, crunched, sipped, supped and the noise was driving me nuts. If one more person masticated in front of me, I was gonna barf.

"Okay, babe," Tracey announced, swooping a

platter down from the chef's pass through to me, "One La-La-Land Special, just for you. Guaranteed you're gonna love it."

I looked at the platter of food and turned green as she placed a ruby-colored drink beside me with little black specks floating on top. I looked at Tracey with a mixture of surprise and disgust. I mean, how could anyone be so damned chirpy in the damned morning? Jeez!

Before I had a chance to resist, the red drink was in my hand. Tracey admonished me, "Down the Hatch!"

Glancing around the counter, I noticed the other patrons had resolutely turned their backs. The only hint of compassion came in the way of a knowing look from one faded out old gal in a shapeless, well-worn flower print dress who said, "Try it, hon. It can't do you any worse."

The mixture of beer and tomato juice topped with fresh black pepper went "down the hatch" with a surprised slosh and almost came back up again.

At that point, Tracey exclaimed, "Hold it!" Miraculously, the stuff stayed down and a flush came into my cheeks.

"Better?" she asked, solicitously.

"Um, well, yeah." I coughed "But I didn't know you guys served beer."

"Shhhh!" Tracey hushed me. "We don't! This is just for special occasions."

"Ahhhh." I did feel a little bit better. Almost human. I dove into the hash after covering it with ketchup.

Tracey left me to my breakfast and continued her daily work. Tracey seemed to keep a weather eye on me. For years, I'd been regarded as nothing more than an inconvenience unless I was needed to fetch the family water–go down to the jail and bail out brother Ed, keep my Mom company when my Dad ran off, take care of Mom when she got sick, accommodate the patrons of the Okefenokee Swamp when they were buying and toss them out on their ass when they were broke. Actually seeing someone care about *me* was a new and refreshing experience.

An ice water wondrously appeared from out of nowhere and, beside it, a couple of pretty white orbs: aspirin. I was saved! Tracey relaxed against the back of the counter next to me.

"See?" she said. "Better, huh, Jersey-style."

"Okay," I replied guardedly. "But what's Jersey got to do with breakfast?"

Tracey grinned. "Well, hon, a while back, we had a governor who mandated all our eggs be well cooked and people learned that a hard-fried egg helped with a hangover–the beer and TJ is an old family recipe," Tracey said.

"I see," I said, "and what about you?"

"Oh, sweetie, I'm in retirement." She leaned closely and said, in a low tone, but high pride, "Three years straight 'n' sober next month and still goin' strong, babe."

She could have pulled down a couple hundred a night at any decent bar in South Florida, she was *that* good. Now I knew why she didn't work that side of the street. Damn. I nodded to show I understood. She winked and went back to work.

I left Dana's at about one-fifteen and headed back to the bungalow to don my new work duds. Dud–singular or plural–described the outfit to a tee. One more breakfast at Dana's and I wouldn't fit the outfit, it was so beyond skimpy. The "uniform" consisted of a scanty white spandex leotard which fitted suspiciously like a cat suit, over which were black spandex panties, little more than a G-string and thong in back with things that looked like suspenders and slipped over my arms. Of course, the boobies bounced right out on either side of the black straps and would be even more prominent if I found the one push-up bra I owned. Jeez, the thing was skanky and needed a washing but good.

So did some other things of mine. The frequent costume changes over the last few days put my simple wardrobe through hell.

Approaching The Captain, I asked about laundry facilities and was told there were a washer and dryer in the back section of my bungalow. Aha! *That's* why the little hovel was shorter inside than out–mystery solved! However, and too bad for me, Dhani had the key and only used it when his three kids were visiting on alternate weekends. If the facilities weren't being used (with three kids? Gimme a break!), perhaps I might get in a load.

Given The Captain's proclivities, I asked about bars in the immediate area. This was a subject on which he knew much.

"Well, now, Missy Stacey," he began, "there's the Sandy Sea over on Ocean Avenue, and the Fisherman on the Pier…"

How quaint, I thought, as the Captain droned the litany of bars in Pompano. Every pier in every sea town has a bar called "The Fisherman" and every "Fisherman" bar has a dish called "Fisherman's Platter" if they serve food. We were going nowhere in a hurry and I had to wash my "uniform."

"…then there's the Bee Sting Bar, Stinger's, and, oh, hey, they serve pretty good pizza…"

Argh! I was getting fed up already!

"…and they have a launder-mat next to the pizza place…"

Bingo! "See ya, Cap'n! And thanks!" I exclaimed, blowing him a kiss as he kept on talking and I gently turned away towards my bungalow to collect my clothes and jump in the Mir for the Bee Sting and points south, namely, the "launder"-mat. I peeled out in the Mir and slung her into the Bee Line Shopping "Centre" parking lot in about two seconds. I found the Bee Kleen Wash-O-Mat, got change, duds were in the suds within three minutes, and then had about a half hour of time on my hands until the dry cycle.

The Bee Line Shopping Centre is a thin little L-shaped strip mall anchored by the distinguished law firm of Bumble & Bumble. Okay, that explained the Bee Line Shopping Centre but... the Bee Kleen Wash-O-Mat? The Bee Beautiful Boutique? The Busy Bee Salon? The Bee Thrifty dollar store and the Hive Convenience Mart and Liquor store? Conveniently, the Bee Sting, known as Stinger's Bar, was located right next door to Bee Kleen.

Typical Florida kitsch: a shabby, somewhat rundown strip mall with themed businesses. It was probably a bit much on the theme part, but perhaps it served as an ego boost for Messrs. Bumble & Bumble, Esquires, Attorneys at Law.

Walking into Stinger's, I sat down on one of the impossibly hard, impossibly high, and impossibly uncomfortable bar stools and ordered up a Coke. I was the only person in the place except for the old bartender, who looked at me suspiciously, as if I were road kill—perhaps he was kin of the waitress at the diner in Lauderdale-dash-by-dash-the-dash-Sea. Like her granddaddy. I laid a ten on the bar. He took it and gave me back nine ones. Yeah, Charlie. Rotsa Ruck. But I just left the ones where they were just to yank his chain and see what he'd do.

I sat sipping my Coke and waited for the half hour on wash to go by, aimlessly watching some talk junk on the cheap TV that was bolted to the ceiling on high. I swear, if anyone ever excavates this place thousands of years from now they'll surmise the banks were where we prayed and the bars were shrines to the God TV. May not be far off the truth anyways.

The dryer turned out to be a real a pain in the ass. Ten cents for ten minutes and you had to put the dimes in one at a time, flip a switch, wait for the ten minutes, and then put in another dime and so forth until the clothes were dry. So, I walked the line between Stinger's and the Bee

Kleen Wash-O-Mat about three or four times until the bartender, whom I lovingly now thought of as "Older than Dirt" asked me what the hell I was doing.

"Wash," I said flatly. I was down to about five or six bucks, having a dollar lifted off the pile every time I got a Coke. I used to give Cokes for free back at the Swamp. It was severe temptation to resist ordering ice water, daring Mr. "Older than Dirt" to charge for that! He filled my used glass with more Coke and a few chunks of ice, but didn't lift another buck off the pile.

"Most people enjoy a beer or two when they wash," hinted Mr. "Older than…"

"I work tonight. Geoffrey's," I explained.

"Nice place," he said in a sarcastic manner. "You should do well. Cocktail waitress?"

"You got it. I'm a bartender usually, though." I replied. Mr. "Older than Dirt" smiled. I had a feeling he knew more than he was letting on.

"You're a little older than the usual gals in there, but you'll do real well–say, what's your name?" he asked.

"Stacey," I answered, extending my hand across the bar for a friendly shake, 'tender to 'tender. I got a limp wrist and the fishy eye. "And yourself?" I asked.

"Charlie," said Mr. "Older than Dirt." Well, Goddamn. Charlie the bartender. I'm psychic.

We passed the time exchanging bartender talk: the pain of daily chores like hauling ice and glass, what our favorite drinks were to make, who made a better Bloody Mary or the recipe for *the* perfect dirty martini, a few jokes about some stereotyped customers who, no matter where you worked, were the same in every bar. We laughed at their animal nicknames, the cougar, the wolf, and the lounge lizard–make up your own animal, I'm sure I could find a barfly to fit the description–and had a little competition of who could outdo whom coming up with outlandish characters. We pretty much tied, but he had a small edge on me. I let the game die into silence and didn't push it. At that point, my laundry was done and we were kinda sorta friends.

"If it doesn't work out at Geoffrey's for ya, Sparky's Pub over on Briney Street is looking for a good 'tender. Maybe you want to check it out. Richard Sparks is the owner over there."

"Why wouldn't it work out?" I asked.

"Well, you're a bit older, as I said before, and you don't seem to be a flighty bitch, if you'll pardon my French," Charlie said.

"Yeah," I said thoughtfully, nodding my head, thinking *Old! I'm not OLD! Thirty isn't old*–then... "You know, I will have a quick beer–got a short one?" I asked.

"We do," Charlie answered, pouring me a quickie.

"Would you join me?" I asked.

"A pleasure," he replied, pouring one for himself and downing it quickly, lest someone walk in and catch him drinking on the job. Most bartenders drink on the job; it's the smart ones who don't get caught. The brew steadied me and I left the small pile of dollars for Charlie.

I thought about the "good old days" in South Florida as I collected my clothes from the Bee Kleen Wash-O-Mat. In the mid-sixties, Charlie had been a bartender at the Castaways Resort in Miami Beach, *the* hotspot of the season. He promised some stories next time I was in and, 'tender to 'tender I shook his hand again and received a good firm grip and eyeball-to-eyeball direct level look back in return.

I headed home to put the finishing touches on my new look for work. Nothing helped, even decent hair. The gold sequined bow tie worn choker fashion around my bare neck totally trashed this cheesy-to-begin-with costume. Even though I wore my classy little black Etienne Aigner low-heeled pumps with the peau-de-soie bows and gold signature "A", I still looked like a slut wanting to party. Off to work I went. Some party.

Arriving at Geoffrey's about five minutes to four, I was ushered into the kitchen by Susie, the buxom blonde hostess at the front desk who brought along a half-finished bowl of salad drenched in thick, creamy whitish dressing. The place buzzed with activity. The Bee Line Shopping Centre was still in the back of my mind and I replayed Charlie's *"if it doesn't work out…"* in my head. There were six other cocktail waitresses besides me, all of them tricked out in the same cheesy getup I was wearing.

Susie intro-ed me with a big toothsome smile. "Hey everybody! Meet Stacey! Our New Golden Girl!" She left to fill up her bowl again with more greens and a generous ladle of white goo from the salad bar in the kitchen. "By the way, Stacey, salad's free! All you want all night long," Susie called to me, stuffing a forkful of drippy greens into her mouth before heading out to her hostess stand at the front of the nightclub.

"Oh, goody," I thought, sarcastically. I met Dianna and Bevvie, Dianna's "partner in crime" from the looks of it. Then Laurie and Lori, cleverly distinguished from one another as "Laurie" and "Lori with an 'i'. Next up were Jennifer, and Tracy (not *my* Tracey, of course). Except for Dianna and Bevvie, none of the "old Golden Girls" looked one whit over 16. I would have carded them if they set foot in my bar, but they were working, not drinking, so it made no nevermind to me. The "new girl"–me, Dianna and Bevvie were thirty-somethings, although I thought Dianna might be on the shady side of thirty if not in her forties altogether. It was the perfect moment to shut up, so I did and smiled sweetly.

Geoffrey was nowhere to be seen and I'd been whisked into the kitchen so fast, I didn't even catch a glimpse of Mr. Cold-As-Ice behind the bar if, indeed, he was working that shift.

I wiggled uncomfortably in my getup, pulling the

bottom down past my butt, I hoped. The tall, lanky girl introduced as Dianna, with flat brown hair, flat brown eyes, no butt and skinny legs strode up next to me and handed me a large bucket of lemons.

"Hi, Stacey," she said crisply. "I'm Dianna. You'll be following me until midnight, then you're on your own. Start by prepping these." She went out the back door, struck a match to light her cigarette and inhaled deeply, Sulphur fumes and all. She lounged next to a pile of plastic milk crates and watched me lazily through narrowly slit eyes as I began to cut lemons.

"Following" is a term in the restaurant business, which meant I got to step-n-fetchit for another waitress while she collected all the tips–hers and yours. It's a whole lot of fun for nothin'. But a job was a job and, after prepping the lemons into neat little slices, twists, and twirls with which to garnish the pricey cocktails, I took a deep breath, pulled down the bottom of my getup again, and went to look out over the club area on the pretext of telling Dianna I had to use the ladies' room. I didn't know if I would dare pee in this outfit. It was like a Roach Motel, you get into it, but you don't get out.

Everything gleamed. The brass and chrome reflected my image against the bar and, given Dana's breakfasts, I still didn't look half bad. Pretty good for cheese 'n' sleaze, I thought. In fact, I could have been topless, or nude, the way things go on in the Fort Liquordale bar biz. I was lucky to be dressed at all. The two Lauries, who I thought of as a matched pair of Lorikeets, those colorful little parrot-like birds who chitter and shit all over you at zoos and bird parks, came out whispering to each other as they sidled into the coffee service alcove next to the kitchen.

Although I overheard the whispering, I could not make out the words. It seemed rather urgent, however, but I was rudely awakened from trying to listen a bit harder by

Geoffrey breezing into the club, giving the bartenders, including Mr. Cold-As-Ice, high-fives and a warlike whoop, smacking me on my somewhat covered butt and saying, "Hey, kid! Good to see ya!" and, with a nod of his head toward the kitchen, "In here." To the Lorikeets, he said, "You two–over here," and pointed to a spot a several feet in front of the kitchen doors which were closed and quiet.

I trotted obediently in the direction of the kitchen; I was–after all–the "New Girl" and wanted to make a decent first impression–*oh, goody–as if I could be decent in this getup anyway,* I thought to myself. Curiosity got the better of me, though, so I ducked and slipped into the shadows of the coffee service alcove.

The Lorikeets beamed at Geoffrey, who said, "Ladies, please," while putting up his hands in an "I surrender" gesture. "We need to talk."

The Lorikeets twittered and cooed.

"It's not good," Geoffrey continued. "Your cards came up okay, but when I ran your socials I found you were born in 1892 not, say, 1972–maybe? Your last names are even the same. You related?"

The Lorikeets visibly slumped, their uniforms sagging on their supple young bodies. I wasn't budging from that alcove unless Dianna came out and dragged me back into the kitchen by the roots of my hair. They looked at each other tentatively then Lori, a tough-looking little blonde, put her chin up, smiled softly at Geoffrey and said quietly, "I know there's a way we can work this out."

Laurie slumped even further, as if she wished her uniform would swallow her inside of it and suck her through an invisible hole in the carpeted floor.

"Come to my office after shift," Geoffrey said and, putting his arms around both girls and drawing them to him. "We'll find a way to work this out."

Lori snuggled close to him. Laurie shrank away, but

put on a good face and pulled her uniform down over her butt.

Lucky for me, I escaped Dianna's wrath by coming into the kitchen right behind Geoffrey and the Lorikeets. I slipped next to Tracy. Dianna's long nails were bared and she had a grim look on her face. I suspected she was just itching to catch me goofing around and tell me off. Or worse.

Assembled in the kitchen with Dianna reeking of her recent cigarette, the cocktail waitresses clustered around Geoffrey. He looked dashing, dapper even, a far cry from the soggy guy I freed from the freezer the previous afternoon. The gray suit I had met him in was swapped out for an up-to-the-minute tux with white tie. He was The Host of the Moment, the Man of the Hour, and the Man of the Minute. Maybe, but he was still too pimped-up looking for me. I knew how that moussed hair could wilt and the stubble show after just a short time in the freezer. Besides, how did he get in there, anyway? I had to pop a lock to get him out. I just kept to myself and kept my mouth shut. I smiled beguilingly at my fellows and Mr. Geoffrey himself.

Geoffrey struck a pose, then another. The girls oohed and aahed like hens preening before the cock o' the walk. I'd seen this in henhouses before, with chickens picking and pecking at each other until the cock walked in. I wondered if this was the reason Mr. Geoffrey got himself stuck in the freezer. Mr. Cock, that is, with too many pickin' chickens in his hen house.

"Ladies, please…" Geoffrey demurred. Yeah, right. They were hanging on every word, even the cynical Dianna and her bud, Bevvie. How much of *that* was an act, I wondered.

"This is pre-weekend, ladies. We're gearing up for party time!" *Jesus*, I thought. "We want to rock 'em and roll 'em." I didn't know at the time, but truer words were never spoken. "Let's hear it for the hottest spot in town!"

"G!" the girls squealed.

"E!" they squealed again.

"O! My!" Another synchronous squeal.

"Double F! And you know what that means! (giggle)" I was feeling actual stirrings of nausea.

"R! We're born ready!"

"E–Yeah! We are!"

"Y! Because we love it!"

Then they all wigged their butts in place of the apostrophe for Geoffrey's and squealed: "Squiggle!" with a giggle at the end. I pulled down my uniform again and checked to see who else was pulling down their getups and spied Laurie struggling to cover her ass with the skimpy black material. I gave her a compassionate, knowing look and received a slight smile for my trouble.

"S! We love it even more! Whoooo hoooo!"

One more cheer and I'd throw up.

The applause and cheers died down as Geoffrey put up his hands, like a rock star placating his audience for quiet before a performance.

"Ladies, ladies–this is too much!" He blushed. "Thank you!"

Blush? Did the man actually *blush?* Shit. What an act.

The doors opened and the patrons streamed in. Most headed for the bars, but a few took tables. We were held in the kitchen for another ten minutes. A fanfare blared from the speakers all over the club, and the DJ announced Geoffrey "The Host with the *Most!*"

Geoffrey emerged on cue with much applause and cheering from the club crowd. He took the mic from the DJ and announced–"for his patrons' *pleasure*" of course– "Geoffrey's Golden Girls!" Meaning us.

"Hey," I said to Laurie, getting behind her, "Isn't 'The Golden Girls' a sitcom about a bunch of old ladies?"

"Hush, you!" she hissed at me.

Lori came right up behind, cutting in front of Laurie. "We're on! Get behind Dianna! And smile, damn it!"

I fell in as I was told, but I thought it was a pretty good joke. I bared my teeth in more of a grimace than a grin, doubting if anyone could tell the difference. Our happy little troupe of trollops marched single file out of the kitchen to a blare of more fanfare and a blast of spotlight.

"Heads up kids! It's show time!" Dianna snapped. "Show what you own! Brightly! And with feeling!"

She had to be kidding. My grimace got bigger.

It was my turn: "And our New Girl! Stacey!" Oh, goody. I went out to the middle of the floor, pretending to haughtily catwalk-stomp like the models do on TV, did a little twirl in the middle, flicked my golden bow tie and stomped off into the kitchen. If they wanted a show, okay fine. Someone in the shadows of the coffee service alcove popped out and flashed me with a paparazzi-type camera. I tried not to flinch.

As embarrassing as it was to be in this cheesy getup to begin with, imagine marching around a busy nightclub, under spotlights, having your name called out as you crossed the dance floor alone! With your ass ogled by a wolf pack all the way back to the kitchen. I enjoyed it more when the Captain wolf-whistled me.

"Show off," Dianna hissed. Well, I could have just curtsied, I thought.

Arriving back in the kitchen, Geoffrey instructed us in our roles: "Laurie and Lori with an 'i'—you do Jell-O shots! Red first, then purple, then green, then back to red. The staff will help you figure out which is which. Got it? Two bucks each." The Lorikeets nodded in assent, a look of awe on their faces.

"Bevvie, Jennifer—you do tube shots." Geoffrey continued, "Rum runners are pink, Bahama Mamas are pink, Alabama Slammas are pink—should be a no-brainer.

Four bucks–got it?" Bevvie and Jennifer nodded and took off for the service bar.

"Tracy, you do food service tonight." Tracy looked at Geoffrey as if he had just bestowed sainthood upon her. This was sheer idiocy!

"Dianna…" Geoffrey gave her a 'come hither' look and a wink, "Stacey…" I got the same treatment, and it took every ounce of strength not to sigh and roll my eyes skyward. I sidled up to Geoffrey in the manner of Dianna, "You have cocktail service tonight."

Dianna looked levelly at Geoffrey and said, "Thanks, Geoff." This was the easiest service job of all, just go around taking drink orders and collecting tip money.

Geoffrey took off for the clubroom and its patrons. The clubroom was a small room off to the side of the general nightclub, reserved for private parties and VIP's. He closed the door behind him. I could hear muffled laughter and clinking glasses.

Dianna turned to me, "Watch, listen, keep your mouth shut and stay out of my way. At midnight you're on your own. Got it?"

I stood there, looking as acquiescent as I could, and nodded. Little ol' dumb shit, me.

The first part of the evening was spent mostly trotting after Dianna, smiling sweetly as possible. I made the evening's mission seeing how downright sweet I could be while wanting to thump the piss out of the miserable bitch. She worked the room like a pro and had her regulars to prove it. The chick must've picked up a C-note an hour, which wasn't bad for such cha-cha work. I wondered if maybe there was something to this, if you could put up with the bullshit.

I watched the Lorikeets. They were like chittering little birds, sweeping the room with Jell-O shots. From time to time, they took a shot on a friendly invite from a customer and a bill slipped down the front of their costume.

Jell-O shot detail also had its moments, it seemed.

In the kitchen, I caught a smidge of conversation between the Lorikeets.

"My Mom finally tracked me down, the bitch," said Laurie.

Lori slumped. "No way. You so need to get rid of your phone now. You think she'll tell on us?"

"Yeah, most likely."

"So, we've both gotta get new phones. Maybe move again. Great."

"What are you going to do about Geoffrey after work?" Laurie asked.

"Whatever it takes, honey. I'm not afraid of my Mom, she's dead," Lori countered. "It's my *Dad* I'm never going back to." Laurie nodded sympathetically.

Bevvie and Jen traveled back and forth to the service bar to dump the empty tube trays and pick up replacements. I knew the bar biz was cash flow, but I'd never seen the likes of this back at the ol' Okefenokee Swamp–usually, you had to use all your wiles to get one of the guys to pony up for the draft beer he'd down in one good guzzle.

Tracy ran food from the kitchen to the bar, so we didn't see a whole lot of her. Dianna and I worked the main room and the bar, like the other girls.

Our "job" was to make sure anyone standing not directly *at* the bar was never with less than a half-full drink in hand, preferably with a backup on the side. The tables, floor, dance floor, DJ area, patio, and five feet off the bar rail was our responsibility. The dirty ashtrays were endless. Just as soon as you'd do the magic trick of swapping the dirty ashtray for a clean one, some turd would just have to mark his territory with a flick of the butt–boom! It was dirty enough for Mr. Geoffrey to demand a replacement if he had seen it. I was told, pointed to, directed, and hissed at to ensure compliance with their standards of ashtray cleanliness.

The empty glasses were relentless and–heaven forbid!–no bus trays or cartage were allowed. I'd put them discreetly on my little cocktail tray, doing the "Geoffrey Dip" as I'd been instructed to do, which involved something of a backward lean with a twist to maximize the show of cleavage through the cat suit. The little tray held a total of four glasses max and I returned to the bar. The tray couldn't get wet, either, so much was made of drying the tray after visiting the bar.

Dianna would serve and I'd dip 'n' fetchit. Dianna would smile and I'd dip and dump an ashtray. Dianna would wiggle a twenty into her cleavage and I'd and pick up a spilled drink. Dipping, of course. I was sick of smiling and dipping and sicker of not making any dough while Dianna breezed around the room without a care in the world. Well, maybe one care: if I let anything go for less than a minute–like for trying to take a cocktail order–I was treated to a sharp look and a long, blood-red fingernail pointing to a spilled drink on the floor, dirty ashtray, or empty glass to clear. Dianna would sashay over to scoop the drink order and the tip. Thanks, girlfriend.

For a moment, I thought it might be fun to suddenly upend the cocktail napkin and bar stirrer dispensers throughout the bar and spill some dirty ashtrays on the floor just to make a rumpus and everyone's life miserable. In the end, that would have cost me my job. I wouldn't have made anyone miserable except myself. Mr. Geoffrey probably wouldn't fire me until I completed my job, picking up the never-ending supply of soggy cocktail napkins and stirrers strewn throughout the bar by the patrons at leisure. I wondered how the joint got so clean after an evening of such bedlam. Oh, yeah–I was dipping and picking up all night.

Finally eleven-thirty rolled around and Dianna regally summoned me. To end my formal training, I guessed.

"Okay, girl," she started, "I'm going to say this only once, so pay attention. If you screw up and Geoffrey catches you you're out." Nice. No pressure. I liked that.

"Work the room, catch six drinks, go to the bar to fill 'em up. Call the whites first, the ambers next, the mixed drinks next, then the cordials, then the beer and wine. That's how the speed racks are set up. The bartender will have your head if you fuck it up. Got it? Now get to work, and I'll be watching."

I nodded sweetly and thought of murder in the first degree–reason enough to smile. Six drinks, I was going to need a bigger tray.

Pleased with the amount of confidence Dianna had shown me, I approached three guys, who had just emerged from the clubroom with no drinks. Two were tall and one was short. They stood at a high-top table, ogling the Lorikeets making the rounds, and making conversation with each other when I sidled over to catch their order.

"Where's Dianna?" one of the guys asked.

I cocked my head in her direction, "She told me to come and say hi. Do you need anything?"

"Yeah, Dianna," said the short man.

I towered over him, "Don't get short with me," I quipped, smiling idiotically, towering over the little dude, as the two taller men blankly stared off into space.

"Dianna!" The short guy called over to my so-called compadre. Dianna shot him a look then nodded at me. Shorty shrugged. "Okay, two beers and a scotch rocks, and send Dianna over with the drinks."

In the corner opposite, I spotted the gentleman in the black leather jacket, who had been speaking with the Cold-As-Ice bartender the previous day. Since my goal was six drinks, I approached him hoping he'd make number four.

"May I get you a cocktail, sir?" I asked politely.

He stood in the shadows and nodded once. "Booker's. Neat."

I headed to the bar and faced the bartender. His frigid stare chilled me.

"Name's Brian, hon. What do you need?" he said brusquely. I ordered the cocktails and beer. He poured the drinks. "That's twenty-five to you."

"Okay, I'll be right back," I said, moving to take the drink tray.

"Uh-uh," Brian said, grabbing my tray and almost pulling a spill. "Now, please."

"But I don't have any money."

"So, get the money, honey, then you'll get the drinks. Looks like you're short all around. Six drink minimum order to you, but you're new, I'll let you slide with four." He priced out the drinks for me.

Drinkless, I walked over to my three gents.

"Seventeen dollars, please." I asked, standing beside them patiently, idiot smile still in place.

One of the tall ones got a twenty out of his wallet and handed it over.

I walked over to the black-leather clad gent, "Eight dollars, please."

"Tell him it's for me," he said flatly. "I don't pay."

"And your name would be…" I started, hoping he'd finish. But he just stood there and casually slid a toothpick from his inside pocket, inserted it in his mouth and twirled it around a little with his tongue. He seemed to look through me, not at me, not away from me. Just stone cold, as if I were completely insignificant. It was an attitude I recognized in my brother Ed when he was cooking up a new scheme and I asked him to help me with my homework or take me to the store. Best leave it alone; I'd get nowhere fast. So, I shut my mouth and studied him for a moment, hoping he was so absorbed in ignoring me he wouldn't notice. I'd done that trick with Ed, too. I realized I couldn't tell the color of his eyes in the dim light of the club. They were dark, though, and he looked as if a dark cloud shadowed his face when I asked for money to pay for his drink. Under the black leather jacket he wore a dark blue collarless shirt, and his ensemble was completed with fitted black jeans and scuffed black boots. This was a man you don't turn your back on. The feeling reminded me of a similar day when I'd faced off a coral snake in the 'glades when I was a kid. Eventually, it moved.

"All right, Mr. Smith it is," I mumbled under my breath, as I finally felt safe enough to step back and head for the bar.

"That's better," Brian said, handing me back my tray, but still keeping a hand on it, stopping me from moving along. Jennifer got behind me and scowled for my being so slow. "You're still short," Brian said.

"The Booker's for Mr. Smith over there," I said, indicating the gentleman in the black leather jacket. He nodded and let me take the tray, "uh, change?"

He scowled and handed me three soggy dollars. I tucked the bills into the top of my cat suit, peeking out so I could easily grab the money and hand it off to the men as I had seen the other girls do. I observed some of the men would just finger the money and leave it where it lay. I wasn't going there for three bucks. They could have it back. All of it.

My idiot's smile was getting harder and harder to maintain. "Thanks, Brian."

He turned his back on me.

Under the assumption Mr. Smith was a "friend of the house," as they say in the biz, he got his drink first without incident.

I walked over to my guys and handed out the drinks.

"What, no napkins?" Shorty sputtered. I turned around to go back to the bar for napkins and bumped smack into Geoffrey and his overstuffed smile.

"Hey! Tracy!" He put his arm around my waist and sneakily copped a feel on one of my butt cheeks.

"Uh, Geoffrey, it's Stacey." I wiggled smartly out of Mr. Geoffrey's reach.

"Riiiiiiight. Hi guys!" to the gruesome threesome. "How's our new little Golden Girl doing?" Then, looking down at the drinks on the bare table, "No napkins? Tracy!"

I hurried back to the bar, threw a few napkins on my tray, and made my way over to the pack of men. Lucky me. Plopping the napkins down on the high top and the drinks down on the napkins, I expected a nod of approval as I fished in my cat suit to pull out the three bucks to give to the men.

Geoffrey grabbed my hand, full of soggy cash, and said "Well, well, what have we here?"

"Bar change," I replied.

"A likely story," slurred Shorty. "She was gonna keep it."

"Now, now, it's her first night," said Geoffrey. "Let's give her the benefit of the doubt." Geoffrey was holding me by the wrist in an excruciatingly tight grip. He twisted it smartly and the bills fell to the floor.

"Oh, my dear," said Geoffrey, tisk-tisking, "now you'll just have to pick them up. Bend over, won't you?"

Something in me just snapped. "That's it!" I snarled, pulling free. "Are you calling me a thief?" Looking square at Geoffrey and the three amigos, I bent from my knees, picked up the bills, counted out the three soggy dollars and threw them onto the table where they landed with a soft splat and half hung off the side.

"Oh, sweetie," Geoffrey oozed. "Nobody's calling you anything, darling."

"Get Dianna," Shorty demanded, peeling the bills from their precarious position. Geoffrey signaled to her and she came over.

"Here," said Shorty, handing Dianna the three bucks, "this is for you." He wobbled drunkenly, crossed his eyes and said, "Nothing for you!" And to Geoffrey, "Just keep her the hell away from us!"

Deciding life was too short for this bullshit, I hissed to *Mister* Geoffrey "This is for you," I flipped a bird. "Next time, I hope you freeze your balls off." I marched directly out of the nightclub into the kitchen and grabbed my purse. On my way out, the tune of giggling Lorikeets half drunk from too many jello shots rang in my ears in that stark white echo chamber of a kitchen. Brian, cold as ice and utterly indifferent to everything around him, was in the kitchen getting ice–what else? He looked up as I passed him.

I held up one finger–the forefinger, not that other one, pointed it at him, and said in that flat and dangerous tone that brooks no insolence, "Don't." He coolly shook his head and went back to shoveling ice. His French cuffs weren't even damp.

Susie, the buxom blonde hostess, was back in the kitchen and watched the whole exchange through squinty eyes while stuffing her round chubby face with salad.

I slid out the side door and slipped into The Mir. As I slithered The Mir out of the parking lot, I saw Mr. Smith casually leaning up against the side door, lighting a cigarette.

I'd show them by sending the Captain back with my uniform and plenty of drinking money. Cooler heads prevailed, though, on my way home, and I decided to be nicer to the Captain than that.

I returned home to peaceful silence at the compound. Not even the palm fronds whispered in the stillness. I collected myself and passed the Captain happily snoring on his chaise in front of Edmund's. There was no other sign of human life on this part of the planet.

Letting myself in to home-sweet-home, I peeled off

the moronic costume and took a boiling hot shower. Clean, dry and in my favorite sleepy-tee, I donned my Tigger slippers and padded to the garbage cans behind the bungalow. Lifting the lid of the first can, I unceremoniously dumped the uniform, gold sequined bow tie and all. It laid in a doleful heap at the bottom, sharing space with some old fish bones, coffee grinds, fruit peels and some hungry Palmetto bugs. Plopping the lid back on the can, I headed inside, stretched out on the sofa, and planned not to know anything until morning.

Chapter Four

I was rudely awakened at six A.M., to the ruckus of Dhani and Edmund getting ready for work. I poked my nose out of the bungalow to see what all the noise was all about.

"Hey, stranger!" Dhani called. "How was your first night?"

"Over," I grumbled.

The Captain gave a bleary chuckle, and slumped back down to his chaise snooze. Edmund shambled out of his apartment to go to work. He was a groundskeeper for an old age home, also known as an *Assisted Living Facility–* which meant the people who lived there weren't hurting for dough and didn't want to be thought of as living in an old folks' home.

Playfully punching the Captain on the shoulder, Edmund said, "Hey, Stace! How goes it? Did you have fun? Make lots of money?"

"Oh, yeah. Call the Brinks truck, Edmund."

"That good, huh? Well, weekend's coming."

"I'm not going back, I'm afraid."

Dhani and Edmund just shrugged. I guessed not working is nothing new in this neighborhood.

"Hey! I've got an idea!" Dhani said brightly, "Come to work with me!"

"And you do… exactly what, Dhani?" I asked.

"Contracting. General contracting. I build buildings."

Oh, great. It was six-fifteen A.M. Well, at least I'd get a tan. Jesus! What was I thinking?!

"Nah, that's okay. I'll pass for now."

"Well, if you need beer money…"

"That's okay. I don't plan on drinking this morning…" and I waved Dhani off and headed back into the bungalow. Hell.

I didn't feel like going to Dana's, partly because I didn't feel like explaining last night to Tracey. I wanted to put some time between last night and me. More like a lifetime.

I pulled a semi-cool Coke out of the fridge–breakfast of champions, when one didn't feel like a beer–and scarfing down some sugar-frosted flakes by the handful straight out of the box. I was starting to feel a little brighter. Sugar does that to a person.

I turned on the TV and watched the weather bimbette ply her trade. Hot and muggy at night, hot and muggy during the day, maybe some rain. Florida weather is a real no-brainer unless there's a hurricane, then the meteorologist takes over. I didn't think it was really all that hot, but the TV hacks are prone to exaggeration. The tourists watching this shit in their mildewy hotel rooms would probably think this was something special. I popped a large, comfy navy blue hoodie over my sleepy-tee and sat on the edge of the bed, munching sugar flakes and taking long pulls on the Coke. I wondered if the weather bimbo had gotten a recent boob job or if the wardrobe department got a kick out of making her clothing uncomfortably tight.

By six-forty-five a.m., I'd had it and decided to lay down for a nap. I tossed and turned for a few minutes, but the sugar surged through my system and kept me wide awake. Oh, well, the beach was a block away.

Tugging some shorts on under my sleepy-tee and sliding my feet into the surfer-girl flip-flops, I headed out to make sure the Atlantic Ocean was still there. It was.

A soft, cool breeze blew off the ocean and ruffled my hair. I walked up the beach, focusing on the pier until I reached it. Turning around, I walked closer to the small waves on the way back, getting my toes kissed by the sea and doing a great job sogging up my new sandals. I found a lonesome bench at the end of the beach, before the street, and sat down. *Now* what was I going to do?

Well, I lived–if not in, near–Fort Liquordale. I'm a bartender by trade. This is the season. So... find another job, I guess. I tried to keep my best interests at heart and truly wanted to work someplace high-end and nice. The long and the short of it was that I'm just a simple woman and fancy clubs don't suit me at all. I thought they had a rotten underbelly that made the little dives smell fresh by comparison. I saw that last night for myself and briefly thought about how the Lorikeets had "worked it out" with Geoffrey after their shift. Throwaway kids are part of a "grow your own victim" mentality, a unique byproduct of the Me-Generation culture. I knew. I was one myself.

I decided to pay a visit to crusty old Charlie down to the Bee Sting and get a line on this Sparky's. I was going to be cagey about this one, though. I was going to do my homework this time and not get hooked into anything too deep first time out.

The sugar was wearing off and I decided some coffee might do me, so I headed over to the outdoor bistro and got the worst cup ever. Two swigs and I trashed the half-full cup. It was so old you could have sung *Happy Birthday* to the coffee a couple times over. My stomach was growling, empty from the vast speed at which sugar metabolizes in one's system, leaving nothing inside except maybe wanting more sugar, so I headed home for a PBJ sandwich, a cool shower and a damn good think. Somewhere in the middle of thinking, I fell asleep.

I walked to the Bee Sting at about one in the afternoon. Charlie was filling sinks and polishing bottles. I was the only one in the bar and hopped onto one of the bar stools.

"Short one today, sweetie? Or a Coke?" Charlie

asked. Ah, he remembered. A good bartender never forgets a face or the drink that goes with it.

"Yeah, please, but make it a regular–beer," I said, focusing on one of those forensic TV shows.

"Can do," he said, pulling a draught with my name on it. I laid a ten on the bar and got eight back. My lucky number. I put a one on the rail, leaving me with seven, and felt better instantly.

We watched TV for a while. Charlie puttered with this and that, I pulled on the draught now and again, the forensic team had begun a minute examination of someone's big toe. Fortunately, the TV was silent.

"You like watching this shit?" I asked Charlie, as the forensic team gathered around a forefinger, most likely matching the source of the toe. They reminded me of pilgrims seeking a relic in a church shrine.

"Nah, that's why I've got it on mute. I can't see for shit without my glasses." He gave me a snaggle-toothed grin and leaned over the rail, "What's the matter, girl? Lost your best friend?"

"Nah, just my job."

"Geoffrey's, right?" he asked.

I nodded.

"Didn't lose much."

I looked up, questioningly.

"That's a rock and roll bar," he said. "They rock the drinks with too much ice and roll the customers by not giving them their change back."

"Oh," I nodded glumly, staring deeply into my beer as if it held the answers to truth, justice, and the American way. Super Beer.

"Most of the chicks have sticky fingers, too. They look nice, but don't give 'em no more than you owe or you'll never see it back."

No wonder the three stooges from the night before were so antsy about getting their change. It also explained why Geoffrey was so eager to smooth things over–maybe that's how he got to wear those sharp looking suits and use a day's pay worth of mousse in his hair. Maybe that's why I had to unlock him from the freezer as well.

He set me up with another, "That's with me." I smiled.

"Thanks." The forensic team was now full swing into an autopsy, and Charlie turned the set off.

"So, what now, girl?"

Nobody had called me "girl" that way since my Dad, and he'd run off years ago. I still remembered the way he said it, though, and my heart gave a little twitch. Charlie was too old for a proper "Dad" fit, more like an older uncle or a grandpa. I shrugged it off and worked on my beer.

"Another job, I guess."

"You're not goin' back down there, huh? You'd be a glutton for punishment," he winked at me.

I winked back, "Not sure, Charlie. You never know what a woman's going to do. Sometimes even the woman isn't sure."

"Why don't you take the day off? Seems like you're halfway there already."

I looked down at my watch and saw it was a little after two. I explored my options: I could sit here for a while, spend down the ten, and go home nicely buzzed; I could go home with some dough in my pocket and get nicely buzzed with The Captain; I could just go home; or I could go to Pizzzazzz.

Life is a compromise, my mother always said. So, I decided to have one more, then go to Pizzzazzz, then go home.

"One more, Charlie."

"All rightee," he said, dipping down to get me a fresh-frozen mug from the cooler.

We passed the time with idle chat. He was from the panhandle area, I was from the southern central part of the state, so we were pretty much on the same wavelength. True Southern conversation is mostly an agreeable exchange, and when enhanced by a few beers, it gets more understated, yet best said.

"So, Charlie," I said, after I'd thought we'd made a pretty decent acquaintance, "what was it like? Back in the day... say, at The Castaways?"

"Well," Charlie started, "the mid-sixties were interesting. Miami was just coming into its own and Miami Beach was the place to be. There was even talk about table games in the big hotels and the boys from Vegas bought up a few choice properties and slung hotels on the beach quick as you please. The Desert Inn, the Sahara, Tangiers. Flashy nightclubs, headliner acts. They were all offshoots of Vegas. Nobody owned Miami just like nobody owned Vegas, so it was a free-for-all, mob-style. Then table games got voted down by the Babble-thumpers, so all these places became just write-offs and hand-me-downs. Even the big-shot entertainers stopped coming. Hell, the Beatles partied at the Castaways that year they stayed at the Fontainebleau. It was that hot of a place. When it cooled down, the mob guys stayed because it was a good place to escape from the heat up north—New York, Chicago, if you know what I mean, and charge it on the cuff to their boys in Vegas. A lot of them stayed, they're still here. They don't so much run things anymore, but they own them."

I nodded as if I understood. *Was Geoffrey one of "them"?* I wondered. Then I thought he'd be too young. In the mid-sixties he'd be just a kid. It wasn't a good time to ask about the connection, if ever it would be, so I just shut up.

"You ought think some about Sparky's," Charlie said as I stood up off the barstool and slung my bag over my shoulder. "I know Rick. We used to work together back in the day."

"Yeah," I sighed. "I'll think about it."

"Let me know," Charlie said as I headed out the door. I left the remainder of the ten on the rail. "Much obliged," he called after me.

I walked up the A-1-A and looked across the street at the huge, old cement and phony sprayed-on stucco high-rise condos lining the beach side. They contrasted dramatically with the squatty little motels, apartments, and bungalows on my side of the street. I wasn't sure I wanted to go to Pizzzazzz after all, but decided to go anyway because something new is always a good way to get your chin up again.

Pizzzazzz was cool and pink inside; kind of like a womb, I thought. I looked over the shoe selection, but couldn't bring myself to muster more than a passing glance to any one pair. Too many beers, I decided, and headed across the street to the drug store to pick up some aspirin just in case of a hangover later. I also picked up a pair of 98-cent rubber flip-flops in a really bright day-glow orange, so the day wasn't a total loss, after all. At least I had something to wear to the beach and could save the surfer-girl flip-flops for "good."

I needed something for dinner. I dropped by the Mom-and-Pop store. Mr. and Mrs. Kim provisioned me with a pack of bologna, a loaf of white bread, some mayo and another six-pack of Coke. I could get beer from the guys if I wanted, but quite frankly, I didn't want. I was in no mood for anything, not even a beer.

I slapped the bologna, bread, and mayo down on the table in the center of the compound and headed to my bungalow to stash the Coke in the mini-fridge.

"Hey, Cap'n," I called to the lump on the chaise. He looked up bleary-eyed and gave a half-wave. "Feast time."

The Captain turned over, snorted and rolled off the chaise. He ambled unsteadily towards the table.

"Mornin' Missy."

"Uh, actually, afternoon, Cap'n," I said. There were

probably more attractive dining companions but hell, what was I gonna do? Eat this shit by myself? I spread some mayo on a slice of bread, laid a couple of pieces of bologna on top, put more mayo on the second slice, slapped them together and voila! Dinner!

"Here, Cap'n," I said, handing the first sandwich to him and building another for myself.

Chomping his sandwich gratefully, The Captain looked up at me and asked, "Drink?"

"Nah, no beer today. Got Coke, though."

"No, you." He said and pulled a bottle out of his shirt. He took a good long swig, then tried to hand off the bottle to me.

I finished my sandwich, passed on the beer, and headed into the bungalow to take a whiz and get a Coke. "Be right back." I said. The Captain nodded and took another pull off the bottle.

Emerging from my bungalow refreshed and fed, I decided to have a bright idea. I needed a telephone. After all, if I were to land a job, how would they call to let me know to let me know I was hired? What if I made a friend? I had Tracey's number, but all I could give in return was my address, such as it was.

"Cap'n," I asked, "where's the nearest phone booth?"

"Gonna change into Superman?" He laughed uproariously at his joke.

"Nah, not today," I replied, not half as delighted or amused with his humor as was he. Resorting to my prior tactics, I asked, "Where's the closest bar?"

The captain snorted, coughed, and said, "Whaddaya wanna bar for? We got stuff right here."

"Don't worry, Cap. I just need to make a call."

"Oh, okay then. There's a pay phone at the Kim's store, but that's out on the street. Then there's a pay phone at The Asylum, but they're not open 'til seven. Oh!" he said, hitting his head with the heel of his hand. "There's a pay phone at Sparky's. It's even in a booth and it's private."

"Sparky's?" I asked.

"Yeah, over on Briny Avenue. Just head up Atlantic then walk up to the ocean. Before you get to the beach, you get to Sparky's."

I stood up.

"You gonna eat that?" The Captain asked, eyeing the bologna longingly.

I sighed, looking at the almost-empty package. "Nah, I've had enough and there's not enough to put away. You want one for the road?" I made him another sandwich with the last few pieces of bologna–I'd swear there was more before I'd hit the head.

"You?" The Captain asked generously, holding out his much-used bottle.

"Nah… gotta make a call, you know?" And I winked.

"Yeah." He winked back, as he took the proffered sandwich and bit into it greedily. I winced and reminded myself I wasn't staying at The Ritz. Never had, either.

I followed the Captain's directions and found Sparky's to be a "landmark" site on the corner of Briny and Atlantic Avenues. Actually, it was a fucking eyesore. The "landmark" was a garishly bright mural, which looked as if it were titled "Jaws Meets Nemo in Jurassic Park", painted on the Atlantic Avenue side of the building. Worse, it continued all the way around to the Briny Avenue side, with the piece also encompassing "Jaws Meets Nemo in Jurassic Park at 40,000 Leagues Beneath the Sea." Oh my aching eyes.

I walked in. "Nice mural," I said to the bartender wiping glassware behind the bar.

He nodded. "Thanks, owner's son did it. He's an art major at U.M.," referring to the University of Miami.

Inside was cool, dark and inviting. There was a large bar running the length of the place and on the east and north sides were tables and booths. The décor was nautically themed in what I'd call Early Obnoxious–anything else would have been insulting. It was not unlike the Okefenokee Swamp; it needed to be hokey and funky. I was thankful it didn't have a freshly killed gator skin curing on the wall, like The Swamp, just a few old stuffed fish. I sat at the bar on one of the comfortable captain-style barstools. I decided if I had the option to work at a job or hang here, hanging here definitely had merit. I was closer to understanding why The Captain decided to take the rest of his life off. I ordered a beer and asked where the pay phone was located. I got change, hoisted my beer to go with me, and went to the payphone to call the phone company.

What a pain in the ass. Press one and wait. Press one if you don't want to wait any more, press two if you want to find out more about not waiting, press three if you want to wait. Run out of change. Get more. Call back. Press one and wait. Finally, a really nice lady came on the phone–my first break of the day–and I arranged to have my phone service hooked up on Monday morning. The Gods smiled. I decided to celebrate with a shot to go with my beer and ordered a "ta kill ya" Gold with lime and salt, polishing it off like it was breakfast.

"New to the neighborhood?" the bartender asked.

"How did you know?" Always answer a question with a question, it's a better policy than honesty, especially when talking to strangers and cops.

"I heard you call the phone company."

Between him and Edmund, I was surrounded by sleuths.

"Yeah. Pain in the ass, isn't it?" I asked back, smiling but quietly seething–hell, The Captain said that phone booth was private. I was glad it was just the phone company I was calling and made a mental note never to use that phone for anything else.

He agreed, "I hate the phone company. But they're not as bad as the power company."

"Oh, tell me about it!" Coming from Lake Okeechobee and a trailer park to boot, the power was off more than on, even if the bill got paid more than two months in a row.

I studied the bartender, who went back to polishing glassware. He was about my height, or maybe an inch or two taller, which would make him short in a man's world. He had sandy brown hair, a boyish face complete with lopsided grin, denim-blue eyes and a nice butt. That's right—I noticed. I'm not dead yet, okay?

"So, what's your name?" I asked him.

"Rick. What's yours?"

"Stacey." Could this be the Richard Sparks that Charlie had mentioned? "Rick Sparks?" I asked.

"How do you come to know Rick Sparks?" Rick the bartender asked. Okay, he was obviously not *the* Mr. Sparks.

"I don't."

"You will when you see him," Rick laughed, "but I'm not him. Wish I was. Wish I had his money, anyway." He laughed again. I joined him.

"Yeah, true—what do they say? *'If you want to drink for a living, buy a bar.'*"

"But make sure it has a restaurant, too, so you eat once in a while." We both laughed and I ordered another beer. What the hell.

There were now a few other people decorating the place: a couple of couples, a few baseball-cap guys in well-worn jeans, and a handful of elderly tourists living it up. The wait staff and second-string kitchen crew were making their entrances. Happy hour was about to begin. There was no frenetic rush to get ready here like at Geoffrey's. Time would come and time would go and the bar would be busy or not. Sparky's would just continue, eerily similar to the way waves ebbed and flowed across the street.

I relaxed with my beer at the bar and looked out the windows at the Atlantic Ocean. Briny Avenue was getting a little more traffic, now that people were coming home from their daily routines. Sparky's started filling up, and by five-thirty, the bar was crowded and the tables were rapidly getting there.

"Happy Hour, Stacey–two for one." Rick smiled. I nodded assent and continued to watch the ocean.

At six, a tall, lanky silver-haired man strolled in. He was dressed in khakis, a light blue golf shirt and boat shoes with no socks. He moved like he owned the place. As it turned out, he did own the place. You knew it just by looking at him.

Rick cocked his head my way and mouthed, "Mr. Sparks."

I mouthed back, "Oh," and dipped towards my beer.

Mr. Sparks made his way casually around the bar. He not only knew his customers, but liked them as well, usually a contradiction in terms for a bar owner. Many bar owners think their patrons are just a bunch of drunken shits, but a fool and his money… well, you know the rest.

Then he headed towards me. Jesus. My first time in the place. I liked it fine, but wasn't sure. Maybe I could work here, so I sure as hell don't want to be known as a regular customer. Damn! He was one fine fish for an older fellow. My mind swam, my knees knocked, I didn't dare stand up. In a moment, he was standing beside me.

"Well, hello, you… first time here?" Mr. Sparks drawled and smiled, extending his hand for a gentle shake.

"This is Stacey, Mr. S," Rick explained, as I took Mr. Sparks' hand–and got shocked. An electric buzz current made its way from my fingertips to my toes, surging up through my hair and probably frizzing my eyelashes if I were ever brave enough to look. I could tell it was an electric current because, just as he took my hand, I saw a flash of mini-lightning pass from his palm to mine. The spark continued through my body and right down to my bones.

Mr. Sparks howled with laughter at my surprised dismay, "That's why they call me Old Sparky!"

The rest of the bar, being in on the joke, of course, howled along with Old Sparky.

I had two fresh beers in front of me and no clue what to do. Taking a tip from my old Tough Luck Lane days, I stayed perfectly still and kept my mouth shut.

When the howling subsided, I smiled weakly at Mr. Sparks, and then promptly passed out on the floor.

Next thing I knew, I was propped up on the soft leatherette of one of the booths in the back being ministered to by three waitresses and Rick, the bartender. I was happy to see Rick, even though his boyish face was clouded with concern. A cool bar rag had been placed on my forehead.

I levered myself up on my elbows and waited for the room to stop spinning. I used the cool rag to freshen my face and handed it off to Rick. Mr. Sparks appeared, towering over people clustered around the booth. He looked both amused and contrite.

"Young lady," he said, parting the sea of people around me and gently escorting me up to a sitting position in the booth. "Are you quite all right?"

I shook the cobwebs out of my head and nodded "Yes." I tried my best to give him a baleful look at the same time. That was dirty pool and he needed to know it.

"Aw, she's going to be okay." The people in the bar stomped, clapped, and cheered to welcome me back. Gee.

Dismissing the waitresses, he invited Rick to sit down in the booth with me and slid in beside him. Calling a waitress over, he ordered three "Irish straights" and some menus.

"It's the least I can do to make it up to you," Mr. Sparks said. "It's just a joke."

"She's not from around here," Rick said. "She doesn't know the place."

"I gathered. Everyone knows my old trick. Give me a palm up when I go to shake hands with you, that's all." Mr. Sparks advised.

"I'll know better next time. You're pretty good for an older guy," I said.

"She speaks!" he announced to the bar. The crowd applauded with gusto.

Our waitress brought the "Irish straights"–Jamison's Irish whiskey, straight up, and menus as requested. We decided on fish and chips and a pitcher of Black-and-Tan. Rick and Mr. Sparks took the whiskey straight down while I took a ladylike sip, which was a far cry from how I'd handled the shot of tequila earlier.

"So, where are you from?" Oh, boy–here we go again. I sighed and gave the abbreviated version of my Tale of Woe. I'd been telling it so much lately that I was able to come up with the Reader's Digest Condensed Version, which was a lot more interesting and easier on the ears. Pompano, I found out, is a very small town and Ricky (Mr. Sparks), knew Geoffrey and Tracey; and Rick–our friendly local neighborhood bartender, had a running acquaintance with Dhani and Edmund. Everyone knew and loved Charlie, Ricky did work with him 'way back when. The Knotts' men? They were in a class by themselves.

The fish and chips were crispy and tasty, although I wasn't sure if I could get used to the taste of malt vinegar on French fries. I'm more of a tartar-sauce-on-the-fish, ketchup-on-the-fries kind of girl.

At the end of the meal, Ricky ordered coffee (Irish, that is), and some Olde Irish Bread Pudding. It was old Irish bread all right, but the coffee was passable, so I focused on that until we got to the topic of conversation:

"What Does Stacey Do For A Living?"

I was leery of telling them I was a bartender off the bat, since I didn't want anyone to think I was angling for a job. Everyone was so nice to me and I really felt welcome there–finally. But I am a bartender; I didn't have a job and needed one. Who knows why things happen when they do? So, I told them what I did and Ricky asked if I'd mind doing a few fill-in shifts to see if it might work out. I agreed and we all had another Irish whiskey.

I went back to the bungalow and passed out again–this time, with a very happy smile on my face. I didn't even know I had gotten undressed and ready for bed in my sleepy-tee 'til morning.

For some strange reason, however, I dreamed about Geoffrey's that night. It was a crazy-mixed up dream where Cold-As-Ice, Brian the bartender, had his back to me. I walked to work–even though I don't work there anymore and it's too far to walk. Cold-As-Ice turns around and, to my dismay and disgust, it's really not Cold-As-Ice, but brother Ed, looking juiced-up for the kill on seeing me. I woke with a start, disoriented because I expected to see my dingy bedroom in the trailer on Tough Luck Lane with Ed standing in my doorway, shadowed by the backlight of the bare bulb in the hallway. I turned on the light and staggered to the mini-bath for a splash of lukewarm water in a feeble attempt to freshen my face. Still buzzed, I flopped back on the sofa bed and spent the rest of the night in an intoxicated dreamless slumber.

Chapter Five

I woke up feeling as if I were wearing my Tigger slippers on my teeth. Groggily, I punched my pillow, flipped over, and noticed the alarm clock hadn't gone off. It was 10:30 a.m. and I had a shift at Sparky's at eleven. Yikes! Instantly sobering up–or so I thought–I stumbled to the bathroom and hauled my ass into a cold shower. If I wasn't sober when I went in, I sure was when I emerged, and freezing, too.

Jumping into jeans, some real comfortable black leather boots, and a black tank top, I gave my hair a quick brush-through, applied some mascara, eyeshadow and lipstick and was out the door, fresh as a daisy and hungry as hell by 10:45. I dashed into Dana's for a muffin and black coffee and a puzzled look from Tracey.

"How the hell are ya? Busy, I see…" she asked as I dashed in and out with a blueberry muffin.

"I'll call you!" I said with a quick wave and headed out, wolfing my breakfast en route to Sparky's.

She blew me a kiss and went back to work.

I headed up Atlantic to Ocean and ducked into Sparky's just in time for Rick to look at the clock, look at me, look back at the clock and say, nodding, "Good sign, on time. C'mon back." He lifted the gate to the bar allowing me access to Sparky's inner sanctum.

I cleaned beer traps, filled sinks, wiped bottles and glasses, learned where all the booze was (standard racking, whites, ambers, colors), memorized the beers on tap (6) and bottled (10), learned the wines (boxed or bottled), checked out the menu, and by 2:00 p.m., I was serving regular. It wasn't hard, mostly jerking beers and running shots with a few frozen slops thrown in for the tourist chicks–no umbrellas, though, thank God.

Around three, Loretta came into the bar. Loretta was a middle-aged, pudgy, redheaded woman whose mid-length hair bordered between bumpy and frizzy, as did her skin tone. Too much sun and not enough sunscreen, I guessed. She had breathtaking aquamarine eyes, which gazed at Rick in utter adoration.

"Oh, boy, here we go," Rick whispered, leaning down to grab a glass while I was slicing a lime for a couple of Coronas at the end of the bar. I smiled knowingly at the all-too-familiar scenario and stepped back to watch the action.

I was impressed. Rick was cordial, nice and playful enough to encourage the woman to have a drink, yet distant enough to deflect any oncoming advances. Smooth, I thought. He introduced me to Loretta who told me she was down from Canada for the season and just *tickled* (her word, not mine), to meet a real native Floridian and from the *wilderness*, yet. Hey, it was a trailer park, not a tent. Okeechobee is a lake, not a swamp–contrary to popular belief, and we are part of Palm Beach County whether they like it or not in the actual Palm Beaches. I smiled sweetly at all the misconceptions and brought her another Tanq 'n' T with lemon, saying "y'all" as much as I could without sounding too stupid and hoping it would result in a decent tip.

Loretta was married and her husband was up in the northern wastes of Canada–well, Toronto, if you must know. As she got more "socially lubricated," her tongue got looser, and I had a whole lot more insight to the life of the moneyed beach residents of Pompano by the sea. Turned out, she loved the beach and her hubby loved his mistress. So, hubby bought Loretta this little getaway and tucked her down here from November to April. He had his shits 'n' giggles back home while she lived her life down here. It was an even-steven trade-off, she felt, and she got the better bargain. After all, she knew he'd dump the mistress, eventually–she'd seen him through about three or four of them already. But he wasn't dumping her since she sat on a pile of dough bigger than his. Bigger than his you-know-what as well, she added with a sly wink. So, she comes down and falls in love for the season and goes back home and they both play dumb for the summer with their country club crowd.

This season, she's picking on Rick and, girl-to-girl, she asked me, "Isn't he just a stud-*muffin*?"

"Oh, yes," I replied, and winked back at her, thinking Rick is more like a bourbon-soaked fruitcake, never mind no muffin, given all the shit he's been sneaking behind the bar. Oh, well–he didn't take any dough from the till as near as I could figure–sticky-fingered bartenders are the worst to work with. Who cares if they sneak a shot or two? If they sneak from the till and you're new, you're most likely to be blamed for it and they skate Scot-free. That's usually what happens with a steady bar turnover. The one who stays is most likely the sneak thief. The poor Joe just learning the trade for a day or two doesn't know enough about the daily take to fudge it.

Loretta and I had a real good girly-girl chat about men (make up your own, they're all pretty much the same), as I fed her Tanq 'n' T's all afternoon. Every time Rick passed by, she'd wink, he'd wink back, and I playfully smacked him on the butt and told Loretta, "That's for you, babe." He laughed and slid some ice down my back. We put on a pretty good show.

By five, she'd about had it and I was just about off shift, so I cashed her out and wound up with a ten spot. Not bad for some chitchat and just a bump of one round to the lady. As she headed out the door, steadier than I would have imagined, yet not dead-on straight, she tossed another ten on the rail and a whispered aside to Rick that she'd be "open tonight."

I shot Rick a look and he mouthed "later." I went around the bar, cashed out all my customers, gave them plenty of time to order another and leave me a tip. By six, I was free as a bird and with solid cash in my pocket as well. *Not bad for a first day's work,* I thought as I clocked out in the kitchen next to Rick.

"We hang at Loretta's at about nine or ten," he said. "She has an open house party a few nights a week," he said. Ah, hah–mystery solved. "You want to come? I'll introduce you around." Was this a date?

"Um, yeah, maybe," I said thoughtfully, acting like maybe I was checking a mental calendar for other plans, which, of course, I didn't have.

"If you want, come by here around eight thirty, I'll buy you a drink." Now he was speaking my language. For the first time since our busy shift, I sized him up–cute, but not obnoxiously so. A bit shorter than me in heels, so I made a mental note to wear flats. Nice smile, lazy eyes. The kind of guy who could lead you into trouble a little too easily, but you wouldn't mind a bit.

"Okay, you're on." I thought it's never a good idea to shit where you eat, but what the hell. A girl needs a friend and, besides, maybe he just wanted some female company to stave off Loretta's eager, smitten gaze every time he passed by while working the bar. We were co-workers, buds, trainer and trainee besides, there was some bonding going on this afternoon between us. He didn't ask for my number, or where I lived, or any other of the first-date small-talk bullshit, pretending they're interested in you to soften you up so they can get what they want. I decided to take him up on his offer and check out the local cast of characters. If Loretta was any indication, the rest should be a hoot.

I passed on my after-shift drink. I had beer in the

fridge at home and I'd be back at eight-thirty, anyway. I headed home for a good soak in the shower and relief from my boots. Damn. I thought they were comfortable. Not.

I entered the compound to a wolf-whistle from the Captain, comfortably installed in his chaise lounge. I waved back. "Hell-o, Cap," with a jaunty salute. "Where are 'the kids' tonight?" Meaning Dhani and Edmund.

"The boat, fishin'," he answered.

I rolled my eyes skyward. "Oh, Jeez. The Minnow." The Minnow was a little dinghy with a motor bigger than the boat. Usually, it was parked under my window with a hole in the bottom about the size of the motor. "You mean they actually fixed it?" I asked.

"Yeppers," answered the Cap'n. "Put a Bimini on top, too."

"How come you're not out with them?" I asked.

"Easier ways to drown," he replied, hoisting a beer in my direction. "Hey–you got an extra beer ya could spare?"

"Sure, Cap," I sighed.

Emerging from the bungalow barefoot and with beers, I handed the Captain his, we clinked cans, said "cheers and beers", and drank thirstily.

The Captain downed his beer in three swigs. I took a couple more than he to finish and then went inside for my shower.

Emerging, clean, fresh, and towel-clad, I almost electrocuted myself with the blow dryer by almost dropping it into the sink upon hearing the most ungodly bumping on the wall of my little hovel and felt the bungalow shake.

"For the love of Christ!" I yelled. "What the hell y'all doin' out there? Smashin' my walls in?"

I peered out from under a window shade to see Dhani and Edmond stowing The Minnow up on blocks.

"Damn, guys, no wonder you have holes in that thing the way you throw it around. Go easy, will you?

Before I have holes in my wall like you have on your boat, okay?"

Edmund just grinned, "Okay, boss-lady."

"Yah, yah, right-ee-oh," added Dhani with more than a touch of sarcasm.

I'd grown up around little boats like The Minnow in fish camps on Lake Okeechobee and they didn't take kindly to rough handling. The fishing guides who earned their living on the little boats were sometimes gentler with the boats than with their women. Paid more attention to the boats, anyways.

"So, what'd you catch for dinner?" I asked.

"Oh, we got good fish," said Dhani.

Edmund laughed. "Yeah, from the fish market. We didn't catch nothin' but a sunburn."

"Okay, okay." I lowered the window shade and tossed on a tee shirt and shorts. I came out with a couple of beers for the unlucky fishermen. "Here's a consolation prize."

"Oooh!" Dhani cried, looking over at Edmund, arching one eyebrow, "a prize!"

"Yeah," said Edmund, "I hear some consolation prizes are a box of Rice A Roni. Guess we're getting lucky with Stacey, getting a beer."

I gave them both the fishy eye for making that joke. That was the closest they'd get to getting lucky from me. They finished stowing The Minnow and toasted to me. How nice. I did a mock curtsy in their honor.

"So, okay," I said. "You sharing the fish? I shared my beers."

"Okay, sure," said Dhani. "Give us a couple of minutes." They busied themselves getting out plates, forks, knives, cocktail sauce, hot sauce, napkins and–what else?– more beer.

They came out with a platter of raw oysters.

"I thought you guys got fish!" I grimaced. I hate

raw oysters.

"It's from the sea, lady," said Edmund, shucking one open and sticking the little critter guts 'n' all, in my face.

"Ugh! No, thank YOU!" I said, and wheeled around towards the bungalow.

I can eat raw clams–I grew up on them–and stone crabs, and regular crabs, and soft-shelled crabs, and shrimp and lobster but one look at a damned raw oyster and I turn positively green. It's probably because the one night I tried them I was with my brother Ed. He got me good and drunk so I'd work up the courage to eat some, but being only fifteen and having no clue how to handle beer, wine, or a mix of the two as well as raw oysters, well–your imagination can put it together as well as I can say it. Ever since, I've hated raw oysters and can still hear Ed's sadistic laughter whenever I'm around them and get that sick feeling in the pit of my gut.

"What'cha doin' tonight, Stace?" called Edmund as I headed back to my bungalow. "We're goin' to the Asylum."

I turned around to face Edmund and Dhani from my mini-stoop.

The Asylum was down the street from Sparky's. It was a dingy, dirty, but very large and noisy bar where some local denizens hung out. On Sunday afternoons, Buckets O' (mini) Beers were $5 and everyone caught a buzz, more often on stuff other than booze. I had learned this afternoon at work Sparky's was one of the "better" bars of the Pompano scene. The "upper crust" patronized The Wharf and the bottom of the food chain hung out at the Bee Sting.

"I'm going out," I said, with a glint of mystery in my eye.

"Anyone we know?" Dhani asked.

"Yeah, probably," Edmund enjoined, "we know everybody." As Dhani and Edmund guffawed and high-fived each other at my expense while downing raw oysters one-two-six, I slipped into the bungalow and began to get ready. My blow dryer dried up enough to be safe to use and not short out the miniscule electric system. Two plugs in one socket at the same time shorted out the place.

I slipped into my skinny black jeans, donned sexy black flat sandals with glittery hammered silver buckles, a black lace and purple satin tank with a silver cuff on my arm and a long silver chain with a silver totem set with amethyst and aquamarine. I had picked it up from a witch-woman who was a friend of my Mom's. She told me it would heal and protect. I just thought it was cool looking. Silver stiletto earrings completed the ensemble and I was ready to rock. Tossing a black-fringed suede jacket over my arm and tugging my black satchel to heel, I was on my way.

When I reached Sparky's, amid a flurry of a few appreciative whistles and toots from car's horn. *Yeah,* I thought defiantly, *I've still got it.* I gave them all a little "bite me" twitch of my butt and went into the bar.

Rick was there–Mr. Rick Sparks, that is. He came over with a kiss and a handshake (no fireworks this time), and said, "Good job today, Stacey. Welcome aboard."

I smiled and thanked him and looked for Rick the younger. There he was, smack in the middle of a gaggle of girls, so I just hung out waiting to see if he'd see me. He did, winked to me (what else, right?), excused himself from the posse and headed my way.

We ordered vodka and water, a time-honored bartender's cocktail, and grabbed a high-top table so we could chat. The guy was amazing. He was fresh as a daisy, even after all that drinking in the afternoon.

"So, what'd you think, Stacey?" inquired the young Rick.

"Okay," I said carefully. "What did you think? Moreover, what did Mr. Sparks think?"

"I think, you know–you're okay. He thinks you're okay, too." He nodded over in the direction of Rick Sparks and ducked his head and grinned. Damn. Guys are just too cute when they duck and grin. I enjoyed a partial meltdown then chilled out to control this feeling. I thought of Ed and Cold-As-Ice. Rick was nothing like them, but I couldn't afford to screw up first time out. I ducked and grinned back, hoping I was just as adorable as he was cute.

"Cool bar," I said. "Nice people."

"Yeah," he answered, "Loretta's a trip."

"So, what's up with her?" I asked.

"Loretta is older. She doesn't have a lot of friends, so she hangs out here. She's cool, she likes a drink, and has this beach place where she lets us come up. We all hang out and party and, you know, whatever."

"What's 'whatever'?" I wondered what the hell I got myself into.

"Well, you know, some people party. You know, 'stuff'. I don't–ex-Marine, Semper Fi and all that." Rick grinned.

"Semper Fi," I said back, thanking God. He tipped an imaginary hat at me.

"Thank you, Ma'am," he nodded. "But I drink like a fish," he said openly and laughed.

I laughed along. "That's okay, I have my vices as well."

"Ohhh?" The question remained open.

"Well, to start, I drink like a fish, too." We grinned, "Hey, do fish drink?"

"Nah, I think they just swim in the shit."

"What a life."

"Yeah…" and a few moments were spent in companionable silence contemplating, no doubt, the peaceful life of our finny friends swimming serenely, awash in a sea of vodka. We finished our drinks and he motioned me out.

Slinging my jacket over my shoulder Frank Sinatra–style (yeah, I like old movies and I think he's the bomb when it comes to style), I followed him to the door then waited for him to open it, went out, and he followed me.

"Okay," I started, "where are we going?"

"I'm following you, pretty lady."

"Har-dee-har. No, really? Where is this place– Loretta's Den of Iniquity?" I deepened my voice to a low boom for the den-of-iniquity part. Then, for effect, I stopped short so he'd bump smack into me. He did and caught my shoulders and arms in a semi-embrace. It was nice.

"Oh, yeah... go left, straight ahead. It's the first building you see."

"Le Club? Looks expensive."

"Yeah. It is."

It stood smack-dab on the beach, twenty-five stories of concrete, chrome, and glass walls floor-to-ceiling, with wraparound balconies on the corner units. Yeah, it was expensive. La-De-Fucking-Dah.

"So, where were we going?" I asked.

"She lives on the top, northeast corner."

Okay. I decided to shut up and just enjoy the ride.

The security guard in the lobby nodded us in (well, Rick, actually, I got a fishy eye which took me down a peg from my *Oh, So Hot* mindset en route to Sparky's). We took the elevator to the penthouse and stepped from there into a quiet-as-a-tomb hallway. There was no indication of anyone even living there, let alone throwing a party. Rick escorted me down the hall to Loretta's—a pair of enameled doors festooned with fancy scrollwork. He rang the bell. One of the doors opened, and we entered Loretta's apartment. No one was on the other side of the door.

"Automatic," Rick said with a wink. "Neat trick, huh?"

I nodded and stepped behind him into a long mirrored foyer with a black and gold marble floor. A small door, off to the side, was cracked open and revealed a small powder room.

Loretta stood at the end of the foyer and gave Rick an open-armed smile with a quick embrace, then she saw me. Her face dropped from here to the floor. I tried the duck-and-grin maneuver on her to no avail. She turned away quietly, her lips pressed together in a thin straight line. She walked stiffly down the large entry hall to the living room, her back to us both. Loretta wore a flowing floor-length caftan in a modern print of jewel colors with an open back and cascades of fabric fluttered like wings as she walked. High-heeled golden sandals clicked briskly as she covered the expanse of marble tiled flooring. Loretta's perfect pedicure flashed bright orange toenails beneath her caftan as she pivoted towards the party.

"They're all in here," she said, more to Rick than to me, motioning to an oversized living room overlooking the beach.

I wanted to tell her I wasn't Rick's date, but he grabbed my hand and pulled me forward, putting his arm around my waist and guiding me in to the main room.

It was a large, airy room, decorated in beige, cream and mauve. Mirrors graced certain strategic walls to enlarge the appearance of the room and amplify the view of the beach and ocean. The pier with its restaurant glittered below. If I peered out, I could see Sparky's and the intersection of Ocean and Atlantic Avenues. A large, horseshoe-shaped built-in mauve 'mica wet bar with some high barstools and a few chairs were in the corner by the kitchen. A low-slung modern sectional sofa in cream-colored leather and chairs covered in mauve and beige striped fabric faced out towards the wraparound balcony and the ocean. The "art" on the walls was probably expensive, but tasteless–it went "with" the room's color scheme, but food for the soul it was not. People buy that schlock at hotel sales thinking they're getting *The Deal of a Century* right here in South Florida not knowing the same shit is being sold in hotel art "shows" everyplace from Kalamazoo, Michigan to Poughkeepsie, New York. A few people were at the bar, a couple was snuggled in a corner on a cuddle-chaise for two upholstered in mauve velvet, and several people were on the sofa facing the balcony.

Loretta went behind the bar, gamely winking at Rick and ignoring me.

"What'll it be, sailor?" she directly asked of my escort, rolling her hips in a sea-wench fashion.

"Beer for the lady here and the same for me."

Loretta, clearly not pleased, opened a beer and set it on the bar by me, then opened another beer and lovingly handed it to Rick. Rick took the beer from Loretta, handed it to me and took the beer off the bar. Loretta's smile did a slow fade.

"Welcome to my home," she said. She didn't sound very welcoming. The flat look in her eyes backed up my initial take on her feelings about me. I set my beer on the bar and shrugged into the black-fringed suede jacket to ward off the chill. I was not looking for trouble here and thought about inventing a sudden emergency at home. Maybe The Minnow sprung a leak and I was needed to help plug the hole. *Hey lady, thanks for the brew, but I've got a leaky boat at home, so I've gotta go*, I thought.

As I was looking to beat feet and not be shy about it, a young, willowy dark-haired beauty sidled up to me and whispered, "Are you Rick's date?"

I shook my head no, and she said, "Don't worry then. The dragon-lady will warm up to you once she realizes you're not after her prize." I took a pull off my brew and watched Loretta eye Rick.

"I'm Kat," she said, clinking her fluted champagne glass to my bottle. "Cheers."

"Bottoms up yourself," I rejoined, taking another swig.

I eyed Kat. Skinny, but a sexy broad. She was wearing a cutout black minidress, which minimized the fact that she had very little in the boob department by sumptuous gathers of fabric in strategic places. But her legs went on forever and ended in stiletto-heeled black leather shoes with spikes and chains.

"Like them?" she asked, noticing me noticing her shoes. "I got them at Pizzzazzz."

"Ahhh." I nodded sagely. "Cool place."

"You new here?"

"Yeah. Had my first day at Sparky's, today."

Kat smiled, "I like Sparky's. You from around?"

"Just recently in town. You?"

"Michigan," she answered.

"Cold up there, huh?"

"Colder here, since my booty split back for home."

"Oh, shit. What did you do?"

"I get by, I dance."

"No shortage of booty there," I said without thinking. We both snorted into our drinks. I tried to picture a titless go-go broad and couldn't do it without a smirk. Hopefully, she thought it was at the booty joke. She did.

Rick managed to pry himself loose from Loretta and joined us.

"See you've met our Kat," he said, hanging on her like she was his property. I was glad I didn't invest a date in this guy. This evening was getting real interesting. I watched Loretta glare in my direction, but she was too busy fixing drinks for the couple in the corner who had disentangled themselves from their embrace on the chaise and made their way over to the bar.

Rick put his arm around me as well and drew me into an ersatz threesome. Loretta didn't know who to glare at first when the doorbell rang.

No one had told me to make myself at home or anything, but I believed discretion was the better part of valor. I tricked myself out of Rick's snare and sat in one of the low-slung chairs by the bar. I was hoping to be out of sight and mind of Loretta while I figured a graceful way out of there. Rick and Kat were busy gossiping about who was in jail, who was out, who got busted and who got busted up. You know, normal South Florida cocktail party chatter. Time passed, and Rick got me another beer from behind the bar and started bartending. Loretta seemed to be elsewhere, I visibly relaxed.

More people drifted in. Kat wandered off, presumably to the ladies' room as I saw someone waggle a small white packet in her direction out of the corner of my eye. I nodded and smiled like I belonged there, but I was good at that, having been a nuisance to big brother Ed in my younger days. I quickly learned how to be invisible while Ed was at a party when he was supposed to be "babysitting" his little sister, me.

Two a.m. rolled around and the bar people started rolling in. There was Grace and Joey—Grace was the night bartender at Sparky's, a hot little Italian chick from New England and Joey her on-again-off-again lover who came down with her seven years ago, I learned. The Lorikeets from Geoffrey's made an entrance along with the cow-eyed Jennifer and Tracey. Tough little blonde Lori seemed in her element as the softer, more timid Laurie seemed to blend into the background. An uneasy feeling started to bubble from within and I hunkered down in my chair, turning my head so as not to be noticed. I pretended to watch the ocean that couldn't be seen in the dark. Rick left the bar and Geoffrey's crew descended on the kitchen and busied themselves with making shots and snacks for mass distribution.

I could see Rick was hot on the trail of Grace and Loretta couldn't take her eyes off them. I felt saved by

Grace. I started loosening up after a few more beers I snuck from the bar and time was drifting by in the easy, boozy way of parties. I felt as if everyone was watching me, but I was, effectively, invisible. I tried to do some people-watching myself, but no one was terribly interesting. I wasn't keen on the Geoffrey's people noticing me, anyway. About halfway through the party, Grace and Joey fought, predictably, over Rick's drunken groping at Grace. It was mundane and pathetically sad.

The doorbell rang again and Loretta, now the eager, happy Queen of the Ball, went to answer the call. I went to answer the call of nature in the powder room off the foyer entrance when I was stopped cold in my tracks. The light shone in the hallway through the open door on the face of none other than Mr. Cold-As-Ice and Geoffrey himself. I felt more than a touch of chill when I saw them and wondered if my new life here was to be ruined forever by that one fucked-up night at Geoffrey's? Hoping they wouldn't notice me, I skittered into the powder room and locked the door behind me.

I could hear the clatter of Loretta's heels on the marble entry floor and the soft shuffle-step of men's highly polished Bally loafers behind. They stopped outside the door of the powder room for a moment then ambled on, stop-and-go, in the direction of the party. I heard muffled voices in the foyer as, I assumed, greetings were exchanged.

Taking care of business, I hung out long enough to let them pass, then let myself out the front door with as little noise as I could manage. The door clicked softly behind me as I left, and I didn't really care if Rick minded or not that I deserted him. I half-ran down the lushly carpeted hall and into the elevator, but thankfully, I didn't see a soul. I hit the wrong button, got off at the basement and found a side door out to the garage parking lot. A few tries at zigging and zagging–not too hard with all the booze

I had swallowed, I soon breathed the crisp sea air and sighed with relief.

Getting my bearings wasn't too hard. I was just up the street and around the corner from the compound, my bungalow, and my Tigger slippers. Unhitching my sandals, I toddled home barefoot and free, thanking my lucky stars– or that witch-lady's charm around my neck? I had escaped at last.

I banged the stove hard with my fist to boil some water for tea. Tossing an English muffin into the toaster oven–the only oven in my mini-kitchen that worked–I pulled open the sofa bed, unhooked myself from my evening's getup and slipped into an oversized, clean, comfy sleepy tee and my slippers. Tea and muffin in hand, I flipped the tube to an old John Wayne-Kate Hepburn western and watched them raft down a river as I munched greedily on the muffin. I washed it all down with the hot, steamy tea and then drifted off myself, alone, in a deep, dreamless slumber.

Chapter Six

The next morning, I awoke wanting Dana's and the company of a kindred soul, Tracey. It was 8:30 a.m. and there was plenty of time for hot coffee. I decided not to blow into work late and headed to Dana's Diner as soon as I was decent.

Tracey was bright-eyed, bushy-tailed, and disgustingly perky as she poured my coffee and warmed my blue muffin. I ordered breakfast and in an unusual moment amidst the busy-ness, Tracey took a break to sit at the corner counter seat next to me.

"You've got something on your mind, girl," she said in a mock-southern accent.

"Yeah. Strange night last night," I told her, and spilled everything from the misunderstanding at Geoffrey's up 'til last night, including my mixed feelings about Mr. Cold-As-Ice and Geoffrey.

"Life's harsh at the beach, sweetie," she advised, "It'll eat you alive if you let it."

I thought about that for a moment and nodded. Nothing grows on the beach but the hardiest and most resistant plant life. No flowers in bloom, no delicate orchids. Only the tough old coconut palms, sea grapes, and sand grasses seem to thrive. I thought of the soothing sound of the waves and how soft the sand felt under my feet. What a lie.

"C'mon," she urged, "I'm off at two, how about a trip to Pizzzazzz?"

"I've got to work," I replied. "Start my shift at eleven."

"Okay, that's cool. But I'm off Thursday. Why don't we meet at Pizzzazzz and grab lunch after shopping?"

Thursday was the day after tomorrow, so I decided that would be my day off as well.

"Maybe in the afternoon we can hit the beach and work on our tans?" I suggested.

"Well, maybe. How about just a nice, long walk on the beach instead?"

"It's a date!" For the first time in weeks I was looking forward to carrying out a plan.

I finished breakfast and paid my tab, leaving another ten for Tracey. I got home to a quiet Compound. Even the Captain was peacefully snoring in his chaise lounge. Everyone else was off to work and I got ready to go myself.

I decided casual attire would be best and donned some comfy jeans, sneakers, and a loose pink tie-dyed tee I bought off the rack at the drug store chain across the street from the Compound. I pulled my hair into a ponytail and applied lipstick and eye makeup–hey, a girl's got some pride, you know? I headed off to work. A job is just a job. Not my life.

I tended bar, tended my patrons, left with more money than I walked in with and considered it a good day. Rick was off, so I was paired up with a dud named Jon. Married, kids, in the biz forever and a day–probably sticky fingers in the till as well, but it wasn't my problem, I had my own cash drawer to work with. I came out even-steven at the end of my shift, and considered myself ahead of the game, in general. I squared Thursday off with Mr. Sparks and headed out.

On arriving home, I found the Captain and opened us a couple of brews. We relaxed in the shade of the huge, old, mostly used-up mango tree in the courtyard and drank our beer in companionable silence. The sun set in the west and the night bugs started up their nightly chorus. Dhani and Edmond arrived home, had a quiet beer with us then went their own way.

I headed in for dinner, a call to the local pizza parlor, curled up with some TV in my Tigger slippers and just hung. The local news didn't seem half as bizarre as the events of last night, whatever they were, I didn't remember. At ten-thirty p.m., I'd had it with the news and, eyelids drooping, I packed it in and fell asleep with the crickets gently chirping at my doorstep.

Chapter Seven

Wednesday, I woke up early and in a pretty chipper mood. Dhani saw me poking around in the courtyard and came over with a hot cup of coffee.

"Hey, stranger," he said. "You live here?"

"Yeah, sometimes," I said. "Only when there's nothin' better to do."

The Captain stirred on his chaise.

"Shhh…" Dhani cautioned, holding a finger to his lips, "unless you've got a beer for him."

I nodded silently, and followed Dhani around to his stoop.

We sipped good coffee and talked until Dhani had to leave for work.

"Working today?" he asked.

"Yeah, 'til six."

He grinned at me. "Shall I tell the Knotts boys to come by tonight? I'll be seeing them later."

I laughed, "Don't do me any favors," adding a roll of my eyes skyward, as if in prayer.

"Okay, maybe another night."

"Yeah, the 32nd of the month should be good."

"Okay, bye." He laughed. He stood up, stretched, and made ready to head out.

"Bye, sweetie," I called. "Have a nice day." On impulse, I went up to him and gave him a friendly peck on the cheek in jest.

"You too. See you later."

I shrugged. Yeah, the moment was over.

Since I had so much time on my hands, I loaded up

some dirty clothes into The Mir and headed over to the Bee Kleen. It was too early for the Bee Sting, which was too bad. I could've used a beer. Of course, the Bee Quick was only a few steps away. I thought I could get a can of beer there and sip away while keeping my part of America beautiful. Besides, if I wanted to enjoy my day off, it'd be best to get my chores done early.

After laundry, I scrubbed the little bungalow top to bottom. I discovered that I hadn't locked the door when I left and the Captain had casually availed himself of my facilities. The bathroom badly needed a good scrubbing. He'd used the shower, too, with similar results. Fortunately, I was happy a simple cleaning did the trick and I didn't have to resort to arson as a method of cleanliness.

Two hours later, I stepped outside, smelling of dirt, sweat and the other unmentionable odors of a deep cleaning. "Mornin' Cap'n," I said flatly, smelling the sweet aromas of shampoo and soap on him–both mine, of course. "Glad to see you've made yourself at home."

"Mornin' missy," the Captain tipped his dirty commodore's cap in my direction. He peered at me sheepishly as he donned his cap and pulled the brim over his eyes.

"Cap," I stated flatly, trying to keep the anger out of my voice, "I can let it go this time, but *next* time…"

"Yes, missy?

"Use the damned hose! It's right there!" I said impatiently, and pointed towards the rubber snake attached to Edmund's outdoor spigot.

"What am I gonna do? He turned it off!" The Captain cried.

"I'll get him to turn it back on, okay? But from now on, stay out of my house!"

"Okay, missy. You got a beer?"

I closed my eyes in surrender and figured, *what the hell*, and went in to grab a beer for the old boy. He put out his hand to take it and I held it out of reach.

"Okay," I reasoned, "I give you this beer, you stay out if my house, deal?"

He looked at me.

"And if you stay out you'll get another when I come home tonight."

He looked at me again.

"…and another one in the morning. Deal?"

He continued to look at me.

"Okay," I held up both hands out in despair, "Captain, sir, you've got to respect a lady's privacy."

"I do."

"No, you don't. When I'm not home you can't just stroll in when you want. When I'm home you have to ask first. That means whether I'm home or I'm not home, you don't go in there! Is that crystal clear enough for you, Captain?"

He shrugged.

"Okay, so how's this. I wake up in the morning, you don't go in, you get a beer. I come home at night you don't go in, you get a beer. I go away for a while you don't go in, you get a beer. Fair enough?"

"I don't have to pay nothin' for the beers?"

"No, you just don't go in my house."

"Deal."

"Fair enough." Considering the time, effort and shit I had to scrub out of the place, a six-pack a day was cheap insurance. I could buy cheap beer, special for the Captain. And now I had to get to work and smile at people. Jeez! I put on some three-inch shitkicker-heeled boots and tucked them into my jeans. A Sparky's tee shirt completed the ensemble. I had arrived, when Mr. Sparks handed it to me after leaving work yesterday.

I ducked into Dana's to confirm tomorrow–ten a.m. at Pizzzazzz with Tracey–and headed off to work. I even whistled a happy tune, if you can believe it, until I hit the door.

Rick was there.

"Hey, you!" he snapped, sounding like the Marine sergeant he had been once upon a time. "Where the hell did you go the other night?"

I looked around. Except us, the bar was empty and dust motes were floating endlessly in the sunbeams through the windows. I decided this was another perfect opportunity to shut up and kept my mouth closed. Tight.

I lifted the gate to behind the bar and started filling sinks with hot water. Just me, the dust motes, and Rick.

"I'm talking to you!" He was almost shouting. Oh, Christ. Summoning all my strength, I gave him a level gaze. Thank goodness for the three-inch heels on my boots. If I had worn my sneakers, we would have been eye to eye. Instead, I stood a half-head taller than him, which definitely helped.

"I had to go," I said calmly.

"What," he sneered, "mother waiting up for you?"

That did it. "My mother's dead," I said flatly.

"Oh," he deflated instantly, "I'm sorry." He opened his mouth to add something appropriately contrite. I held up my hand to stop him.

"Don't be. You cut limes yet?"

"No."

"I'll get 'em." I went into the kitchen, leaving him to the sour and cocktail mixes the seasonal tourist crowd readily slurped up every afternoon.

I took my time with the limes, the lemons, and peeling the little strings off the celery, cleaning the scallions for the Bloody Marys. Whatnot chores and side-work kept me busy until the first patrons of the late-morning drifted in. Rick and I worked silently, in tandem, trying to stay out of each other's way. I saw him sneak a couple of shots and thought about one myself, but that only would have made me tired later, so I gave it a pass.

"My dates don't leave me," he hissed, when we were washing up at the same sink together, "and this water isn't hot enough."

"I wasn't your date," I hissed back, twisting the hot water all the way over, scalding his hand.

"Yow!" he yelped, jumping back and wringing his scalded hand.

"Here's some ice," I said, wrapping some up in a bar towel and placing it on the reddened hand. "Excuse me." I left him to tend his wound while I took care of a customer and snagged a tip.

"Damn you," he said through his teeth and watched me post the tip into my cup.

Arrogant bastard, I thought to myself and smiled sweetly at him for the customers to see.

Then Loretta walked in. She lumbered up to the bar with all the grace and dignity of a lead female elephant in charge of her herd.

"Rick!" she snapped. "A T 'n' T!"

Knowing she was good for at least a twenty in his cup, Rick immediately proffered her the chosen drink and solicitously asked after her health. He listened to her whiny complaints with the perfect mixture of solicitude and sympathy. That woman would complain there was sand on the beach along with everything else.

I was happy to have him off my back for the next few minutes. He'd earn that twenty for sure, and maybe twenty-five if he could get her in a good mood before she left. I kept snagging little tips for my cup. A dollar here, two dollars there. It's all the same and they add up. Some tips you have to work harder for than for others. Me, I'll take the easy way out every time.

By the end of shift, Loretta was still calling for "T 'n' T's" and Rick was saying "Dyn-O-Mite" in that old Jimmie Walker style, keeping her on the hook.

It was call time for the 6 p.m. staff and she still

showed no intention of leaving yet, a marathon complaining session with a willing ear knows no bounds.

Rick had no time to heckle me, busy as he was bowing and scraping to Loretta while in-between trying to play fast and loose with a couple of touristy gals in halter minis and fresh sunburns. He was burning it at both ends, and I gave even-odds under the bar rail to a few customers in the know he'd go down in flames at shift's end. The night shift straggled in and I cashed out, collecting my winnings, as Rick showed no signs of relinquishing his shift until Loretta left. I was happy to be rid of the place until Friday.

Grace took up my end of the bar, with a little nod and ducked out of Rick's way. I could see she had carefully applied heavy concealer to cover a beauty of a shiner on her left eye. Well, it was none of my business, so I nodded back at her, kept my mouth shut, and took off.

When I got home, the Captain was waiting for his promised beer. My place was as pristine as I had left it, and I was happy to join him myself. Eventually, Dhani and Edmond returned home, so we all chipped in for burgers and chips and enjoyed a hell of a feast. Sometime after dinner, someone brought in a big old bottle of mellow red wine and we spent the remainder of the evening talking about the sun, the moon, the stars and the sea. I relaxed in one of the chaises, letting the wine spread a pleasant warmth through me, listening to Edmund and Dhani swap fishing stories. I wondered how much they were exaggerating. Eventually, we all drifted off to our little homes, leaving the Captain to enjoy the orchestration of evening bugs and beasties of the smooth, sultry south Floridian night.

Chapter Eight

I woke up rarin' to go. I had money in my pocket and a trip to Pizzzazzz planned. After a quick breakfast at home of tea and an English muffin, I jumped into the shower and got ready. For once, the humidity backed down enough to allow a good hair day and I was even showing a few sun-blonde streaks in my normally dirty-dishwater light brown hair. I put on a cute little red and white mini polka dot number I own, those sweet little red wedgies with the little white hearts bought at Pizzzazzz when I first hit town and a red-and-white big-beaded necklace. I shook my hair loose and free and took a good look in the mini mirror of the bathroom and I was pleased as could be with the result. Late nights and sleazy living agreed with me.

I smiled at my reflection and swallowed a little extra mouthwash for extra freshness. It was time to head out the door for my date with Tracey.

It had been awhile since Tracey had been at Pizzzazzz, so she found a few things for her closet. Tracey has olive skin and short curly dark hair with a sleek petite frame, so the purple leather platforms she picked up added to her height and showed off her curvy legs. The gold chains across her slender ankles were a nice touch. I picked up a pair of round-toed pink ballerina-style slippers and black leather stiletto heels with silver fringe dangling from the instep to the high heel, something like I'd seen on Kat the dancer. Strippers know their shoes since they're pretty much all they wear. The ones I purchased were more graceful and stylish than Kat's though, since dancers tend to pick a chunky heel for balance and comfort. But I didn't think I'd be dancing much in them.

A few pounds lighter in the coin department, we headed out in The Mir to Oceans, a toney lunch spot she suggested in Deerfield Beach, up coast a town. The Mir behaved herself, fine ship that she was, and we made quick time. The young, good-looking valet took the keys, gave The Mir an admiring look and vaulted into the driver's seat. We sauntered into the coolness of the air-conditioned restaurant. I turned, leaned out of the doorway and gave him one of those "you-know-what" looks as he revved the engine and put The Mir in gear. The valet took his foot from the pedal. I smiled and winked at him, he saluted me with a thumb up, a show of respect for The Mir.

We had girly-girl salads with minted sweet iced tea and then headed for an after-lunch walk along the beach.

The ocean isn't as blue in Deerfield as it is in Fort Lauderdale. Deerfield was more cobalt, while the water off Fort Lauderdale beach, on clear days, is a fresh, clean aqua. The grassy banks dotted with palm, sea grape and fichus trees along the shore gave plenty of shade. We took off our shoes and walked in the soft sand, squiggling our bare feet deep into the coolness of the shaded beach.

I kicked a little sand her way, "Hey, what the hell was up with that Geoffrey's?"

"What do you mean?"

"Okay, I find the guy himself in the freezer, I get him out, get a job, and next thing you know, I'm parading around like a show pony then get my ass kicked out on a bogus stealing accusation by two assholes who were obviously amused by my monkey-in-training step 'n' fetchit routine for some dominatrix wannabe named Dianna and thought it would be a night of fun for them. And who the hell is Vinny?"

Tracey grinned. "Any more questions?"

"One more. Who the *hell* is that chilly bartender? I don't think the ice he spends half his life chipping would melt in his mouth. Is he human?"

"Oh, you like him, then."

"Jeez, no!" I shuddered and kicked sand at her. "Besides, I was kicked out, remember?" I exclaimed, kicking a little more sand at her. She kicked some back.

"No good deed goes unpunished. So, you let Geoffrey out of the freezer?" She chuckled then dodged nimbly as I aimed a playful punch at her.

"Come on," I said, "what's the story with this place?"

She went deep into thought then came out of it just as quickly.

"Yeah, you're right. I knew it was kind of crummy, but I hadn't realized the place changed so much. But I warned you to watch your ass."

We found a street vendor, an old guy, brown as a coconut with a wrinkly face, like wizened little monkey, and one of the cheeriest smiles I'd seen in a long time. We bought a couple of bottles of ice-cold water then settled ourselves under a royal palm on the grassy bank. The grass wasn't like usual Florida scrub grass like, or crabgrass, they call it up north. It was real honest-to-goodness sit-on-your-ass grass and cool as a cucumber in the shade.

We both took a long sip of the water, then held the cold dewy bottles to where they did the most good, she to the back of her neck, me to my chest, then placing the bottles between our wrists to cool us down a little more. I lounged back on my side and took a hard look at her.

"All right," she started, "it's not easy 'cause it'll bring a lot back, but I'll tell you what happened."

I kept my mouth shut and waited while she collected her thoughts.

"I had just come down from Jersey. If you say 'what exit?' I'm stopping right now and you can figure it out for yourself."

I crossed my legs and twirled my ankles, looking

down at my bare feet, the cute red and white wedgies casually kicked to the side. I wasn't saying anything.

"I didn't know what I was going to do, so I took a job cleaning boats and lined up a little room at the marina, right here in Deerfield, next to the inlet." She paused, looking out over the water.

"It was okay for a while, but kinda smelly and you wouldn't believe the kinds of messes you get to see on a daily basis. Seems the richer the owner, the dirtier the boat. But clear everything out, take a hose to it, polish and shine it up again, and it's just as good as new for next time.

"Well, this captain would come in and he blew me away. He was young, handsome, and real Florida, you know? Well, I thought like most captains, he was getting it on with the owner's wife. But it wasn't so and we sort of struck up an acquaintance, you follow?"

I nodded. It's all too easy for a handsome face in a uniform to get over on you. Just look at my big brother Ed when he came home from the Navy. Of course, nobody knew he was actually AWOL for about a month and due for a stint in the brig. He just strutted around town in his Navy dress uniform, flashin' his pearly whites at anyone who'd look–and more than a few tootsies did, too. Then the MA's showed up and took him. We didn't see him for a good year or so. It turned out he smuggled gun parts to the same drug dealers who smuggled drugs to some junkies who were helping out the dealers for free shit. The whole thing came apart when one of the guns blew up on itself when one of the junkies put it together wrong. He'd sold the gun to a junkie instead of the dealer, who probably would have known what to do with a gun. When the stoner blew his foot off, he screamed bloody murder to anyone who would listen and spilled it about Ed at the hospital. It was pretty easy to find Ed, seeing as how he hadn't kept his whereabouts exactly a secret. All the girls knew where he was.

Tracey continued, seeming to notice my musings had ended. "Well, one thing led to another and when the owners weren't around, he'd get to take the boat out for a spin to check it out. One day I was off, so I just went with him. Next thing you know, we're going off on weekends. Then I got canned for being away so much and couldn't pay for my room. I couldn't live on the boat 'cause he didn't own it. So, he intro-ed me to Vinny, a friend of the owner of the boat to see what he can do to help me out. He sailed me down the Intracoastal to this big white place right on the water in Fort Lauderdale, someplace with a pool and tons of patio furniture. I mean, the place is gorgeous! I can see inside from the patio and the living room is all decorated with crushed velvet sofas in gold and gold lamps and white tile with real wood everywhere. There's sculpture and fancy paintings, too. I mean, you know the stuff is real art, right? There are big high windows draped in what looks like golden silk, I mean, everything is just drop dead beautiful.

"The captain takes me inside and Vinny shows me to a little room off the living area. This room was different from the rest of the outs. It was decorated like a doctor's waiting room. There were cheap chrome and gray fabric chairs lining the walls and a cheesy particleboard coffee table in the middle, loaded with all these golf and travel magazines. So, maybe the guy is a doc, what do I know? They asked me to have a seat and they go out on the patio and talk awhile. Then they came back and ask me a couple questions, like, do I have a boyfriend and what about the folks up home–stuff like that. I'm getting a little edgy. I mean, whose business is that? So, I tell them there's nobody up home and I'm on my own, looking for something to do.

"Then they said they just want to make sure I'm safe and ask would I be happy here because Vinny is some sort of big shot distributor who travels a lot on business and he could use a house sitter to watch the place. I'd have my own room in the house and just do a little favor for Vinny from time to time, like help him entertain his friends or set stuff up around the house like call the plumber or something like that. I could come and go as I pleased with the captain when he came around and meanwhile, I hang with Vinny. Seemed like a piece of cake to me, I mean, *live* there?

"Now, Vinny was a good guy to take me in, but he seemed a little shady. Do you follow?"

I nodded.

"When it came to matters of discretion such as this, he would keep a secret from the owners of the boat, even being friends with them, you know what I mean? It would get this captain canned if they knew he was screwing around with some boat maid.

"So, Vinny takes me to his place to keep me on tap for this captain, okay? This way, Vinny has something on the captain, he has something over the owners of the boat, he gets me to house-sit and hang out when he needs sandwiches and beer served at his poker games, so everyone's quiet and everyone's happy."

She took a long drink of water and set the bottle down. I took a sip and thought of our Captain back at the compound and wondered if he had gotten the rest of his life off because he was screwing some Mrs. and the Mr. found out.

"It was pretty good for a while," she said thoughtfully. She cast her eyes down towards the grass and started making little circles with the wet water bottle in the greenery, plucking a stray strand to perfect a circle she created.

"I was told I didn't need a car, so I sold mine for the dough and got to drive Vinny's Cadillac when I needed, like to go to the supermarket or the liquor store. Vinny was cool with me, and I thought of myself as sort of like a

'Higgins' from 'Magnum' at Robin Masters' place, you know? Vinny gave me money to tip the gardeners and the pool boy and always gave me a little extra for myself.

"Once in a while, he'd have me go out golfing with him and the guys. I didn't golf, just drove the cart around, and when I did that, he always took me out beforehand to buy me a cute little outfit. Then he started buying me other shit, like jeans and tops and stuff. He said what I had didn't look really 'nice' when his friends came around for poker games, you know?

"The captain would come around from time to time and take me out, but it wasn't like before. We'd cruise down the Intracoastal to some quiet bar off a canal or on the river, have a few drinks and maybe something to eat, but mostly drinks, screw, and then back to Vinny's. Maybe the owners got wind that something fishy was going on, so they kept the captain on a pretty short leash. Besides, they were planning an extensive trip to the Caribbean for a few months, at least, and needed the captain to read charts and shit to plan it out for them.

"Meanwhile, Vinny's telling me now when to go to the store and how long I have to stay there. That meant I had to go to the store at two in the afternoon, not ten in the morning like I like to, you know? Then he told me I have to stay until at least three then come home. First, I figure he's got a girlfriend and doesn't want me hanging by the pool or anyplace she can see. Maybe he wants his alone time with her. He was out most nights and when he was in, he was in his den, I didn't see him much. Besides, I knew how to mind my business, so I stayed low to the ground and just enjoyed the digs, the cool clothes, booze whenever I want and no demands except for my captain, right?

"But one day, I got real bored with being told when to go where. So, just one time I thought I'd go for a little joyride in the Caddy instead and blew off the store. I was still gone from two to three, so who gave a shit? Vinny had enough food in the house for a hundred sandwiches, believe me.

"Well, when I got home as scheduled, Vinny didn't say a word. He just gave me one good smack across the face and then got in the car and took off. Hell, I didn't even know where I lived, exactly, what the phone number was, or anything. Talk about a wakeup call. There I was, lounging my life away by his pool, cruising with the captain, drinking everybody's booze, eating whatever the hell I wanted, and one time I don't do one little thing, I get smacked like an Eighth Avenue whore. Jeez. I took a hot bath and curled up in bed with some chocolate and tried to figure out what I could do about this. All I got was a stiff headache, or maybe it was the couple of stiff vodkas I had after Vinny left, so I fell out completely and really didn't know shit until morning.

"Vinny must have come home late that night, but the next morning, I woke up to find a gorgeous Louis Vuitton Speedy bag on my nightstand with a red bow. And it wasn't a knockoff and the Louis Leather was real.

"I got dressed and went into the sunny breakfast room off the kitchen. Vinny was there with a fresh cup of coffee in his hand. There was a glass and silver coffee carafe, steaming with a fresh aroma that was too good to pass up, and another mug on the table. As I poured myself a cup, he motioned me to sit down. I did and cradled the hot steamy mug in my hands, ready to toss it in his face if he got nasty then run like hell someplace else.

"'Little girl,' he said, 'am I good to you?'

"'You weren't yesterday,' I replied, a little amazed at my answer.

"'That aside, honey,' he said, as he brushed his hand in the air as if waving off an invisible bug 'am I good to you?'

"I shrugged. 'Yeah, you're okay.'

"'I buy you shit, I give you money, that 'Louie Vee'

handbag didn't grow on a tree you know.'

"I shrugged again. 'Yeah…'

"'I don't bug you in bed, you got your own nice room, you come and go on that boat as you please…'

"Another shrug, 'Yeah…'

"He got in my face and said softly 'So, girly-girl, when I ask you do some little thing for me, I'm not doing any harm, am I?'

"'I guess not.'

"'And when I ask you to be someplace, can you be there for me? Because if you can't, you can't live here any more.'

"'But…' I started.

"He backed off from me and held up his hand, 'Ah-ah! No buts. Can you do me a favor when I ask? I do them for you all the time and you don't have to ask.' He was almost, but not quite, looking sheepish now. 'I'm sorry about yesterday, but you peeved me, little girl.'

"I thought to myself, *Peeved? I'm glad I didn't piss you off.* I would've hated to see that.

"'And if you gotta leave, you gotta leave at midnight tonight. Decide what you want to wear and go. Leave the rest. Take the pockabook if you want.'

"'But my captain…'

"'Honey, he's gone, he left yesterday.'

"I was totally deflated.

"'He wanted me to tell you we can work something out if we want, but he's not sure he can see you anymore. At least, not like you were.'

"'I don't believe you!' I said, knowing in my heart of hearts it was true.

"'Yeah, well, believe what you want. It is what it is and you're done. Besides, what's so bad about here?'

"'You hit.'

"Now it was his turn to shrug, 'Yeah, well…'

"'I don't want to get hit.' I told him.

"'Okay, so we have an understanding. You just obey and you don't get hit. You want leave, go at midnight, not before, not after. You want to stay, you do as you're told. I can't be any fairer than that.'

"I looked out over the Intracoastal through the sunny breakfast room and wondered how it was possible to be so miserable in such a gorgeous place. Welcome to Florida, Tracey. I took a bottle of Stoli out of the freezer and put a shot of vodka in my coffee to take the edge off. I took a long sip, thought for a second and said, 'Okay, I'll stay.' And decided to figure out my options at my leisure. At least overnight.

"'Good,' he said, smiling. 'We're going golfing this afternoon and I got a game on tonight.'

"It was going to be a long day. All day I tried to forget the night before, but his slap stung me, so I thought the whole world was able to see the bright red slap mark on my face from many hours before.

"The week passed uneventfully. I was still wary, but he was mostly out. Then the dreaded request came.

"'You gotta go to the store this afternoon,' he said matter of fact like.

"'I do,' I said, trying to sound agreeable, 'we need a few things. Two o'clock, as usual?'

"'Yeah. How long will it take you?'

"'About an hour, I guess.' I shrugged noncommittally.

"'Okay, good girl. Stay at the store until three. Be home by three-thirty.'

"'Sure, anything you say.'

"'Vinny,' he added, and looked at me through hooded eyes.

"'Anything you say, Vinny,' I said.

"I spent the remaining time relaxing by the pool, gazing over the Intracoastal and wondering if I could swim away. At the appointed time, I showered and left for the store.

"As I pushed my shopping cart around the stupidmarket, I glanced out the enormous plate glass windows in front at the marvelously sunny day, feeling absolutely miserable, and I thought about what I might do about my situation. I could scream and everybody would think I was some crazy housewife gone postal. I could call the cops–yeah, sure. What would I tell them? Like, I'm living with this guy who demands I go to the supermarket between two and three on Tuesdays? 'What's your point?' they would say back to me. Well, he hits if I don't. Well, when he hits you, *then* give us a call. Great.

"I came out of my fog long enough to look up again and saw someone at the Cadillac. A well-dressed man I'd never seen before. He opened the back door of the Caddy with a key, pulled out a brown plastic supermarket bag and put in an identical bag. The old supermarket bag switcheroo. Hell, I thought everyone had an extra supermarket bag of shit in the back. Ours was being changed on a regular basis. But I definitely should not have looked at that car at that time and seen that man with those bags.

"I realized this was the first time I'd gone to the store actually somewhat sober and not quite as buzzed as usual. Since the slapping episode, I found it was easier to sneak a little now and again to maintain all day, and I saved the big buzz for cocktail hour. Now I needed a drink. What was I driving home with? What did I drive *from* home with? All kinds of crazy shit raced through my head. The bags could have held everything from human body parts– maybe Vinny killed an ex-wife from once upon a time or a "business" associate and I was schlepping them piecemeal to be carried away by one of his cronies. But what about the return bag?

"*Okay*, I thought, *numbers tickets and money? Or drugs and guns?* Hells bells, I was scared shitless and scared more-than-shitless to ask, so I drove myself home. When I got home, I told Vinny I didn't feel so good and asked him to unload the bags for me. He said he would.

"I went to my bathroom, threw up, then had a drink from my secret bottle in the back of the closet. I curled up under the covers and shook until it was time for another drink. I had the drink. I curled up under the covers some more and slept. Drunkenly. Stupidly. Thank God.

"I woke up the next morning deciding I had to do something about my situation.

"'Vinny,' I started, 'I need a job.'

"'For...?' he raised his eyebrows.

"'I want to earn my own money...'

"'For...?' He was not making this easy.

"'I need stuff.' Oh, brilliant, I thought to myself.

"'Such as...?'

"'What is this? Twenty questions?'

"He got that 'hit' look in his eye and I backed off quick.

"'Vinny,' I started again, 'a girl needs stuff.'

"'Like... *what* stuff?'

"'Okay, Vinny, if you must know, like tampons.' He looked mildly amused, and so I continued, 'Hair spray, haircuts and manicures. My own clothes, shoes. You know, stuff.'

"'What, I don't take good care of you?'

"'Sure you do, Vinny. But a girl just needs her own.'

"He thought it over a moment then nodded.

"'Okay, I can see your point. So, what would you do? There's no boats around here to clean.'

"'I thought maybe waitress, or bartend. I could work part time, right? And be here whenever you want.' I had pretty much accepted that my captain was a thing of the past. Working in a restaurant in South Florida–well, there's plenty of them, it's all cash, and I could stash a few bucks to make the split from Vinny maybe a month down the road. Maybe I would hook up with another waitress or something.

"He put his finger on one side of his chin, trying to look thoughtful. I could see the wheels turning.

"'You ever do this sort of work before?' he asked.

"'Well, I bartended for my cousin a time or two up at his place in Lodi,' I answered. 'It seemed pretty easy. You know, beers and shots, nothin' like I don't know.'

"'You've got me there, girly-girl,' he said. 'Okay, lemme make a couple calls and line something up. I got a friend or two in the business. I'll square it wit' them.'

"*Oh, great*, I thought. *Out of the frying pan into the fire*. Then again, maybe not–it was worth a shot, if it ever came along, leaving it to Vinny.

"One thing I'll say for Vinny, though, is that he is a businessman. When he tells you he'll take care of something, it's good as done–no matter what. I've seen the respect his cronies give him at the poker table and it wasn't just for playing good cards.

"So, I wasn't surprised when Vinny came up to me later that afternoon as I was lying by the pool, nursing my mid-day buzz. He ordered me to get dressed and ready to go out.

"'Golf again?' I asked, 'It's been three times this week.'

"'Maybe later. Right now we gotta go see Geoffrey. I have some business there and maybe he's got a job for you. C'mon baby,' he said, and smacked me squarely on the ass. 'You're gonna be a workin' girl now. You better hustle better than that.'

"I quashed my buzz and marched smartly into my shower. We left in short order. Vinny parked me at the bar to talk to Brian, the guy you call Cold-As-Ice, while Geoffrey and Vinny sat at a back table. I felt like prime Angus beef being looked over at the slaughterhouse.

Geoffrey and Vinny shook hands. Geoffrey got up and, with a little bow to Vinny, headed in my direction."

"Oh, Jesus," I said to Tracey, thinking more than a little about big brother Ed and what it felt like to be under someone's thumb–and forefinger, pinky finger, fuck-you finger and, from time to time, the whole ham-fisted hand. "Hey, you want to rest a bit and head on home?"

Tracey shook her head. "I want to get the rest of this out. I'm almost done."

"Okay," I said, "but let's find a shadier place, it's getting hot here."

Tracey acquiesced and we moved to grassier, higher ground in the shade of a few sea grape trees. Tracey looked around, as if to make sure someone wasn't listening to us.

I hopped up on a low-lying sea grape limb and leaned against the trunk. Tracey followed suit, climbing up beside me and perched next to me on the branch, looking like a frail, frightened bird about to take flight at any moment.

"Well," she continued, "you know what it's like there…" She trailed off.

"Sort of, but I don't think I got the whole story."

"Yeah, I should have warned you more strongly. I'm sorry." She looked at me with an almost haunted expression.

"It's okay. I survived. Won't make no nevermind since I don't work there now."

"You're lucky," she said. "You start working there, you're not likely to leave..."

"So, what's the scoop?"

"You really want to know?"

"Probably not." We sat in silence for a moment, "So, go on–what happened?"

"I worked as a cocktail waitress for a while, made pretty good money…" She drifted off again, looking out over the beach to the ocean and beyond.

"Eventually, I became a bartender…" She was talking in drifts now, like the waves washing ashore.

"I made really good money then. I was able to fool Vinny into thinking I was blowing it left and right on hairdos and clothes…" She spoke in a halting fashion, stopping for a moment in between each statement. I shut my mouth.

Tracey continued, "I stashed the money in my pillow. He found it one night when I was out… he kicked the crap out of me, kept my money he found, and drove me to a street someplace… he kicked me out of the car and I wandered around for a while, trying to figure out where I was. The cops picked me up sometime later. After a time in the tiger tank, they realized I was beaten up, not drunk or on drugs… so they sent me to the hospital… I started going through the DT's and then I got shafted to detox, rehab, and a halfway house for a few months. Now I'm on my own, working at Dana's."

She looked like she was going to fall off the limb. I steadied her and we jumped down together.

"Let's get outta here."

"Yeah…" she was still drifting. We wandered over to where The Mir was parked and I had to help her into the passenger seat. I tucked her into the seat belt and slid behind the wheel.

"So," I said, "Where to?"

"Home, I guess. Need to make a call."

I hoped she wasn't thinking about getting in touch with Vinny again or, worse, her friend the wayward yacht captain. "None of my business, but…"

"My sponsor. I'm gonna need a meeting now."

"AA?"

"Yeah," she answered. "Seemed like the thing to do at the time, I suppose."

"I suppose." I sighed. My mind swirled with everything she had told me and everything I had experienced at Geoffrey's.

"But why did you recommend Geoffrey's in the first place?" I asked.

"The money's good and if you're not one of the 'players' they're not gonna hassle you."

"Wanna bet?"

There was real pain in her eyes when she turned towards me, "I'm really, really sorry. Besides, I know where Geoffrey's concerned, all bets are off, anyway."

"Huh?"

"Yeah, well, that's how I got in. You see, Geoffrey had a little gambling habit, loved the sports book, poker... you know. So, he had a little action with Vinny. No big deal to Vinny, but Geoffrey got in over his head. Vinny agreed to cut him some slack if he took me on–under certain circumstances, you understand."

"Yeah, like you had to be able to do the shopping." I said.

"Yes, and tend to the poker parties and golf outings and all the other sundry stuff I did for Vinny."

"So, what the hell was in the supermarket bags?" I wasn't sure I wanted to know but had to ask.

"I never found out. Hey, make a right here, we're home."

I let her out in front of a long strip of tidy-looking white apartments with a small pool in front. The grass was well maintained and I could tell the place had just gotten a fresh paint job. I handed her the shoe bags from Pizzzazzz– somehow, they looked a little wilted after sitting in the car for a few hours. So did she.

"Well, thanks for driving," Tracey said as she opened the car door to get out. "'Bye...'" She was drifting again.

"'Bye,'" I drifted, too, leaving way too much unsaid. I was too overwhelmed to say much of anything. There are times when being close-mouthed has nothing to do with meaning to be.

I headed home up the street in an uncertain mood. Dhani, Edmund, and the Captain were in the courtyard, putting down cold ones and talking over the day. I parked in the back lot and slipped in through the side gate, straight to the bungalow.

They looked up, but must have sensed I was in no mood for a chat, so they just went back to their beer. I could hear them discuss the merits of a courtyard poker game and would Mike or Red Dog be able to come by and make it a foursome, since the Captain was not actively considered under any circumstances to be a particularly skillful player.

I listened to the soft brown voices of the men with half an ear, packed away my Pizzzazzz shoes without trying them on again as I usually do when bringing home new shoes, and stepped into a steaming hot shower. For once, the balky showerhead cooperated and I reveled in the sensation of steamy-hot water, the sensuous lather of shampoo and emerged considerably more refreshed than when I came home. I started plotting tomorrow's adventures.

I was actually looking forward to going back to Sparky's and the more mundane world of drunk wrangling. The fancy club scene was not for me, and Tracey's story made me happy I hadn't cut the mustard at Geoffrey's. I thought about her, a little sadly, hoping she'd gotten with her sponsor and made her meeting. I remembered what Mom went through when she had to quit after the cancer came. AA sure made quitting a whole lot easier than drinking. I popped a beer and headed out barefoot into the courtyard, wearing denim shorts and a loose-fitting blue tee shirt, my dripping-wet hair wrapped turban-style in a towel.

"Hello, boys," I said, Mae West style to the guys in the yard. The Captain wolf-whistled low and long, while everyone else told him to shut up and said hello to me.

"Can you tell my fortune, swami?" asked the Captain.

I looked off and beyond, put my hands up to my head and said, "I see... I see... a beer in your future," and took out the cheap can of beer I had cleverly hidden in the towel wrapping my hair.

"You play poker?" Edmund asked.

"No thanks, not tonight. "I said as the towel fell off my head onto the path between the bungalows. "Maybe I'll look in on the game later, though, if that's all right."

"Cool."

"Yeah," I said and picked up the towel as I sat down to enjoy my beer in the companionable silence disturbed only by the chirping of skinks in the distance. Skinks are lizards that look like snakes. They have little bitty arms and legs and real long tails. Some of them chirp like crickets in the darkness, a soft, soothing song for those of us who grew up with them, like we had under our trailer. Some skinks are native, others are introduced here from God knows where, like too many Florida critters. As a kid, I thought they were kind of fun to play with and if you caught one they didn't bite. They're skittery and slithery, so now I don't think I'd go out of my way to catch one. I was pretty sure we had a permanent resident skink behind my bungalow in the makeshift laundry room. Too many people buy premium critters for a fancy price, get a permit to keep them at home and then let 'em loose when they get bored. I was pretty sure that's how we'd come by this skink since skinks don't usually make noise but this one sure did.

Eventually, Mikey and Red Dog ambled in, six-packs in hand, and the game was underway. I got up to free my spot at their table and headed back to my bungalow. I was restless, but didn't feel like going out. I was thirsty, but didn't feel like drinking. I figured the best thing to do was to say the hell with it all, turn in early and be happy for a full night's sleep. I stowed my Tigger slippers under my bed and that's exactly what I did.

Chapter Nine

I woke up at dawn, unrefreshed, but happy the night passed. I had tossed and turned for hours with Tracey's story echoing in my mind like a swarm of bats sealed in a dank cave.

A major case of homesickness washed over me and I wondered why I'd ever left in the first place. Not that there was anything to go back to. Almost everyone I knew grew up and left, seeking greener pastures, which they usually found, given where they'd come from. I felt I stood on ground that was constantly shifting and tilting. At any moment, it would fall away and I would follow into endless emptiness. The old familiarity of knowing what's what, where it is, how to get what you want and from whom was sorely lacking in my new life. I felt raw, lonely, and hollow inside. The loneliness creeping in on top of the homesickness made me decide the best thing to do was get the hell out of the house and get something to eat. Besides, I wanted to check up on Tracey.

Musing on what I did have to be thankful for, steady work at Sparky's and the safety of the Compound, I realized it wasn't bad, even though it wasn't home. *Home is where your Mom is*, I thought, caught myself thinking I should give her a quick call, and then quickly realized exactly where my Mom was. The rawness was giving way to a meltdown, so I stood up and shook it off.

Since it was only about quarter to seven in the morning, I had several hours before work. I tied my hair in a scrunchy ponytail, threw on a pair of shorts, a hoodie and old comfy flip-flops to head over to Dana's. Tracey was the closest thing I'd had to a friend in a long while. I didn't want the fire to go out just because of our talk the day before. Sometimes, people reveal too much and then back off. I hoped she didn't feel that way. I wanted to believe she was confiding in me more than venting through a handy conduit for her hurt. It's easy to talk to people you don't know very well–they're less likely to judge and, not having been there when you actually went through the pain, more likely to listen. It's easy to listen to a painful story when it's not your own.

The Captain snoozed peacefully in his chaise next to Edmund's. There were stirrings in the Compound of people waking up. Morning smells–breakfast, coffee. My stomach growled. I glanced at the table in the center of the courtyard and saw it strewn with remnants of last night's poker party. A few stray plastic chips had landed on the bare dirt floor around the table and chairs, one of which had been tipped over the night before. The Ace of Diamonds stuck out from the trunk of the big old mango tree. A couple of near-empty beer cans smelled of the dregs of stale beer and a cigarette butt or two. Some pocket change was strewn about and I spotted a fin on the ground. *Cap'n'll have a field day*, I thought, and smiled, leaving the fin where it lay. I wondered what the Captain would do first, take a pull off one of the old beers or pick up the fin.

Slipping out back behind the bungalow, I headed over to Dana's. Man, it was going to be hot, steamy already and not a stirring of breeze through a single palm frond. A person can blow in the direction of a palm tree and it'll sway in the "breeze." This morning, there was nothing. I could huff and puff as much as I pleased, but I had a feeling the fronds wouldn't budge.

Dana's was packed for that hour of the morning. I'd never been there before eight, so this was a whole new experience for me. As a rule, I don't like crowds, but felt better seeing Tracey behind the counter plying her trade. I smiled, waved, and ducked through the crowd, trying to get a precious seat in her station. Finding a stool next to a somewhat beefy gent quickly downing a plate of eggs and hash, I ordered my usual coffee and blueberry muffin and watched the action around me.

There were a lot of men in there, and more than a few of them were the police. Even the beefster next to me had the telltale bulge of a shoulder holster under his armpit. Dana's was obviously a hangout for the local cops–*too bad*, I thought.

Tracey swooped by, coffee and muffin in hand, lightly perching them in front of me on a small corner of the counter as my personal space was greatly diminished by the blue plate special next door.

"Hi," I said. "You okay?"

"Hey… I'm okay. You're up early, huh?"

"Yeah, couldn't sleep. You're pretty busy yourself."

"Yeah. Case over on Briny Avenue last night. Most of these guys were up all night solving a 'death by natural causes.' The cops hate the word *murder* around here." She cocked her head in the direction of the uniforms and then said under her breath, "I think the guy next to you is a detective."

I didn't dare look and continued to keep my mouth shut by effectively stuffing it with a bit of muffin. After a sip of coffee, I looked questioningly at Tracey.

"You know, there's never a murder in Pompano," she said. "One time, they found a guy shot dead and stuffed in the trunk of a car and ruled it 'Death by Misadventure.'" She rolled her eyes in my neighbor's direction, but he seemed to be paying more attention to his breakfast than to us.

"Helps with the tourist trade here," she went on, "they think they're staying someplace safe."

Remembering yesterday's conversation, I gave a small snort of derision, "Right."

"Yeah." Tracey agreed and then slipped into the kitchen. She flipped back out through the swinging saloon-style wood doors just as quickly with three steaming plates in hand, loaded with bacon, sausage, eggs, and home fries. I was almost tempted to order a plate myself.

Taking a refill on my coffee, I looked around quietly at the uniforms. My Mom always said there was something about a man in uniform. Seemed to make him more handsome or something. I tried the old speech class trick of picturing them in their underwear and I guessed Mom was right. Most of these guys you wouldn't look at twice if you bumped your supermarket cart into theirs or saw them with the wife and kiddies in the local home and hardware store. Just plain old guys who happened to be dressed in lots of blue with a gun in every holster. Now there's a campaign slogan: "A chicken in every pot, a gun in every holster." Just livin' the American dream. Yeah.

Tracey hopped back to my spot and took a breath. "Whew!"

"Big day, huh?"

"Both, I guess. This is way more than I'm used to."

"Weren't you this busy at Geoffrey's?"

"Different kind of busy." The subject was closed as she locked her eyes into an impenetrable stare across the diner.

"Sorry," I said, "I didn't mean…"

"No, no, it's okay," she waved the apology away, patting my arm. "Really."

"Actually, *I've* got a story," I said.

Tracey raised an eyebrow and her eyes started to thaw.

"Bet you do, hon."

"If you want to listen, I'd like to share."

She raised one eyebrow cautiously, "You don't seem like the sharing type."

"I'm not, really. But I would like to talk to

someone."

"Yeah, sure, you listened to my tale of woe. I'll hear yours."

I was dubious. She didn't know me as well as I thought I knew her at that point. Maybe she just didn't believe I could have a 'tale of woe' or tell it fully. She'd been through enough and looked like she wasn't too sure of making it all that much further. Or, maybe, she was just tired from being so busy all morning.

Seeing a signal from Louie in the kitchen she said, "Look, I gotta go…"

"Yeah, I'll see you."

"Sure, hon."

I paid up and headed out, less than satisfied with my morning mission. Well, sometimes it happens that way. There was a sourness in the steamy air outside which mirrored my mood. I took my keys out of my purse and decided to blow the Mir out on the highway for a couple of minutes. It would help to clear my head as well as the Mir's exhaust. You can't run a thoroughbred like the Mir at twenty-five miles an hour all her life.

The Mir's air conditioning had conked out some time ago, and I remembered seeing little battery-powered fan at Knott's Hardware. It wasn't expensive and I thought if I bought a couple and clipped them onto the visors, I could drive without breaking a dirt sweat from the heat in five minutes or less.

The Mir and I danced down the Dixie Highway until we crunched into a parking spot on the gravel and dirt lot at Knott's. Howie, Mr. Knott the younger, was somewhere out in the dusty yard, and cussed up a storm as a load of lumber tumbled off of one of the trucks directly onto the dirt.

I walked into the dry cool yard shed. It was dark as usual inside, cobbled together of planking and spare lumber but sturdy as a treasure chest. That shed would probably outlast all of us if allowed to stand on its own with just minor maintenance from time to time. Mr. Knott the elder was seated in an old worn out executive chair upholstered in tattered black leather. It creaked as he leaned forward to look directly at my chest.

"Help you, Missy?" he asked my chest.

I ignored him, turned and gave him a view of my butt in shorts for good measure–dirty old bastard–and said with my back to him, "Need a couple of those little fans."

"Whoo hoo," he hooted. "I can bet for what and I've got just the thing. C'mere, girly, I'll fix you right up."

I looked at him suspiciously, not wanting to get any closer than I absolutely had to.

"It's for that car of yours, isn't it?" he asked.

"Yeah. The a/c went on the fritz awhile back."

"Yep, round about the time Howie came into business with me, I reckon. Been about ten years or so now. Them T-birds are nice, but a/c's a bitch to fix when they blow."

"Don't I know it."

He stood up from the creaky chair and reached over to one of the shelves on his left, producing two little fans on clips.

"Will this do?"

"Perfect." I gave him $13.00 for a $12.98 purchase and told him to keep the change.

"Big spender." He smiled, "Penny in penny out. I'll remember this if you're ever short."

"Yessir, and take care not to spend it all in one place." I winked at the old buzzard and he winked right back. Howie came in just then and looked down my tee. He was disappointed that the crew neck blocked his view, but he just shrugged and headed toward his dad.

"Don't be a stranger, y'hear?" the old boy called after me.

"Yessir," I said, trying to quietly exit the shed. The

crude screen door on hard spring hinges refused to cooperate and slammed me in the butt on my way out.

I headed to the Mir. I bet the Knotts had that rigged on purpose and rubbed my butt. I was sure they were watching me. I wouldn't swear to it, but I thought I heard chortling noises from inside the shed. I opened the door to the Mir and before I stepped inside and made a real show of rubbing my sore ass knowing full well the car door blocked the Knotts' view of this action. I slid in behind the steering wheel, giving a beep and a wave. A Knott–I couldn't tell which–sullenly slipped from view behind the ornery screen door. *Damn*, I thought to myself, *I just gotta find a Home Depot.*

I clipped the two little fans to my visor and pointed them in the direction of my face. They did the trick; now all I needed was a decent pair of cool sunglasses. I stopped at a Stop 'n' Cop convenience store and got a really cool pair of shades. These crappy little convenience stores usually have the coolest shades for cheap and who cares if they last only a month? There's always a newer, hotter style out and you don't want to be stuck with the same pair of sunglasses forever, do you? Not in Florida, anyway.

I fumbled with the radio dial and finally found a station I liked playing head-banger music. It made me want to slam the gas pedal as Axl Rose welcomed me to the jungle and I thought, "You're not kiddin' bro'." Metallica screamed after Guns N' Roses, and the Stone Temple Pilots warned me not to get stuck in the Vaseline. The Smashing Pumpkins then reminded me "What I choose is my choice" as I blasted up I-95 to Boca, then turned around on Glades Road and blasted back. Rush hour was just starting to wind up by the time I peeled into the dirt lot of the compound. I took extreme care not to fishtail into the spot with the cable sticking up. I felt refreshed, cleansed and with no desire to go home to Lake Okeechobee. The Mir felt better, too. If I really had wanted to go home, I would have slammed down to I-595 then out to 27. Not today.

The compound was quiet and still as I headed towards the bungalow to get ready for work. Even the Captain was gone. I showered, washed and styled my hair, got dressed and headed out to my shift at Sparky's. My shift was 11 to 6, but it's more 10:30-6:30 by the time you have to fill sinks, do side work and shit then cash out at the close of your shift.

Ricky was at the end of the bar, quietly talking to the kitchen crew when I came in. I just dropped my bag behind the bar and busied myself with side work: first, I ran the water to get hot in the sinks. The left sink filled with hot water and I dropped in the chemical tablets, which fizzed into soap to clean the glasses. I dropped the scrub brushers in the soapy sink which removed lipstick and other gunk off the dirty glasses. The right sink I filled with clear hot water to rinse after dipping dirty glasses in the chemicals. This makes a good case for drinking beer straight from the bottle.

I wiped down all the bottles on the speed rack with a new bar cloth wetted down with club soda. I cleaned the beer taps and got the yeasty stale beer wiped off the bottom of the drip. It *stinks*. I cleaned the drippers. I put new liners in the trash tubs. I filled the ice in just three trips to the ice machine in the kitchen. I stacked napkins, straws, and then I cut bar fruit. Keep busy-busy bee and stay out of Ricky's way. I checked the mixes and ducked down to check the reserves as he chocked the front and side doors in the open position to air the place out and let the customers know they're welcome to start drinking with us. I nodded as he entered behind the bar to take up his place and gave me an acknowledging nod back. I watched him test the sink temps and got an approving nod. I kept a straight face. Bartenders loathe the public knowing their tricks and secrets so they either hiss or nod to each other. They almost always keep a good poker face, unless they're courting a tip. I counted my bank in the register, it was all there.

I stood at the other end of the bar, away from the door and near the kitchen. Customers dribbled in soon after. By noon, we were in full swing with the lunch crowd, mostly barflies and a couple of construction crews working on the A-1-A nearby. Seems like they wait until the most inconvenient time to rip up the roads and plant new pavement. Usually, this means the end of season or the hottest part of the summer. Then by next season, it's ripped to shit again.

Some of the hardcore barflies drink until closing. Others come and go, depending on errands they have to take care of or the level of functionality they choose to maintain. But they're always good for conversation and happy to make the acquaintance of the barkeep hoping to score a free drink. Usually, a good bartender cultivates this steady trade and oblige with a bump or two of a free drink for regulars or people they like on shift, thus ensuring repeat business and a decent tip. This conversation kept me busy and out of the line of fire from Ricky. I really needed this job and just didn't want the hassle. Ricky occasionally glanced in my direction, but he was too busy to talk.

Finally, the inevitable happened and our worlds collided. I was filling a sink, again, and he was trying to get a reserve bottle of vodka. As he tripped over me on his way to the reserve bin, I caught him by the shoulder and unobtrusively righted him, saving him from a very messy fall on the sloppy rubber "comfort" mat beneath our feet.

"Good save," he hissed. "What happened to you the other night?"

"Had to go. By the way, where's your girlfriend? Isn't she late for her shift?"

The world seemed to stop. It was as if time stood still and I had stepped smack in the middle of it. Even the running faucet on the sink seemed to stop. Actually, it had. Rick turned it off. The bar was silent as a tomb. Rick turned towards me. Even the barflies weren't sipping away. No one was gnawing a burger. Nothing. It was as still as the sour morning air I stepped out in earlier that day.

"That's crude, Stacey." Rick said flatly.

"What do you mean?"

"She's dead."

"*What?*" I blurted. I didn't believe it. I shut my mouth quickly.

"Last night. Late."

I put my hand on his shoulder, "I'm sorry, Rick, I didn't know."

"Yeah, well, Kat found her." He shrugged off my hand.

"Oh, man, poor Kat."

He nodded. "Yeah, the cops were up there all night, making it out to be a stroke."

"You think it's something else?"

"I don't know. Kat said she was bleeding from her ear."

"Poor Kat." My vocabulary was getting more and more limited, but at least I could open my mouth a word or two. "Poor *you.*"

"I gotta go have a cigarette." Rick said, as he downed a quick shot surreptitiously behind the bar. Bartenders were only allowed a couple of smoke breaks outside, if they took them at all. Even though smoking was allowed in the bar, bartenders had to keep smoking to a minimum.

"I'll watch the bar, you go ahead." I refilled drinks and cleaned ashtrays as the bar slowly got back to normal after witnessing the little drama that had just taken place. Loretta was dead. Jesus. And I knew Rick didn't smoke. Usually. The whole thing seemed surreal.

I faithfully watched the bar as promised and Rick came back about fifteen minutes later, looking a little hotter and fustier than usual. As I suspected, he did not reek of cigarette smoke. His eyes were red and bleary. He'd probably just stood on the sidewalk, trying to sort it all out. I felt rotten for opening my mouth, but the deed was done. Shit. We continued our shift in silence toward each other, but busied ourselves speaking only to those customers who seemed disposed for conversation.

Many of the regulars asked about Loretta, since she usually came in around mid-afternoon. She was a fixture at the bar feeding on Ricky. I saw little bar faces crumple when faced with the news and I played dumb and kept my mouth shut. It was going to be a couple of tough days ahead for Ricky. Several extra shots were poured and consumed. Rick took his fair share. I took nothing, figuring Rick was entitled to his day.

Kat came into the bar around four and sat at my end. I was surprised, thinking she'd look for service from Rick.

"Hey, Kit-Kat," I said, trying to be friendly. She looked up with her blue eyes shadowed with purple underneath from exhaustion and ordered a double Jack Black rocks. I set the chilled amber liquid down in front of her and said, "On the house, my dear."

She smiled in thanks and took a long draught. Kat set the drink down in front of her. She crossed her arms, leaned on the bar, and sighed.

I busied with the other customers in the house and left her in peace. Her glass would stay full all day, on the house, as long as she wanted–or needed.

She reached her hand out to stop me on my way around the bar yet again, "She was my friend," she said.

"Loretta? Yes, I know," I replied softly. "That's where I met you."

"Yeah, well you don't KNOW…"

"No, not really." I met her gaze with mine and saw the alcohol beginning to take hold. This, obviously, wasn't her first of the day and her last wasn't coming any time soon, either.

"Look," she said, "I gotta smoke." I flipped up an ashtray from behind the bar and placed it in front of her with a phony-baloney magical flourish, which usually can cheer up the gloomiest Gus. Kat didn't even notice. She slid off the bar stool, drink in hand.

She jerked her head in the direction of the door, "Outside," she said. I looked towards Ricky who motioned me to go with her.

"Hey, Ricky, I need a break anyway, okay?" He nodded in my direction and lifted the gate of the bar to let me out. I walked around to the back entrance and found Kat. Outside, leaning against the building, her lanky form silhouetted against a garish undersea mural painted on the wall facing the beach. Some local *artiste* who possessed more energy than actual talent had created it. I thought about my bungalow wall and decided whoever painted this wouldn't be allowed within a hundred yards of my place. The next Scott Weiland he wasn't.

Kat lit her cigarette and blew a smoke ring in the stillness. To be able to do that right next to the ocean meant it was totally still. Lake Atlantic it was sometimes called, and by the tiny wavelets, it was flat as a flapjack. The bit of the shade provided by the overhanging roof on that side of the building did nothing to diffuse the heat of the intake fan generated by the kitchen.

"It's a hot one," I said as an opener. One thing about Florida—you can always talk about the weather.

"Yeah, but at least I can feel it. Loretta's in cold-storage by now." She inhaled, held the smoke, and French-inhaled it again—a small puff out, a quick intake, and another exhale, full out. It tastes good, but its hell on the lungs, especially when you blow it like dragon smoke out of your nostrils. The wall was doing a wonderful job of holding Kat upright.

I stood there, taking the air, and she offered me a

cigarette. I took it. I really don't smoke, but I know how and can stand there holding a lit one, looking like I'm smoking in dire circumstances such as these.

"I'm freaked. It was a woman thing, you know…" she trailed off. "Loretta was really good to me. Helped me out of a jam once. "

I nodded and wondered what kind of jam this skinny stripper could have gotten herself into and how Loretta had gotten her out of it. I kept still, though, and let Kat go on.

"I found her, you know. She was on the floor in her foyer, bleeding from her ear. I touched her to wake her up. She was cold. There was so much blood… she looked so small…"

I wondered if Kat was going to offer any more. I thought about the large, cold, and almost-empty marble foyer, which served as the cavernous entry to Loretta's inner sanctum. We both stood there and held our lit cigarettes as we watched them burn down to the filter. Well, I watched mine; I doubted Kat watched anything besides the scene that played over and over in her head.

"Hey, let's go back into the a/c," I said, stubbing out my butt on the curb and tossing it into a storm grate. "I'll buy you another round."

Kat nodded quietly and flicked her cigarette into the street, which was something I'd never learned to do. I never copped all the cool moves that automatically go with the habit, maybe that's why I don't smoke. We walked back into the bar.

"Thanks…" said Kat, drifting off. I wasn't sure what she thanked me for.

Ricky nodded to me as I ducked under the gate and took my place by the cash register in the back. A few more rounds, then time to cash out. Kat looked more bedraggled as each drink wore on her.

"Ricky gonna take you for something to eat?" I

asked, thinking how sorely she needed it.

"Nah, dunno," she replied.

"Okay, where do you want to go?"

"I-HOP," she answered.

Oh, goody. Pancakes on top of sour mash. Sensible choice. Well, it was her day, not mine.

"You taking her out for a bite?" I asked him.

He shook his head curtly and hissed, "Stuff to do. Going home."

"Then I'll take her to the I-HOP after we're off," I said. Ricky shrugged.

I went back to Kat and parked an ice water in front of her.

"Look, I'll take you. I'll be off in a couple and my car's just around the corner. Okay?"

Kat nodded wordlessly, stared at her ice water and shrugged.

For a friend who just died, there was a whole lot of shrugging going on.

I was able to pour Kat out of the bar after I closed up, rang off shift, and fetched the Mir. We headed over the Intracoastal to Federal and south on Federal to the restaurant. Kat seemed to perk up a little in the overly cool climate of the I-HOP and almost acted as if she were interested in eating.

We ordered pancakes for her and an omelette with hash browns and bacon for me. Coffee for both of us and I gave thanks to the Coffee-God. It was a bottomless pot.

Kat looked down pensively and played with her napkin, unfurling it from the cutlery then rolling it back up as if she were deciding whether pancakes were an appropriate finger-food or not.

"So, look," I started, "You don't have to tell me if you don't want to, but I'm just curious…"

She smiled bleakly, her wan face looked markedly more drawn in the harsh fluorescent restaurant lighting,

"You mean, what's a nice girl like me doing in a place like this?"

"No, not exactly."

"It's okay. I know–I don't look anything like anyone's idea of a stripper and the fact that I take my panties off for a living doesn't exactly endear me to most women."

I shrugged, "Hey, it's what you do. But that's not what I meant. I was wondering about Loretta."

"Yeah…" Kat looked horrid and there was no shot of whiskey to be had to smooth things over. I poured more coffee and fixed it for her, having watched her prepare her initial cup with three sugars and just one creamer.

"Take a sip," I said. "Did I do it right?"

She sipped and nodded it was okay.

"Look, there wasn't anything between Loretta and me," she started. "I mean, not *that* way if you know what I mean. She had her own things going on the side and, like I told you, she helped me out once, so I was just a friend. At least, I thought I was until the other night."

"The night of the party?"

"Yeah. There was that stuff going on with you and her and Ricky and I knew for a fact that she was screwing Brian. She wants to screw Ricky, too, but he likes them young. Well, younger, anyway."

"Whoa–wait a minute. Brian–the handsome guy on the way in as I was on the way out?" I did not want to tip my hand to her that I'd had a run in with him at Geoffrey's already.

"Oh, I thought you'd left by then."

"Yes, well, I was leaving, but had to make a pit stop. I ducked into the bathroom just as they came in. Doesn't this Brian work at Geoffrey's?"

Kat snorted, "Yeah, if you can call it work."

"He's a bartender there, isn't he?"

"Um, yeah. That and a whole lot more. How do you

know all this? I thought you weren't from around here."

Now I was really curious. I wanted to find out more if she'd give it up, but I had to clear the air first.

"You know the bar biz." I shrugged easily. "You pick things up. People come and go. But I don't know that much."

Kat took a thoughtful sip of her coffee and gave me a measuring look. I guess I passed muster because she took another sip and started to talk.

"Okay. Here's what I know. Geoffrey hires the girls to work in his place. Brian cozies up to them, promises he'll teach them to bartend, so they'll make so much more money and he gets over on them that way. Bartending pays a lot better than waitressing, besides, it's a whole level up on the food chain."

"I've been told that," I said, remembering some of the drunk-wrangling I'd been forced to do in the past and wondered how that could be considered 'one level up' from just laying down a few plates and collecting the money after the meal. The Jello-shot brigade I'd seen at Geoffrey's didn't seem all that much fun, either.

"Well, the girl isn't really gonna be a bartender, it's just a line to get close. So, he feeds her the line and, like, he does her. Next thing you know, he's telling her she needs to be 'nice' to this customer and that customer and it's all in the line of work. If she doesn't do as he says, he'll rat her out to Geoffrey and she'll lose her job because she's been slacking off trying to make time with him."

"Cute," I said, remembering my hasty retreat from the place and thanking my lucky stars I hadn't gotten in any deeper. "But why don't the girls leave? They can get other jobs. It's not the only bar in town."

"If you're the right type, they're the only bar in town that pays $500 a night and gives you your own place, scot-free."

"Wait a minute," I said, tipping my hand, "I worked

there and I didn't make no five hundred dollars."

"How long were you there? A week?"

"A night."

She laughed. "You're smarter than the average bear."

"No, they said I stole a customer's change, so I walked out."

"I hope you kept the money."

"Nope, I chucked it on the floor. Before I was actually accused."

We both laughed. "Bet they had some time digging it out of that lush-plush carpet," Kat said.

"Ick!" I replied, shuddering. God knew what was regularly spilled, spit, dropped or otherwise deposited on that floor. We both rolled our eyes skyward and laughed again.

When the waitress brought our food a few minutes later, Kat attacked her plate with gusto. She just needed a little time to recover, I figured. I started thankfully on the omelette.

"Okay," I said as we started eating, "tell me about Loretta." Sometimes, it's easier to talk with a plate in front of you while you're shoveling the food in than to directly face a subject.

Kat started, "Loretta was from Canada…"

"I've heard that," I answered, filling her in on what I already knew.

"I was working at Geoffrey's and I was one of the 'it' girls, if you know what I mean."

I had an idea, but I parroted, "'It' girls?"

"Yeah, choice of nights, choice of shifts, $500 a shift and my own place, free and clear. A car. I was on my own for clothes and shoes, but they paid for the upkeep."

"Upkeep?"

"Yeah, the hair stylist a couple times a week, facials, manicure, pedicure, massage at the spa, you know.

'Upkeep.' Even offered me a boob job," she said wistfully.

"Oh, upkeep." I thought about how good some of the ladies looked during my brief stint. "So, what's the hitch?"

"I think Brian selects who's going to be who for Geoffrey. He does the bartending thing, then he says they don't have a spot open at the moment, but since you've been such a good trainee, they'll pay you $500 a shift–about what a good 'tender makes a night there–and you do your waitress job and they'll take care of you and give you the first spot when it opens up.

"But," she added, "They tell you not to tell the other girls because some of them may have a similar deal, but they're just not as good as you are and they really want you. If you open up to the other girls and you don't go along, they'll make your life miserable until you quit, and they just couldn't bear to lose you after you've done such a good job. Then they tell you you're going to be a tremendous asset to them once you start bartending. They say they're going to be expanding and that will mean more customers and more money. Hell, maybe even a grand a night if you work with them. Of course, there's the angle with Brian, too. By that time, you think you're in love with him and he's in love with you." Kat snorted.

I thought about Dianna and what bill of goods she'd been sold. Expand? They were fronted on the east side by the water. Opposite the water, on the west side, was a high-end popular restaurant which had been in business for many years and clearly wasn't moving anyplace any time soon. On the south side was the bridge over the Intracoastal and on the north side was a canal. Where, exactly, were they going to expand–up?

Presenting this to Kat, she looked down thoughtfully at a half-eaten pancake and said, "Guess I'm not smarter than the average bear. I never thought about that."

We ate in silence for a few minutes.

"Okay," I said, "that tells me about you and Geoffrey's. Where does Loretta come in?"

"Well, I bought their story and next thing you know, I'm 'entertaining' customers when I'm not working." I nodded encouragingly, stuffing my mouth with omelette in an effort to keep it closed and succeeded.

"At first, it was fun. I'd sleep in late after a shift, wake up late on my day off, get a call from Geoffrey asking me to go on a boat ride with him and some friends. It'd be a party on a big yacht–one of those really fancy motor yachts–and after I got drunk and stoned, one thing would lead to another and I'd get it on with some guy. Then we'd all dock at home and I'd get in, conk out and go to work the next day like nothing ever happened. I didn't know then, but now, I think it was all arranged. I think I was set up and went with who I was *supposed* to, not who I might have wanted to be with."

I felt my blood start to curdle in my veins like the dram of sour half-and-half I'd just put in my coffee. I asked the waitress, who came to check on us, for a fresh cup and cold creamers.

"Damn, girl," I said, "you were in a fix. They had you coming and going up, down and sideways."

"You could say they had me coming and coming…" We both laughed hollowly at her feeble attempt at a joke.

"Well, one day, I just felt sick. Maybe I drank too much or partied too much, maybe even had a little bug, but I just wasn't up to a trip one day." This was sounding vaguely familiar to me. "So, since I was warehoused in Pompano for them–that's what it was, you know, warehousing, even a fancy place on the beach can be a cage if you're not free and I wasn't free, but I landed at Sparky's that afternoon and bumped into Loretta. We got to talking. I'm from Michigan, not too far from Canada myself, but nowhere near her neck of the woods–but it was a comfortable fit. So, we had a couple drinks and I told her what I did and pretty much how I did it. She told me I'd be used up in a year or two, if I wasn't approaching it already, and what would happen then?

"Then she asked if I knew how long the other girls had worked at Geoffrey's. I told her I was pretty new myself and didn't really talk to them. I thought we all were pretty new and I had been there longer than some of the others. She bought me dinner, gave me her address and number, and asked me to call or come over in a couple days, whatever I liked."

We finished our meal and the waitress cleared the table.

"Did you go?" I knocked myself on the head. "Dumb question. So, what happened when you went?"

"She told me I was being used, like a fork or a knife or another utensil at the restaurant. She'd gone there for a drink and, since she's not a babe or anything like that, she just has some money and can 'walk the walk and talk the talk' that way. She could blend in to the crowd and chat up the waitresses without being perceived as a threat. She made it a point to go when I wasn't working and found out that none of the girls had worked there for more than a few months. They didn't have any family or friends in the area and it was just assumed when they left Geoffrey's, they'd gone elsewhere to other jobs or back home. Now, I wonder about that."

"So, how'd you get away?" I thought she had to be special to pull off a stunt like leaving Geoffrey's unscathed.

"Loretta told me to tell them I was gay and coming out of the closet to shack up with her. They'd figure I was useless and just let me go. They did. Of course, not without trying to change my mind and making me be with a 'real' man."

I felt a small tinge of nausea. "Then what?" I asked.

"I left."

"Just like that?"

"Pretty much. I didn't take a whole lot of stuff with me and kept a pretty low profile at Loretta's until I could set myself up. Someplace cheap and easy to split from if anyone came sniffing around. Of course, Loretta didn't tell me that Brian was doing her, too. Getting her to be with a 'real' man."

"So, why strip? You could do something else."

"Why not? I don't give a shit. The money's good and when I get home, I live my life, my way. Someday, I'll have enough saved up to go home and maybe go to school or something. Get a real job down the road."

"So, right now, this is a means to an end for you?"

"Yeah. Is there ever an end?"

"We live and hope," I said, downing the rest of my coffee. "You know, these other girls…" I said thoughtfully, "How can they get out?"

"Maybe they can't, or don't, or don't want to," Kat replied.

"What if they want to? It's a helluva way to live, if you can call it that."

"Yeah." Kat, considerably sobered by warm food and good coffee, took the check.

"I'll get that," I said.

"No, it's mine. You listened."

"So, what about Loretta passing on so suddenly?" I asked, biting the bullet and getting to the nitty gritty before we left.

"I don't think it was all that sudden. Maybe she had medical problems. Maybe somebody caught on to her. She had a rich husband in Canada who sent her down here. She figured it was because he had something going on the side and a beachfront condo was a small price to pay for a free and easy winter up north. She didn't seem to care all that much. I don't know. I'm just sorry she's gone."

I nodded, thinking back to the night of Loretta's

party. Poor, desperate, smitten Loretta. I wondered if her husband would miss her. I thought about her sudden departure and wondered if it was due to 'medical issues', after all. I also thought Kat, coming up to me, might have meant I had gay tendencies, so Loretta let me be for the night.

I took Kat home and dropped her at a set of bungalows not too different from ours at the compound and not too far from there, either.

"There's a bunch of little places like this around here, aren't there?" I asked of Kat.

"Yeah... my hideaway." I thought of Tracey and where I'd dropped her the night before. Was everyone hiding out in Pompano? "Don't be a stranger, okay?" she said. "I don't have a lot of girlfriends and I'd really be happy to have one. Want to come in for tea?"

I declined, thinking I didn't ever want to be there if Geoffrey or Brian got wind of her whereabouts. I didn't think she was the safest person to be around right now and opted to beat feet to the Mir.

"Well, thanks for listening."

"Sure. Thanks for dinner."

"You're welcome," she said, and gave me a slow, soft smile, "I'm off on Saturdays, you can find me by the pool with a book. Come by sometime..."

"I might do that. See you around."

She shut the door and I drove home. Funny how I was already thinking of the compound as "driving home" now, when this morning I was so homesick and lonesome.

I got back to the compound and the Friday Night Freakies were holding court. Sunday through Thursday it was usually low-key in the courtyard—just the Cap'n and us regulars. Friday to Sunday morning was its own entertainment. There was a short stretch of tarmac from Atlantic Boulevard bypassing the A-1-A from the back of Sparky's. There was also the Club Oasis–a rough-monkey type of place with the smelliest carpet in town. Next door was a dive called the Beach Club, which seemed to be the hangout of choice for every stoner in Pompano. The Compound, because of its location, was a combined refuge and transfer point for the patrons of these two beacons of SoFla nightlife. Everyone avoiding John Law passed through our pearly gates to this little piece of heaven. Not always on foot, either. Until the cops moved on, sometimes they stayed, sometimes they crashed. Sometimes, they puked or peed in the bushes. They could be total pains-in-the ass, but they were never boring.

A few folks were hovering in the back of Edmund's, passing a joint while others were seated around the table front-and-center engaged in a lively debate over the next beer-and-cigarette run. I waved to Dhani, got myself a beer and sat myself down on my stoop to watch the action.

I listened to the crickets chirping behind my bungalow and hoped Palmetto bugs, a.k.a. cockroaches, didn't make that identical sound. I sat and thought about what Kat had told me. Something was fishy in Pompano and it wasn't just at the pier. I compared Tracey's story to Kat's and came up with the same conclusion. Given my limited experience with Geoffrey and his restaurant, there was nothing I could prove, but it bore looking into as long as I didn't risk life and limb in the process. I was curious, but not *that* curious.

Dhani pulled up a piece of stoop and sat next to me, beer in hand.

"You're making too much noise here, we gotta ask you to keep it down."

I looked at him morosely.

"Wow. Lose your best friend? Come on–it can't be that bad." He tipped his beer skyward and drained the dregs. "I need another, want one?"

"No, thanks," I said, hoisting my Bud tallboy.

"Suit yourself," he said. "Save me a seat, I'll be right back." He padded back to his apartment.

A moment later, one of the goofballs wandered up to me and delightfully announced, "Oh, man, I am *tripping*."

Oh goody, I thought. This was Curt, one of the laborers who occasionally worked for Dhani when he wasn't working a buzz or tripping out. I was not favoring his company at the moment, however.

"Hey, Curt," I said, "I just saw Dhani and he said he was looking for you. Something about pay day and Friday."

"Oh," Curt answered stupidly, "is it Friday already?" I wondered if he was hallucinating at that moment. Did I look like a giant radish or something? It gave one pause. He waved vaguely to no one in particular and turned around, tottering towards the main building to seek out Dhani.

Dhani came from behind Edmund's bungalow, startling the pot smokers as he edged over to my place. They scattered like chicks at the sight of a fox.

"Nice trick, Stacey," Dhani said, laughing as he sat down next to me. "He'll be wandering for hours."

"Yeah," I grinned. "Wait'll he gets a look at some sea grapes–he'll think the space aliens have landed."

"So, what's on your mind? You've been deep in thought for hours now."

"Has it been that long? Seems like about fifteen minutes to me." I got up to fetch another beer from my mini-fridge. I came back out and sat down on the stoop next to him, then took a stick and aimlessly traced circles in the dirt next to the stoop. We looked like two kids drawing out the rules for a game of kickball.

"I'm not used to this, you know…" I trailed off, leaving him to finish the thought.

"To what?" He frowned.

"All this big city intrigue."

"What, Pompano? Big city? Ha!"

"You know Loretta? Older woman, redhead. Hangs at Sparky's?"

He nodded. "I've seen her once or twice. Older lady–she's got a thing for Ricky the bartender, right?"

"*Had* a thing for Ricky–she's dead."

"Dead?" He stared at me, genuinely shocked. "Oh man," he hung his head and crossed himself. "Jesus! What happened?"

"I don't know, but something strange is going on…" and I spelled everything out for him, starting with my stint at Geoffrey's, Tracey's story, and ending with Kat. It was all I knew, but it seemed I knew more than I should. Even being more hearsay than fact, I'd heard someplace that even a little knowledge could be dangerous.

Dhani heard me out then put a sympathetic hand on my shoulder. "I think you need to step away from it for a while. Have another beer, chill."

I drained the tallboy and thought I might do well to take his advice. But I just couldn't leave it alone.

"You know a guy named Vinny? Developer?"

"I've heard things. But I don't know him personally."

"What things?"

"Look, I really can't say. I've just heard stuff, but I've never seen it for myself."

"But you're in construction," I trailed off.

"Yeah, little stuff. Someday, maybe, I'll get to be big time, but I'll have to have a crew that shows up and works regular."

As if on cue, Curt came stumbling out of the sea grapes behind the bungalow and spied Dhani.

"Ah-hah! There you are," he said with bleary triumph, spotting Dhani on my stoop and, as his six-foot four-inch frame trundled in our direction, he suddenly stopped and I was tempted to call out "Timmmmmberrrrrrr!" as he flopped face down into the grassy area next to the Minnow beside the bungalow, not ten feet from us.

"Down for the count," Dhani said. "Well, he'll be no good for work tomorrow. Just as well to leave him here."

"Yeah, he'll keep the Captain company."

"Some company." We both laughed.

"Help! Help! The inmates are running the asylum!" We clinked beer cans and laughed some more.

A half-naked girl came running from the main building calling "Catch me if you can!" with her boobs jouncing freely in the breeze. A fully nude male chased after her. I won't describe his personal anatomy, since it pretty much defied description, anyway. Make up your own version–they're all pretty much the same.

"Alex and Alexis–their usual chase, slap, and tickle game." Dhani grinned and shook his head.

"Who?"

"Alex and Alexis. They live downstairs from me. You've never seen them?"

"Once before. I guess we're not strangers, anymore." I shrugged and took another pull off my beer.

"So…" Dhani began.

"So… what?" I finished.

"What is it you want to know about this thing? It's none of your business, really."

"No, it's not. Guess I'm just curious."

"Life is harsh at the beach, Stacy." Edmund's voice came from behind his apartment. I jumped and turned to him as he emerged from the shadows. He smelled strongly of Panama Red and probably more than one vodka martini.

"You were listening the whole time?" I accused.

"Most of the time. The rest of the time I was enjoying my buzz, but you were just droning on to Dhani."

"I wasn't droning, Edmund. I was talking."

"Talking, droning–it's all the same when you're

buzzed." He chuckled. "At least you weren't whining, that's a real bummer. Hey, want some?" He held out the stub of a roach half burnt to ashes. I shook my head "no" and he pulled it away, taking the last hit for himself and tossing the roach into the shrubbery behind his apartment, where it bounced off the shrubs and landed squarely into the parking lot of a bank. The ember dimmed out on the roach. Edmund nodded to us and toddled off amicably, in search of more weed or perhaps a martini.

"Look, Stacey, this Vinny, you don't want to go there," Dhani said.

"But what about Geoffrey's? I think they're doing something with the girls."

"Both of them—bad company. Look, there's a guy with a boat down at the dock. I think he works for them."

I remembered seeing Brian, Mr. Cold-As-Ice, down at the small marina behind Dana's. A chill ran up my spine. He'd been working on a boat there. A shadowy figure, dressed in leathers and dirty blue jeans had been on deck nearby—not working, just watching. It was someone I'd seen before, but I just couldn't piece it together.

"I don't *want* to go there."

"Good girl," said Dhani. "Some of us live in the sunshine, some of us live in the shadows. I wasn't sure about you."

"Does that mean you're sure about me now?"

"Well," he said and smiled, "not completely. You can never be sure of any woman." He laughed. "But I think you're out in the sunshine now—wherever you were before." I smiled and we clinked cans again.

Oh, boy, here it comes, I thought. "You asking?" I queried. "I mean, about before?"

"No, not really. You tellin'?" His eyes gleamed mischievously.

I kept my mouth shut. We drank silently together.

"Hey, speaking of sunshine, is it gonna be nice

tomorrow?" I asked.

"Red sky at morning, sailors take warning–red sky at night, sailors' delight," Edmund called out from his place.

"You eavesdropper!" I teased.

Edmund popped out of his door, martini elegantly in hand, announcing, "I saw a red sky tonight. Let's take the Minnow out tomorrow and catch our dinner! You gotta work tomorrow, Stace?"

"No, but Sunday I'm on." Saturdays were for senior bartenders at Sparky's and I had a ways to go before I rated that. "Let's do it!"

"Yeah, you could use a cruise. Fresh air, sunshine. Maybe you'll catch something."

"Hope it's a buzz." I replied.

"Oh, that's for certain," Dhani chimed in. We laughed.

The one wonderful thing about Edmund is that he is just happy being Edmund. No more, no less. True happiness with oneself is one of the universe's greatest gifts, and you get a little piece of that just hanging out with Edmund. He works as a simple groundskeeper for an upscale condo down in the Fort. All that grass and landscaping at the beach is a constant battle someone has to fight and Edmund fights the good fight on a daily basis. But when he comes home, you can find him bouncing around, joint and/or martini in hand just living life and enjoying the hell out of it. He has up-to-date credit cards, a legal car, a savings and checking account. All these details were gleaned from the communal mailbox where we all collect our daily bills. Okay, I admit it–I peeked.

"How many people are going?" asked Dhani. He whispered to me. "The boat only holds three or four, but sometimes ten or twelve show up–then it's a mess."

"Just us, Dhani. You, me, and Stacey here."

"Cool," I said. "What time?"

"Ten? I don't do anything on Saturday morning before ten," Edmund said firmly.

"Make it eleven, I gotta work till ten," said Dhani.

"Eleven it is, then–even better!" Edmund agreed. "Okay with you, Stace?"

"Sure… I can get some laundry done."

"Want some of mine?" Edmund and Dhani asked in unison. Great minds think alike.

"Sure–I'll do the laundry, you guys buy the gas for the boat and give me a rod and reel. Oh, yeah–you clean and cook the fish as well."

"Want us to eat 'em for you, too?" Dhani asked.

I grabbed a nearby fallen palm frond and went to swat them both.

"Ah, an exotic fan dancer." Edmund laughed, in his best Curly of The Three Stooges voice.

"Yeah, I'll fan you, all right." I responded in my best Moe, taking another swipe in his direction. Just leave the laundry in pillowcases on the stoop in the morning, okay?" I was beginning to feel more like my old self again.

"I better start getting it together now," said Edmund, grinning. "There's a lot."

I laughed, blew them both a goodnight kiss, and headed in for my shower and nighty bye. The Friday Nite Freak Show was just getting started and I wanted to beat feet before it got into full swing.

I took a couple shots for medicinal purposes only and, with Tigger slippers stowed securely underbed, I slipped off quickly into a deep, dreamless slumber. After a while, the last of the freaks departed and the quiet woke me up. It was so quiet, I heard the ocean waves brushing against the shore a block away, with thoughts of Vinny and the smarmy Geoffrey's even farther away than across the sea. I closed my eyes and drifted off to the music of the ocean waves from the calm safety of my little home.

Chapter Ten

I was rudely awakened the next morning by an incessant thumping against my door.

"Oh, go away!" I called out, half hungover. The thumping continued then abruptly stopped.

"Guess that's it," came Dhani's voice.

"Yeah, me too," said Edmund. I heard one final thump against the door.

Oh no, I thought. *Laundry pillowcases. Shit.*

I struggled up and stumbled to the door, gingerly opening it to see a pile of laundry blocking my view of the courtyard. As my vision cleared, the pile was reduced to about five or six pillowcases stuffed to overflowing with dirty underwear, t-shirts, and wads of dirty socks. I slipped outside to organize them, trying to separate Dhani's wash from Edmund's. It was still early and the sun hung like a gold ball in the azure Florida sky. I got my own dirty clothes together and loaded everything up in the Mir.

Dhani was nowhere to be seen. I heard Edmund puttering about his bungalow as he made breakfast. The Captain was snoring heavily on his chaise and Curt was no longer face-down on the grassy strip beside the Minnow.

"I'm going now," I called to Edmund. "Just don't leave without me!" If they took off to the marina and left me behind with the laundry, I'd pray for a squall or a swarm of hungry sharks.

I had enough change this time to use the Shifty Coin Laundry, a big, wide open field of washers and dryers south of Knott's Hardware on Dixie Highway. The beauty of going to a large laundromat is you can get a shitload of laundry done in about an hour if you have enough change. Being in the bar business, my tips yielded plenty of coins which I saved up in a jar on top of the stove (which was good for little else). I could get it all done in short order and still make it to Stinger's for an early beer and a slice before we left for the boat ramp.

There was *Love at the Laundromat* that morning between a handsome Brazilian couple and I wondered about the drama in their lives. I cast them as a modern day Romeo and Juliet, imagining his father as head of some major South American cartel and she, the daughter of a housemaid, so they had to meet illicitly at Shifty's to carry on their affair. A dirty little girl came out of a house across the street. A man, probably her father, followed a moment later. He was a scowling young man with dog tags hanging from a buckeye chain around his neck. He was bare-chested and wore soiled trousers tucked into worn black army boots. Shouting angrily to the little girl in some Latin language, Spanish or Portuguese, I couldn't tell the difference, he grabbed her by the arm and dragged her back into the house. Ah, memories of a happy childhood. I wondered if he had murdered his wife and stuffed her into a footlocker somewhere. Before I knew it, the laundry was sorted, washed, dried, and folded. I loaded fresh laundry, myself, and my overactive imagination back into the Mir.

I headed over to Stinger's to see Charlie at the bar. It was too early. They didn't open until noon on Saturdays. I shrugged it off and headed to the little Mom and Pop market to score a six-pack of tallboys and something to eat on the trip. I thumped the clean laundry cases against Edmund and Dhani's respective doors. Then I changed into my swimsuit, pulled on some shorts and sandals, and scrunched my hair on top of my head, loading up on conditioner and sunscreen and announced in general to the courtyard that I was ready to go.

The Minnow was still parked next door, so the boys

hadn't left yet.

Edmund bounced out, toting a tallboy of his own as well as a couple of rods and reels, and a cooler filled with bait. He grinned happily at me, casually tossed the pillowcases with his clean laundry into his apartment, and stowed his gear in the Minnow.

Dhani came out with a rig fancy enough to hook a marlin and I brought over my six-pack—now a five-pack.

We hitched the Minnow to Dhani's truck and we were off to the local marina park and boat ramp. We shoved off in no time and headed up the Intracoastal to the cool blue water of the Hillsboro Inlet. The sea sprayed over the gunwales of our little boat and provided a cooling mist on what would prove to be an unstintingly hot day. I rubbed salt water into my hot skin, thinking it might deepen my tan. It would also remove the sunscreen, but I didn't care.

We fished all morning to no avail. Even though we had our hooks in the water with tasty morsels dangling below, no one was biting. So, we headed over to a little place on the beach, dropped anchor and waded in to Lah-de-dah by the Sea and a cute little restaurant adjoining a public "beach club." We ate, drank, and made merry. I got to go to the bathroom in privacy and comfort. We waded back to the Minnow and more fishing, and hoped we caught something by suppertime.

Actually, we caught a pretty good buzz from a heady mix of sun and alcohol. Dhani almost fell out of the Minnow when Edmund heroically guided the little Minnow through the swell of a six-foot trough.

"More fish this way," Edmund said. And while Edmund didn't have Loran, he claimed to have "inner radar," that would guide him unerringly to a rich trove of pompano, mahi-mahi or grouper. Having grown up on the shores of Lake Okeechobee, I'd hung around the fish camps and heard stories of how schools of fish can "call out" to some people and lead them straight to the jackpot.

There was also the usual horseshit about the really big one that got away or a fish had actually jumped into the boat of its own accord. I had tended bar long enough to know a fish story when I heard one. I smiled secretly to myself.

I sat quietly with my hook in the water, thinking *"Here, fishy fishy"* over and over. Half drowsing with the chant, the warmth of the day, good beer, and food in my belly, I suddenly got a hit. The line played out very quickly with a vibrant swish and a jerk on the rod, waking me from my reverie. I pulled up on the rod and played the line out again. I hoped I hadn't snagged a diver. I hadn't. The poor thing was fighting for its life. I could see flashes of its sleek gray and white body as it struggled beneath the surface. I hoped it was big and tasty. I shifted my grip on the rod and pulled a little harder.

Dhani and Edmund both yelped with my success and leapt to my side of the boat, almost tipping the little vessel over in the process. It was all I could do to maintain my balance and my grip on the rod and reel–not mine, so I had to be doubly careful–and my stance in the Minnow.

"Play him out," yelled Edmund.

"Reel him in," called Dhani.

I fished my own catch and brought in quite a respectable grouper.

"Lucky catch," said Edmund.

"Luck had nothing to do with it," I replied smugly.

Dhani's line took off with a whispering whirr and his rod bent down with a jerk. "Ah-ha!" he shouted triumphantly.

"Reel him in!" I called.

"Play him out," Edmund advised. As Dhani played out his catch, Edmund's line caught fire with a tug on the end. I got busy watering down the lines, getting the gaff ready, trying to keep centered on the boat so it wouldn't tip over, and getting the cooler of ice ready to receive the catch.

Dhani pulled up a feisty little shark, which he quickly tossed back after cutting the hook and cussing a blue streak. Meanwhile, Edmund pulled up another grouper. Not as big as mine was.

I put my hook back in the water and caught an eel. Edmund snagged what looked like a tire and then had to cut bait. Finally, just before we were ready to call it a day, Dhani hooked a lovely snapper. Oh, we would feast at the Compound tonight. We celebrated by toasting to each other with the beer we removed from the cooler to make room for the fish. Heading in, I felt the first sting of sunburn creeping over my skin. I looked down at my bare red arms and knew there'd be hell to pay. I got another beer. Anesthesia for the burn.

When the sun goes down, the tans come out—and this day was only half over. I hoped I had aloe at home. If not, there was an aloe plant growing out back. No self-respecting Florida home should be without one.

Edmund cleaned the fish at the dock as Dhani hitched the boat to the trailer and brought it out of the water. I stood there and felt like a cooked lobster. *Stupid!* I fumed. I should have put on more sunscreen. The salt water wasn't worth a damn in developing a tan. I planned on wearing a bed sheet wrapped softly over my parboiled body and yelling "To-ga! To-ga!" all night, so it'd look like I was toga partying and not tender to the touch. If the guys found out how burned I was, they would never leave me alone. I'd be the target of overly hearty backslaps for the rest of the night.

As I stood on the dock, I saw a sleek, low-slung Italian yacht moored nearby, the "Golden Girl." At the stern, standing just outside the salon, I could make out Geoffrey, Brian Cold-As-Ice, and a large, flashy looking fellow. The side of the boat that faced us was decorated with about half a dozen young lovelies in various stages of undress. Some were sipping cocktails and chatting gaily;

others were leaning over the railing, jibing the captain to get the party underway. I recognized a couple of them as the Lorikeets I had known from my stint at Geoffrey's. One of the Lorikeets, the soft blonde one, sat a little apart from the others and just watched the goings-on aboard the Golden Girl. I turned my back to them and walked towards Edmund and Dhani, who waited for me at the truck.

I had almost forgotten. Now it came back. I felt my blood turn to ice water and tried to blame it on the sunburn. As quickly as I could, I slipped into the truck beside Edmund as Dhani. I was silent during the ten-minute drive home.

"Stacey, you okay?" asked Edmund as we got back to the compound and started unloading the Minnow and the fishing gear.

"Yeah, fine–why?"

"You looked a little sick back at the dock."

"Yeah, well, maybe I caught a bit too much sun. I'm gonna take a cool shower."

Edmund nodded and turned away, continuing to unload the Minnow.

"I know what you saw," said Dhani quietly. "We'll talk tonight."

I nodded and walked into the bungalow. The interior was cool from the shade of the huge ancient mango tree in the courtyard, for which I was grateful. I took a shower and draped a soft old white sheet around my nude body in the form of a toga and padded out barefoot into the uncovered soil of the courtyard. I had no plans to wear any kind of shoe any time soon, even if somebody handed me a free pair of evening Choos.

I really wanted just to lie down in the cool of the bungalow and roll a cold can of beer all over my naked body, but Dhani said we'd talk and I was getting curiouser and curiouser. He knew something–that was obvious. The sensible side of me wanted nothing to do with it, but the other side, that cross-grained, stubborn side that just had to go looking for trouble, wanted the whole scoop and nothing less would do.

One thing about Dhani—he always appeared fresh as a daisy, no matter what. When he came out of his apartment and bounced my way, I marveled at the amount of sun and alcohol he had absorbed without apparent effect.

He sat down in the old, beat-up metal chair next to me and casually slung his leg over one of the armrests. It creaked alarmingly, but didn't collapse.

"So," he said with a grin, "had a little sun, I see."

"Yep."

"And you saw..." he said, pausing briefly, "some people maybe you didn't want to see."

"Yep."

"Do you know them?"

"Not all." Now it was my turn to pause. "You?"

"Well, pretty much..."

I took a pull off my beer and looked at him questioningly. Keeping shut is the first rule–he who talks first, loses.

Dhani spoke, "Well, Geoffrey, he owns that big place on the water, but everybody knows that."

I nodded, taking another pull off the beer.

Dhani continued, "...and the girls, they pretty much come and go with the wind, but the wind is more predictable."

I nodded again, contemplated my beer by picking it up and setting it back down again.

"But they're interchangeable. They're not players."

Looking levelly at Dhani, I said, "Okay, so..."

"The big guy in the flashy suit, that's Vinny. He owns it all."

"Yeah...I thought he was a big-time developer." I tried to sound skeptical, not wanting to look too interested at the mention of Vinny's name, but my ears pricked up and I was curious as hell. I don't like gossip as a rule, but knowing who's who and how they fit together is quite another matter altogether. There are times when that sort of knowledge was worth more than an M.B.A. from Harvard.

"And everyone is there for him. There's one guy who wasn't on the boat, and he hangs out with that good-looking guy. That good looking guy works Geoffrey's and handles the cash for the big guy."

"So, Geoffrey…"

"Is into the big guy for something, but I don't know what."

Big help. "And the good looking guy manning the cash drawer at the bar?"

"He's keeping Geoffrey honest for the big guy."

"I see." I didn't really, not yet. But something in my brain started putting one and one together, and it added up to a hell of a lot more than two. "So…"

"You can figure it out," he said with a chuckle.

"What's to figure? I don't work there anymore."

"What about your friend, Tracey?"

"She got out, too."

"Yeah, but they still know where she is."

I felt a chill. "Are they watching?"

Dhani sipped his beer, thoughtfully. "No, I don't think so. They just know where she is. She's not doing anything, so they don't have to watch her closely. I think they just like to know where she is."

I wondered why a big guy like Vinny would be so interested in a small-potatoes waitress in a diner. Then it dawned on me. Oh, Jesus. I had to get to Tracey right away. I started to get up, but my raw, sunburnt skin stopped me in my tracks.

"Hey, where you running to?" Dhani held up a hand. "He's not going nowhere, he's on the boat. They may not be back for days."

I shrugged. Dhani was right. I eased myself back

down into a chair, pissed at myself for tipping off my intentions so transparently. I picked up my beer and took what I hoped seemed a nonchalant sip. It had turned warm, just like the sultry night around us.

Edmund emerged from his apartment, freshly showered and pink as a newly-boiled lobster.

"Anybody hungry? I've got some fresh fish we can grill." He started his industrial-sized propane cooker.

I sat quietly and still felt a little woozy from the sun and the beer. The other tenants in the compound converged on Edmund's apartment, attracted by the aroma of fresh grilled fish. Someone handed me an icy brew, I sipped at it silently and picked at a perfectly filleted piece of grilled fish. I listened listlessly to courtyard talk about this and that, politely biding my time until I could say goodnight.

Dhani tapped me on the shoulder and it stung like hell. "Oh, sorry."

I looked up at him through what felt like blistered eyes.

"Look, whoever you were running to see, see him tomorrow. He can wait through the night."

"Who did you think I was running to?"

"Weren't you going to see Rick?"

"Rick? No…" I was fading fast.

Dhani looked puzzled. I smacked myself on the forehead, painfully, and explained the Rick thing to Dhani.

"Then get some rest. You look as if you could use some," Dhani said.

The Captain staggered in and it couldn't have been better timing. "Here, Cap'n. Take my seat."

The Captain sat down. "Thanks, missy."

"Finish the rest of this, too," I said, handing off the lukewarm beer to the captain. Nodding gratefully, he took a long swallow and I was only too happy to bow out.

"Leaving already?" Edmund chuckled. "You only just got here."

I smiled back wanly at Edmund and a few of the others laughed quietly. I was relieved my "toga" had decided to stay in place as I stood up and gingerly eased back to the bungalow.

"'Night," I called, to a response of many hearty cat-calls and party roars of good cheer. The Compound was thriving, full of fresh fish and beer. I was plumb tuckered out, but my brain shifted into overdrive, full of whirling images. People, places and things flickered in my mind's eye in an endless procession of synaptic overload and something told me there was something extremely important, if not urgent, that I fit them together in the right pattern.

I looked at my Tigger slippers under the bed and ruefully examined my dirt-smudged feet. Slipping off my toga, I used it as a sheet over my clean bedding and settled in. I was asleep almost before my head hit the pillow.

I dreamed I was on a boat—not the Minnow, but a large, white yacht with beautiful people all around me. The water was deep-water blue, a dark, intense navy blue. The ladies wore elegant dresses and the men were in black tie and tails. The crew wore monogrammed uniforms with navy blue crew shirts. I struggled to make out the monogram over the left front pocket of the crew shirts to no avail. I couldn't see through the searing sunlight. I was burning. My skin was on fire and I discovered I was strapped on the deck, naked to the burning rays. I struggled to get free, but the leather straps held firm, cutting cruelly into my skin. Then someone threw a bucket of seawater on me. I could taste the water and salt through dry, cracked lips. My bound wrists and ankles were rubbed raw with my fight to try to release myself from the deck. I writhed in pain as my wrists and ankles bled. More seawater was thrown on my overheated flesh by one of the deck hands, and I awoke to find rain coming in through the window above my bed. I closed the window, untangled myself from the toga I'd slipped over the clean bedclothes the night before, and dried myself as best I could. I lay down and pulled up the covers, shivering, and fell into a fitful, but thankfully dreamless sleep.

Chapter Eleven

I woke earlier than I expected, mostly because I felt as if someone was rubbing every inch of my body with a huge piece of sandpaper. Then I realized it was just the bed sheets, lightly draped over very bad sunburn. I got up and headed for a cool shower. After drying off, I pulled on sweatpants, flip-flops, and a light nylon hoodie. Outside, dawn was just airbrushing the sky with thin streaks and swirls of amethyst and cerise.

I remembered my mission to get to Tracey as quickly as possible. I slipped out of the bungalow and ran across the courtyard into the alleyway leading to the boulevard and Dana's. My watch said six-thirty, a half hour before Dana opened her doors to coffee and muffin lovers everywhere. I headed for the beach.

Crossing the A-1-A, it was deathly still. I could hear the waves at the beach across the street and the palms weren't stirring a bit. The sand was damp from last night's rain and the air was still, heavy and humid. More storms on the way, I guessed. I walked along ocean's edge, my flip-flops making little plopping noises as they sucked up bits of sand and water before they dropped back into the oblivion of the Atlantic Ocean.

Just ahead, I saw someone lying full length on the sand. Probably some homeless person who had to sleep on the beach. Thinking that easily could have been me, I kept my distance and fixed my eyes on the horizon. But curiosity pulled at me, and I moved towards the figure and affected a nonchalant saunter. After a moment, I made out the pallid blotches on exposed flesh. Drawing closer, I could see it was a woman. She was on her side. The curve of her waist sloped gently from her breast to her hips, mountains and valleys in a flat sandy landscape. She was pale and still as an alabaster statue, and then I realized she wasn't breathing. I crept closer, slowly. Her face was half-buried in the sand. At first, I thought some of her fingers and toes were covered by the sand that had washed in with the tide. They weren't. Several digits were missing altogether, chewed off by fish of some other hungry inhabitant of the Atlantic. I noticed she was wearing a skimpy polka-dot bikini. I felt a flutter in my gut as I recognized that bikini. It was one I had seen the day before on a girl hanging off the side of the fancy yacht.

Spotting several other beach walkers, I did the sensible thing. I started jumping up and down and yelling for help. Within five seconds I had a crowd of about ten people around the body.

"Don't touch her!" someone cried.

"I've got a cell. I'll call 9-1-1," another voice echoed.

Lifeguards came to watch over the body. Eventually, sirens could be heard in the distance. An older couple in matching dark blue windbreakers, wearing jeans, stood on either side of me, offering comfort and support.

"There, dear," the lady said in a soothing, grandmotherly voice as she held my arm gently, "it's all right."

About thirty minutes later, the cops showed up.

"Who found the body?" One of the cops asked the bystanders. A finger was obligingly pointed in my direction. I backed off and hoped the elderly couple could screen me from view long enough for a quick, discreet exit. The lady's grip tightened around my arm perceptibly as if to hold me back from flight. I shook her off and moved away.

"Hey, you! Hold it!"

I stopped and slowly turned around. *Shit.* The cops

turned the dead woman over on her back. The gay red and white polka dotted bikini fell apart off her body like an old dishrag. Another cop was kneeling beside a tiny red and white polka dotted shoe ten feet down the beach. I had seen those shoes at Pizzzazzz, thought they were cute and considered buying a pair myself. The absurdity of the thought brought up a bubble of hysterical laughter and I grimly clamped down on it just in time.

The crowd backed off in horror. For the first time, I got a good look at her as she lay there, bloated, pale skin mottled and bruised, staring sightlessly up at the brightening sky. I recognized the face. It was one of the Lorikeets I had seen on the Italian yacht yesterday. The soft one. The sad one. The one who wanted no trouble. I thought of her the day before, young and pretty, standing at the rail sipping her drink with nothing on her mind but a boat party and a little harmless fun. Now she was sprawled on the sand, bloated and lifeless, a pathetic little strip of a bikini still clinging to her. My stomach knotted and I felt a cold wave of nausea course through me.

I staggered down to the water's edge, rested my trembling hands on my knees and threw up into the sea. My head spun and I was bathed in sweat. The salty tang of the ocean filled my nostrils. I retched violently and nearly pitched headfirst into the water. Suddenly, two strong hands gripped my shoulders, steadied me and pulled me upright. I was guided back from the water's edge to a level spot a little further up the beach. I tried to pull away, wiping my mouth with the back of my hand.

"I'm all right," I said in a strangled half-whisper.

"No, you're not," a man's voice said from behind me. I knew the voice, even if I didn't know the man. A professional, brisk, no-nonsense voice; a voice that brooked no argument or insolence. A voice of authority. The voice of a cop. He continued to hold me by the shoulders in a strong but gentle grip, and just then I was glad of it. If he'd let go, I was sure I would have folded like a piece of newspaper.

"Take it easy," he said. "Look out at the horizon and get some air."

I felt suffocated and put my head back to take a deep draught of brisk ocean air. I focused my gaze on the horizon and tried not to think of what I had seen.

"Better now?" he asked.

I nodded, trying not to tremble. My body didn't want to cooperate and I trembled anyway.

The area was sectioned off with yellow crime scene tape and deputies milled around, trying to keep a small crowd of curious beachcombers away while they waited for the Medical Examiner. Deputies in crisp white shirts and hunter green slacks with dark gray stripes down the sides were trying to disperse the crowd, which wasn't cooperating. I wished I'd been standing with the crowd instead of where I had been. I would have gladly left.

Someone handed the cop who had steadied me two steaming cups and he handed one to me. Coffee, strong and black. The rich aroma enfolded me, blotting out the smell of the sea. I took a tentative sip; it was hot, but good. Life seeped back into me. Someone put a rough gray blanket around my shoulders and I burrowed into it as the man and I walked slowly along the shore.

"Detective Dan Gowan," he said, indicating the badge hanging from a nylon strap around his neck. I nodded.

He was of medium height, with regular features, light brown hair and hazel eyes. He wasn't tan, but he wasn't tourist-white, either. He wore a blue shirt and dark blue tie, with dark gray trousers and loafers. Normally, you'd see this guy in a bar and wouldn't look twice at him. He wasn't handsome, but he wasn't scary, either. There was a little bit of stubble on his face, like he hadn't shaved that morning, but not enough to look like a five o'clock shadow after an all-nighter the morning after. There was no sign of a hangover or the telltale cloudiness in the eyes and puffy lids that give a heavy drinker away without question. His hazel eyes, while lively, seemed soft and gentle. But I didn't doubt those eyes could probably cut through leather if the situation demanded it.

Climbing up a sand dune not too far from the body, he motioned me to sit on a bench. My legs were still unsteady; as I moved towards the bench I stumbled, nearly spilling still-hot coffee on my hands, but scalded my sunburned arm through my thin nylon hoodie. Detective Gowan took the cup from me, sat down, and handed the coffee back after I'd wiped my hands on the blanket.

I watched an army of people surround the body. Some paramedics from Fire Rescue knelt down and hooked the body up to a machine.

"What are they doing?" I asked the detective.

"Looking for a heartbeat."

"But she's dead."

"They do it all the time," he said and shrugged.

A news crew pulled up but they were shepherded by the cops about a dozen yards up the strand, on the sidewalk, far from the body. I supposed zoom lenses on their cameras would be working overtime. They started setting up lights and equipment, talking excitedly amongst themselves. *That's showbiz*, I thought. I just hoped they wouldn't turn their prying photographic eyes on us, two anonymous-looking figures on the beach with their backs turned, looking out to sea. I ducked my head and quieted my fluttering stomach as best as I could.

"You'd think this was something special," Detective Gowan said, nodding towards the television news crew. "Walk up and down this beach every day for a month, and you're bound to run into a body." He shook some sand off his shoe.

"Yeah, that's the thing about the beach. It's loaded

with sand."

He smiled at me. "A sense of humor, that's a good sign." His eyes turned towards me in seriousness. "We need to talk about this."

"Well, you're the nicest cop I've ever met."

"You meet many cops?"

I shrugged. "Not that you'd notice." I studied his face and recognized him as one of the detectives I'd seen in Dana's a few times before.

"What's your name?"

"Stacey." I knew better than to lie, but I wasn't parting with all the information yet.

"Stacey, then. I'll have to take a statement from you."

"Here?"

"Yes, just a verbal, then you can come downtown and sign it."

I nodded understanding and took another pull at my coffee. I looked out over the water, and tried to ignore the scene below. The news crew started to converge on the body, but the deputies stopped them and the Medical Examiner's SUV pulled up. At that moment, all I could think about was that forlorn little shoe, lying half-buried in the sand.

"Okay, I was walking along by the water and thought it was just someone sleeping on the beach."

"Start with your name first, Stacey."

"Okay. Stacey Longacre."

"Where do you live, Stacey?"

"Around the corner."

He almost smiled. "I'll need the address."

Then it hit me. I hadn't memorized it yet. I knew it was on Second, but as for the number, I was at a loss. My zip code was zipped tight in my memory as well.

"Um, I just moved here. I live over on Second Street. The address is on my driver's license. Can I bring it when I come downtown?"

Detective Gowan nodded. "Northeast, or southeast?"

"Southeast."

He took out a cheap little memo pad and a pen and started writing.

"Phone?"

I gave him my number.

"Okay, so that's a start." He looked levelly at me. I was looking over at the body; it was as if I could not pull my eyes away. I started trembling again. "It's not going to help if you get emotional about this. Focus on yourself and what you were doing at the time."

I shrugged and stared down at my feet. "I just thought I saw someone sleeping on the beach and went to take a look. I thought they were sick, so I hollered for help and then I puked into the ocean when I saw who–what–it was." Oops. Hastily, I added, "I mean, that it was a dead person and not just someone sleeping."

"Who it was? Did you know her?"

Damn. Busted. "Well, yeah. I mean, not well. I mean, I knew her to see her around, but we weren't friends or anything like that." Remembering Lori, or Laurie's, giggly fresh-faced wholesomeness, I wondered if this girl was really wholesome or just plain dumb as your garden-variety rock. Maybe both. Either way, it had cost her. An enormous wave of sadness rushed over me, obliterating everything for a moment. The sky, the beach, the ocean–it all seemed to turn gray.

"Focus in, Stacey. We have to do this now, while it's fresh in your mind. When did you last see this girl?"

"Yesterday," I said.

"Where?"

"I was coming in from fishing with some friends at the boat-launch marina over there," I said, pointing north, "and she was on a yacht, heading out. Looked like a boat party."

"What time?"

"Four, five o'clock, maybe."

"Four or five, Stacey?"

"I'm not sure, I had a lot of sun and some drinks. It was late afternoon, though, maybe early evening."

"Do you remember seeing the name on the yacht?"

"Yeah, the Golden Girl." I spelled it out for him as he took down the name. How could I forget, having been one of those "Golden Girls" myself, even if only for a one-night stand?

"Do you remember seeing anyone around on the beach?"

"Not really, I was just walking alone. By myself." *Oh, God,* I thought–*duh.* I shut my mouth and planned on keeping it shut until I could put my thoughts together. I kept sipping my coffee, knowing as long as I did that no words would inadvertently escape my mouth. I wished for a shot of whiskey in the coffee. That would help. Yeah, right. With a cop right beside me.

I thought about Tracey. "Oh, my God, I have to go." The sun was up in the sky now, so it was probably close to eight-thirty or nine. I didn't dare check my watch.

"Hold it, young lady. Not so fast." I tried to stand, but Detective Gowan's hand pulled my sunburned arm and brought me right back down again.

"Hey! Am I under arrest or something?"

"Not at all, but are you going back *that* way?"

I looked over and saw a technical team finishing photographs of the scene and the Medical Examiner positioning a beach gurney to remove the Lorikeet's body. The television news crew had finally been given clearance by the deputies and was closing in fast.

"I really don't need to see this," I said.

"Okay, then, let's walk. You can walk and talk at the same time, can't you?"

"I can walk and chew gum, so yeah, I guess so."

We went down a couple blocks on the beach, south of where all the action was. We passed Loretta's apartment building and I shuddered secretly to myself. *A lot goes on in this town*, I thought. Most of it pretty nasty. Okeechobee was starting to look like Mayberry with a tropical twist.

Making sure we were below where I lived–that was all I needed, bringing a cop to the compound–I headed toward the street and the A-1-A. Finding a bench just off the beach, I sat down and shrugged off the blanket.

The detective stretched on the bench and visibly relaxed. That relaxed me as well and I wondered if it was some kind of cop trick to lull you into spilling everything you know. If circumstances had been different, you would have thought we were just two friends sitting on a bench at the beach whiling away the morning.

"So, you haven't lived here long?" he asked.

"Nope."

"How do you like it?"

"It's okay, I guess."

"What did you do when you saw the body?"

"I looked at it. I didn't know it was a body. Well, I knew it was a person, but I didn't know she was dead."

He nodded thoughtfully. "You work?"

"Yeah."

"What do you do?"

"Bartend."

"You working today?"

"I'm supposed to."

"Where do you work?"

"Around the corner." This could have meant anyplace, given the amount of bars, hotels with bars, clubs, and restaurant establishments along the beach.

"Where?"

"Sparky's."

The detective nodded. "Maybe you should think

about taking the day off. Can I call anyone for you?"

"Nope. That's okay. I'd rather work."

He shrugged. "What made you call for help?"

I shivered. An uncontrollable chill had now come over me in spite of the sunburn. Pulling the blanket around me, I replied, "I could see she wasn't breathing."

"How close were you to her?"

"Not far."

"Ten feet? Fifteen feet? Five feet?"

"About five feet away, I think."

"Did you notice anyone else standing around right away?"

"No. Lifeguards and stuff. Some people came over when I started hollering. Then they turned her over and I had to puke. Is that normal?"

"What, hollering or puking?"

"Puking."

"Sometimes. Usually not, though."

I took another sip of my coffee, it was down to lukewarm dregs and bottom-of-the-cup coffee grounds. Well, it was better tasting than barf.

"Look, are we done?" I asked.

"Come down to the station any time after three. We'll finish up there."

"Okay."

"You know where it is?"

"I'll find it."

He handed me a white business card with his name and number on it in green lettering with the Sheriff's Office star on the right side and the website below. *Slick*, I thought. Everyone seemed to be going in for what they called "positive brand imaging" these days. "Call before you come." Gowan continued, "Ask for me or Sergeant Douglass."

"What'll I have to do?"

"Finish your statement, bring your driver's license,

give us your information."

"But I didn't do anything wrong."

"No, but somebody might have–wouldn't you want to help? You knew the woman, even if only a little. We might want to talk to you again."

I shrugged, trying to make it casual. "Yeah, okay. I can do that. I get off at six."

"Rethink taking the day off, Stacey. This is tough on anyone."

Slipping out from under the blanket, I tossed the empty cup in the wire basket next to the bench. "Okay. Thanks for being so nice, Detective. Nice to meet you."

He smiled tightly and nodded once sharply, "Sorry you had to." He turned and headed towards the street.

Our business finished, for now, I walked briskly to fend off a chill I felt under my skin and headed over to Dana's. I hoped I would be able to catch Tracey and the place wouldn't be crawling with cops.

The warm smells of coffee, breakfasts, and muffins filled the diner and brought a sense of almost-normalcy to my state of mind. The shakiness in my stomach was quelled. It was as if the beach didn't exist, the body of the Lorikeet didn't exist, and the day didn't exist except as just another one in the life of yours truly.

Aside from a few deputies, it was much quieter than I expected. I guessed the cops were still working the scene, but they'd probably pack the place for lunch. I wondered if the television news crew would discover Dana's, and hoped like hell they'd bypass it for La-de-dah-by-the-sea. Maybe the bar would snag a few leftovers and lookers-on.

I silently thanked God for my job bartending at Sparky's, and the fact that most cops don't drink on duty. They don't even like to come into a regular bar, they have their own hangouts. Like coffee shops, they have their little cop bars, usually small holes-in-the-wall patronized exclusively by–and sometimes owned by–the local gendarmes. Civilians don't normally go in a cop bar to drink. If they do stumble into one by mistake, they get the fishy eye from everyone present, have a quick one, pay up and get the hell out. When a place is crawling with cops on a bender, it's very damn serious and can be pretty dangerous for the average civvie. It works in reverse in bars where criminals hang out. In some towns, the good old drunks don't have a place to go, so they just stay home and get toasted in front of the TV all by themselves. The old Swamp where I used to work in Lake Okeechobee, was neutral. Both sides of the law came to that watering hole because it was the only game in town. Like the watering holes that are far from anything else you see on the Serengeti Plain on TV nature shows, the lion drinks with the wildebeest out of sheer necessity, leaving them to their business. After that, the game is on and survival of the fittest is the law of the jungle. Any jungle.

I caught Tracey's eye as she worked the counter and she motioned me over to the corner seat. She placed a steaming cup of coffee and a warm blueberry muffin before me right as I sat down.

"You hear what happened?" she whispered out of the corner of her mouth.

"Yeah," I whispered back. "I found the body."

She gave me a wide-eyed look and whisked off with a coffee pot to quiet her customers. Then she flew right back to me.

"So, what's going on?" she asked, still in a half-whisper.

"Plenty. We have to talk. It was one of the Lauries from Geoffrey's."

"No!" Her eyes grew wider. "Yeah? Well, are you okay?"

I took a piece off my muffin and stuffed it in my mouth. It's just not polite to talk with a mouthful of muffin. It was a great way to keep my mouth shut without offending my friend. The muffin, while it smelled delicious, tasted to me of sawdust, just like the woody smell at Knott's Hardware. I hoped the feeling would pass.

"I'm okay, I get off at two."

I nodded. "I'm working 'til six then I have to go sign a report or something at the police station downtown."

"Come on over my place when you're done. You want dinner?"

"No, I don't think I even want breakfast."

"Tough. Eat. On the house." she said, shoving the rest of the muffin closer to me.

I picked at the crumbly top crust of the muffin, stuffing tiny bites into my mouth.

"Okay," I said, "I'll come over."

"I'll make some tea. I'm a real tea nut these days. Teapot, tea cozy, tea leaves, the works. You like vanilla?"

"I like iced tea."

"No problem. It'll be ready when you get there. Do you remember where I live?"

I shrugged, so she scribbled some quick directions on a napkin and shoved it into my pocket.

"There. Now eat."

The muffin was actually getting easier to eat. The bites were getting bigger and it no longer tasted like sawdust. I loved those blueberry muffins. I washed down a bite with some more coffee.

"You got a couple hours before work, right?"

"Yeah," I said between bites.

"Get some rest. Don't worry about the food. I told you, it's on the house and if you even try to tip me I'll throw you out on your ass."

I grinned. "Tough Jersey bitch." I muttered under my breath.

Tracey grinned back. "Later."

I walked back to my bungalow slowly, my mind empty of everything except an overwhelming urge to burn my clothing. Why was it every time I had something to do with anyone at Geoffrey's all I wanted to do was burn my stuff?

Slipping out of my flip-flops, I peeled off the soggy sweats and damp windbreaker, hanging them to dry over the stove. I smelled like an old salt, so I hit the shower pronto, toweled off, and dressed in slick black slacks with cigarette legs, a soft purple pullover top and what I now considered my "working" boots, black leather shorties with about a two-and-a-half inch heel, high enough to be flattering, but thick enough to be comfortable. I twisted my hair up, laid on a little makeup, and sat on the sofa–all dressed up and nothing to do. I paced for a while then decided to get in the Mir and take a short spin to clear my head. There was probably still too much action at the center of the beach, so I headed south and landed at Stinger's.

Charlie was behind the bar, as usual, wiping glasses and cleaning up after imaginary patrons. There was no one in the place except him and me. I wondered if this might be a cop dive after hours. There didn't seem to be enough daytime action to suit a more criminally bent mind and it was too far off the beaten path for the tourists to frequent. They preferred the beach, where the action was

I pulled up a stool and he set a beer in front of me. We quietly took in a daytime talk show, something about a divorcing couple breaking up over his having an affair with her father. She was heartbroken, but it turned out she was bedding his brother; so as long as it was all in the family, I guess everything worked out in the end. During commercials, I watched people come and go about their business through the smudgy windows of the bar. The Bee Kleen Laund-O-Mat and Bee Kwik convenience store were a hive of activity. Even Bumble & Bumble, Attorneys-At-Law got a few elderly stragglers wandering in, maybe to cut the kids out of their wills and leave it all to the Humane Society. Who knew? Nobody came into the bar.

"Little action down to the beach today, eh?" asked Charlie.

"So I hear. I dunno." I shrugged.

"Found a dead girl, I think. At least a couple of 'em wash up on the beach ever' year. Young ones, too. Usually pretty."

I nodded, signaled for my tab, paid up and left the bar.

Work, for once, was normal–if you can call drunk wrangling in any way, shape or form normal. I guess what happened had cowed everyone into submission. Little Ricky was even nice to me, for a change. For one thing, he was quiet. He'd come to work, then leave and live his life. I wasn't all that interested in his affairs, but I missed the fun-loving party-boy I'd thought I'd found at the beginning of my job at Sparky's. Even Mr. Sparks himself seemed flattened. He came in at six o'clock, rang out the tills, gave instructions to the kitchen and split.

I left the bar and headed west in the Mir to the police station. I really hate police stations. They stink of urine and sweat with an underlying odor of fear. On Saturday night, when the drunk tank's full–perhaps thanks to someone like me, in part–there's the unmistakable smell of vomit hanging in the air. Lovely. I couldn't wait to leave and I hadn't even gotten there yet. I realized I'd forgotten to call the moment I stepped in the place.

"Help you, miss?" the desk sergeant said to his work log in front of him he was busily attending to.

"I'm here for Detective Gowan or Sergeant Douglass."

"Oh, yeah. You're the gal found the body on the beach."

I looked around to see if anyone had heard him. Short of a few people snoozing on the bench, no one seemed to hear or care. I nodded and he pointed to a door to the right side of his high-top desk.

"Wait for the buzzer and go right in. Someone'll meet you."

I did as I was told and, after a cheap feel on my soft black leather shoulder bag as a preliminary frisk, I was handed off to a man in shirtsleeves and led down a long, brightly lit corridor. I couldn't help but notice the obvious gun in an arm holster. I guessed this was the one place cops can just be themselves and don't have to worry about concealment. I secretly wondered how tough it would be to grab the gun and yell, "Stick 'em up" to the cop–just as a prank to yank his chain a little, you understand. It was tempting, but I wasn't a lunatic, either. It did, however, make me smile and I was clutching at anything to help forget the day.

Shirtsleeves led me to a raw-boned room on the left side of the corridor and left. The door wasn't locked, just closed behind him. Maybe it locked automatically, I mused. I wasn't testing my theory because a large mirror, which I assumed was two-way glass, would show my every move. The mirror faced a battered and scarred rectangular table. The room wasn't as brightly lit as the entryway or corridor and everything was scuffed and shabby. The floor showed countless scrape marks where cheap plastic chairs had scoured the linoleum and some long, greasy black marks; cop shoes, I thought. The air seemed dry and stale. I saw a tin of DampRid in a corner. The room had windows reinforced with chicken wire in the glass and metal bars on the outside. There was a wooden ledge going around three sides of the room, bench height, and I was starting to feel distinctly uncomfortable and itchy. I sat in one of the cheap plastic chairs and tried not to look nervous. I scratched my left shoulder and waited for someone to come into the room. Ten, fifteen, twenty minutes passed.

Finally, after forty-three minutes, a round, stoop-shouldered cop in a deputy's uniform came into the room. His sparse light colored hair was poorly combed over his balding scalp, and I saw a sunburn through the greasy strands which covered the top of his head. I felt sorry for the guy, having been in a similar predicament yesterday.

"I'm Sergeant Douglass," he said as he stood over me. "You Stacey Longacre?"

I nodded and looked up at him from my section in The Cheap Seats. I could barely see his face over the substantial sweep of his belly. When he straightened from his stoop, I saw he was tall, at least six-two.

He brought a sheaf of papers over to me and I could smell Brut cologne over the stench of other, less pleasant smells.

He pulled another cheap plastic chair across the table from me and sat down wearily. "Look these over and sign at the bottom if they're okay." He sighed as if he had done this for about two thousand years. "You bring ID?"

Tempted to reply, "I have no idée what you mean," but taking this prime chance to shut up, I pulled my wallet from my bag. I took my license out carefully and put my wallet on the table in front of me–why not? Where could I be safer laying out my wallet than in a cop shop? I looked over the paperwork and was amazed at the detail and accuracy at the report. Furthermore, it seemed Detective Gowan had done a little digging and learned about my fiasco at Geoffrey's. Somewhat relieved, I signed the papers and watched as the sergeant entered my information where it belonged at the top of the report.

Handing my license back to me and watching me put it in my wallet, he picked up the completed report, stood up and motioned it was all right for me to do the same. He bent over to look square at me with the sweetest, softest blue eyes I had ever seen. He could have been a teacher or a poet with those big soft eyes of his. Why the hell was he a cop?

"Be careful," he said. "You're luckier than you know not to be working at Geoffrey's anymore. It's not a crowd you want to start up with, if you're just getting into town."

I nodded and picked up my purse.

"You're free to go."

"Uh-huh," I nodded.

A lock clicked on the door and it opened with Mr. Shirtsleeves standing by the door, ready to escort me out. I took advantage of that opportunity and briskly left the room. Now I had an idea of what my dear brother Ed might have suffered at the hands of John Law, and was just a little bit more forgiving and understanding than I had been five minutes ago. I took the long walk back down the corridor and out the front door of the station. I took great care to park the Mir carefully when I arrived, so I was blessed not to have a ticket waiting for me on the windshield when I emerged. The Mir is a wonderful car, but sometimes cops like to ticket the thing for shits and giggles because it's so old. Maybe they lay bets the car will fall apart with the weight of a ticket. However, no such games were played tonight and I headed into the darkness and over to Tracey's.

I turned the interior light on and pulled out the directions, smoothing out the napkin. I had inadvertently used it in the cop shop to wipe my sweaty palms and scrunched it back into by bag. I got my bearings and wound up at Tracey's apartment with little more than a superfluous U-turn and a left on red.

Tracey's apartment was a row of look-alike units, all painted white with black shutters. There was ample parking on a gravel strip in front of the place and I silently prayed for no cable wires sticking out to flatten a tire on The Mir. A fenced-in pool gleamed quietly in the moonlight and I could see some people sitting on their tiny porches outside. A young couple was walking their dog in the street, taking care to keep the dog on the lawns and watch for traffic in the road.

"Nice neighborhood," I thought to myself as I

headed over to Tracey's unit, which was second from the left.

I rang the doorbell and waited as I heard a scuffle of slippers, then Tracey opened up and with a warm smile, motioned me inside. She was wearing puffy pink bedroom slippers and jeans, with a soft pink gauze top.

"Hi! The iced tea is waiting." She remembered! How sweet. I nodded and stepped into a clean, pretty efficiency. It was a little bigger than my bungalow, but not by much. It looked bigger, though, because the whole place was painted white, even the floor. Brightly colored scatter rugs were strewn about, and yellow and white checked café curtains festooned the windows. A small daybed in a corner was dressed in white fluffy ruffles and fresh flowers were on the glass coffee table in front of the daybed. A couple of simple metal folding chairs, the kind you see at any random church or civic function, were draped with white covers and tied with bows in back. The whole room was "pulled together" (as tone-y interior defecators like to say), by a colorful flowered border like a garden, hung at the top of the wall next to the ceiling. A couple of well-placed, store-bought full-length mirrors in white frames completed the look, enhancing the illusion of space.

Leading me to the day bed, Tracey settled me in with a few soft pillows. She went into the kitchen nook and a moment later brought me a glass of crystal clear iced tea, sweetened Southern-style, just the way I grew up with, and a lemon wedge. She settled down beside me with her own cup of steaming hot tea.

"So…" She looked at me levelly. "…you've had a hard day."

"Bro-ther! You're not kidding," I sighed and took a sip of iced tea. It was as refreshing and delicious as it looked.

"Want to talk about it?"

"Not really… I just want to forget about it."

"I don't blame you." We silently enjoyed our tea. "So, tell me," she said, cocking her head with attitude, "what's a nice girl like you doing in a place like this?"

"For a girl like me, where I'm from, this *is* a nice place."

Tracey smiled over her steaming teacup, taking a small sip and pursing her lips with pleasure, saying nothing.

I stretched out and enjoyed the coziness of Tracey's tidy apartment.

"I'm a 'native'," I started. "Florida born and bred."

"Okeechobee, right?"

"Yeppers. Grew up on a street called 'Tough Luck Lane.'" I waited for the response thinking, "here it comes" and got absolutely no rise out of my friend save an encouraging nod.

I continued, "It's got a trailer park on it. Streets are named all 'lanes' or 'paths' or 'ways'. You're probably the first person who's believed 'Tough Luck Lane' is a real street, or you're too polite to say otherwise." I smiled at her. Tracey nodded back.

"Let's just say I believe you're the kind of person whose word is good. That's one thing that I like about you. Can you tell me what it was like down here? Growing up?"

I shrugged, "Not much to it, really. The streets are real little, with everyone living in trailers almost on top of each other so you get to know your neighbors real good and pretty fast. You also learn to keep quiet and mind your own business just about as quick."

"Any brothers or sisters?"

"One brother, older," I replied.

"And he is…"

"Whereabouts unknown," I said, downing the last of my sweet tea and longing for something stronger, having to contemplate Ed for the first time in a number of weeks.

"Don't like him much, huh?"

"I don't know. I didn't mind him so much. I mean, I was little when the whole Ed thing was going on. He didn't like me much, I guess. I was always a pain in the ass to him, a burden slung around his neck like a dead skunk and just about as welcome, except when he could use me for something."

Tracey looked up from her tea. "More?" she asked. I held out my glass for a refill.

"I don't mean to pry, but what'd he do?"

"Well, Ed was into a little bit of this and a little bit of that, if you get my meaning." Tracey nodded. Given what she had told me, I was certain she knew exactly what I meant. "We didn't have a lot," I continued, "but Ed always had something. He would buy me a treat or give me a few bucks if I'd run an errand for him now and again. Never had any idea I was doing anything wrong, that's how Ed was. Ed could talk you into just about anything and make you think it was all forthright and aboveboard. Then later on, you find out you're just working Ed's hidden agenda and you want to be gone from him right quick."

"Was he a lot older?"

"By about ten years. I figure where we lived and all, what you hear day-to-day, at ten. When I came along, Ed was more or less living his own life and didn't want to be bothered by a little bitty baby, let alone a baby girl. I just made too much noise and took up too much space. I think that's how he saw me. I got our parents off his back, though, so he was pretty much free to run as he pleased.

"When I got older, about five or six, he caught on that I could be of some use to him, so he'd bribe me. It wasn't hard to do. I looked up to him, you see. He'd be nice and give me treats and ask me to do him just one little bitty favor. Like when he was in the trailer with Suzy Ortiz. When Mom came home from her job, he had me rustle the bushes outside the back window like I was playing to warn him and run around to the front real quick. That kept Mom at the front door while he ran out the back with Suzy.

"He had the girls all over him. Ed's real handsome. Blue eyes, black hair, and a nice straight nose. 'Course, the girls would find out, sooner or later, he wasn't just with them only like he said and all hell would break loose. Then everything would simmer down after a whole bunch of hollering and visits by the girls' parents to our place."

"So, who looked after you while your Mom was at work?"

"Neighbors, friends, anyone pretty much available. Seems once I could walk, I'd like to go all over the neighborhood to explore and someone was always picking me up and taking me home."

"Whew." Tracey whistled. "You were a lucky little girl. Anyone could have taken you."

"Pretty much," I said. "I mean, we had a funny uncle, but we knew to keep our distance from him."

Tracey gave me a wicked smile, "I think there's one of those in every family. Did you notice, as a kid, you just knew to stay away from them?"

"Yeppers, you just had your own way of knowing who was nice and who wasn't, kind of like a dog knows who's gonna pet him and who's gonna kick him down."

"So, what happened to Ed?"

"He got into trouble–pretty bad, whatever it was. I was a little kid, so I didn't know a whole lot about it. My Mom never mentioned it and Ed left home to join the Navy. He never finished high school, just went over to Pensacola and shipped out of there for a while. Mom was really sad but kind of proud, too, with Ed serving his country and all. She and Dad fought about it a whole lot. I was about eight or nine at the time Ed left. I didn't miss him so much as I missed the few bucks or the ice cream. By that time, I had a few kids I hung out with on my own and we pretty much stuck close together. After suppertime, we'd all meet at the end of the lane and just sit around and play or talk or hide away from our parents until it got dark.

"That went on for a while, and Mom and Dad kept fighting. Then I got wind of Dad drinking maybe more than just his regular couple of beers after work, and Mom started hitting the sauce herself. Maybe it was just to keep him company. But then the fighting got really bad. They'd keep at each other almost all night, and didn't even notice if I was home after dark or not. Some nights when I got home, it was all dark and quiet inside the trailer and I'd just climb in my bunkbed, happy it was peaceful."

"What about school?" Tracey asked.

"I went, if that's what you mean. What about it?"

"What was it like down here?"

"Well, I think as I got older, it got more important to me. I'd say I was studying at the library or at this one's or that one's house. No questions were asked as long as I said I was going out to study. If I said I was going out to play, it was the whole third degree. Who was I going with, where was I going, when would I get there, when was I coming home."

"Oh, yeah, the usual interrogation," Tracey chuckled.

"So, if I said I was gonna go study stuff, they'd say okay and leave me alone."

"Bet you were really smart."

We both rolled our eyes skyward and laughed, "You betcha, I was real smart." Actually, it was nice enough to talk to Tracey about this. She seemed to understand, and talking about the past made the events of the day fade a little bit into the background.

I continued, "We had a history teacher who taught us the Holy Bible, and said since it was God's Word, it was true history. Then we had a science teacher who told us about the Tom-foolishness of believing we were descendants of monkeys and that we needed to know that we were actually made in the image of our Holy Lord and descended directly from Adam and Eve their holy selves. We had an English teacher whose main mission in life seemed to be to make us say please and thank you kindly all the time and a P.E. teacher who was a regular bull dyke."

"Jeez! The Southern System of education."

"When I was about fourteen, I'd had enough shit to last me a lifetime, so I kind of quit going to school except for the dances. I would go enough to pass, but by the time I was sixteen I wanted o-u-t out."

"So, you didn't finish high school, either, like your brother?"

"Actually, I did finish. There was this library lady who was really nice to me. I remember her name was Betty Johnson. Seems I was sleeping at a library table and she just let me be. When I woke up, the library was dark and Miz Johnson was sitting at her desk with a little lamp on, reading a book. I wasn't sure where I was for a few minutes, but she came over and said everything was okay, she just thought I looked like I needed the sleep. Mom and Dad had been fighting pretty bad lately, and even my sneaking a beer or two couldn't shut out the noise.

"So, me and this nice library lady talked for a spell and she dropped me at the corner of Tough Luck Lane, since I didn't want to explain anything about being brought back to the trailer in a car. Miz Johnson said I could stop by whenever I liked. So, I did now and again, and sometimes there was stuff there for me to eat and there were always books and shit to read. There was always stuff to talk about, and it was kind of like playing with my friends. She never told me not to read this or that, or tell me something was 'too old' for me to understand. A lot of the stuff I didn't understand, but I read it anyway.

"I still hung out with my friends and all, but passing class was getting easier for me. Once I learned stuff and how to give the teachers what they wanted, school got pretty easy and I finished with a diploma.

"But in-between then, Mom and Dad were just living in a pissed-off state with each other. One day, I came home and the trailer was dark, like it usually was late at night, but it seemed quieter, somehow. I saw Mom in the morning and she acted like nothing was wrong. It was quiet and peaceful over the next couple of days and I just figured my Dad found a bar and was drinking there instead of coming home and making a big deal.

"When the weekend came, I asked Mom where Dad was on Saturday morning and she just shrugged and said she didn't know. I asked when he was coming home and she shrugged again and said she didn't know that, either. Then she sat down and poured herself a drink and one for me, too. I never had it before and I hated the taste of the stuff. Puke! Like medicine, man. I mean, a little beer, cool. Wine's nice, too. But the hard shit? Man, I think it was scotch or something—my first taste, and it was rough. By and by, though, Mom'd put out a little beer for me and pour herself a stiff one after day's end. We'd sit together in the kitchen and have a drink. One day, I got real bold and broke out a pack of smokes and she didn't say a thing. I just smoked in front of her, easy as you please."

"But Stacey, you don't smoke, do you?"

"Not now, I gave it up. My friend, the library lady, gave me this book on cancer and how smoking at a young age made me more prone to it than if I'd started as an adult, since my lungs weren't yet fully grown. She said to just think about it, but maybe decide to smoke when I was eighteen instead of fifteen. Either way, there was no smoking in the library and that was that! She didn't even like it if I hung around the building outside with a butt, and told me, either to go elsewhere or stub it out and come on in, but no hanging around the building with a lit cigarette."

"And you listened to her?"

"Well, yeah, she was my friend. I could hang out

with my buddies and smoke and drink all I wanted. It was kind of fun when the boys came buzzing around, and a little making out in the swamp was okay. But then I'd think about Ed and how I didn't want to get caught up in something like his girls did. They'd come around the house, begging and pleading just to see him even when he'd be out. Mom or Dad would say he's just not here, or with Bobby-Joe or Billie-Sue or whoever the hell they thought he might be with. But most of the time, they didn't know for sure. The poor girl would go away crying. I was not going to be one of *those*."

Tracey gave me a sympathetic glance and I backpedaled, remembering the story she'd told about her and the Captain.

"It wasn't so bad, actually. In time, the girls would get over old Ed and wind up with some nice guy named Mike or Steve, who'd take them to the movies or the Prom."

"Do you look like Ed?"

I laughed. "Hellll...no! As you can see, I have dishwater hair, but it's getting blonder!" I held out a strand of butter colored hair, I was happy to say.

"Yeah, so I see," Tracey agreed.

"...and I have hazel eyes. I tend more to tawny than tone-y, if you know what I mean." I smiled wistfully. "Ed was–well, maybe still is–gorgeous. I told you he had black hair and blue eyes and black eyelashes that were really long. They made his eyes look a little smudgy all the time. He would get pretty tan and those blue eyes would stand out like blue topaz on a sandy beach. He had a gift of gab, too. He could talk you six ways to Sunday while pickin' your pocket and you wouldn't mind a bit. That's how good he was, and probably still is.

"Anyway, I think Dad had enough of Mom crying over Ed, and said she thought she should be proud of Ed serving his country and all. But she hated war and that her kid might get killed over something stupid. War's just people squabbling big time over something one has and the other one wants. Dad was all for Ed joining the Navy, so they fought some more. Once in a blue moon, we'd get a picture back, with Ed more gorgeous than ever in uniform. Sometimes, he'd be standing next to a ship, but usually, he'd be standing next to a girl."

Tracey laughed at that. "A girl in every port, huh?"

"Yeah, they're all pretty much the same, I'm thinkin'."

Tracey got up to re-heat the water for another cup of tea. I was itching for something stronger, all this talking was putting a thirst on me. I needed a beer.

"Hey, Trace," I said.

"Yes, ma'am?"

"I know how you feel about drink and all, but it's been a helluva long day for me and I'm a bit thirsty. Would you be put out if I went out and had a beer?"

"Store's up the street. Why don't you get yourself something and bring it back?"

"Won't it bother you?"

"No, I'm over it. You just go ahead. I'll be right here when you get back."

"You're sure?"

"Positive."

"Okay, then." I grabbed my purse and the keys to the Mir.

"You don't need the car. It's just on the corner." And it was.

I got back with a six-pack of standard-issue all-purpose beer. I popped one open and stashed the rest in her fridge. "I'll take 'em with me when I leave."

Tracey shrugged. "I don't really like beer, never have," stirring a fresh cup of hot tea.

I took a pull off my beer–it was heavenly. Icy cold, wet, and refreshing as hell. I sat on one of the folding chairs across from Tracey on the daybed.

"So, it sounds like Ed pretty much raised you."

"Not really. I'd hold that to Miz Betty Johnson."

"What happened to her?"

"I think she met someone and got married. The summer after I graduated high school, I went by to look in on her at the library, but she wasn't there anymore. I asked around, but nobody knew. If they did, they weren't telling me."

"Did you go to college?"

"I thought about it, even registered for a class. Then I got a job tending bar. The money was okay and living home didn't cost me anything. Ed was gone, Mom was okay, so I just hung out with the status quo and things pretty much went on as they were. Mom and me, having drinks at the end of the day, a drink at the end of her day before I went to work, then a drink at the end of my day, when I got home. I'm sure she had a couple more between Point A and Point B, and so did I, with maybe something a little stronger now and again, but things were so peaceful, I didn't much care. We kept pretty good company for a while and then she got sick."

"What happened?"

"Cancer. It came and went for a while, then she got really sick and finally passed. I looked after her until the end and then landed here by a sheer twist of fate." I told her how I came to Pompano, by way of Fort La-Dee-Dah by the Sea, and now had gainful employment at Sparky's and was just living the life I dreamed. Well, almost, anyway.

"So, what are your plans for the future?" she asked.

"To own a pair of new Jimmy Choos."

"Now, wait a minute. That's one thing I don't understand. Here you are, from some backwater swamp hole in the ground. How the hell do you know about Jimmy Choo?"

I laughed. "You can thank Miz Johnson for that,

too. I told you I read everything with her–that included high-fashion magazines, trashy tabloids, everything like that. It was like candy–a little went a long way, but it sure was fun going down. Then, just before I graduated, she took me to a mall in Boca–kind of a field trip outside the library–and we got dressed up and visited all the high-end department stores. I saw all the famous designer clothes, and shoes, and a bunch of cheap shit as well. She showed me how to tell the difference between the two. She helped me 'start a wardrobe' as she called it. I got a dress and some shoes. All I've been able to do is more shoes, but some day…"

"Bet you were a quick study."

"Bet you're right!" I held up my beer in a toast to myself and downed the rest as we both laughed.

She took the five beers out of the fridge and handed them to me, along with my purse and keys that I'd set down earlier. "Okay, Chicky-dee, while you can still drive and my resolve is still firm, outta here."

I took the beers, grabbed my purse and keys and headed out with a hug and a laugh to Tracey.

"Today, 'True Confessions'–next week, Pizzzazzz!"

"You're ON! Now outta here–I've got an early call."

The drive home in the cool stillness of night was uneventful, even the Compound was quiet. I headed in and stashed my beer in the fridge, but not without popping one first and headed outside to savor the sweet evening stillness. I reveled in the soothing fragrance of night-blooming jasmine. Even though it had been the day from hell, it was a night of peace. Finishing my beer, I placed my Tigger slippers under the bed, slipped into my sleepy tee and tucked in for a good night's sleep.

It was not to be. I tossed and turned, dreaming of the morning on the beach and the drowned Lorikeet. Just at the point where I walked up to see her, she turned to me with her half-eaten away face and pointed to the sea. I ran and ran and ran and fell off the edge of the ocean. Thumping soundly on the floor, I woke up and paced awhile. I looked out over the Compound to see if anyone's lights were on. All the buildings were dark. Maybe someone else was up, but no. Even the Captain wasn't snoozing in his usual chaise. I locked my door and paced– three steps this way, four steps that–until, finally, I thought I was tired enough to bed down for the night. I stared at the ceiling. I stared at the moonlight coming through the window. I saw shadows on the wall of the bungalow. I turned on the light, hoping the garish brightness of the bare bulb would chase away the demons of the dark. It just made some other horrible shadows on the other wall, so I snapped it back off again. I wondered where the palmetto bugs and lizards were hiding in my tiny abode. I wondered where the other Lorikeet might be.

I decided it bothered me a lot. I resolved to go to Geoffrey's and satisfy myself the next day. After all, he owed me a night's pay and I was just more than a little curious about everything. I'd learned at a young age that curiosity was not something to be encouraged, like reading or knowing how to do your sums. But something was nagging at the back of my head and I just had to make the connection between those pesky neurons if I didn't want to drive myself crazy.

Chapter Twelve

Dawn finally dragged its ass up from the east and I had a reason to pull myself out of bed. Daylight seeped dolefully through the bungalow window. Looking at my meager hovel in contrast to Tracey's place, disappointment was a gross understatement. I made the bed, tidied up, decided on coffee instead of beer and headed over to Dana's for a cup of Joe to go.

Tracey was there, bright-eyed and bushy-tailed as ever, slinging her hash and plying her palaver on any and all of the court she held at the counter. I waved and the cashier handed me my coffee and a fresh blueberry muffin wrapped in bakery paper. Happy with my booty, I walked back to my place, taking in the sea air, but with no desire to go near the beach. I had a few hours to kill before work.

I opened the door to the bungalow and set down the coffee and muffin. Splitting the muffin in half, I took a half with my coffee outside to look at the bungalow interior. Outside looking in is a certain perspective, which showed the bungalow could definitely use some work. Where to begin? I could rip out the rug and lay down some faux tile flooring. Simple and cheap. It would be easier to keep clean than the sorry old carpet decomposing on the floor. The old "Honeymooners" era wallpaper would take a bit of doing, though, and I wondered if Dhani and Edmond would lend a hand. I could get my hands on a case of beer and let loose with some of my industrial-strength "good" stuff, which might get them in the mood. On a moment's reflection, I decided I was not going to let the good ol' boys at Knotts Hardware help me with my interior decorating plans.

Downing the last of my coffee and wiping the few crumbs of muffin straight into the mini-garbage can I kept under the sink, I put the second half of the muffin in the fridge, locked up and headed out in the Mir. I stopped for gas and paid a king's ransom for a full tank. I was going for broke and headed to the new glitzy home store on the highway across the bridge. Things seemed a bit more normal on the other side of the Intracoastal. More permanent, somehow. Solid, and meant to last more than a season or two.

For the next couple of hours, I filled my head with color swatches and home decor. I selected a few to bring home to look at in the light of the bungalow. I found an inexpensive fixture that would make a better statement than the bare bulb now hanging from the ceiling. I purchased a new faucet and looked at the oven ranges. A bit out of my price bracket for now, but a new Weber barbeque grill and new barbeque tools were in line. Besides, a new barbeque meant a celebratory feast at the Compound and I could live off the leftovers for a couple of days. Finding some "place and press" tiles, I took a few samples to go with the color swatches I'd selected. Loading a flatbed cart with my purchases, I left with the smug look of satisfaction only a home fixer-upper can know. I also knew I'd be back–there's no such thing as "just one" trip to these places.

I loaded up the Mir and went to the major market all-purpose store to look at bedspreads and shit. I spent the next hour or so defining and refining my sense of style. I decided I wasn't a ruffles-and-lace person like Tracey, as much as I wanted to be. I found a little lamp for the small night table next to the sofabed and a clock-radio alarm that made sounds like rain and nightfall in the jungle. After I'd had enough, I drove home and proceeded to place my new goodies to see if everything "worked." It clearly didn't. I tucked the samples under the sink and decided to wait for the right moment of inspiration. A fleeting thought in consideration of the leopard print border crossed my mind and I resolved to ponder on it some.

I showered, dressed, and left for work. The Captain was peacefully snoozing in his usual chaise. I wondered where he had been the night before.

Work at Sparky's was nothing special; just the usual drunk-wrangling, infighting, and bartending bullshit that goes on day after day in a small pub. A small pub is like a small town, everybody crawls up your butt sooner or later, but for stretches of time it's just old humdrum routine. Rick was warming up to me again, but quickly sensing I was having none of it, slunk off to make time with one of the tourists having too much already. I pulled beers and poured shots and BS'ed my way through the day. At six, I went home as usual, but my mind was on the BBQ party at the Compound and Geoffrey's.

At the Compound, things were progressing at a sedate, steady pace. The Captain was already in his cups, Edmund and Dhani were contemplating my new barbeque, and assorted characters were drifting in and out of the courtyard. I changed into shorts and a tee, beer in hand, three-pack in tow, offering drinks all around and hoping someone had some charcoal and a steak or two.

I made out better than expected. Edmond had taken off early that day to go fishing and had landed some nice-looking mahi-mahi. At the Compound, whenever someone buys a new barbeque, everyone pitches in and the first meal is cooked "on the house." My neighbors and friends contributed what they could, from charcoal and starter fluid to food and drink. Someone, probably Edmund, had arranged the charcoal in a perfect little pyramid and lit them "just so" to make the perfect fire, which burned long and evenly. I was happy to supply a few paper plates and utensils as I watched the goings-on in comfort and ease. I felt the beginnings of a very happy buzz a few beers always accord at a party and my fellows seemed same in spirit.

Someone had put some potatoes on to boil to serve with the fish. Another resident supplied greens for a salad and yet another some salad dressing, salt, and pepper. Fish is simple: grilled, brushed with butter, a squeeze of lemon and a sprinkle of dill. Everywhere there was beer. We ate, and talked, and toasted one another on everything from fishing skills to superb barbeque technique.

As dinner wound down, I sat on my stoop with Dhani and Edmund came over and stood in front of us.

"So, what are you doing tonight, Stacey?" Dhani started.

"Not sure," I replied. "Guess I'll go try to pick up my pay at Geoffrey's."

"I thought you were done with that place," Edmond said. "Let it go. How much could you lose anyway? Twenty-five bucks?"

"It's the principle of the thing," I said. "They trumped up some bogus stealing charge and I've got that old business to straighten out. I'm not a thief."

"No," Dhani said. "You're not a liar, either. But do you really need to go back?"

"I do. I feel as if I got slapped in the face."

"You really didn't deserve it," Edmund said. "But some things you just need to let go."

"There's no warning her, Edmund," Dhani added. "It'll fall on deaf ears. She's going to do what she's going to do. But, Stacey," he continued, "we've been around here longer than you and don't want to see you bite off more than you can chew, yes?"

"I'm not 'biting' anything, Dhani. I'm just getting what's mine." I was sick of getting the short end of the stick and, besides, something just felt wrong about the situation. I felt I was set up and dismissed too quickly. What had I seen, or heard, that made them want to get rid of me so fast. Hell, I didn't even finish out the shift. Couldn't have been much, then again...

"Okay, guys," I started, "here's the deal. I get this job at Geoffrey's, am just standing around, and minding my business. There's trouble with a couple of the younger girls, and I overheard some broad hints about 'working it out' with Geoffrey. Next thing you know, one of them washed up dead on the beach a few days later. Loretta, you know, the older woman who hung in Sparky's and had a crush on that bartender Ricky, she dies. I know Geoffrey was at her condo because I saw him there as I was leaving. It doesn't make sense. Or it makes sense, but the wrong kind of sense, if you get my drift. I saw Geoffrey and the girls going out on the Golden Girl yacht when we came in from our fishing trip that day on the Minnow."

"That's why you stiffened up, Stacey," Edmund observed. "It wasn't sunburn."

"I had a feeling," I said, "and I felt uneasy. One girl, the girl who was dead on the beach, stood off from everyone and didn't look completely comfortable with the situation."

Dhani and Edmund looked thoughtfully at each other.

"Do you want one of us to go with you?" Dhani asked. "I could drive you there and just hang in the truck, yes?"

"No. I have to do this myself."

Edmund shifted uneasily. "You're just going in to get your back pay, right?"

"Of course. I just want what's mine." I stood up from the stoop. "Well, I have to get going, thanks for dinner."

Edmund and Dhani shrugged, turned, and walked over to the courtyard with their heads bowed in quiet conversation. Edmund shook his head and Dhani nodded. I wondered if they planned on following me in spite of my protests then went inside the bungalow to change.

I donned cigarette-slim jeans, black stiletto-heeled

sandals, a mirror encrusted black leather belt and slinky black tank. I gave my hair a massive fluffing, squirted some perfume throughout, applied too-smoky eye makeup being sure to include a thorough coating of mascara, and sauntered out the door on a mission. My outfit elicited several loud wolf-whistles and a round of applause as I strode through the courtyard of the Compound en route to The Mir. *How nice to be appreciated,* I thought. Dhani and Edmund didn't budge. They didn't whistle, either. They sat stone-faced with nothing to say to me.

I arrived at Geoffrey's by eight-fifteen, clearly too early for the night crawlers, but late enough for everyone who was anyone in the place to be there, getting ready for the night's festivities. Dianna came out from the kitchen as I approached the bar.

"Oh, you," she said flatly. I leveled my gaze at her and did not nod, speak or smile. I stepped up to the bar and was ignored completely. Brian the bartender, whom I could think of only by the sobriquet I had given him on my first and only night there, Cold-As-Ice, began discussing something at length with Dianna. It was nothing that was making her happy. Whatever it was, it was nothing I had any business overhearing, much as I wanted to eavesdrop. Their heads were close together as they conducted the whole exchange in terse, angry whispers. I waited until it was over as Dianna stalked into the kitchen looking as if she would spit nails. Cold-As-Ice straightened himself up, gave a tug on his cuffs, and proceeded to polish the bar, still ignoring me.

"Sir?" I tapped the bar rail gently with my fingernail. Cold-As-Ice spared me a glance and continued polishing the same spot he'd been working over the last couple of minutes.

"Excuse me, please," I said.

"We're not serving yet."

"I'm not here for that. I need to see Geoffrey."

He nodded. At least that had been received and understood.

"I'm Stacey, I used to work here."

"I know."

"Your name is Brian, right?" I asked, boldly and feigning supreme indifference; assuming the rule if you give information, it's fair game to expect some back.

"Brian," he answered flatly.

"Brian," I started, resulting in a reflex of his looking up from the bar to me levelly, as if it were sheer effrontery to use his name. "I'm here to see Geoffrey."

"He'll be out. Just wait around."

Girls flurried about in the abbreviated costume I had trashed not so long ago. None of the girls had shared a shift with me that fateful night. The hostess, however, was the same porcine blonde who stood at her station, inevitably stuffing her face with some unidentifiable variety of salad. She looked up, glanced in my direction then just as quickly looked away, shoving a massive forkful of dripping greens into her mouth, which was edged in bright ruby red lipstick. Lipstick smeared her fork, she rubbed it off with a finger then wiped the finger on her too-tight little black dress. She shifted in her high heels, giving the impression she was extremely uncomfortable; one of those people for whom everything is too tight, too short, and never fits quite right. The dress pulled across the bust line and seemed to cut a bit under her pale fleshy arms. Another ginormous forkful of salad made its way into her mouth. This time, she saw me watching her and used a napkin to daintily wipe her lips clean.

I didn't have to wait long for Geoffrey. I didn't see any smoke signals or other means of silent communication, but expected there might be a button under the bar Brian could press to summon Geoffrey from his inner sanctum for one pesky reason or another he didn't want to deal with. Like me.

Geoffrey emerged in full feather, navy blue pinstriped three-piece suit, crisp white shirt with diamond and gold cufflinks, which sparkled as he shot his French cuffs in my direction. His purple tie gave away his concession of cheesiness, but he looked much more put together than the first time I had seen him. Black Bally loafers made no sound as he traversed the brown and gold marble flooring to the bar. I wondered if he had gone to the airport for his jet-plane blown out hairstyle and I felt a little *snick* in the back of my brain, as if a gear had just connected.

"Geoffrey," I said, walking up to him slowly, but not so slowly as if to be fearful. I saw he definitely had too much bronzer on his face as I drew near to him.

"Tracey. Good to see you again."

"It's Stacey."

"Stacey, then. How nice."

"You owe me a night's pay."

"You owe me a uniform. Bring it back to Brian here and he'll take care of you."

"That piece of crap? It was garbage when I got it and it's garbage now."

"No uniform, no money, sweetie."

"Geoffrey, that uniform was *used!*"

"Sorry."

Damn, I thought silently to myself. This wasn't going to get me anywhere.

"Geoffrey, Tracey told me to come to you originally," I lied. "I assumed you were friends or, at the very least, acquaintances."

"Tracey, right. Good kid."

Yeah, really? "Geoffrey, look, I need the money. Can't we work something out?"

"Want your job back?"

"Um." Stalling for time, although I really didn't need to think up an answer to that one. "I have a job,

Geoffrey. I've just come for what's mine."

"Didn't you steal some money from one of our patrons? I believe that was why you left."

"No. I didn't steal." Bad move, he had put me on the defensive. I had to backstroke quickly if I was going to get what I came for. Remembering his exchange with tough little Lori, who was nowhere in evidence this night I said, suggestively, "I want to work something out with you."

"What did you have in mind?"

"I'm not sure. There must be something I can do. I really need that money and don't give me any crap about that old uniform." Then, softly, leaning up to speak in his ear, "I did you a favor when we first met, remember?"

Brian looked up and over at Geoffrey. Geoffrey made a motion with his hand to dismiss Brian, who polished bottles then moved away from the bar to give Geoffrey some space to deal with me, or twist in the wind, it made no difference to him. I thought Brian was a reptile. Cold-blooded with ice water for blood in his veins.

Geoffrey sighed, looked over at Brian and motioned him to come back to us. "All right," he said, "Brian, give Miss Stacey here a C."

Brian opened the register and handed me a hundred-dollar bill. That about covered the day's trip to the home improvement emporiums. But something in the back of my mind was nagging at me. This was just a little too easy. It *felt* fake, as uncomplicated as it seemed to be. I told myself to tread carefully and remember to shut up more than I spoke. If I overdid it, I'd be sunk.

"Now, what else can I do for you? And forget the uniform."

"Oh, Geoffrey, thank you. Perhaps I could do something for you now." I sidled up to him, gently running my fingertip along the sleeve of his jacket. "I haven't seen the girls, I really liked some of them."

Geoffrey snorted, "Yeah. Well. Crews come and go

in this business, honey."

"Don't I know it."

"Hard to keep a good crew in line anymore. We have a new crowd these days."

"The patrons? They seemed pretty steady to me."

"No, the help. We're always looking for good girls. It's easy work, not like they have to dance or anything. I need a drink. Would you like a drink? Brian, get the lady a cocktail. I'll have my usual."

Brian stood at the ready. I ordered a white wine spritzer. Geoffrey took a Cuba Libre, I suspected not his first of the day.

He nodded appreciation of my choice. "Good girl, I like a lady who doesn't overdo."

So far, so good, I thought, silently breathing a sigh of relief in overcoming the first hurdle, as Brian topped off my spritzer with a flourish and a twist of lemon. We clinked glasses together and Geoffrey treated me to a sly, knowing wink. Sheesh. I tried not to roll my eyes.

We sat at the bar together, talking about absolutely nothing. I had the feeling I was up for General Inspection like a boat, car, or some other commodity bought and sold on the open market. I mostly let him talk just smiling sweetly and responding appropriately when the time was right. Good, sweet, patient Little Stacey.

"So, how have you been doing? New in town, aren't you?"

"Yes, I am. I'm doing okay, but I could do better. You know." I drew little dollar signs on the bar with my fingertip. Obvious, but maybe he'd take the bait.

He took a sip of his drink and nodded. "We could always do better, I agree."

How nice. I sighed softly and looked up at Geoffrey, slyly, from beneath hooded eyes, "Like you say, I'm new in town. But I know *you*." I gave him the largest cow-eyed look I could muster without cracking up.

"You sure you don't want your job back?"

"Oh, Geoffrey. I was thinking of something a little better than just a job. Something, you know, maybe, extra?"

Geoffrey signaled Brian for another drink. I took mine with a resolve to have just half and switch to club soda with a twist. I needed my wits about me now. Geoffrey owned the place; he could afford to chuck half a light wine with what I was bringing to the table.

I clinked my glass against his, "To bright futures and sunny days." I whispered to him gently.

Another wink and a clink. "I think maybe you might be able to do something for me."

I gave him a sidelong look and arched one eyebrow.

"Not really for me," he said, "but a friend of mine."

"Oh? Who?"

"Just a friend. He needs someone to do his shopping for him. You can use his car, it's a nice, new Cadillac."

A flash of Tracey went through my head. "Just shopping?" I asked.

"Yeah, that's it. A favor for an old friend. And me."

"And?"

"You do the shopping, drop off the car, and come see me."

"Well, I work during the week, you know."

"No problem. You can do it Saturday mornings."

"Just shopping? That's it?"

"That's it. I'll make it worth your while. Come by here Saturday morning for directions and the shopping list. My friend will be eternally grateful."

I'll bet. I nodded in agreement and stopped at the half-level of my drink. "Driving. Can I get a club with a twist for the road?"

"Sure, sweety, anything. Brian?" he called the bartender over. "The lady needs a new drink." After placing the order, he said, "I've got to get ready. Ten-thirty

Saturday okay for you?"

"Eleven would be better. I'm in the middle of redecorating."

Geoffrey nodded, "Are you decorating do-it-yourself?"

I nodded.

"Done," he said. "You'll be able to decorate professionally if you like, and if this works out."

"Okay," I said and sat at the bar watching Brian watch me.

Geoffrey got up to leave at nine o'clock, adding, "Brian, whatever the lady wants, on the house." Oh temptation, get thee from me! He put his hand on my back and I stifled the impulse to shiver. I wound up having another club and lemon, then left just as the lights were dimming and the introductions of the new crop of Geoffrey's Golden Girls were about to begin.

As I left the bar, "Mr. Smith" was standing in one of the back corners, watching my every move. I didn't see him come in. As I left Geoffrey's parking lot in The Mir, I could see Mr. Smith standing in the shadows cast by the front awning. An ember glowed in the dark from the cigarette he clenched in his mouth. A puff of smoke curled through the air, then he was gone, as was I.

I got back to the Compound and the crowd was mellow. Not one word was mentioned about what happened on the beach the previous day. Most people, I found, who live at the beach witness a couple of drownings a year, sometimes more if there's a bad hurricane that attracts aspiring surfers with more courage than sense. They just deal with it and move on. Life on the beach can be harsh. I'd already had my share with Loretta and the Lorikeet and was just as happy to let it rest as well.

Dhani and Edmund looked me over as I came into the courtyard. I guess I didn't look much worse for wear so they left me alone as I went into the bungalow to change and grab a cold beer. I went two doors down and sat with Maricella and her Mom.

As the evening wound down, people went back to their apartments and bungalows with wishes of good cheer, prosperity, and good catch. Maricella and her Mom went inside. I sat with Dhani at the table in the center of the courtyard as Edmond "scrubbed" the grill with tin foil.

"It's been quite a run for you since you've come here, Stacey, yes?" Dhani asked with a smile.

"Yes, Dhani, it has." I sighed.

"How did you make out?" He winked as if the double entendre was extremely funny.

I shrugged. "I got my pay, it's fine."

"Ah, yes, always it's fine."

"Agreed."

We sat in companionable silence. No one asked where I'd come from, where I'd been, or what I'd been doing. Not that they didn't care; they just knew how to keep mum and mind their own business. I hoped it wasn't a trait I'd be sorry for down the road. I hoped Dhani and Edmund would consider the business concluded and wouldn't press for any more information.

We briefly discussed some inconsequential news item Edmund had seen on TV, capped with Dhani's keen observation the female anchor reporting the story, obviously, had a boob job. Then the talk drifted toward the weather, with a general hope that it would remain warm and sunny at least through the weekend. The scent of night-blooming jasmine hung languorously in the air. They were just coming into flower. Edmund decided to pack it in. Dhani sat next to me on the stoop of my bungalow.

"Stacey, I'm not going to pry, but we can talk, yes?"

I nodded. When people ask if you can "talk", it usually means they're going to talk and you're going to listen. When they say they don't want to pry, that's exactly what they're doing so it's a fine opportunity to shut up and hear them out without giving anything up yourself.

"This, Geoffrey's–you know, it's not a good place."

"How so?"

"Before I say anything, your business is finished there, yes?"

I nodded again, "I got my pay."

"It wasn't always Geoffrey's, you know. I built that bar about ten years ago. A guy named Vinny owned the place. He was from up North and came down because he was a little bit of a fuckup where he was. He started the club–it was called something else then, I don't remember what, but it wasn't Geoffrey's. It was a private club back then and it was a good place to stay out of. Geoffrey took over a few years ago and Vinny kind of disappeared. I know who you saw on that yacht and I wonder what you're thinking."

"I'm not thinking anything, Dhani," I said.

"Just don't get involved. I did the job, got paid, and didn't look back. You do the same, yes?"

I nodded yet again. Dhani got up and left.

I stayed for a little while longer, but not so long as to let the sweet scent of the jasmine become sickeningly cloying. I went into the bungalow and safely stowed my Tigger slippers safely under my bed. I drifted off, dreaming of color swatches and the bungalow's interior resplendent in stylish leopard-patterned wallpaper. There were touches of purple in the décor, which for some reason, jarred me half awake. I rolled over and tried to dream about something else.

Chapter Thirteen

I arose feeling a little shaky but felt a need to go to the beach. I wanted–no, needed–to make sure everything was okay and get rid of the bad taste from a couple days ago. The sand, the endless ocean, the jetties, drifted through my mind. It wasn't good enough just to think of this. I needed to *be* there. To feel the spray on my face and the sea air in my lungs. I walked up directly from the bungalow, passed the bench where the cop and I had coffee, and ventured onto the sand. So far, so good. No real memories yet, and I turned my gaze southward, in the opposite direction of where Laurie's body had been found two days ago. The Atlantic kept churning, waves ebbing and flowing onto the shore. I felt as part of a larger continuum; the sea kept on as it had before I was born, and would go on long after I ceased to be. It was as looking into the galaxy on a deep night. I felt awe and respect. I kicked off a flip-flop and traced a line with my toe on the sand, waiting for it to be erased by the ocean. People are no different, I thought. So many of us come and go unknown. Just sand washed away by the tide.

I walked up to the jetty and braved a stroll on the rocks in my flip-flops. One got knocked off going over a big rock, but it floated in a tide pool and was easy to fish out. I went out as far as I dared, I peered into more little tide pools showing an occasional starfish or mullet captive within its grasp until the next tide. I hoped it wouldn't be long until they reclaimed their freedom back into the ocean. I looked across the water and pretended I could see England. Of course, if we looked across the water in South

Florida, we'd sooner see the coast of Africa, where hurricanes are mostly born, but I imagined England and dreamed I could see clear across.

Right down the street, however, I caught a glimpse of Dan Gowan, the cop from the other day. He was just standing there, watching me pick my way along the oversized dark brown rocks of the slippery jetty. I finally reached land. He didn't say anything to me. After a moment, he turned his back and started walking towards the A-1-A. *"No, I'm not returning to the scene of the crime, Sergeant Friday,"* I thought to myself.

I headed home and (finally–hurrah!) decided the colors of the beach would be good for the bungalow. I set out in the early morning once again for the home improvement store. I stopped at a fast food place for a cup of the world's most awful coffee and longed for Dana's Diner. I promised myself a stop at Dana's would be my reward if I found what I wanted to feather my mini-nest. Sipping the hot, bitter liquid, I reached the home store in no time flat and got busy roaming the aisles picking colors and styles with a fresh inspiration.

I found a paint chip the color of windblown sand. Floor tile in darker beige, almost the color of wet sand. Some other tiles were textured like sand etched with seahorse and starfish designs. I decided I would not do cheapie place 'n' press, but ask the guys about laying actual tile–this was Florida, after all. Finding a sea-themed border that tied it all together, I totaled up the tally and got a real wakeup call. Whew! It would have taken my life savings and selling off the rest of the liquor I had stashed to pay for all that stuff.

Hell's bells–I was just renting the place, not buying in Boca. I decided to go the cheaper route. I opted for the sea-themed border and figured on some pretty new curtains I might pick up cheaply at the discount store. The rest of the ideas I'd save up for "Fred", my imaginary mansion. I could hide the "Honeymooners" style wallpaper with travel posters, maybe from a cruise line. Or I could always I might talk Big Rick out of a Key West or Longboard Beer sign, since we no longer stocked the brews due to lack of interest. Even folks in the keys drink good ol' Bud and Corona.

Curtains and rods were no problem. I found a ruffly café set in a seafoam blue to go with the border. Damn. I realized I needed a hammer and some nails at the home store and was loathe to return. If you're a girl, and you return in fifteen minutes or less, you're greeted with smirks and snickers and usually one or two "can't pour piss out of a boot with directions printed upside-down on the heel" comments from the male staff. I steered the Mir towards Dixie and went to tangle with the good ol' boys at Knott's Lumber and Hardware. Oh, well. I figured it was a chance to patronize small American business.

It must've been a nice day for fishing, since the Knott boys were gone and just old man Knott was kicked back in a battered wood and leather office chair. He leaned over so far to stare at my chest I thought he'd tip over, but he miraculously kept his balance as he hauled his carcass up off his throne and rang up my few simple purchases.

"Anything else, Missy?" he asked my chest.

It was at that moment that I made it a mission to learn how to throw my voice. If boobs could talk, I imagined, it'd set him back in his chair a bit.

Shifting my bra and slinging my shoulder satchel in front to block the view, I lifted the petty amount of cash he required out of my pocketbook and sauntered towards the door.

"Uh, Miss," he called. "Your hammer and nails." He shoved the bag towards me as I turned back to the counter. Not surprisingly, the bag thumped into my chest. I turned around and strode to the door, only to be half knocked over by two exuberant Knott boys.

"Hey, Pop! They got a bikini girl sellin' hot dogs 'n' beer on the highway!"

"Ain't it against the law to drink on the highway? At this hour of the mornin'?" The old man scowled.

"Well, you can't drink when you drive, but you can sit on the grass and drink all you want," the bigger of the two Knott boys explained, towering over his dad.

"I can see you did that, son. Maybe you need to work some o' that off..."

The other Knotts' boy grabbed me by the shoulders and hopped me up and down a bit.

"Hey, girlie!" He shouted as if I were five blocks away. "What's shakin'?" Both boys howled in amusement.

I smacked bouncin' baby boy on the shoulder, "You know what's shakin', now quit makin' it shake!" He let go, lifting up both of his soiled hands in a gesture of injured innocence. Before he could speak again I slammed out the door trying not to grind my teeth into rubble. So much for patronizing small American business.

As I stomped through the dusty parking lot, I saw a figure of a man leaning slackly against a low-slung black Jaguar on the far side, near the highway. He took a drag of a cigarette then flicked an ash off his worn black leather jacket. I thought it was a bit hot for leather, but his choice of ensemble was none of my business. His eyes slid sideways, giving me the once-over. I lifted my chin and stared right back. After a moment, he looked away toward the street.

Hopping into the Mir, I thanked God for the Mighty Eight and couldn't kick up enough dirt to get out of there. With a crunch of gravel and the squeal of good tires hitting hot pavement the hard way, I hauled ass and only breathed a sigh of relief as I scooted over the Intracoastal Bridge on Atlantic. I caught my breath and realized I had just bumped into Mr. Smith. Again.

Wheeling into the parking lot, but damned careful

not to hit that stupid metal cable, I brushed myself off and decided to concentrate the redecorating project instead of wasting energy on those stupid Knotts. Good name, got me all tied up in knots, all right. I swore never to darken their door again and even that would be too soon for me. Mr. Smith hadn't followed me to the bungalow either, so I figured I was home free.

The courtyard was cool under the shady mango tree and little flowers were starting to bud from the branches. The coconut palm was still stubbornly unyielding, but the whisper of fronds could now actually be heard since the Captain was not on his chaise lounge, snoring like a demented foghorn. I drank in the cool stillness of the day, took a seat at the table in the center of the yard, and reviewed my purchases. All present and accounted for, I was eager to get going on my new project. I thought about Dana's, but time was of the essence.

There's something about popping open a cold beer in the still of the morning just before a bit of work around the house. My rule, however, was just one. More than that and I'd wind up hammering my hair to the border and hanging my skirt on the window instead of the curtains. Though I could sustain a pretty good buzz on occasion, there comes a time when one turns into six. Besides, I still had to go do that errand for Geoffrey.

I decided to begin with the self-stick border, or so they said. I filled a pan with cool water and set the border to soak. After the allotted time, I picked the soggy mess up and crawled on top of the sleeper sofa to begin installation. Unfortunately, the directions were somewhat misleading and I wished mightily they had spent more time explaining this stuff in English than providing me with equally incoherent instructions in French, Spanish, Swedish, German, and Japanese. *What the hell.* I wondered if they planned for this cheap shit to be the official wallpaper of the United Nations. I struggled, sweated, and swore as I sloshed the soggy mess all over the place. I was barely able to get it up after wrangling it similar to a king bull, not that I've ever had the pleasure, but some of the drunks I've worked with could have earned that dubious distinction. Anyways, I got it all up then stood back to take a look. It was crooked as a country mile and just about as sloppy. I crawled all over the furniture to get it straight and got the self-stick adhesive in my hair, on my shirt–hell, I even glued my boobs together. But it got done and it worked even better once I nailed the damn border up on the wall– okay, they were *little* nails; you could hardly see 'em.

I looked like hell and was a hot, sticky mess. I popped another brew and took a break. I still had about an hour and a half before I had to get to that errand. I took a minute to open the curtain rods and figure out those directions in God-knows what language. Thankfully, they were in–Spanish? Right. I flipped over the instruction sheet and found the English side. I decided they were clearer en Español. There were better pictures on that side, too. I measured and hammered, ruffled and fluffed. After about half an hour, I had fresh, pretty new curtains. The bungalow was beginning to look a little more fit for human habitation, namely, me. Since it was so easy, I decided to have another beer and sit down to admire my handiwork.

About the middle of the third beer I started to feel a little buzzed, maybe from no breakfast, so I took my beer into the shower with me and hosed off. It's a real art being able to shower with a beer, even if you aren't a past master at it as I am. A few soap bubbles won't kill you, besides, it cuts the heat that wells up in your throat from the steam and keeps you clear. By the time I finished, I was almost sober and the half-beer was warm. I chucked the contents down the toilet and crumpled the can. I thought I'd like to do that to the soggy-bottom Knotts brothers. I felt a bit ashamed for breaking my rule and imbibing as much as I did. I used a few tricks of the trade to straighten out the rest of the way. Afterward, suitably chastened, I got dressed.

I knew I had to look good enough to pass for, say, a suburban housewife, but a touch on the hot side (that's Florida, baby). However, I couldn't look as if I was a working girl. Settling on a pair of slim white jeans, a cool blue blouse, and white kitten-heeled thong sandals, I tied my hair into a ponytail with a blue and white scarf and fastened a couple of simple, small gold hoops in my ears. Switching my purse to a convincing imitation "It" bag, I locked up and headed to the Mir.

What a mess. My beautiful white Mir was a dusky brown. I must have kicked up a shitload of dirt at the hardware store. I grabbed a hose lying on the lawn, turned on the water and very gingerly sprayed the Mir, miraculously managing not to drench myself in the process. Okay, I was a little damp, but I'd dry. It took me about ten minutes to get to Geoffrey's at that hour. Once I entered the cool polished lounge, I almost didn't want to leave.

Brian was at the bar as usual, polishing the already gleaming countertop. I walked up to him, trying to keep it cool and casual. When I asked for Geoffrey, he uttered a curt, "Not here," and handed me an envelope.

It was one of those every day white business envelopes that could hold anything–in this case, a set of keys and an address typed on a plain white piece of paper.

I thanked him and left a fin on the bar. Service is service, after all. This merited a peremptory nod and a nearly imperceptible half-smile.

"Come back when you're done," he told me. "There will be another envelope waiting for you when you get back." It was my turn to nod coolly. Whether or not I managed that half-curled smile back at him, I'll never know, but I tried like hell to give what I got.

Coming out of the bar, I clattered across the patio and wondered if flatter shoes might be more in order for a trip to a stupidmarket. Oh, well, too late now; I was stuck with it, so I pressed on, climbing into the Mir and heading toward the address given.

The home was on a quiet street in Lighthouse Point. Like so many other neighborhoods, this once-pretty street was being eaten alive by houses. The houses were too big for the modest lots they occupied. Most of them were painted a hideous mustard yellow–I'd seen the same bilious color on mansions in Palm Beach on an occasional sortie down Ocean Avenue. Perhaps this was their way of living like the Rich and Famous, even though they usually were not. I thought about my dream mansion, "Fred": white exterior, black shutters, black iron grille work, a plaza in the center of black and white checkerboard marble and, of course, plenty of lush green, landscaping all around. Except for the ocean behind the mansion, of course.

The house to which I was assigned seemed to be bucking the trend. It was a single-story, yellow and white stucco house with a white tiled roof. A white paver drive was bordered by a painted white iron gate, massive enough to guard the residents from any who didn't belong and wanted to get in. No encyclopedia or vacuum cleaner salesmen here, I thought, quelling a grin. I slung The Mir onto the swale in front of the house. I alighted, walked up to the gate and contemplated the location of a bell, or buzzer. I stood there for a full two minutes, hands on hips feeling slightly foolish and increasingly annoyed. Just as I was about to mutter "Open Sesame," the gates swung open. A pale yellow Cadillac was tucked off to the side of the drive. A slight beep came from the gate's left pillar next to me, then the metallic hiss of a P.A. speaker. After a few seconds, a voice came on.

"The directions are in the front seat of the Cadillac, Miss. Just put the groceries in the back seat and drop off the car when you're done. You shouldn't be more than an hour and a half. Leave your keys in the box here."

The voice was fuzzy, decidedly not Southern.

Definitely male, though, and tough. I took the key from the Mir off my key ring and slipped it into a small metal box on the gate. I gave a small nod and walked toward the car. A tiny camera on top of the gate whizzed and hissed as it followed my path.

The Cadillac opened with a soft click. Even that sounded expensive. The rich leather interior still smelled new. I slid in behind the wheel, kicked off my sandals and sunk my toes into the plush pile of the carpet as I adjusted the seat. It purred like a boxful of Persian kittens, instantly shaping itself to me for maximum comfort. I felt my eyelids start to droop in the warmth of the car. If I sat there much longer, I'd be curled up like the Captain on his chaise, sawing enough logs to fill a lumberyard.

Another businesslike white envelope was on the front seat with the address of the supermarket and parking directions. There was also a grocery list that would take about an hour to fill and more than enough money to take care of it.

The key slid into the ignition with an oiled, almost sensuous smoothness. Turning over engine, it rumbled with the sleek power of some big jungle cat, flexing its muscles for a run. *Wow*, I thought—*sexy as hell*. I considered taking the beautiful beast for a spin along the A-1-A and giving the boys at the Compound something to stare at, but thought better of it. Time was money, after all. I shifted the Caddy into gear, curling my bare toes luxuriously around the gas pedal.

Tracey had told me she did this every week for quite a while and no harm came to her save for a hit from Vinny. Hell, I got more than that for less than an off-track adventure at home. I figured I could just go do the deal and get done and home in time for a nice drinky and a chat with the Captain. Maybe there would even be a supper of fresh fish if I were lucky. I prayed I'd be lucky. I prayed I could figure out how the hell to drive this thing after checking out all the buttons and gadgets on the dash. Was that a TV beside the radio or a GPS? Maybe that's how Vinny knew Tracey took a side trip–the damned thing had been *tracking* her!

I drove to the store sedately. I know a cop-magnet when I'm in one and, as nice as I may have looked I knew I didn't look *that* nice. So, I took it slow, easing into a parking spot close to the back of the parking lot as directed.

Slipping my sandals on, I stepped out of the car and took a hard look around the parking lot. I even looked into all the cars nearby to make sure there wasn't anyone in them. I popped the trunk to see a grocery sack on the floor. Pretending to stow my "It" bag, but on second thought, I snuck a peek in the sack. I did a double-take and pursed my lips in soundless whistle. Thick bundles of bills were in the sack. A shitload of money, in other words. I suppose I half-expected it, but actually seeing that much cash was something else again. To me, a hundred bucks was a windfall. This was like waking up in Shangri-La.

I slung my bag over my shoulder and headed inside to hunt down the food. Now, when you're a regular at a grocery store, you get in and out quick. You know where everything is and most of the time it's always there. You even know a couple of helpful locals to ask where to locate hard-to-find brands or new stuff on sale. When you're in a foreign store–one outside your neighborhood–it's a stupid market and you're the stupid in the market.

I fumbled around and managed to find most of the stuff on the list. Anything I couldn't find, I made up as I went along. At one point, the hairs stood up on the back of my neck and I had that creepy, uncomfortable feeling as if someone were watching me. I looked left, right–and nothing. It seemed kind of suspicious–in a crowded supermarket, wherever I looked, there was, well–nothing. On checking out, I had way more money than I needed. I awkwardly sorted through the bills for something less than a C-note. I tried not to sweat and adopted the bored, slightly bovine detachment of the average weekly supermarket shopper. It worked. The cashier didn't look twice at me. She continued to talk on her cellphone tucked into the crook of her neck while she made goo-goo eyes at a bag boy pushing a cart out of the store for a little old lady: a twig-thin crone in a paisley-patterned housecoat who looked three heartbeats away from a defibrillator.

I glanced through the store's front window as the cashier finished ringing me up. The entire parking lot was clearly visible and I found the Caddy without difficulty. I heard the muffled slam of the trunk and saw someone step back from the rear of the car, merging quickly and seamlessly with the crowd of shoppers approaching and exiting the store. *Ah-ha!* I thought. *Someone just took delivery of something.*

Dumping the grocery bags in the back seat as instructed, I headed out the same route I came. All that money must have gone to my head because I didn't even notice the lion-like purr beneath the hood of the Caddy. I wondered if whoever opened the trunk had taken delivery or made an exchange. The desire to see if I was right became overwhelming. Then I had an idea. I noticed a construction site on the right and pulled over in an adjacent vacant lot. I got out of the Caddy and checked the tires as if I were checking for a flat. Left side front, rear, right side front, rear. I opened the trunk to check for the spare tire and stood in front of the open trunk, hands on my hips like I was looking for a jack. I even stamped my foot and swore - and noticed a flat paper bag had replaced the fat plastic sack with all the money. *Ah-hah!* I thought to myself again. A rueful grin threatened to spread across my face, but I quelled it in time.

Gingerly, I opened the paper bag and saw pictures of pretty young women. I flipped through them quickly and paused with a cold tingle in my gut. There was a snapshot of Tracey, sitting in her front yard on a sand chair. It wasn't a very good picture. She was wearing a two-piece swimsuit–not even a bikini. But it was she, all right. I could tell by the haircut and her face was clearly visible. I replaced the photographs and closed the trunk, just in time to hear a car pull up behind me, and the muted squeal of brakes. The cold tingle in my gut became an icy lump. I turned around, hoping I didn't look too nervous. Inside the car was the guy I'd seen lounging beside the black Jag outside of Knott's. Same guy I'd seen at Geoffrey's. Same guy I'd seen a little too much of lately. Mr. Smith. The Jag sat behind the Caddy, its twelve-cylinder engine thrumming powerfully. It was dusty and needed a wax job, but those wide high-performance tires looked new and probably cost five hundred a pair. After a second, Mr. Smith got out and walked over to me, his gait unhurried, but purposeful. He had left the Jag's engine running.

He took his time walking towards me. Same height and build as my brother Ed. His right hand was clenched in a fist or held a small cellphone.

"Got a flat, miss?" he asked. His raw, whispery voice wasn't helpful or even particularly friendly; it sounded insinuating and suspicious. He had a British accent, but not the smooth, precise tones of Oxfordshire you hear with English actors in old late-night movies. It was flat, harsh and reminded me of New England Patriots fans who'd vacation at the Fish Camps and watch the game at Okefenokee Swamp bar if the Pats were playing the Fins that weekend. He wore a weathered black leather bomber jacket, black jeans, and dusty square-toed black leather Frye boots. A black t-shirt with blood red trim completed his ensemble. I noticed a large diamond stud in his left ear as he swept a shock of straight black hair behind his ear. *Straight*, I thought, like my brother Ed's hair.

"No," I said, "Thanks. I'm fine. I thought I ran over a nail or something, but everything looks okay."

His narrow black eyes never left me. "Why'd you look in the boot then?"

"Boot?"

He pointed to the trunk.

"Oh–trunk. I wanted to make sure there was a spare. You know–just in case."

He mulled this over for a second and seemed satisfied, because he relaxed a little and said, "Then you'd best get where you're goin', luv. It's not safe around here for ladies who stop on the street."

"Okay, sure. Thanks." I said and with a nonchalant wave I stepped back into the Caddy and drove off slowly, although, if I had my way, I would have gunned the damned engine. I glanced in the rear view mirror; Mr. Smith leaned against the side of the Jag, cellphone to his ear.

The Cadillac purred into the driveway and the gate opened for me with a snick. *No announcement necessary this time*, I thought to myself. I pulled up next to the Mir, which had been moved from the swale to the driveway, and a bulky-looking man came out of the side door next to the garage. Maybe this was the guy I had heard on the speaker when I first got there, which seemed so long ago. He wore a black and white polyester print pointy-collared shirt over khakis. Sandals showed bare feet that were too clean and too soft to be Floridian. He had the look of a Northerner, not quite comfortable in Florida gear, but wears it all the same thinking it was the stylish thing to do. He looked like he'd be more comfortable in a three-piece suit with a diamond stickpin and Gucci loafers. With socks. If he had worn a Panama hat, I would have been hard-pressed not to giggle. He moved swiftly for his bulk and, opening the door for me with a flourish, tendered me out of the car with a hand as big as a Honeybaked half-ham. This was the big cheese I saw on the yacht that day.

"Right on time," he said, glancing at his watch.

"Good girl."

He plucked the envelope with the change and receipt from the grocery store off the front seat and carefully counted the remaining money. Removing the receipt, he handed me the envelope with the money.

"That's for being on time." Then he smacked me. Hard. White agony exploded through my skull. I blinked, hard, willing the tears welling up in my eyes not to show. I was shocked speechless by the casual brutality of it, like he was swatting a fly. I heard him say, in the dim recesses of my mind, still reeling from the sting of the slap, "You get any car troubles, you call. You take that money I just gave you and get yourself a cellphone. Go to the mall." He mentioned a specific cellphone store. "Call if you have any trouble."

Taking the envelope out of my hand, he fished in his trousers and found a small golf pencil. Writing the number on the envelope, he handed it back to me and repeated, "Get a phone at the mall, call when you get it. You got any trouble next time, you call." That was it. There wasn't a trace of anger or even annoyance in his voice. He might have been talking about the weather.

After a strangled moment, I looked at him coldly and said, "Who should I ask for?"

"Nobody. Just call the number."

I nodded and collected myself, heading back to the Mir. I tucked the envelope into the center console and slipped into the Mir. I turned the key in the ignition and, hearing the familiar rumble of my own big eight, felt a bit safer. I backed out of the driveway and out down the street. I looked back and saw the gate closing slowly. Tears were freely streaming down my face now, and I reached for a paper towel in the console to clean up before I got back to Geoffrey's. It was five minutes before I realized I was wiping my tears with a twenty. I endured a white-knuckle ride; every few feet I checked the rearview mirror to see if I was being followed. I wasn't, but that didn't make me feel any less vulnerable. I just made straight for Geoffrey's and pulled into the empty parking lot.

I clattered over the parking lot asphalt and across the patio. Geoffrey met me just outside the bar and handed me the promised envelope.

"Call me when you get your cellphone," he said. "I'll need the number as soon as you get it." I nodded. "Just go to straight to the house next week. You don't have to come here anymore. In fact, I'd just as soon you didn't." There were no smiles, nods, or knowing winks now. This was business and I'd just become a little spoke on a big wheel.

"Okay, I'll call you," I said, inwardly astonished at how calm I sounded.

He ducked back into the club and I went back to the Mir. Pulling out of the parking lot, I felt soiled and rotten, like an old deviled egg left out at a picnic for too long. I couldn't wait to get home and have a nice long boiling hot shower. I thought I'd never feel clean again.

Arriving at the Compound, I brought all three envelopes inside. I grabbed some of the good stuff from under the sink, poured a shot and downed it quick. I wasn't shaking nearly so badly then, and I sat on my sofa-foldout-bed and kicked off my shoes, not particularly caring where they landed. Putting my bag down on the bed, I opened the first envelope. A hundred dollars. I opened the second envelope from Geoffrey. A hundred dollars. I opened the third envelope, which contained the change from the supermarket: two-hundred thirty four dollars and sixty-eight cents. I guessed the two hundred was a "sign on" bonus and I'd get what was left over from the shopping trips from that point forward. The cash felt dirty. Blood money. What the hell kind of cellphone did I need for hundreds of dollars?

I peeled off my outfit and stuffed it into the hamper

at the back of the closet. Grabbing a couple of fresh towels and a cold beer, I padded to the bathroom to indulge in a long hot soak in the shower. I immersed myself in the water, spilling some beer in the stall, not caring. I felt the cold liquid slide down my throat as my body burned and pinked in the steamy heat. On exiting the shower, swaddled head-to-butt in fresh, clean-smelling towels, I was feeling a bit more like myself. I curled up on the sofa and finished my beer. Padding to the sink in my Tigger slippers, I downed another shot and fixed a water-back. Stretching out on the sofa, I nuzzled into my pillow and slept.

I dreamed I was in an enchanted jungle. There were macaws and toucans flying overhead, screeching and scolding in a riot of multicolored plumage. As I walked down the jungle path a python in a tree swayed and nodded as I passed by, his large anvil-shaped head ushered me into his domain. A waterfall was a visible beyond, with wild orchids and jungle flowers everywhere. Up ahead, the turquoise glow of the ocean beckoned. Stepping from the cool, musky embrace of the jungle, I emerged onto the warm, sunlit beach. Something was lying in a shallow tide pool, bobbing gently with the roll of the breakers. I moved closer and saw it was the dead Lorikeet, being devoured slowly by a swarm of busy sand crabs. I leaned closer and the face emerged in the sunlight: it was Tracey's.

Chapter Fourteen

I awoke in a cold sweat, toweled off and donned light blue denim cutoff shorts, a clean white tee shirt and flip-flops. I needed to get out of there. I grabbed my fancy "It" bag–well, who the hell cared now, anyway–and slipped behind the wheel of the Mir once again. I opened the windows and drank in the still smell of a dry day by the sea. I was hungry–that struck me as weird, and I had a cellphone to buy.

I drove to Dana's for a sandwich. Silly, but I was going out anyway, so I brought the Mir with me like a snail brings his shell for safety. Stepping into the diner, I glanced around while my memory flipped through the photographs I'd seen. Pitilessly, it selected the photo of Tracey and held it up to me. There she was, by the pool in her two-piece swimsuit, with a self-conscious smile. I felt a little sick. Meanwhile, the real Tracey was happily plying her trade behind the counter and gave me a hearty wolf-whistle as I walked up to the counter.

"Yeah, thanks a lot," I said and ordered up a burger and a coke. I knew I needed to talk to her, but didn't know what to say. Not there, not at that time. She seemed so happy, just being Tracey. Kidding with the customers, flipping food, slinging drinks and quick quips and smiles across the counter. What could I say?

"What time are you off?" I asked her.

"Three o'clock. Wanna go to Pizzzazzz?"

Now *there* was an idea. "Sure! See ya at three–I'll drive."

"What, a block? We'll walk."

I felt panicky. "No, let me drive, hon. Then let's get something gooey and chocolate."

She rolled her eyes in mock ecstasy, "Oooh–Shoes and chocolate? Now, *there's* a girl's dream!"

"I've got an errand to do at the mall," I said, polishing off the last of my burger and sucking in the last of the Coke, making the same nasty slurping sound kids make to annoy their mother.

"What a lady. I don't know–should I go out with you?"

I burped and said, "Why the hell not?"

"Jeez, Stace–take that outside, will you? I don't even want to be in public with you at present."

"Okay, I'll go burp in the mall, that'll please 'em." We laughed and I paid up, tipping generously–what the hell, blood money could be spread around freely. After all, it wasn't like I earned it or anything. I felt a twinge and hoped to hell Tracey wouldn't be paying for that money; things were starting to come together.

The Mir positively wagged its tail all the way to the mall out on Federal. I looked at Local Piece-A-Shit phones; high-tech phones that did just about everything but go to the bathroom and wipe your ass for you; middle-of-the-road phones and then I saw it: a pink bling-bling phone that just screamed at me to take her home. The guy selling her was tall and cute, a nice bonus.

"Can I help you, Miss?" He said, looking at me through tawny hazel eyes. His nametag indicated his name was Gregg. He wore black trousers and a crisp blue short-sleeved shirt, open at the collar. He had the casual, suntanned look of a native Floridian and his barely-noticeable Southern accent confirmed the fact.

"Yes, please," I said, making my voice soft and Southern to match his.

"Let me guess–you're here for a phone. This phone. It's perfect for you. I just did the skin myself."

I looked down and the phone and back up at him through my lashes. "The skin?" I asked.

"Yes, the pink cover and the rhinestone accents. They're Swarovski crystal, you know." He took the phone out and twirled it around. The store lighting made the little phone sparkle and shine. It positively glimmered. He beamed down at me. I was in love.

The phone was perfect for me. More money than I would have paid on my own, but as I took the cash out of the envelope to hand to Gregg, his hand brushed against mine. I thought I felt a spark ignite between us.

"I'm off at six. Would you maybe like to have drinks and dinner later? I'll show you all about the phone—you can do a lot with it."

I agreed and he said he'd call me on my new number. "Well," I quipped, "talk about having my number from the get-go," and we both laughed. It shook the webs out of my head a little.

"See you later!" he called after me as I left the store. "I mean that! I'll call you!"

The Mir heard me hum a little as we headed back to Dana's to snag Tracey and hit Pizzzazzz. She was ready, willing, and able when I got to the diner, but still in waitress duds.

She took me up on her offer to drive her home for a quick change of costume and we arrived at the shoe store in about a half hour.

I found a pair of clear plastic retro platform hotties suspended on four-inch stiletto heels, festooned with multi-colored hearts on the heel and toe. Tracey snagged a cool pair of high-heeled black suede boots, which cost plenty, but showed off her legs to the city limits. It was too damned bad we weren't the same size–I'm bigger. So, I bought a pair of those boots, too, and we agreed to call each other if we ever went out together to make sure we wouldn't look like Ozzie and Fozzie from Okefenokee.

With our cool pink Pizzzazzz bags in tow, we slammed out in the Mir to Federal Highway and found an ice-cream parlor Tracey was on friendly terms with. I ordered the Peanut Butter Fudge Supreme Sundae with all the bells and whistles. Tracey had the classic hot fudge sundae, but with chocolate instead of vanilla thank-you-very-much. We talked about shoes, guys, and just general girl stuff for a while and then it got serious.

"Hey, Tracey," I started, "I've been meaning to ask you something."

"Anything." She motioned with her long-handled plastic spoon.

"What happened to you after that shit with Vinny?"

She wiped her mouth daintily with a cheap paper napkin and took a sip of ice water.

"Well…" she said, slowly and thoughtfully.

"Hey, if I'm prying…"

"No, not really… after all, I *did* screw up, sending you to Geoffrey's without saying anything much. I should have warned you off the place," she said.

I crossed my eyes and gave her a hokey Evil Eye. She snorted with laughter, nearly spitting her ice water all over me. After a second, she wiped her eyes and daubed at her mouth again, then took a spoonful of her sundae.

"Okay," she said, "it's pretty simple. I realized I was in trouble. After I got out, I went to AA, found a sponsor, and stopped falling in love with drunk men." We both laughed.

"Been there, done that," I said.

"Tell me more…" she urged.

"Uh-uh," it was my turn to wave my spoon at her. "Later. You first."

"All right, I wound up in AA and Al-Anon and it was the best time of my life."

"Really?"

"Yeah, really. It was free. Those private hospitals

cost a fortune."

I nodded. I'd seen enough on both sides. There had been more than a few mornings after when I wondered if I maybe have benefited from a meeting or two, myself. But somehow, I always managed to avert disaster. Some of my friends weren't so lucky over the years.

"Okay, so…" I prompted her.

"Okay, so… I've been clean for a few years now. I'm not seeing anyone presently, although I date from time to time. Haven't found that special someone yet, but I'm more hopeful than I have been. So, what about this Gregg?"

"Well, I don't know, for sure," I said, "but he's tall and cute and he has a job."

We both laughed.

"And I don't know the first thing about him other than he sold me a phone and we're having drinks and dinner tonight."

"Be careful, okay?"

"Yeah…" We faded off into silence, polishing off our sundaes. "So," I asked, "what if you run into Vinny again?"

"I'd run like hell," she said.

"Promise?"

"Yeah."

"Swear to it."

"Yeah, okay… what's up?"

I didn't have the courage to tell her. Maybe if I did, things would have turned out differently, but I just didn't have the heart.

"Nothing," I said. "Just from what you've told me he's bad business."

She nodded fervently. "Boy, is he ever."

"Geoffrey is, too."

"Oh, he's not so bad." Tracey shrugged and took a sip of her water.

"Yeah? How so?"

"He's on the fringes... a wannabe. He hangs out with those guys, but doesn't have the guts to go through with what they do." She grinned briefly. "He's a wuss and anyone with half a brain would know the difference between a real hardass and Geoffrey."

Yeah, I thought. Tell me about it. The guy didn't even want me back in his club after I'd survived Vinny's.

"Okay," I said. "I'll go with that. He can't even handle his girls so well. He had one in there... a real dragon lady."

Tracey nodded. "Dianna?"

"You know her?"

"That's his girlfriend. She's always angling for a bigger fish, but Geoffrey's the best she's been able to land, lately."

Maybe that's why Geoffrey didn't want me hanging around the club.

"Dianna's got four kids by three different guys and if she makes Geoffrey the daddy of number five he'll be stuck for the whole bundle."

I thought of Dianna wearing an apron, surrounded by five wailing brats. Somehow, I didn't see it and shuddered, "Jeez... I hate women like that. Makes you feel sorry for the kids."

"Hey, you got kids?" Tracey asked.

I scowled at her. "Bite your *tongue*, woman."

"Me neither, but my sister does–up north. And she's all by herself, you know? If she could get a guy... well, it's a way out. And if getting knocked up is the way to do it..."

I nodded grimly. I'd gone to school with girls like that. Pregnant at 16, married at 17, divorced at 19 and three kids by the time they're twenty and no man. "Yeah."

"If you get the guy early enough, he'll have a sense of responsibility."

"Yeah, maybe–but later on? There's no guarantee he'll stick around."

Tracey shrugged. "There's no guarantees in life, period."

I sighed. "Don't I know it. Well, I've got to get going." I looked at my watch.

"Yeah–hot date." Tracey grinned.

"Anyways… we'll see, he hasn't even called yet," I said, grinning back. We paid up and left.

On the drive back, I tried to seem casual as I asked Tracey, "Look, if you see anything that looks like Vinny, you'll run, right?"

"What's with all this Vinny business?" Tracey gave me a sidelong glance, "You meet him or something?"

I backpedaled, "Well…" and I couldn't bring myself to lie to her so I did the next best thing and offered up a half-truth, "maybe I saw him at Geoffrey's that one night, but I don't know," I said to get her off track.

"Yeah, maybe," she said. "But I didn't know him to go out much, unless it was with the Captain."

The Captain? I briefly thought of my Captain at the Compound. Could she have meant *him?*

"Yeah," I said, gripping the steering wheel tightly to cover my surprise. "Just run, okay?"

"Sure," she said. "I'll run."

We pulled up to her place and she asked me in for tea. I wanted to, but time was short and I had to get going. I begged off, promising next time for sure and headed home.

My new phone rang and Gregg asked me if I'd be ready at eight. I said sure, then thought–*shit!* I was supposed to call Geoffrey and the other guy after I got the phone. I waited until I got home and unpacked my Pizzzazzz bags, keeping the new boots safely tucked in their box and openly admiring the new platform hotties I was planning on wearing that night.

I dialed the number on the envelope. After two rings, there was a click. "Yeah?" a gruff voice answered.

"This is Stacey." I said.

Dead silence.

I said again, "This is Stacey."

"Yeah, I know," said the voice. "Don't call back."

I hung up, puzzled. Staring at the phone, I decided to call Geoffrey.

"It's gonna be a great night at Geoffrey's!" a young female voice chirped. "How can I help you?"

"Um, Geoffrey, please?"

"He's busy–you want to call back or leave a number?"

I left my name and number, figuring I was done with the whole business. At least I'd gotten a cellphone out of the deal, not to mention a couple hundred bucks for my trouble and one good smack. It didn't seem worth it, I thought. I touched my cheek where I'd been slapped, feeling a ghost of the original sting. I reddened just thinking about it. There was a big ocean and a beach just outside my door and I thought about blowing Gregg off and hanging on the beach, listening to a Tribal Drum Healing Circle that assembled there every night to chant and pray. Then again, Gregg had my number and it could be fun, I thought.

Gregg called just a moment later, while I was still looking at the phone and wondering what the hell was going on.

"So, how do you feel about burgers?" he asked.

"I had one for lunch."

"Not *this* burger," he replied. "Dress casual, okay? I'll pick you up at eight. I know where to find you, but if I get lost, I've got your number."

"Yeah, you do."

"Something wrong?"

"Oh, nothing, just a little distracted getting ready, I guess."

"Okay–well, put on your party-hearty clothes and we'll go out."

A twinge of discomfort went through my veins as we hung up. "I know where to find you," he had said. Okay, I had to give him my address for the cellphone application, but it was still a little presumptuous. He could have asked and, for a moment, I thought to call him back and offer to meet him, taking The Mir instead of getting picked up. But I shrugged it off, discounting the uneasy feeling as residue from earlier and told myself to be happy, no worries. I had a date, he was cute, he had a job *and* a car.

I freshened up, fussed with my hair a little and decided I was definitely in need of more blonde streaks to feel at home down here. That would be something to talk to Tracey about. With her dark good looks she hadn't fallen into the I'm-in-Florida-so-I'd-better-be-blonde trap. But with my mousy dishwater hair, I figured a little more blonde couldn't hurt. Not a lot and in just the right places. I settled on stonewashed jeans with a little moss green tank top, which made my eyes look greener than their everyday hazel. The top must have shrunk when I washed it at the Bee-Kleen, because I was just about hanging out all over. *What the hell*, I thought; he'll think it's sexy. I thought it was too tight, which made me annoyingly self-conscious. More *Vinny or Geoffrey Residue*, I thought and poured myself a beer to relax.

Two beers and a shot later, just before eight o'clock, I put on my new platform shoes and tried not to fall off of them. I teetered a bit then regained my balance. When you're on the short side–not like Tracey, but still no model–you learn to walk in high-heels real young and you have to train yourself not to wobble because it looks stupid. It's a skill, not a talent and can be mastered with enough practice. I hoped I wouldn't be asked to dance, though. Walking steadily was just about manageable. I walked around the bungalow a little to get used to the height and feel of the new shoes.

I managed a passable strut down the alley by the bank next door to avoid marching through the courtyard of the Compound. I stood behind the bungalow, next to a row of dirty gray metal garbage cans which I hoped wasn't a harbinger of my date. Even so, howls and wolf-whistles from the guys in the Compound, the Captain included, found me, so there was no peace.

"Stacey's got a *date!*" someone sang out.

"Woo-hoo! The lady is hot to trot!" Another country heard from. The U.N. General Assembly had nothing on the hot air blowing off from this bunch. Still, it *was* nice to have a Fan Club.

With a wink and a wave, I confidently strolled into the parking lot proper, a few minutes late, to–nothing, except Edmond strolling out casually right after my glorious arrival at the garbage cans, cool beer in hand.

"Stood up?" he asked, a shade too innocently.

"No," I said, "it's his first time here."

Edmond opened his mouth to reply, but I was saved by the bell, literally. My cellphone rang and I nearly broke a nail whipping it out of my handbag.

"You ready?" Gregg's voice asked.

"Yeah, I am," I said with open relief.

"I'm here." A sleek, shiny late-model black BMW convertible pulled up beside us, spinning a fancy half-turn to stop with the passenger door just six inches from my hip.

The passenger window was down and I could see Gregg smile as he leaned over to open the door for me. "At your service, pretty lady" Gregg said gallantly. He wore jeans that fit him just right, faded a little, but not ripped up, what looked to be a pair of new Nikes, and a comfortable-looking navy blue short-sleeved Izod alligator shirt. He smelled real good, too, not like the guys I knew who bathed in Brut and called it a date. He was clean-shaven and fresh and didn't look like he'd worked a full day, unlike me who, most days, felt as if I'd been hit by a tractor trailer after hauling ice, changing sinks, and exchanging clever repartee with the garden variety of drunks of both sexes at the bar.

I smiled at Edmond as if to say, *"See? Told you."* and half sat, half-fell into the small bucket seat of the Beemer.

Edmond threw up his hands in mock-despair. "I'm licked!" he said. "When the lady has a date, the lady has a *date!*"

"Friend of yours?" Gregg asked.

"Maybe," I said. He grinned and threw the Beemer into gear; a second later, we were roaring off down the A-1-A. I threw a wave to Edmund over my shoulder.

There is something to be said for cruising down an ocean road in an open car at a bit more than the legal speed limit. I loved the feel of the wind in my hair and the sound of soft surf not far beyond. We stopped at a red light in a central tourist district and I realized that, for once, *I* was the hot girl with the hot guy in the hot car. It might be for just a night, but what a night it was going to be, I hoped.

He turned on some smooth jazz and I promptly switched the radio to classic rock. He smiled.

"I prefer that, but I wanted to please you…"

"This pleases me just fine." Brilliant repartee, yes? "So, where are we going?"

"You said you liked burgers."

"Well, I said I had one for lunch."

"Okay, so I'll take you for one for dinner."

Visions of the local fast food emporium danced through my head.

"But this is beyond a burger," he continued. "You'll see."

We drove a very long time, talking about this, talking about that. It was actually relaxing. I tried to think about the last time I had been on a real date. I thought it was most likely at my junior prom. Ed had a buddy in my class into dealing drugs for him. Ed was going to help him unload the stuff at the prom, but his buddy didn't have a date, so I got to go. I got a new pink dress for the occasion at a real boutique in West Palm Beach and a pair of ancient pink Manaolo Blahnik shoes at a consignment store in Boca. This was my first encounter with high-end designer shoes and the love affair began. The shoes cost almost as much as the dress and the whole outfit, come to think of it, just slightly less than The Mir. Even though the shoes were old, the dress was new and as the beneficiary of Ed's "generosity," I was lifted to Cloud Nine instantaneously.

Never mind that I spent most of the night alone and watched Ed and his buddy wheel and deal in the corner next to the restrooms. Ed's date and I played The Wallflower Game and wondered if we'd get a chance to dance before they took down the balloons and crepe paper in the high school gym. She looked as if she'd eat her heart out. I knew better and I was eating my own heart out, besides. I didn't care so much about dancing with any guy in particular. I just wanted to step out on the dance floor in my Manolos.

Afterward, we went to some bar with a few of the older kids. A group of us girls hung out together and we actually had a pretty good time. We drank a few beers and danced to some old Patsy Cline and Louis Armstrong records. We kissed the guys a little. Some of the kids, maybe, fooled around, but Ed watched his buddy like a hawk, so as he didn't get fresh with me. Not that I wished he had—ewww. After a couple of hours, it was time to go. Since then, I'd enjoyed a few one-hit-wonders, none particularly memorable. A couple of times, I'd gone to bed at two with a ten and woke up at ten with a two. That about summed up my dating experience in old Okeechobee. A few drunks would try to grope me at the bar after I was leaving my shift, but they were simple to handle: push them off and they'd hit the dirt. Literally. I'd just leave them there. Most of them would just go back to the wifey in the morning after they'd slept it off. There was one guy, however, but I slammed my mind shut on that memory, very quickly.

This was a *real* date and I reveled in it. Gregg brought me back from my stroll down memory lane by telling me about himself. He was Florida born and bred like me, had gone to a local junior college, unlike me. He made so much money at the cellphone company he said the hell with school and worked full time. He loved selling cellphones and believed it was a real "ground floor" opportunity. He had an apartment and a Beemer and he was looking at buying his own condo in the near future. To me, he was a king.

I crossed my legs in the bucket seat and lead in towards him. "Do you have a special lady?"

"Not for a while. Now, you," he looked over at me, "that guy back at your apartment. Is he your boyfriend or anyone I have to worry about shooting me, maybe, when I bring you home?"

I shook my head no and at just that moment the "Don't Worry, Be Happy" tune by Bobby McFerrin chose to come on the radio. I started singing softly and bopping around a little, using the tight ride of the Beemer to bump into him gently now and again. He started singing along, bumping back and we enjoyed a long, leisurely drive down the A-1-A.

Gregg turned into a funky little place called LeTub. We passed under a jungle canopy to enter the restaurant, which reminded me a little of my enchanted dream jungle but without the less pleasant aspects. We were shown to a cozy, weathered wooden booth under some sea grape trees. It was packed and we were lucky to get seated. I wondered if Gregg had greased the palm of the hostess. If he did, I hadn't seen it. Tables were butt-up against one another, but perhaps because each "booth" was enclosed in foliage, there was a feeling of seclusion from the other people in the restaurant. We settled in comfortably and ordered a couple of beers and an appetizer of smoked fish dip.

"What shall we drink to?" I held up my beer.

He shrugged, "I don't know," and he thought a moment. "To sunset and new beginnings tonight." We clinked beer bottles and the sun set over the Intracoastal.

"So, where in Florida were you born and bred?" I asked.

Gregg shrugged. "Down the Keys." It's a given that Keys people are pretty much envied for coming where they're from, but once you know the ins and outs of anyplace, it's not all that. I thought the little tourist girls must have been crawling all over him in Season, like now.

Even I was a little impressed though. "So, why leave the Keys, anyway?"

Gregg leaned closer to me and lowered his eyes, "Depends on which Key you come from. Key West is okay, but little keys, like Big Pine, Cudjoe and them, well, you either have to travel down to Key West or up to Tavernier or Marathon to make anything happen." He took a pull on his beer. "Opportunities were limited in the Keys. But there's a lot of new building going on, that's a shame, but if I keep to it and work hard, I'll come back and maybe have my own cellphone store. Then I'd have a real ground floor opportunity–first cellphone store in the Keys, make a nice living and be with my kin, besides."

"What does your family do? Down in the Keys, I mean," I asked.

"They used to run a little shop. Then Mom and Dad split. She moved back to Miami." He pronounced it the old native way, *Mi-am-uh.* "Dad stayed and was pretty good at fixing boats and this and that. So, he's down there."

"Any brothers or sisters?" I inquired.

"Nope, I'm a lonely only." he sighed as if he'd been asked that question a million times and was sick of answering.

"What about you, pretty lady? You got any brothers and sisters?"

I admitted to having a brother named Ed, that's it, and shifted the topic to life in Lake Okeechobee and around the fish camps, keeping it light and sweet. It's a different life than the Keys–more hard-bit and less touristy. Of course, I thought wistfully, I had nothing to go back to and no family I wanted to be close to. He must have caught my thought and asked me what was wrong. I blew it off and was saved by the waitress telling us good burgers take forty minutes to make and do we have the time because she didn't appreciate anyone bitching her out for waiting so long. We told her we had the time. I thought the burgers must be pretty special because the service certainly wasn't. People didn't come from miles around to be upbraided by a surly waitress–not unless they were professional masochists.

The burgers were *that* good and the beers ice cold.

Of course, drinking beers makes you piss a quart after drinking a pint. I got up to use the ladies room. When I got back, Gregg had paid the tab and the table was seated with another couple. I looked around for Gregg and saw him scrunched down next to the cigarette machine, talking on the phone. I backed off and listened.

"Yeah, it's under control, boss," he said. "I've got her covered." He flipped his tiny phone closed with a skillful flick of the wrist.

I walked up beside him and asked, "Who's covered?"

"Oh, that. Nothing. Just a tricky customer at the store." He tucked his little flip-phone in the pocket of his jeans and motioned to the pool table next to the bar.

We shot a couple games of pool. I was so bad, he beat the pants off me, so to speak, and the platform hottie shoes I was wearing didn't exactly add to the accuracy of my shots. I started to relax. We talked to some locals, some tourists, the bartender, and even the waitress who thanked us again for not bitching her out because the burgers took so long and you wouldn't believe the *nerve* of those demanding tourists as she entertained us "fellow Floridians" with a wink and a few hysterical stories. Make up your own, and they usually get funnier with more beer. We ended up talking with basically anybody and everybody at the bar when we had one-for-the-road before we headed home.

One thing about Florida: if you're a local and know the lay of the land, it's a pretty easygoing state. You can have dinner, a few drinks and even a little fun; and, if you're not an asshole driver or hit with a roadblock, it's smooth sailing going home.

Gregg was totally cool behind the wheel and we drove north past the Compound up the A-1-A. We stopped in Deerfield Beach and had a stroll in the moonlight along the boardwalk. We paused at an overlook where he kissed me gently and I kissed him back. After a bit, things became a little more passionate; we headed back to the Beemer before things got too much out of hand too soon.

He drove me home and asked me what sort of things I like to do, where I worked; the usual stuff. I told him pretty much the truth, omitting my passion for shoe shopping, of course. I also left out some of the more unpleasant stuff from my past, and tried to think like hell of things we could do together. Fishing seemed to hit a chord in him and we discussed a future fishing date.

Walking me to my door, he gently took the key to the bungalow from my hand and opened the door for me. He kissed me goodnight, almost chastely in contrast to the passions we'd felt rising on the beach, and promised he'd call. I asked him to call me when he got home safe and he did. We chatted a bit, and he promised, again, that he would give me a call.

I told him I'd hold him to his promise and went

inside. Tucking my Tigger slippers underbed, I spent a safe
night in dreamless slumber until the next morning.

Chapter Fifteen

Sunday! People went to church, did their shopping, went to Mall-Wart for cheap plastic crap (according to one funny tee-shirt I'd seen), or to Big Lots for even cheaper shit. Me, I had to go to work. No time even for a Dana's coffee and muffin. Besides, they were closed Sunday mornings. I slammed a quick beer, munched on some cheese and headed out the door for Sparky's to work my shift.

It was raining–a cold, nasty, unforgiving rain that soaked me to the bone by the time I got to work. I shook off the droplets on entering and got everything warm, clean, welcoming, and ready to go. Then the boss walked in and there I was–looking like a drowned rat.

"Morning Stacey," Rick Sparks said.

"Good Morning, sir," I cautiously replied and slicked back my hair into a simple ponytail. I hoped he wouldn't notice the soggy patches on my Polo shirt.

"This your first Sunday?" he asked.

"Yes, sir."

"Well, you'll get a lot of strippers, a lot of lowlifes, and thank God it isn't football season or you'd a lot more to deal with."

"Thank you, sir."

He went to check on the kitchen staff then swung around before he reached the door, "How're things with Rick?"

"Sir?"

"Rick. You know, he says you've got quite a thing going."

"Oh. Rick." I turned to the register and started

counting my bank.

"Well, whatever, Stacey. That's your business, but you're doing a good job."

"Thank you, sir."

But he hadn't waited for my reply before heading into the kitchen.

I'd sliced enough limes for a week and prepped enough celery for a hundred Bloody Marys when Ricky sauntered in at noon.

"Hi, Stacey. Glad to see you're holding down the fort."

I mumbled something unintelligible and mentioned Rick Sparks was in the kitchen.

"Oh, Rick," he muttered, then smiled like the proverbial canary.

"Yeah, Big Rick," I said as he turned towards me, "Little Ricky, you've got some 'splainin' to do," I added in a phony-baloney Lucille Ball imitation-Ricky Ricardo accent.

"Oh, that…" He was still grinning.

"Yeah… that," I said, flatly.

"Well, I thought if he thinks you're my girlfriend he won't give you any trouble."

"Yeah. Well, what if I'm not your girlfriend?"

He looked at me with a mock-hurt expression. "You mean you're not my girlfriend?"

"No," I stated. "I'm not."

"Well, not now."

"Well, not ever." Then I realized this was nothing, but a big joke for him. Fun-ny.

"We'll see."

I sighed–there was no use. I left him smirking and humming behind the bar to get some ice.

We tended the bar like a well-oiled machine that afternoon. If one of us mixed drinks, the other filled sinks, and vice versa. We worked our tills, bucketed our tips, played with our patrons, and snuck a shot or two here and there in-between. By the end of shift, we were righteously buzzed and our pockets were lined. It was a good day on the job.

Ricky asked if he could walk me home and I politely declined, stating I could stumble off by myself. We parted friends and I went home to a hearty *"hail-fellow-well-met-got-a-beer?"* from the Captain. Happy to accommodate him, I brought us both a cold one. We sat together and I recounted the day's events. He found the old dirty jokes funniest and would rock back and forth when he laughed, holding his sides. Make up your own jokes; they're all the same to me.

I regaled him with a tale about the stripper from the second-class titty bar down the street who comes in first thing before her shift to get toasted to deal with the job. The fact that she weighs two-fifty plus doesn't seem to daunt her from being a stripper, so she takes her panties off for a living all the same. He regaled me with the tales of strippers he'd seen on hours, off hours, and everything in-between. It's amazing what captains can get away with on the boats when the owners aren't looking.

Eventually, I broke out some of the good stuff and we toasted one another, ourselves individually, and life in general.

Dhani returned home and so did Edmond. We spent the night grillin' and chillin' and deciding what was to become of the world under the influence of a mighty buzz. We decided that the end of the world as we know it would be a whole lot better if we were buzzed, so we opened another six-pack and toasted the world.

After a while, I went home, showered, got into my sleepy tee and watched a little TV. I fell asleep on the sofa without folding it out, and was none the worse for wear on Monday morning. I didn't have to go to work, so I slept in, took my wash to the Bee-Kleen at about noon and had a beer and a slice with Charlie at the bar at Stinger's.

"How're ya doin' girlie girl?" he asked when I entered what he considered to be his inner sanctum.

"Fine, just fine... and yourself?" I asked, feeling accepted at last.

"Fair to middlin'," he replied.

"Oh, yeah? What's up?"

"Things are gettin' strange here. Cops in 'n' out, rich folks where they're not supposed to be, regular folks not being where they're usually at, buildings comin', buildings goin'–it's all changin'."

"Speak English, Charlie–it's all I understand."

"Well, girlie-girl, if I was to tell you that some rich shit was buyin' up all the land and plannin' for Pompano to be one o' them rich-shit hangouts, what wouldya say?"

Slipping into his own lingo of native Floridian, I replied, "Dunno, can't call it."

"Well, girlie-girl, there's money that talks sayin' the beach is gonna come to an end and those that are with it are gonna hafta go, too."

I bought Charlie a beer. "Tell me more," I said.

"Well, there's rich folks comin' in here and talkin' and goin' out there and buyin' and sooner than later there's gonna be a shakedown and I'm not talkin' about boats."

"What, you mean rich guys like Vinny?"

"No, out of towners, like the husband of that lady in the fancy apartment that got killed."

"Who, Loretta? I thought she just died–natural causes, you know..." I drifted off, my finger swirling a meaningless doodle out of dewdrops on the bar.

"Yeah, Loretta. Talk is that it just looked like a stroke. May have been something else altogether." He shrugged and turned his back to me to polish up some bottles–the bartender's universal signal that the conversation is closed.

"But why are you telling me? I've just come in here

to do my laundry and time and again we've shared a drink."

"Because girlie-girl, you're of this place–"

"Pompano? Well, nooooo." I squirmed.

"You're Floridian, aren't you?"

"Yeah, so...?"

"You're one of the few I can talk to. I hear a lot. Can't talk to many. You, I can talk to."

"What part of Florida you from?"

"Me? I'm from New Jersey."

I sat there a minute and let the wheels turn. "So, why are you telling me? Why would I care?"

"Because I think you care about people, you care about Florida, you care about what's right. But that's only what an old man thinks, not maybe what is."

"Charlie..."

He said nothing. He just went about polishing glasses, wiping down bottles, and setting me up with another when I returned from putting the clothes in the dryer. I sat waiting for more and received nothing in return. When my clothes were done, I paid up and gave him a tip. He grabbed my wrist as I laid my money on his bar rail.

"I'll give *you* a tip, girlie-girl and this one's not for nothin'," he said, taking my money from my hand and putting a business card in its place. "You're gettin' in a bit deep, I hear. Call Dan Gowan in Fort Lauderdale if you want."

"Dan Gowan?"

"Yeah, you met him on the beach–the day that young girl died."

I shuddered, tucked the business card in my bag and left the bar to pick up my laundry. For the rest of the day, I felt cold and dreary, even though I went to the beach, soaked up some sun, had barbeque with the crew and curled up later with my Tigger slippers safe underbed.

Something nagged at me all night, but I didn't put it together until dawn and then I put it out of my mind as useless imaginings–"stinkin' thinkin'" some circles would call it.

Tuesday was dead at Sparky's. Football was over and the 'Fins hadn't done much. Sports were generally dead and the local teams weren't all that great that year. The Heat was heating up, but at night and other than a chance game of golf on the tube, there were 500 channels and nothing to watch. I was able to manage the shift alone, since little Ricky called in drunk and I was happy to keep the measly pennies the patrons of this fine establishment left me to myself. The rest of the week passed uneventfully and, after a while, I got lulled into a false sense of security due to the humdrum day-to-day routine I lived. Ricky would show up late, if at all, everybody behaved themselves and the week passed.

Gregg called one night just to see how I was doing– that was all. Then on Thursday, he called to line something up for Saturday.

Other than visiting Tracey at Dana's for my morning muffin and coffee, I had forgotten about the previous week's adventure until Saturday morning rolled around again. At ten a.m. my cellphone rang.

"Eleven's the time, you know where to be." The caller said, simply, and hung up.

Sighing, I shrugged into a shower and shrugged into some clothes, not taking quite as much care as I had the previous week, and shrugged The Mir down the A-1-A to the fancy white house with the fancy white iron gates which opened to grant me access to the fancy yellow Cadillac parked in the drive. I was a minute and a half late.

Vinny came out wearing black slacks with a razor-sharp crease, and a powder blue golf shirt. Sleek black Bally loafers tap-tapped softly on the driveway. He stonily looked down at his watch, probably a Rolex–it was big, gold and very flashy, then looked back at me, arching one eyebrow.

Before I stepped out of the Mir, I thought of my warning to Tracey and choked down the urge to slam the Mir in reverse and bolt like a bat out of hell. But the casual brutality of Vinny's demeanor when he was crossed, made me unsure of myself so I got out of the car, closed and locked the door quietly and walked over to where he stood on the driveway, next to the Caddy. I tried to look as meek as the proverbial Lamb of God. I focused on his face averting my eyes, but his eyes had the cold look of flint. He smiled at me, but the smile didn't go to his eyes. If anything, he bared his teeth and that's what passed for a smile on Vinny.

"This will take an hour in the store," he said very quietly, "no more, no less," as he handed me the keys and an unsealed nondescript white business envelope. I nodded in understanding and took the Caddy out for a spin. Vinny went back into the house and I snuck a peek inside the envelope, and then folded it shut. It wasn't as thick as the previous week, but it was still substantial, however, the list was a bit shorter, too.

The Caddy purred under my feet. I wondered who else had enjoyed the luxury of this car, and decided it was none of my business. I couldn't help but wonder how many "errand girls" came before me and what happened to them. I pulled slowly and comfortably into the same supermarket parking lot I had been to before.

I remembered last week's admonishment, kept my head down, my eyes on my cart, the list, and the supermarket shelves, and was happy things were starting to look a little familiar to me when I filled up the cart with groceries. As before, there was plenty of money and plenty left over after checking out.

I drove back to the big house on the ocean and carefully slung the Caddy next to the Mir. No stops this time or wayward slaps. Vinny met me at the car, opened the door gallantly and, almost with a flourish, handed me out of the car very gently. I was surprised how gentle he could be, having been intimate with the wallop he could wield. It was not necessary this time and he simply handed me the envelope after carefully checking the change against the receipt with a brusque admonishment to return next week–same time, same place, same station. I nodded and slunk into the Mir, cash in hand, thinking that two-thirty-three forty was a bit steep for a grocery trip. Didn't these guys know they could get it cheaper elsewhere? I wondered, not for the first time, what the hell was I getting into and remembered Charlie's words; I was getting in "a bit deep," and shuddered.

It was a little after twelve-thirty and I didn't have anything to do until Gregg picked me up at eight. I'd been to Pizzzazzzz, I'd seen Tracey all week at Dana's for breakfast, I didn't feel like working a buzz with the Captain and I was bored out of my skull.

Deciding a little ride in the Mir might be in order to freshen my head, I slipped out onto the A-1-A, watching the white curlicues of the gate close slowly behind me for another week. They almost shut on the butt of The Mir and I got into traffic just in time to avoid a little shark bite from those massive gates.

As I passed a glorious banyan tree, its canopy shading the road, I reveled in my Mir. One thing about having a big eight under you when it's running right: it's like riding a lion. Pompano was lucky for me and The Mir– she hadn't broken down once since I'd been here and then I put the thought out of my mind so as not to jinx myself. The Mir and I headed south on the A-1-A this time, just meandering along, exploring the territory. I landed at Le Tub for lunch and chatted up the waitress Gregg and I had last week. They weren't so busy now and she was much calmer and even friendly.

"Hey, sister, welcome back!" she called and seated me at a primo table under a palm.

Sitting down with me for a hot minute, we exchanged small talk and I ordered one of "those" burgers and a beer.

"Kitchen's slow today, won't be much of a wait," she said, putting the ice-cold mug in front of me. I nodded and smiled.

"So, my name's Stacey–and you are…" I let the question drift into outer space.

"Elaine, honey." She was one of those women who'd probably been on that side of the dinner table for years and everyone was honey, baby, or toots. I wondered what her story was and decided to mind my own business. I finished the awesome burger, paid up and left.

Tummy happily full, I decided to treat The Mir to a meal of high-test gas, so I boogied out to Federal Highway, found a reasonably priced no-brand gas station and filled up. Taking a hard look around the pumps, I saw an old black truck. It wasn't just any old black truck; it was *the* black truck I had seen at Knotts that one morning and that had stopped to help a damsel in distress last weekend. I couldn't see anyone inside, but drove all the way home with one eye over my shoulder, just in case. I wasn't sure I was being followed, but I wasn't sure that I wasn't, either. I'd explored a couple of side roads, but not too many or too far out of the way and I didn't see anyone in back of me, but then again, I'd gone the whole afternoon feeling free as a bird. I pulled into my parking spot at the compound with a distinctly uneasy feeling.

For once, I didn't feel like drinking. Gregg called to confirm our date and time and asked what I wanted to do. I suggested a movie and maybe pizza afterward, hoping to get my mind off things.

Gregg's Beemer pulled up a few minutes ahead of schedule and, since I'd been raised a Southern lady, thank you ma'am, I primped a little more until I thought I looked really hot and sauntered over to his car.

"Wanna date?" I said in my best imitation-hooker purr.

I must've flustered him a little, because I got a smile of appreciation as he loosened up his shirt and shifted in his seat to open the door for me.

"Oof!" I exclaimed, almost falling off my high heels and clumsily slid into the Beemer's low-slung bucket seat. I thought to myself I'd better cut out the morning muffins at Dana's as I felt my jeans pull a little around my butt. Better forget the pizza afterwards, too.

Gregg laughed. "Some date." I laughed back.

"So, what's playing?"

He reeled off a list of the latest and greatest and we decided on a goofy comedy, thinking we could both do with a good laugh. It was nice someone liked the same things as me.

We got soda (diet, me) and popcorn (him) and settled into our seats to enjoy the show. The movie was okay–no Oscar winner for sure, but who cares? The people were pretty and the locations were cool and a few things here and there flipped over, blew up and flew apart unexpectedly. At the end, everyone lived happily ever after and all was right with the world. Just what I needed to see.

"Pizza?" Gregg asked, after the movie.

"Pass–" I said and vowed to myself to get on a health kick first thing in the morning.

"Beer?"

Okay–start fresh Monday, I thought, and agreed to go for a drink. I could feel myself starting to relax in his company. I didn't bother to look around for anyone nor did I care. I wondered what the hell I did, anyway, to merit all this attention and forgot about it as soon as I thought it, wondering where we were going for a cocktail.

We drove down Federal to Commercial and hit this little bar snuggled in a strip mall on the northeast side. It was dark, the seats were low, and the place looked like it had been there forever.

The hostess checked Gregg in, which I thought odd until Gregg explained this was a private club. The hostess assured me anyone could join and gave me a card to sign up.

"Cool place," I said, giving serious thought to signing up and paying the whopping twenty-five bucks it cost to join.

"Yeah," Gregg agreed. "I've been a member since they had a club in South Beach."

"There's more than one of these?"

"There's about four–or there were. One membership gets you into all of them."

I thought that made it about six-and-a-quarter per year per club. I started filling out the card.

"Do you mind?" I looked up at him.

"Hell, no."

Some guys are really funny about a girl going where they hang out. I saw it with Ed. He had a place to hang with his buddies and a place to take his dates, and never the twain should meet. Given a town with two-and-a-half bars (the half-a-bar was in a restaurant, so it didn't really count), a soda fountain, and a few convenience stores, that made it a bit tough on the lady. Ed would give her the bum's rush and hustle her out the door with a promise to meet her elsewhere, later. Maybe he did and maybe he didn't, but whatever happened, that lady didn't frequent the place all that often if Ed was there, unless he brought her. Sometimes, it made for a couple of good catfights, but all in all, most of the chicks were pretty cool. However, I learned always to ask first.

"I could use a little place for my downtime," I said. "This is nice."

We scootched into the low-slung seats–I'd been careful not to fall off my shoes this time–and ordered a couple of whiskies and a light bite. The prices were unbelievable. Two-fifty for filet mignon tips over garlic toast and three-fifty for snails. I opted for steak tips. I thought the snails were a bit pricey because you can grab all the "free" snails you want at night when they're out and about on the sidewalk. Never gave a passing thought to eating them, though.

"I'm glad you like it here," Gregg said. "Is anything wrong? You seemed a bit edgy tonight."

"Not really. I think I've just gained a few pounds."

"Ahhh," he said, like an old Jedi master. "Passed on the pizza, you did."

"My secret revealed, I've gotta lose a few. Enough about me, what's with you?" I said, rapidly changing the subject.

"Work's good, busy, and it looks like camera phones are on the horizon."

We laughed, toasted to camera phones, and our sizzling platters came out right at the end of our first drink. We ordered another round of drinks. The smoky-tasting whiskey was the perfect complement to the rich, full flavor of filet mignon.

"You ever play sports?" I asked. Guys love to talk about sports, especially when it's about their involvement in them. Every game is major-league, every play of heroic proportions.

"A little baseball, football, nothing special."

"You follow anything?"

"Yeah," he said. "Hockey."

"Weird. Some Floridian, you are." We laughed.

He laughed. "We have the Panthers, and tickets are cheap. I'll take you sometime."

Our conversation continued for a bit as he explained the game of hockey to me. I didn't fully understand, but thought it might be fun to go to a game, especially when it started getting sweltering hot outside. All that ice–and I didn't have to chip it apart or lug any of it to a bar.

Afterward, we played a couple of games of Liar's Poker for the bill, I lost, paid up and we left. What the hell, he sprung for the movie. I didn't pay for the membership, though, just tucked the slip in my bag for another day.

He drove me home and, in the back lot behind the Compound, things weren't quite as chaste as our goodnight kiss of the week before. He was fun, I was yielding and we concluded our evening on a completely enjoyable note.

"I'm off tomorrow," he said.

I groaned. "Shit, I'm working."

"'Til what time?"

"Six."

"Want to get together?"

"You asking me for a date, sailor?" I said with my most lascivious grin.

"Something a little more serious, maybe."

"We'll see. Maybe."

"What's wrong?"

"Nothing."

"Just being mysterious, is that it?"

"Maybe." I winked at him. "Give me a call. On my cell. About four."

"Okay," he sighed. "The games women play."

"Not a game, I might be tired after work."

"We could just hang out and watch TV."

"Yeah, maybe."

He sighed. "Okay, you're gonna be difficult."

"Yep."

"I'll call you."

And he didn't.

Chapter Sixteen

Sunday at four, I looked at my cellphone wistfully, wondering if I had done something wrong by acting a little hard to get. In the good old days, when Ed and I were sort of friends, he gave me some advice about handling men. A big tip–according to him, of course–was to blow a guy off from time to time to make him really hot for you. I didn't exactly agree, but then I didn't want to be too easy, either. We had a nice time and I thought I'd see him again, but I wasn't exactly ready to go off the deep end for anyone. I just wanted to stick a toe in the water before I jumped in. So far, the water was pretty warm, but I still wasn't head-over-heels about the whole thing. It was nice, just nice, and I didn't mind leaving it that way for a while.

Given the climate of the compound, I also didn't think it was a good idea to "entertain" quite yet if I didn't want a whole bunch of ribbing and teasing the morning after from the guys. I didn't give a shit, but I didn't want to deal with it, either. They were like a whole bunch of rough-and-tumble brothers, so I thought I'd play the Little Princess just a bit longer. They did look out for me, after a fashion.

Monday and Tuesday I worked, and Wednesday I went fishing off the pier. We enjoyed my catch-of-the-day at the Compound for dinner. Dhani helped me program my cellphone with all my necessary numbers–even Gregg's, but not without a sly sidelong glance and a quick little wink. For once, though, he kept his mouth shut.

Thursday and Friday I worked with Little Ricky. That was my week. The most exciting thing to happen was when a stripper threatened to throw up on the bar. I sent her packing; either to the bathroom or out the door–take-yer-pick, lady. Nothing is worse than cleaning up bar puke. It feels like a whole day is wasted over five stupid minutes, thanks to some moron.

I studiously stayed away from Dana's and the muffins and walked on the beach every morning, so my jeans fit a little better by Friday. Of course, I'm sure giving up cheeseburgers helped, too. I opted for grilled fish sandwiches or salad at work–we got one meal per shift–and that would tide me over, unless someone grilled fish at the Compound and offered it all around. I considered switching to light beer then dismissed the thought as sheer stupidity.

Gregg still hadn't called. Since Saturday was coming up, I thought about it, but not too much. I was thinking more about my "errand" and if there might be a way to play sick and get out of it.

The call came at nine that Saturday morning. "Eleven, and be on time." It was Vinny. I was uncomfortable I had recognized his voice so easily. He hung up before I could say a word. I'm not a wimp, but I'm not stupid, either. So, I fixed myself up, had a cup of coffee, and thought about a shot of whisky to calm my nerves. Not wanting to lose the edge, I gave the shot the go-by and headed out in The Mir looking like an oh-so-upscale hausfrau out to do her weekly gig. It was like a gig, in a way, all an act.

I remembered the smoky taste of the whiskey and chided myself for being so silly. I should have had the shot–then again, maybe not. I was into something, but nothing, so far, had settled to anything concrete. I hoped it wouldn't. I thought about concrete shoes. Then my brain switched gears and I thought back to the whiskey again and the pleasant time with Gregg the week before. A mere week ago I was looking forward to a date. Now, it seemed I had precious little to look forward to, and a precious lot to hold on to. I decided a trip to Pizzzazzz was in order and made up my mind to call Tracey after the morning's supermarket run was finished.

Everything went smooth as silk, for the most part. "Third time's the charm," I thought to myself, smiling cynically. I wondered if I could hook back up with Geoffrey and quit this deal.

I had a little upset in the supermarket–it never rains, but pours. Tracey called me and I lined up the afternoon with her. Little Ricky called and asked if I wanted to hook up for dinner and I said yes. Gregg called, and I blew him off. Vinny called asking if everything was all right, he had called and needed another couple of stops this time, but my line was busy. I said everything was fine, I was just talking to some friends. I could hear him shrugging on the line as he asked me to stop at a certain tobacco store and pick up a box of cigars. He told me the brand. There was also a large liquor order to be picked up at the priciest liquor store in town, then he explained there would be plenty of money for the purchases. Boy, was there ever, and plenty for me as well when I returned, right on time, according to Vinny. "Mr. Smith" lounged against his old black truck parked next to my Mir in the driveway. I still did not dare to ask his real name.

Pocketing the leftover money, as usual, courtesy of Vinny, I backed out slowly using excess caution to steer clear of that old black truck. As I left in The Mir and wondered when the hell I could hook up with Geoffrey and ask for o-u-t, out. No black truck was in the background following me this time, but it had been there in Vinny's driveway when I pulled in with the Caddy. I hadn't stepped out of line, but I still felt the hair on the back of my neck rise when you know someone is watching you from a hidden position.

I thought about Charlie and even Dan Gowan and

wondered how deep I was in. I didn't know anything, but when you're in this deep, ignorance isn't necessarily an excuse. I wanted to keep shut about it, but I wanted someone else's opinion as well.

Totally torn and unsettled, I didn't even think a trip to Pizzzazzz could make it better. I was right.

Tracey was waiting outside the store when I pulled up in The Mir.

"Where the hell have you been?" she asked.

"You tawkin ta me?" I quipped back in a genuine-imitation New Jersey accent.

"Yeah," she said, sounding oddly tense. "I've missed you."

"Sorry, I've been hitting the muffins a bit too hard lately. I had to cut back."

"Okay," she replied, relaxing visibly. "So, let's go shopping!"

"All-rightee then!" I said and we headed into Pizzzazzz.

I couldn't find a damn thing. Everything I liked didn't fit right or wasn't in my size and the stuff in my size wasn't any bargain, or it was just crappy. I couldn't even score a pair of sandals. I had money, I was in Florida, and in one of the best shoe stores I'd ever had the pleasure, no less. What was the world coming to?

"This is not a good day for you, lady," Tracey said, scooping up three dreamy pairs of shoes on sale.

"That's the understatement of the century," I said, eyeing the racks glumly.

Paying for her choice goodies, she turned and said, "Come over for tea. We'll talk." It was an order, not an invitation and I knew better than to decline.

It was a fast five minutes to Tracey's in The Mir. We rode together in uneasy silence.

On entering her pretty little place, all the shit from the day seemed to just melt away. She put the kettle on, motioned me to have a seat near her in the kitchen and busied herself setting up the tea things for us.

"Okay, kiddo," she started, "let's have it. You're not going to talk unless I ask and I'm not going to pry, so we're at a little standstill here."

I nodded.

"So, if I guess it, will you talk about it?"

I nodded again.

"Okay–is it work?"

I shook my head no.

"Is it that guy you met?"

I shrugged.

"Getting warmer... but still not it." Tracey shrugged and shook her head, thinking. She spooned tea into a large tea ball for the pot and said, "One for me, one for thee, one for the pot and one for luck. Maybe I'll luck out and guess what's bugging you."

I shrugged again.

"Jeez, kid, all that shrugging going on with you I'd think you were from Jersey."

She was trying to cheer me up at least, so I smiled wanly.

"Okay–let me keep guessing. Animal, mineral, or vegetable?"

I shook my head, none of the above.

"Person, place or thing?"

"All of the above."

"Bingo! Start with one–the person," and leveled her eyes at me.

It all came out, and not exactly in order, either. The dead Lorikeet at the beach; the night at the police station; the party at Loretta's and Loretta turning up dead shortly after; Kat's mysterious note; hooking up with Geoffrey and my weekly rides to the supermarket in the Caddy. I also mentioned the black truck and "Mr. Smith", the cop, Dan Gowan, Charlie at Stinger's; Little Ricky; big Rick, my "career" at Sparks', and so on. I rattled it off pretty quickly, so by the time I came up for air, the kettle was screaming.

"Jeez! How long have you been down here? A month, maybe six weeks?"

I shrugged. Tracey went into the kitchen to silence the screeching kettle.

"Yeah, I know what you mean," Tracey said as she poured the hot water into the teapot. Turning back towards me, she walked over and sat down. "It'll keep," she nodded at the teapot and sat down. "Anyway, you've started. Now let's take it apart and put it back together. In order."

With the patience of a horse whisperer, she got the whole story out of me, even the part where I found her picture in the trunk of Vinny's Caddy after my first run.

She let out a long, low whistle that would have rivaled the teakettle. For someone like me who usually likes to shut up, I was amazed how much I had released, much of it unplanned, most of it still unorganized in my head.

"Okay," she said, "for starters, I'm going to have to watch my ass."

I nodded.

"Quit that, will you? All that head-bobbing makes you look like one of those little bobbly dolls on the dashboard of a car."

I nodded, one time. Tracey set out the tea and some thin, crispy little lemon coconut cookies to go with it. Snuggling the teapot in a cozy for Chrissakes, she sat down and pulled up next to me, taking a long pull off the tea and motioning for me to do likewise.

Taking her advice, I mumbled through a mouthful of cookie, "So, I've just been confused, and I put on a few pounds, so I stayed away from Dana's muffins this week. I'm sorry."

Waving me off, "It's okay—you're here now, let's figure this out together, but I'm pretty mad you didn't come see me when you saw that picture of me in the trunk of the Caddy. I'm not going to argue with you and someday you'll tell me your reason for holding out." She shrugged and got up, grabbed a pad and pen and sat down again, brushing a few crumbs off her lap and tapping the pad with the pen. "So... what do we know? Let's make a list. I've found that's always helped me."

I nodded. "Where do we start?"

"We'll start with me. I was set up before you. Let's look at the whole cast of characters." Tracey started ticking off names: Vinny, her Captain, Geoffrey, "Mr. Smith" the thuggy looking guy in the black truck, whose name turned out to be Ian, the girls—especially Dianna the Dragon Lady and the Lorikeets, Loretta, Kat, big and little Ricky, the guys in the Compound, Brian Stone, the bartender at Geoffrey's, Gregg, and everyone and anyone we'd come into contact with in the time we'd been here, including Charlie the bartender. I thought that was a mistake to count him in, but she wrote him down, studied the page and said, "What a mess!"

We had drawn circles and connecting lines to the people and it looked like one of those Spirograph drawings kids make, with stars and hearts thrown in for good measure—good, bad, and people of special note.

I agreed.

"Okay, let's try it another way," she licked her thumb, turned the page and drew a line down the middle of the pad and marked one side Tracey—she'd been here first—the other side mine.

Together, we ticked off the names of the people we had in common. We had a laugh over the captains – her captain would never be mine and vice versa. But then again, you never know.

I thought back to the day I drove down. Leaving Tough Luck Lane for more tough luck, I guess. But there was no family and there was no sympathetic librarian to look out for me. Maybe Charlie at Stinger's could be an ally, but it was too early to tell.

We came up with an abbreviated common list.

"So, tell me about Geoffrey. What happened when you got the job?"

I told her about finding him in the freezer, slightly cool to the touch and a bit mussed, but none the worse for wear.

"Okay, so bottom line is, you unlatched the freezer door," Tracey said.

"Yes."

"Do you think somebody could have locked him in there?"

"I didn't at the time." The more I thought about it, the more likely it began to look.

Tracey confirmed it with a grim smile. "Listen, kiddo, with a walk-in box that big, it's unlikely that accidents 'just happen.' The boxes are rigged, so if someone gets stuck in there, there's a trip device and they can get out. Obviously, our dear friend Geoffrey couldn't use the trip switch."

I nodded.

"Chances are, somebody wanted to chill him for something and you just got in the middle of that. He was probably grateful, so he gave you a shot. It didn't work out because of the Dragon Lady. Then you went sniffing around there out of–what? Curiosity? Not good–remember the cat. You didn't know what you were messing around with and maybe I didn't lay it on thick enough. But these are not very nice guys and the chances are good they're keeping an eye on you, too."

"I'm sure of that, but why?"

"Remember the Lorikeet? You went to the cops."

"They came to me! I was there when they found the body!"

"Yeah, and that cop Dan Gowan has been sniffing

around the beach like a dog after a piece of bacon lately."

"I didn't tell him anything. I don't know anything."

"That's not the point. They think you do."

"Who?"

"*All* of them. And you're now here with me. Oh, brother."

"All rightee, then," I said, slipping into my lazy southern patois, "Now what?"

"More tea, for starters," she said, expertly tipping the pot over my cup.

Cupping my hands around the warmth, I snuggled into her cozy chair.

"Comfy?" Tracey asked. I nodded. "Stop that!" She snapped, half exasperated. "We've got work to do!"

"Oh, sorry. Yes, I'm downright relaxed."

She gave me a sidelong glance and poured out a second cup for herself.

"Now, we put it together," she continued. "So, what the hell are they up to?"

Like a jigsaw puzzle, we placed the pieces, events, characters and places one by one, very patiently, into place. We had the players, the places, and put together the events–the yachting "party" on the Golden Girl that one day, finding the Lorikeet dead on the beach, Loretta's death–which came first? It was a Chicken vs. Egg scenario there. The endless parade of "Golden Girls" though Geoffrey's–turnover of the young and restless or something more. There were more tea and sandwiches. Then dawn broke, figuratively and literally by the time we were done. A small "snick" like the lock on a solid-gold bracelet being secured on the wrist clicked into place. We looked up at each other.

"Oh, my God," Tracey said to me.

"They're selling girls," I finished for her.

Then the weirdest thought popped into my head, given the enormity of our conclusion. I realized I had just stood up little Ricky for our dinner date. I praised the heavens he didn't have my cellphone number as much as he had cajoled, wheedled and bullied me for it. There would be hell to pay when I went back to work.

"You won't believe what happened," I said, and proceeded to tell Tracey about little Ricky. She laughed.

"That's *it?* After all this, this is what you think of? If that's the worst thing you do in this life, you should be thankful, toots."

We sat and looked at the notepad filled with our lists and musings and let the magnitude of what we'd discovered sink in. Especially Tracey. That photograph of her floated in my mind's eye for a long moment, bringing on a chill the hot tea would not dispel.

We were both spent, so Tracey made a bed for me on her wicker sofa and headed off to bed herself. She didn't leave me empty: there was a fresh towel, washcloth, soap and toothbrush waiting for me in the bathroom as well as a comfy terry robe she had as an extra. I showered and tucked in on the couch, daylight seeping in the windows and I barely got to sleep.

Chapter Seventeen

I slept, or thought I did, until I heard some soft clattering about the kitchen. Groggily, I looked over to see a freshly-showered Tracey in her own comfy robe, putting together coffee and drying the tea things to put them away.

"Oh, I'm sorry. Did I wake you?" she asked, with a solicitous look.

"What time is it?" I mumbled.

"Eight-thirty."

"Did you sleep?" I asked, as I knuckled my eyes and yawned wide enough to hear my jawbone crack.

"No. I tossed and turned a little, but couldn't turn the lights out." She peered down at me. "You're still half asleep yourself."

"Yeah, I am. Wanna play hooky?"

Tracey shook her head. "Not a good idea. Business as usual, I think, and I'm due in fifteen minutes."

I roused myself from the sofa. "Want a ride?"

"Nope. I'll walk," she said matter-of-factly. "Business as usual."

"Are you sure? Is it safe?"

She turned and smiled at me. "Look, honey, we just figured all this out last night. It's obviously been going on a lot longer than that. So, let's just forget it for now and act normal. You've got to be at work when–eleven?"

I nodded, forgetting myself, but Tracey ignored it.

"Then just get some sleep if you can," and she lowered the shades. "There's coffee when you're ready. Have a shower and lock up on the way out. It's cool."

"You're braver than I am, girl."

She nodded once, grimly, and shrugged.

Tracey was the epitome of grace under pressure as she glided out the door, apron in hand, and headed over to Dana's. I shuddered and hunkered down under the covers, hoping to get some rest, which didn't come. I made myself lie swaddled up on the couch, begging the gods for some sleep. No go.

A footfall scratched on the sidewalk outside and a shadow appeared through the jalousies. A slight nod and bob, and the footfalls drifted off the sidewalk onto the gravel path. Oh, shit. The Mir was parked right out front. I held my breath, counted to ten and looked. There was nothing, not even the scrunch of a car leaving the swale. I waited an hour and a half to be sure.

I took a hot shower and blew out my hair in real honest-to-God air conditioning—a treat beyond belief. I kept one ear turned to the front and an eye on the window. Nothing.

I put on the clothes from the day before, but they weren't exactly fresh. But I was clean, dry, and heading out the door in one piece.

All was status quo at the Compound when I arrived, five minutes later. The Captain was snoozed off a drunk peacefully in his chaise and stirred gently as I passed. I was happy for the sweet aroma of Tracey's tangerine-mango shower soap and focused on that instead of the Captain ripening in the sun. I did a quick change into jeans, sneakers, and a tee-shirt and headed into work, passing by Dana's to check on Tracey. I watched her for a moment through the window—business as usual. Bubbly, as if there weren't a cloud in the sky. The sky was clear, but my mood was overcast and I headed down to Sparky's.

Oh, man. Why didn't I call in? Little Ricky stood there, hands on hips, filling sinks, scowling at me. He looked madder than a wet hen caught outside the coop a rainstorm. He even looked a little bit like a chicken with his head all stuck from his collar and his short bandy legs in the ready position. Ready for what? Did he think I was going to jump him? Sheesh. Even his buzz-cut hair was sticking up like a rooster's cock-comb.

Keeping my mouth shut, I slid in behind the bar and started counting my bank at the register. He started to say something, but I held up a finger to silence him as I counted. Busily ticking off singles, fives, tens, twenties and the change, I shut the register drawer with finality and headed for the fruit.

"It's all done," Rick scowled.

"Thank you!" I replied, with a sunny and entirely counterfeit smile.

A customer came in and Rick gave me a hiss under his breath as he went to the waiting patron. I sighed and checked the ice and the temperature of the sinks. My sinks were ice cold. Bastard.

Bar sinks need to have hotter-than-hell water at all times to pass the Board of Health inspections. When they deign to walk into the place to check on the sterilization of glasses and shit, they look at everything; even check the temperature of water in the sinks with a thermometer. They never smile. If all goes well, they just leave. If it goes badly, they motion the owner into the back to write him up and levy their fines and, if it's bad enough, a court date. Big Rick would have my head–and my job–if my sinks weren't up to snuff.

I checked my ice. Zero. *Thanks a lot, pal*, I thought and muttered a curse under my breath. Ricky looked up and smiled angelically. I loathed him and was sorry I'd ever agreed to break bread with him, even if I hadn't showed.

I pulled the plug on the sinks to drain them and headed into the kitchen to fill up on ice. The fry cook treated me to a finger-wagging lecture about standing up Rick. The dishwasher, like me, kept silent. As I shoveled gallon-sized scoops of ice into a five-gallon white plastic bucket, I got more pissed off by the minute. Damn. Why, of all days, did I have to pull a shift with Rick? I lugged a couple of buckets full of ice out to the bar and filled my bins. I put the buckets under the speed rack; loath to revisit the kitchen under any circumstances.

I could have auditioned for a job with Ringling Brothers as a tightrope walker, given the day I had. I was friendly and chatty with the customers and gave Rick the cold shoulder after that cold sink job. I didn't blame him for being mad at me for standing him up, but to fuck with a person's livelihood is another thing entirely–it's just plain mean. Luckily, we started getting busy about eleven-thirty and kept it up 'til two. There was a lull until three and then a flurry of business for about a half-hour.

I picked up a dollar bill, folded in half, on the rail of the bar. As I picked it up and unfolded it, I noticed a small piece of paper tucked inside. I tucked the paper into the back pocket of my jeans and popped the dollar into my jar.

Rick was studiously avoiding me and I was just staying out of everybody's way, in general. At four, the regulars started dribbling in and I was happy to get off at six before they had to be poured out of there an hour later. The day after helped me forget the night before, but as soon as I stepped out of the bar, Tracey's and my discovery bore down on me hard. I sagged.

Most bartenders like working nights because the money's pretty good, but I didn't need much. My rent was cheap and with the extra money from Vinny I was just as happy to skip the rowdy drunken rodeo at night. The day shift was as close to "normal" as possible if there is such a thing and, in the bar business, that's highly doubtful. I preferred to work during the day so the nights were my own.

I hung around outside for a couple minutes, hoping to bump into Rick and square things with him. At least I could apologize and tell him my side of the story, if he asked. Not the *whole* story, of course, just that I got busy and forgot about him. Then I saw he hooked up with a couple of tourist gals with Da-Glo suntans and too much makeup. I shrugged, *just as well,* I thought, and walked straight home, thanking my lucky stars the bungalow was close to the beach.

Tracey had my cell number and I kept thinking about her, but she didn't call. I figured she would call when she could, or when she thought it was safe to get together again. I really wanted to tell her about the shadow, but didn't quite know what to say. A shadow? It could have been anybody. Someone looking for an apartment to rent, someone looking for a friend, it was anybody's guess. Yet a faint doubt gnawed in my gut and I itched to get inside the safety of my bungalow and have a beer.

The Captain was awake and downright friendly, even though I wasn't so inclined. He seemed sober, although I knew that wasn't the case. Dhani and Edmond were arguing about what to cook on the grill. I flipped them all a wave, then the bird, in jest, and unlocked my little bungalow. Everything was intact and undisturbed. I popped a beer and emptied my pockets of all the debris accumulated after a day of not carrying a pocketbook. I came across the piece of paper, which by now was pretty well crumpled.

Unfolding it gingerly, very lightly, written in pencil was: *"Loretta dint die naturally. Anemone."* I turned it over in my fingers. It was just a blank piece of white paper. Not a sticky note, not notebook paper. It was ripped on one edge and pretty good quality paper. Maybe it came off one of those free pads they always have in the desk drawer of high-end hotels. I fiddled with it for a minute, shoved it in my junk drawer and focused on my ice-cold beer. I contemplated a shot, but figured dinner would be a better bet.

Heading out in the Mir, I made a pit stop at the bank

to squirrel away some of the cash I had stowed at home. It doesn't pay to have too much lying around in a free and easy environment like the Compound. Courtesy of convenient anytime ATM banking, it took the money, gave me a receipt and I hit a little Italian joint for dinner. I don't care where you're from or what you are, there's just something about a nice hot pizza and an ice-cold pitcher of beer that sets things right when you're out of sorts. I had half the pizza left over and a pretty good buzz from the beer. I decided to walk over to the mall to dissipate the buzz and work off a few calories. Perhaps not the smartest thing to do, given the current state of affairs with Gregg, but I was a little stupid from the beer. Mallward I went.

The cellphone store was open and I waved to Gregg behind the glass. He saw me and waved back. I didn't expect him to come after me, but I wouldn't have minded if he did, either. So, I slowed my pace and affected a casual saunter into the mall. If he'd wanted to catch up, he would have. Oh, well.

I walked around the mall for a while, which leveled off my buzz to the point where I could drive safely. Not actually shopping, I did stop and buy some mango-tangerine shower wash for myself. What the hell, I stopped at the discount department store and snagged a cozy terry robe in pale peach and a couple of fresh towels, washcloths and a matching bath puff. I even bought a new matching toothbrush, pricey, but peach. Back at the Mir, I loaded up my packages and drove on home.

I showered and shampooed and reveled in the new terry bathrobe, pampering my tootsies in my good old reliable Tigger slippers. I made a cup of tea in Tracey's honor, toasted us both, and curled up in front of the TV. Once again, five hundred channels and nothing to watch except en Español. South Florida television at its finest. I finally found a program extolling the wonders of nature and fell asleep to the dulcet tones of cheetahs ripping apart their prey while screeching buzzards wheeled overhead jostling for leftovers.

The annoying electronic trill of my cellphone jolted me awake from my doze. *Oh, shit*, I thought. Now what? I reached over and checked the display. Gregg. I wasn't sleeping all that well, anyway, so I picked up.

"Hi there," he purred.

"Hi yourself." I suppressed a yawn and leaned up on one elbow.

"Up for a little company? I saw you in the mall."

"Yeah, I saw you first, remember?"

"Is it too late? Were you sleeping?"

"Not really, it's not too late and I could use the company." Thinking over everything Tracey and I had gone over together, a little male diversion would be nice.

"Okay, I can be there in say, ten or fifteen minutes. Anything you'd like to do?"

I figured there were a couple of alternatives open to me: allow a pounce off the bat by letting him into my place at this hour or going out first and then allowing a pounce. I chose the latter, figuring I could use a good stiff drink for false courage.

"Yeah, I wouldn't mind a drink."

"Your wish is my command, my lady. What's your pleasure?"

"Really, Gregg. You're too funny." I laughed. "How about a beer at Sparky's?"

"Isn't that where you work?"

"Yeah, but it's cool. We're just going for one."

"Okay. Just park in back and flash your headlights when you get here. Neighbors, you know."

Gregg agreed.

I pretended I was a quick-change artist and spiffed myself up with about two minutes to spare. Gregg pulled in discreetly behind the garbage cans beside my bungalow and flicked his headlights on and off a couple times. I didn't want to deal with the inevitable hoots and howls from my neighbors about having a date, so I slipped out the door and snuck around back.

"Walk or drive?" he asked as I quietly slid in beside him on the passenger seat.

"Drive, if you don't mind."

"Nope, not for just one I don't," he said and we took off for the thirty-second trip to Sparky's.

Little Ricky was off, having worked the day shift with me. Since he'd trotted off after the tourist gals, I didn't think he'd return any time soon.

Gregg and I settled comfortably in a pair of high captain's chairs at the bar and ordered a couple of beers.

We chatted about absolutely nothing. He told me a joke and I laughed hollowly, wondering if he would catch it, but he didn't. He continued to entertain me. I let him.

The bar was half-full, which I guess made me an optimist. Three or four strippers I knew were huddled down at the far corner on the other side. One of them cut loose from the herd and wobbled in our direction.

"Friend of yours?" Gregg asked.

"Probably on her way to the ladies'."

She weaved to and fro, finally landing next to me where she casually sidled up to my side of the bar. I recognized Kat by her gloriously underendowed build. She was the skinniest, flattest-chested stripper in south Florida and I wondered how she made a living at stripping. Well, she had great legs and a pretty good butt, maybe that's how.

"Hi," she said blearily.

"Hi yourself, Kat. How's tricks?"

"That's not nice," Kat said, grabbing on to the bar rail to steady herself.

I grimaced. "Sorry, that's not what I meant."

"That's better. You get my note?"

"What note?"

"The anonymous note–this afternoon."

I blanked out, then the light bulb went off in my head. "Oh–the anemone note."

Kat nodded unsteadily. "I've been drinking."

"Really?" I said dryly. "I'd never have guessed."

"I've had so much, shit, I think I'm gonna puke." She leaned over as if she would unload right then and there on my shoes.

"Oh, no, you don't," I said quickly, excusing myself to Gregg and guided Kat firmly to the bathroom. I looked over my shoulder at the bar and saw Gregg sitting there, watching with an ironic half-smile. Down a little further, I saw Ian Smith slung in the corner behind the strippers, next to the jukebox. He caught me as I watched him, but turned quickly to punch up some selections from the box.

Kat barely made it to one of the stalls and finished her business with due haste and dispatch. I wet down a couple of paper towels with cold water and handed as she stepped–well, shuffled–from the stall.

"Okay, Kat, do you mind?"

She wobbled and blinked at me a couple times and took the cool, wet paper towels. "No, I don't mind, thank you. We need to talk."

I wanted out of the bathroom, but it was useless. I've had my share of drunken conversations on both the giving as well as the receiving end. Once they're off, it's off to the races, so best to hang on and ride it out until you pull up at the finish line.

"I'm listening," I said. "What's all this about a note?"

"Not here."

"Why not here?" I looked around. Not a soul besides us was in the room. How intimately revolting.

She stood very close to me and whispered, "Loretta–it wasn't a stroke."

"How would you know that, Kat?"

"I found her. She was bleeding from her ear and her mouth. A lot. I think somebody came back and cleaned her up."

"Wouldn't the coroner find something like that?"

"Not if he was bought off."

"Okay, but why tell me?"

"You were there, remember?"

I dimly recalled the soiree at Loretta's, and how I couldn't wait to get out of there. I also remembered Kat saving my life, just a little.

"So, what can *I* do?" I asked.

"I don't know."

"I'm not even from here. Why tell me?"

"Because I think you're a friend."

Some friend. "Kat, she was our customer, that's about it. Not even my customer. She was Ricky's customer if you really want to know." I remembered the way Loretta treated me at her little do when I walked in with the object of her desire and how every time she walked into Sparky's I'd think of that old Beatles tune, "Get back home, Loretta," and something about high-heeled shoes and low-necked sweaters.

Kat wobbled again.

"Whoopsy daisy," I said, helping her towards the toilet.

She steadied herself and straightened up. "No, I'm okay. Really. And you are a friend–of mine. I gotta go." She squeezed around me in the miniscule bathroom and made for the door.

"Then Kat," I said and she stopped, "if we're friends, we need to talk, but not like this–when you're straight."

She smiled wanly. "Yeah."

That's the trouble with drunken conversations. When they should talk they don't, but when they shouldn't be talking, you can't shut 'em up.

"Ian's out there," I said.

"Yeah. He's waiting for me."

Oh, boy. "Kat, you come with me. We'll tell him you're not feeling well."

She wobbled some more.

"Okay," she said and half slumped in resignation.

I ran the water and helped her freshen up. We headed out to the bar.

Gregg was there, patiently waiting. The half-smiled had disappeared, replaced with a look of too-polite concern.

"Everything okay?" he asked.

"Yeah, fine," I replied. "Look, Gregg, I need a favor. We need to take Kat home. Would you mind?"

He shifted in his seat uncomfortably. "We just got here."

"I know, but she's not well."

"You mean she's stoned."

"Whatever. Can we give her a ride?"

Gregg shifted again in his chair, but I did not reseat myself. He looked clearly unhappy at the prospect of giving a sick drunk a ride in his immaculate Beemer, but seeing I was adamant, he relented. "Will we coming back?"

"I don't think so."

He threw a ten on the bar and we left. Ian was nowhere to be seen, the strippers still cuddled in the corner together.

Outside, the night was damp and sultry from the warm ocean mist. I thought I saw a figure in a leather jacket leaning against a telephone pole, but the light shifted through a trick of the sea breeze. Nothing. Just shadows and the encroaching night.

Gregg helped Kat wobble to the car while I half-carried her from behind. He sat her in front and I took up the slack in the back going around to Gregg's side to get in.

"She gonna puke in my car?" Gregg whispered nastily. A fair question, though, given the circumstances.

"Nope–been there, done that, flushed the toilet a couple times," Kat said and giggled.

"Where to?" he asked me.

"Down Ocean," Kat said.

"You sure?"

"Yeah," Kat mumbled. She gave him detailed instructions, which resulted in a rather roundabout route with two or three u-turns and missed corners. Eventually, we arrived at a neighborhood not very far from Tracey's place. We pulled up to Kat's apartment and I noticed that it looked almost identical to Tracey's building. I wondered how long ago some builder had a dream of sweet little Florida apartments dotting the city so affluent snowbirds could some down and soak up a little sunshine to warm their bones, sweet little one/ones, barely a cut above a cheap motel room, a block from the beach. I wondered if that builder knew that these days the apartments were used by low-renters who couldn't afford the rents in the suburbs and that, eventually, they would be kicked out because the dirt under their little one-bedroom boxes was worth millions.

Gregg handed Kat out of the car as graciously as he handed her in and walked her to her door. Taking her key, he opened the door and guided her into her apartment. She turned on the light and gave him a little hug goodnight. I decided then and there that Gregg would get more than a little hug from me that night, for being such a sport.

Getting back in the car, Gregg turned to me and said "What was all that about?"

"I'm not really sure…" I drifted off.

"You still want that drink?"

"I do, but I don't think Sparky's is a good idea at the moment." I handed him a ten dollar bill. "That cost you. Let me pay you back."

He took the ten and grinned. "I never like to take money from a lady, but in this case I will, so I can take her out and spend it on her. Where to?"

"How about that club on Commercial?"

"Really? You liked it? I thought you were bored out of your skull there."

"Silly boy," I replied sweetly and shot him what I thought was a smoky, mysterious look.

"Alrightee then! We're off!" To prove the point, he roared the Beemer away from Kat's and down the A-1-A to reach the club in what seemed like nanoseconds.

Handing me out of the car, he said, "It's quiet in here–maybe we can talk?"

Before I could answer, the hostess ushered us in and seated us at a small, low corner table deep in the recesses of the club.

"Do you do this often?" I asked, thinking perhaps I was one of his many and, at the moment, he was my one and only.

"No," he said. "I'm usually alone. Except for the time I came with you."

I nodded.

"So, this Kat," he said. "She's not a friend, but we took her home?"

"She's one of our customers at Spark's. I see her from time to time at work."

"Oh. You don't seem like the mothering type."

"I'm really not. But bartenders talk to people all the time. After a few drinks, they tell us everything. Look, let's talk about something else. I just thought she was in a bad way and could use a leg up, if you know what I mean."

"Yeah, I do. Some guys would take advantage of a girl in that condition."

"Exactly. I'm not a hero or anything, but I work there, too. How would it look? I'd feel awful if something happened."

"Wasn't she with friends? Or anybody?"

"I'm not sure, but she came to me."

"It's not your responsibility."

"If we all thought that, there'd be more trouble than there already is."

He nodded. "I guess you're right. So, other than tonight, how's it going?"

We talked for a while over cocktails, ordered another round, and left.

When we arrived at the Compound, all was silent. He walked me to the door and took the key from my hand, just as he had done for Kat. He clicked the key gently into the lock and gave it a soft twist.

"Before I go..." he took me into his arms and initiated a gradual kiss that deepened in intensity and weakened my knees and any resolve I might have had left. He gently broke our embrace and stood closely in front of me, as if to pull away and leave if I said the word.

"Where do you think you're going?" I asked as I pulled him toward me and kissed him back in the same manner, building, smoldering, and leading him towards the bed with soft wet kisses. He gingerly kicked the door behind us and it closed with a quiet snick. That night, the Tigger slippers were under my bed, Gregg was on top of my bed and I was right in the middle. I wound up sleeping very soundly indeed.

Chapter Eighteen

The next morning, I woke up when the door softly snicked shut. I heard Gregg's footsteps recede down the path. I looked around and found a note next to me on the pillow. "Friday at eight, don't be late. G." I smiled groggily to myself and turned over drowsily for a couple more z's.

The warm sun crept in and served as my alarm. I arose, stripped the bed and put it away, popped an ice-cold soda and headed for the shower. I felt melty all over, like I'd been in a sauna, or had enjoyed a deep massage. The sugar rush and icy-coldness of the soda served to rouse me from my reverie as I lathered myself profusely with the tangerine-mango stuff. I decided it was a little cloying, and switched to good old deodorant soap. I tossed on jeans, flip-flops, a tank top and a windbreaker, figuring I'd hit the beach for a nice long walk after stopping in to see how Tracey was doing.

I breakfasted at Dana's–muffins again–with Tracey plying her trade at the counter as expertly as ever. Nothing appeared to be out of place in the cool blue and white interior of the diner. It was an oasis of sanity in the midst of chaos.

"Hey, lady!" Tracey called out. "More coffee?" I nodded, Tracey poured.

I looked around the place. Tracey seemed way too put together, given recent findings and events. I saw the reason–Dan Gowan was sitting in a corner booth with a newspaper in front of his face.

I noticed Gowan's brown leather jacket and thought it bore a distinct similarity to a leather jacket I'd spotted just last night outside of Sparky's. I didn't know if he was actually reading the paper over his morning coffee or engaging in a little surreptitious surveillance. I wondered what his interest was in this small-potato place, unless it was the excellent coffee and fresh blueberry muffins, a few of which were parked by his elbow. He took a sip of coffee, looked up, spotted me and arched an eyebrow. I returned the gesture and he motioned me to sit with him. I looked to Tracey for some support and she promptly waved me over to Gowan. I shrugged and walked towards him, coffee in hand.

"Hi," I said, standing next to his booth, not sure if the invitation was real or imagined.

"Please, have a seat, Stacey." Gowan said and waved his paper to the seat opposite him. Great, I thought. Me having coffee with a cop. What could be more natural? Well, I'd had drinks with Charlie the bartender, so why not coffee with Dan the cop? I shrugged and slipped quietly across from him. He folded the paper neatly and put it on the seat beside him.

"We have to talk," he said.

For someone like me, who never passed on a chance to keep her mouth shut, it seemed way too many people were trying to pry me open. I believed I now understood how a clam would feel prior to being shucked, and looked at Gowan levelly.

"Talk about what? I went to the station, just as you asked."

"This is off-line."

"Oh, off-line," I repeated, not sure if he meant off the fishing line, off the hook, or off the record. "What do you mean?"

"You're new in town."

Okay, we'd established that at the station, which was probably why I wasn't grilled more intensely about the death of the Lorikeet on the beach.

"You run with some pretty shaky people," Gowan said; then, nodding in Tracey's direction, added, "as well as some good ones. The trick, young lady, will be to separate one from the other and make the right choices."

I stiffened. My mother was dead and he could kiss my ass. He read my expression and sighed. For a moment, he looked weary and resigned: an overworked cop forced to view the underside of the rock once too often.

"I'm not telling you this because I care. I'm telling you this because it's my job."

"Okay, so you've done your job. Thank you. May I go?"

He handed me his card. "This is my cellphone. Twenty-four seven, any time."

I nodded, took the card, and tucked it in the pocket of my windbreaker.

"You don't say much, do you?" he said.

I gave him a hard little smile, pocketed the card more out of courtesy than actual intent to contact the man, and slipped back out of the booth and over to Tracey.

"Thanks, pal," I said to Tracey under my breath. "Thanks a lot."

"What?" She seemed surprised at my tone and looked a little hurt. "What's wrong?"

"Nothing, sorry," I said and waved it aside. "Listen, call me when you can, okay? I get off at six."

"I'll be out tonight. How about tomorrow night?"

"Yeah, tomorrow night's good. Call me, okay?"

"Okay," Tracey replied and went back to slinging eggs, coffee and b.s. at her counter station. She seemed a little put out; I had obviously not done what she'd hoped for. I was thinking maybe she wanted me to back up whatever she might have said to Gowan or give him a clue as to what was going on. In truth, I *didn't* know what was going on, not really. Besides, he was the Sherlock; let him get his own clue.

I hit the beach, briskly walking to blow off steam, all the way to the Lighthouse Point jetty and back. I looked at the Coast Guard lighthouse at the Hillsboro Inlet and wondered what they did to keep our coastal waters safe. Protecting boaters from renegade manatees, maybe? I shrugged and headed south, in the direction of Atlantic Boulevard, and spent some time on the pier, watching the fishermen catch nothing more than an empty belly and a hell of a windburn. Smith stood at the far end of the pier by the open water, looking in my direction.

I looked down towards the other end of the pier and spotted Gowan's now-familiar brown leather jacket in the shadows of the porte-cochere at the entrance to the pier. Smith turned his back to me and towards the sea. Nah, I thought to myself–everybody has to be someplace and they're just here. I'd be a looney tune if I thought it had anything to do with me. Anyway, it was none of my business, or so I kept telling myself. Then I realized I was hungry–again.

I skipped getting another muffin-to-go at Dana's and opted for a ride to the supermarket. Funny, I didn't pick up even a six-pack of beer for myself on the Saturday runs. I had about an hour before work, so there was plenty of time to get my marketing done for the week. Since I was finally coming out a little ahead, I bought a case of beer to share at the Compound, some steaks, salad fixings, and soup. Odds and ends filled out the market basket, along with some Krispy Kreme doughnuts–not as good as Dana's blueberry muffins perhaps, but no cop attached, either. I smiled at the irony in buying doughnuts because I didn't want to be associated with a damned cop.

When I got home, I popped a beer to take the edge off dealing with Little Ricky on shift, put the food away, and got ready for work. I twisted my hair in a knot, exchanged sandals for sneakers and tank top for Sparky's polo shirt. I hated that shirt. It was a deadly green, which made me look like a corpse someone forgot to bury. Maybe with a tan it might look okay, but that shade of bright Kelly green was never my color. Every chance I got, I snuck in with a regular tee-shirt, and opened my Book of Excuses, saying the Sparky's shirt was dirty, torn, whatever. I'd get another one for the next day with a not-so-veiled threat they were going to start charging me if I wrecked any more shirts. I was hoping I would run them out of shirts soon and maybe suggest a different, less nauseating color; sunshine yellow or sky blue pink. Anything but deadly green–well, khaki would be a close second. And what's wrong with black, anyway? The place was painted black, so why not the shirts?

I slammed into work, defenses in place, ready to deal with what must be dealt with and ran smack into Mike, one of the other bartenders.

"Ricky called in sick," he said. "I'm covering. What register do you like?"

I indicated my preference and we got busy getting ready for the onslaught of the two customers who sauntered in at the crack of noon. This was the "noon rush." Same as usual, two city employees who nursed their beers with such miserly reluctance, you'd thought I'd slipped a shot of motor oil into their mugs. Mike gave me a lopsided grin as he watched them as they grimaced over every microscopic swallow.

I liked Mike. He usually worked nights and weekends, kept to himself, and wasn't a goof like Ricky. He wasn't a player and he didn't play. He worked, he was pleasant, clean-cut, and seemed like a decent kind of guy. I'd heard his girlfriend was a secretary at one of the high-end financial offices in downtown Fort Lauderdale, so I figured that probably kept him away from the flotsam and jetsam of the beach scene. We wound up having a steady, easy day, split our tips, rang out our registers, and parted company with a wave, a smile, and "See you next time." I hoped next time would be soon.

When I got home, I shed the shirt, popped a beer topless and didn't give a damn if anyone was looking or not. Then I thought of who might be looking and quickly donned a bright pink tank top. I fired up the grill and announced steaks were on the menu. The boys gave me a heartfelt cheer and gratefully emptied their refrigerators of any leftover beer and food as a gesture of goodwill. I broke out some of the good stuff and offered shots before dinner, so we were about as grilled as the dinner by the time it was ready and it never tasted better. We managed to put up corn on the cob in my bungalow, even though I had to give the stove a good beating to boil water. I fixed salad, sent out steaks to Dhani and Edmund to work their magic with sauce and spices, and we all enjoyed a feast.

"What's the reason for the party, Stacey?" Dhani asked, between bites of steak.

"No reason, just thought I'd share, that's all."

"She had a *date* last night," Edmund offered with a mockingly schoolyard simper.

Everyone but me let out a prolonged "Oooo-oooo."

I playfully smacked him on the shoulder. "Enough. No talking out of turn," I warned. He shut his mouth when the stern look I shot him told him I meant business.

"You know, Stacey, you could have been one nasty school teacher with that look of yours," Edmund said.

"Yeah, I'll teach you something," I replied, threatening him playfully by grabbing the barbeque tongs from him, nipping them open and shut menacingly towards Edmund and almost, but not quite, spilling some of my ice-cold beer.

He backed off, held his hands in the air and gallantly gave up. "Okay, okay, I'll stop."

Everyone moaned with manly disappointment and called Edmund chickenshit. We laughed.

Dhani contributed some chocolate chip cookies for

dessert. My ardor for the cookies cooled somewhat when Dhani admitted they'd been sitting uncovered on his counter for five days. Given his casual approach to housekeeping, it was anybody's guess who had taken a bite of them before we did. I passed.

My private stock of Krispy Kremes was stashed in my kitchen cabinet, safe from friendly neighborly plundering after dinner.

Fully sated and happily buzzed, I went home, pulled on my Tigger slippers, a sleepy-tee, and settled in to watch TV. I turned off my cellphone and very comfortably dropped off to sleep on the sofa covered with just a clean sheet, so I wouldn't have to make up the bed.

Chapter Nineteen

Morning dawned fresh and sunny again–that's Florida for you. Everything over the past couple weeks seemed almost surreal, evaporating in a blaze of sunlight and blue sky. I heard the murmur of the ocean and the stirrings of the Compound crew getting up and at 'em.

Stirring myself, I put up a pot of coffee, got the Krispy Kremes down from the cabinet and wondered what Kat might be up to. I hadn't seen her for a while and was curious.

Kat had told me she worked the day shift at the Booby Bar, so I figured eight a.m. was just about right since she had to report in at ten-thirty.

I fired up the Mir and scattered a healthy load of gravel onto my neighbor's cars inadvertently as I wheeled out of the driveway. It took about two seconds to get to Kat's and the sleepy little apartment strip looked undisturbed. A stripper living in a strip of apartments, I mused inanely. I parked the Mir and scrunched along the gravel parking strip. The Mir shuddered, sighed, and turned off of its own accord. I hoped it would start up again with no problems.

I walked up a front path of worn concrete imitation flagstones to Kat's apartment, having remembered it from the other night. When I knocked on her jalousie door, it swung slowly open with a soft squeal of unoiled hinges. I paused a moment, not quite sure of my reception. After all, I'd been taught it wasn't good manners to just prance into someone's home unannounced or uninvited and I was both, but since it was open, anyway, I stepped inside and saw the place in a shambles. The setup of the apartment was similar to Tracey's place, but with shabbier furnishings. A chair was overturned in the kitchenette and random clothing was strewn about living room. Either the lady lived like a slob or there had been one hell of a party.

"Kat?" I called out tentatively.

The bathroom door was closed and I could hear the shower running. The hair on the back of my neck stood up, I felt a cold, tingling sensation as my shoulder blades did a little twitch to shake it off. My skin prickled and my stomach flipped a little.

"Kat?" I called again. Silence, except for the murmur of water in the shower.

There was no answer from the bathroom, so against my better judgment, which told me to leave quickly, I hedged over towards the door.

The water was running, but it must have been on for quite some time because the bath didn't seem steamy. I couldn't hear the sounds of someone splashing as if they were having a good wash. I poked my head in and all seemed in order. The toilet lid was down and there was a towel lying on top of the closed lid. A thin, faded yellow bathrobe was slung over the doorknob on the inside of the bathroom. A cheap, plastic floral printed shower curtain hid the tub.

"Kat?" I called out yet again, a little louder so as to be heard over the running water.

A moan floated from behind the curtain.

I flung it open to find Kat slumped in the tub, water running randomly over her long, angular body. Her ghost-pale skin was bruised and mottled. She'd been given a good going over. Half-hidden by the tangled streams of her long black hair, her face was swollen and purple. Her thin chest rose and fell in regular, but shallow breaths. I breathed in suddenly, not realizing I'd been holding my breath. She was alive.

I shut off the water and grabbed the bath towel and gently daubed at her face as I gently brushed the hair away. I wrapped the towel around Kat as much as I could and eased her out of the tub. Her body looked so small and fragile, but it was almost more than I could manage, pulling her out of the tub. I remembered my Mom, after I'd bathed her. Her body was wet, unresponsive and heavy, like a waterlogged piece of timber. Just like Kat's. I tried not to shudder.

Kat struggled to get onto her feet and sagged against me. I reached for another towel on a rack above the toilet and wrapped that around her shoulders. She managed to shift the first towel around her waist like a South Seas pareo and we stumbled together towards her couch.

I shook like a wet dog and droplets of water splashed about her unkempt living room.

Kat moaned again and almost slid off the couch. I caught her and got her into a half-seated position.

"Where's your phone?" I asked.

"What?" she mumbled, looking up at me wearily.

"Your phone," I repeated, shaking her gently. "Where is it?"

She pointed to a small table in a corner with some clothing piled on top. Picking off the frou-frous and gewgaws of stripper's gear, I found the phone and dialed 9-1-1.

"Someone's hurt, there's been an accident," I reported.

"What is your location?" the dispatch operator asked.

I gave an approximation of the apartment's address.

"Stay right there, someone will be right over."

"I'll see you later," I said to Kat as I headed out the door. I really wanted out of there—now. In spite of myself, I turned back to her, knelt down and gently put a hand on her shoulder. "I'll call your work for you, where's the number?"

Kat lifted a bruised, bony arm and fished a matchbook off the lamp table next to the couch. I quickly took it from her and, stuffing it into the pocket of my shorts, wasted no time getting out the door. I jumped into the Mir, which started right up to my sheer delight, and got the hell out of there. I drove as slowly as I could manage, so as not to draw any attention to myself.

When I got home, I downed a quick shot to steady my nerves, plucked the matchbook from my pocket, and walked to the payphone on the corner. The fates were with me–it worked. I called the Booby Bar to report Kat, whose stripper name turned out to be Yvette after much back-and-forth with the bartender, as being too ill to work, and I was just a girlfriend looking after her today.

"Hung over, again, huh?" the bartender sneered. I closed my mouth so I did not state the appropriately emasculating rejoinder, which came immediately to mind, and gently hung up the phone. There's nothing as satisfying as a good hard slam of the phone when you're good and pissed off, but a gentle click is a completely indifferent way to disconnect. My hackles were raised momentarily, but I really didn't give a shit.

I walked back home and sat on my little couch, surveyed my shabby but tidy bungalow and opened a beer so I could have a good think. My hand shook as I popped the tab. I heard a siren in the distance and wondered if it was an ambulance for Kat.

The Compound was eerily quiet and I could hear my thoughts tumble around in my head. It was days before I had to make a run for Vinny. I didn't want to call Gregg on this, didn't want to see Tracey at the moment and was in no shape to go chat with Charlie at Stinger's. I called in to work and left a message that I was taking the day off, and popped open another beer.

I opened my bag and found Dan Gowan's number

tucked into one of the inner compartments. I never had any use for cops and they usually had less than no use for me, save to shake me down from time to time about brother Ed when they had nothing better to do.

I turned the card around and around in my hand, flipping it, trying to skate it across the room as I had done with Ed's baseball cards when I was a kid, and finally decided there weren't too many other alternatives to calling the guy and coming clean–at least about this Loretta thing. Maybe everything else would fall into place if he could get the lowdown from Kat, who seemed as if she was ready to give it up, but why to me? I dialed the phone.

"Gowan."

I hung up. My phone rang right back at me and I looked at it for about four rings before picking it up. I said nothing, just held the little cellphone to my ear.

"Gowan," the voice said at the other end of the connection.

"It's Stacey," I said, "from Dana's, the other day."

"I know."

"We need to talk–off the phone."

"Okay–tell me where and when."

I named a little breakfast joint right outside downtown Fort Lauderdale I had seen, but had never been to. I figured if he was a Pompano dick, I'd have him outside of his jurisdiction and he couldn't lay a finger on me. He agreed and we set a time in the almost immediate future.

The Egg and You is an institution and has been in Fort Lauderdale for years. It's cozy, serves good breakfast on the cheap, and you can go there and mind your own business with whoever you please since everybody else there is either a regular or minding their own business as well. It's not a place anyone would remember seeing you, but it's a place where everyone goes. I didn't think anyone I'd be taking about would go there and even if they did, I didn't expect it would be before the ungodly hour of nine thirty in the morning.

I dumped the remainder of beer number two in the sink, quickly brushed my teeth, used a generous amount of mouthwash, and changed into jeans, a tee shirt, and sneakers. I twisted my hair into a modest ponytail and demurely left the bungalow for the Mir, but not without a hard look around for any person or persons known or unknown who might be watching me. I felt stupid, but safe.

Dan Gowan was sitting in a corner booth when I arrived and motioned me to slip into the seat across from him. I was tempted to slip next to him so I could also watch the door, but I did as asked and tried to relax. I looked down at my hands and noticed I had a couple of broken fingernails–must have been when I was stumping around with Kat after pulling her out of the bathtub.

"Rough morning?" he asked. I nodded.

He ordered coffee for both of us and asked if I was hungry. I shook my head no. He ordered himself a generous breakfast, enough for two, and I wondered how he kept himself in shape to do a cop's job between the muffins at Dana's and breakfasting here.

"Stacey, you've got nothing to worry about," he said. "Not from me, anyway. If you haven't done anything, you can't get busted for what you didn't do."

Famous last words, I thought to myself. I'd seen too many people get busted for little or nothing and I had no intention of being one of them. But this situation was more than I wanted to handle, my being from nowhere and not knowing anybody. I needed a friend, and Kat was out of commission for a while, and Tracey was out of the question altogether after seeing her photo in the trunk of the Caddy.

I drew a deep breath and told him about finding Kat this morning. I showed him the note she left me at the bar. It was crumpled but readable. I told him about Loretta, and Loretta's "thing" for Rick, and the soiree at her place the night before she died. I talked about how drunk Kat got over Loretta's death and that she was trying to tell me something about it through that note.

"Unfortunately, Stacey," Gowan said, "Loretta's a Canadian national. Her husband had her body quickly cremated and flown back home."

"Wasn't there an autopsy?" I asked, hoping against hope something might have been yielded to point at the motley crew polluting the beach.

"In cases of death by natural causes, especially on a national from another country, we try to disturb as little as possible. It looked like she had a stroke. Simple and plain, so why make more of it than it is?"

"If she was having a stroke, why would she bleed from her ear and her mouth?"

He shook his head and shrugged. Breakfast arrived.

All of a sudden, I got insatiably hungry and asked if he wouldn't mind if I had his English muffin. He nodded and shoved it in my direction. Next thing, he had shoveled some eggs and potatoes next to it on the plate and I was eating like a starved she-wolf in the desert. We washed down our meal with several cups of steaming hot coffee and it was as if I was purging the morning's despair with hot food on a sunny day with a sunny type of personality.

Dan Gowan radiated good health and a robust love of life. He seemed like a good guy who liked good healthy food, good healthy sport, good healthy women, and a good healthy life with lots of excitement. He was also patient and stealthy, like a large cat coiled to spring, but waiting until the exact moment for the prey to be caught. Being a cop seemed like a natural path for him and being a detective seemed second nature. He seemed to instinctively know how long to wait things out as they unfolded and press just the right buttons at just the right time to mix it up a bit. Well, now seemed the time.

"Tell you what I'll do," Gowan said. "Loretta's

apartment is still sealed up and the husband isn't making any noise about coming down and closing it up any time soon. I'll take you over there and you can show me who was where and what was what before you left. Then we can see if we can figure out how Kat's version comes into play. If we find anything, I'll start digging. If not, it's a done deal and we'll talk some more. Are you in trouble, Stacey?"

I shook my head and said I didn't think so, but I was loath to let go about the stuff with Tracey and Vinny and Geoffrey just yet. I could wait things out, too.

We got into Gowan's brown sedan and headed up to Pompano. I sat in the front seat with him and tried to remember I wasn't under arrest and actually going someplace willingly with a cop. We got to the luxury Beach Palace apartment complex and he pulled into the underground garage, waving himself past the attendant with his badge. We went in through the service elevator in the basement and up to Loretta's floor. From the outside, it looked like just another apartment. As we opened the door, a strip of yellow CRIME-SCENE-DO-NOT-ENTER tape festooned the foyer inside the apartment.

The apartment felt stuffy, as if it had been closed up for longer than it had been. The air was stale and warm because the air conditioning had been turned off. A taped outline of where Loretta must have lain was on the left side of the foyer, opposite the bathroom and half up the hall. I thought it was odd that if she fell on the floor from a stroke, why was she half up the hall?

I walked through the foyer, listening to my sneakers make soft plopping sounds on the tile floor.

"So, if it's not a crime scene, Dan, why the tape?"

Gowan shrugged. "Precaution, I guess."

I walked around and showed him where everybody had stood, where everybody had gone and when and how, especially how I had slipped into the foyer bathroom and hid out, making my getaway out the front door after I heard the click of highly polished shoes on the highly polished floor.

We looked over the foyer and Gowan had me stand where Loretta might have stood when she was having her stroke. He moved me a couple inches over, then a couple inches more. He turned me a little, towards the wall and away from the bathroom and looked up.

He looked down. There were very tiny red dots on the wall and an even tinier red stain on the grout between the polished marble tiles.

Gowan sighed. "Shit."

I looked and saw what Gowan did. "That's blood?" I asked. He nodded.

We walked out of the apartment. Gowan removed a small roll of the yellow CRIME-SCENE tape from his pocket and fastened it outside the front door of the condo. I felt pukey and really, really wanted to go home.

"I'll run you back to your car and I'll have to come back," Dan said. "Where can I find you later?"

"How about if I find you? I'm not feeling very well right now. And, please–don't come to my house."

Gowan nodded. "But find me, okay?"

I nodded and we headed back to the Egg and You in the sedan. I shouldered the door and couldn't get it open fast enough when we got to The Mir. I opened the sedan's door and promptly vomited on the pavement. I tried not to step on it as I alighted with as much dignity as possible and exited the car. I looked at Gowan sheepishly as he reached over from his side and closed the passenger door. He began talking to somebody on his car radio and I took that as my cue to get the hell out of there.

I steadied myself in The Mir and drove back to the bungalow. I hid there for the rest of the day on the sofa with my head tucked under a pillow. Where had I come to and what the hell was I doing here? Moreover, how was I going to get the hell out? I tossed and turned for a while, turned on the TV, put it on mute, and tossed and turned some more. I didn't want a drink; I wanted company, but could think of no one I wanted to be with. I wanted my Mom and tears welled up. Loretta's death seemed to hit me like a sudden dowsing in cold and dirty sink water I emptied at work. I thought of a forensics team like I saw on TV going over the apartment, now with a fine-toothed comb. I wondered if Gowan would reveal where the tip came from and mightily hoped not.

I padded barefoot to the bathroom to wash my face and brush my teeth. I decided to slip out of my jeans when I found a twenty in the pocket. I thought the corner drugstore might have something to help me sleep. I slipped the jeans back on and donned a pair of flip-flops and marched over forthwith.

The drugstore was empty, save for a few tourists getting ripped off for suntan oil and flip-flops. I selected my sleeping medication of choice and wandered aimlessly among the garishly colored beach chairs, tee-shirts, and water noodles. Down one aisle, I found a cheap little battery-powered radio to take home with me. Ah, company at last.

Having a radio on is like a houseguest you don't have to pay attention to. The DJ yammers on and on about the latest promotional contest while music plays in the background of your life. I set up the radio, kicked off my flip-flops and popped a beer, ready to listen to everybody's comings and goings without taking part, if I didn't want to. I found a station where the DJ wasn't offensive, the music was standard rock-and-roll, and settled in to work up a good buzz and forget the whole day.

Eventually, the soft rustlings of people coming home from work and preparing to spend an evening at home disturbed the still, empty silence of the Compound. Car and truck doors opened and shut, audible sighs of relief could be heard, people popped in and out of their apartments and bungalows cheerily wishing one another good evening, and is anybody coming out for a beer?

After a decent interval, with a familiar face or two at the table, I emerged from my sanctuary and flopped down into one of the mismatched patio chairs around the central table in the courtyard. Someone put a beer in my hand and we sat around and chatted amiably about the day's happenings.

"Day off, Stace?" someone asked.

"Yeppers," I replied. "How sweet it is." Lying through my teeth.

They all agreed I "had the life", going in at eleven, coming home at six, making a bundle in-between at a pretty cushy job. I agreed and seemingly reveled in living the SoFla dream come true–bartender at the beach. Loretta, Kat, Tracey, Vinny, and Geoffrey tumbled to the back of my mind, and I thought about Gregg.

"What's up with that boyfriend of yours, Stacey?" Edmund asked, gaily popping out of his bungalow, freshly showered with martini in hand.

I just looked at him and nodded. "He's just a nice guy."

"Don't we get to meet him?" someone else asked.

"Hey, gimme a break, guys! It's just starting!" I cried and was answered by a bunch of hoo-haws and back slapping amongst the guys of the Compound.

Tony the Portuguese Tiger came over from next-door and tried to slip me some tongue and Edmond playfully, but effectively smacked him out of my way.

"Hands-off, sport. She's got a boyfriend!"

"Ah," Tony smiled at me, giving me a slow wink on the side and charmingly kissed my hand in courtly fashion. "Congratulations to you, lady."

I laughed and had to agree it was about time.

One of the guys came in with some fish and admitted sheepishly that he'd bought them, not caught them. It was another one of those collective meals we frequently shared. Edmund cleaned the fish and filleted them for cooking, someone had a few limes to soak the meat in, I had some stuff left over for salad from the night before, more beer flowed, and we all enjoyed a hearty repast in the shade of the huge old worn-out mango tree in the Compound. A scrawny mango from last season managed to fall on the Captain's head and he claimed to discover the laws of gravity. We all said it should have been a coconut to knock some sense into him and explained Sir Isaac Newton had discovered the same thing, centuries ago, with an apple.

"Yeah, but a mango's more exotic!" the Captain rebutted, doing a little hula-hula dance in his chaise looking at the wizened piece of fruit.

We all laughed and went back to our beers and good-natured jokes. The current joke was to wonder when I was going to run out of shoes–no one claimed to see me in the same pair twice.

"Hey, you see me in sneakers and my Kino's sandals all the time!" I protested.

"They don't count, everyone has them," Edmund said.

"Well, then wait 'til the end of time, boys," I said, "I'm never gonna run out..." I gazed off dreamily into space, as if contemplating a never-ending supply of footwear.

Somebody got the bright idea it would be fun to take a walk on the beach, so we packed up our moveable bar and headed out to make sure the Atlantic was still there. The sun had already set in the opposite direction of the Atlantic and it was dark on the beach. We found a spot in front of the dunes where the streetlights were muted so we could see the stars.

Healthy dunes are a boon to a beach, and serve to preserve it for generations to come. The wealthy developers who insist on building immediately on the sand for a quick profit doom their even wealthier customers' palaces in the sky to wash away in just a mere matter of years and, no matter how close they get or how high they are, it still doesn't change the fact that there is still absolutely nothing to see at night. Mother Ocean will reclaim everything back to her bosom, given half a chance.

We looked at the constellations and had another drink among the grains of sand of the beach. We felt a strange kinship with those little beige specks, sitting on the dunes as small grains of sand ourselves locked into the vast voyage and mystery of the Milky Way. I felt very small and insignificant and wondered if anything I had been experiencing was real.

The job at Spark's was real, the guys at the Compound were real, and these evenings were real. I was buzzed. And, yeppers, the other stuff was real, too, and as I snuggled my back deep into a dune, I decided that what doesn't kill us makes us stronger and somehow it would all be dealt with–in my favor–if I was just lucky enough.

We poured ourselves home and said our respective goodnights–not without a bear-crushing hug from Edmund to me and Dhani threatening, but not quite, to get a bit fresh. I turned on a light in the bungalow, flicked on my radio, and fell into a deep, sound sleep with the strains of music in the background. The sleeping pills went unopened.

Something must have triggered me in the middle of the night because, suddenly, I was sitting bolt upright and completely disoriented. I felt for my Tigger slippers under my bed and they were just where I'd always put them. I listened to the radio for a moment and heard the same song they'd played at Geoffrey's to introduce us "Golden Girls". That was what had woken me up.

I quickly remembered the events of the day and that garish yellow tape marking where Loretta lay stuck like a logjam in my memory. The song playing on the radio stuck good in my head, too. I ran to the shower to wash all the bad stuff away and was haunted by the mental picture of Kat as I'd found her earlier that morning. There was no getting away from my self-torment. I threw on a tee-shirt and shorts and headed out into the Compound to spend the night, until dawn, if necessary, in the warmth and light of the other bungalows and apartments deep in the throes of slumber. The Captain, on his chaise, was still up.

I fetched out a pair of brews for both of us. We sat among the crickets and toads as they gently serenaded the Compound. A large bullfrog boldly leapt across the courtyard, fearing no man–as no man, or woman–if they had any sense at all, would be out at this hour. We watched him softly plop across the bare courtyard, kicking up little froggy fistfuls of dust as he continued on his nocturnal mission, perhaps to find a lady frog, or avoid a hungry dog.

The Captain, contrary to his usual red-eyed rheumy gaze looked almost clear and alert. We clinked bottles and toasted our mutual health, for today, anyway. We sat in companionable silence for a while. He only turned to me when he was ready to reach for and open his second bottle. I nodded assent and opened another one myself.

"Stacey, right? It's Stacey, isn't it?" the Captain said.

"Yeppers, Cap'n, that's me."

"Stacey, you bring a little life to this place."

"Oh, yeah? How so, Cap?"

"Well," he said, setting his bottle down gently next to his chaise, "there are more people around now than when you weren't here."

Other than Gregg, I'd had no visitors, so I pressed him for more.

"Haven't you been dating a bunch of guys? You know, playing the field?"

I advised I had not, and explained I didn't play the

game that way.

"So, who's the guy in the black truck?"

I looked at the Captain very slowly and guardedly asked, "What guy in what black truck?"

"There's a guy in a black truck who comes around during the day like he's looking for you."

"Am I here?"

"Sometimes yes, sometimes no. He was here today."

"And…"

"Today he came in the courtyard."

"I was home."

"I know."

"Why didn't you get me?"

"I don't know. Just something, I guess." He shrugged. "Maybe it was me. Is he a friend?"

"No…" I exhaled softly.

"Then I did good."

"Cap'n, you did more than good. Who else has been around?"

"Well, two guys in business suits, that Gregg fella you've been seeing, and another guy drove by a couple times in a brown four-door."

Dan Gowan, I thought.

"Captain, you're a wealth of information," I said. "Look, if anyone else comes around, and you tell me they've been around, the beer's on me."

"What about the good stuff?"

"Yeah, okay, that, too–but just a shot now and again. I'm not a liquor store."

"Fair enough." He nodded. "Do you want me to say anything to anyone?"

"Nah." I tried to act nonchalant. "I'm sure it's nothing."

"Yeah, just bees buzzing around the honey hive."

"Yeah, you're probably right–and speaking of

buzzing…" I hoisted my bottle and downed it. The Captain did the same and hunkered down into his chaise with his cap over his face. He was done for the night and so was I.

Passing on the sleeping pills, I played the radio softly, lit a candle, and waited with an ear cocked toward the road to hear any suspicious footsteps or vehicles at that late hour. When I couldn't stand watch any more, I drifted off into a semi-sleep until the first fingers of daylight gently touched my eyelids and roused me at dawn.

Chapter Twenty

The candle had burned down to a nubbin, so I blew it out and set it on the kitchen counter. I switched the radio to a livelier station, turned on the TV news, but hit the mute button, and brewed a fresh pot of coffee. I popped a Krispy Kreme in the microwave. I sat down with my coffee and doughnut to look at the news. I couldn't abide the shrill harpy the TV had as its anchor, so I hoped the radio would fill me in on the rest.

It was too early for the Compound to be stirring, but I heard a footfall on the alley beside my bungalow. It wasn't the soft shuffle of a beach-goer's flip-flop, but the harsh crunch of heavy leather boots unaccustomed to treading sandy sidewalks at the beach. The scuffling continued around the side of the bungalow until it was by the front door and abruptly stopped.

An opening between my bungalow and Edmund's exposed the alley between the buildings. There's so much discarded junk in Edmund's alley, there is no pass-through at that end.

There were no windows on the alley side of the bungalow, just a small opening holding the little window shaker air conditioner in place. It wasn't secure, so I very slowly and quietly crept on a foldup stepstool I used to reach my pie-in-the-sky kitchen cabinetry and peeped through a chink left by the cheesy, poorly installed plywood facing. It was Ian, a.k.a. Mr. Smith. I quickly slipped back before he could see me, turned up the radio to blasting, found a hard rock station and bounced out of my bungalow, chilled beer in hand, and made enough noise to wake the dead, which startled the Captain sleeping peacefully in his chaise.

"Mornin' Cap'n! Rise 'n' shine!" I sang out. "Edmund! Mornin'! Rise 'n' shine!" For good measure, I banged lustily on Edmund's window with the bottle of beer hoping like hell I hadn't cracked the glass.

"Dhani! Victor! Up and at 'em! It's Morrrrrrrrrrrnin'!" I continued to sing and dance to the strains of Led Zeppelin's "Immigrant Song", and made a general rumpus in the courtyard until, within moments, the denizens of this jungle roused from their slumber and came outside to see what all the fuss was about.

Suddenly, I heard the rumble of a truck starting up and the subsequent squealing of tires peeling out of the parking lot behind the bungalow. It seemed Ian had decided to retreat.

Naturally, everyone was cranky and sore at me for the early wakeup call, but I brought out fresh coffee and Krispy Kremes cut in half so there'd be enough to go around. When I filled them in on my lurking visitor they more than understood. Everyone agreed I may well have saved the Captain's life by my noisy exit from the bungalow. Not to mention maybe saving my own ass–this time. I didn't tell them everything, of course. I just let it drop that this was a hanger-on at the bar and had asked me out several times. I said he'd made a thorough nuisance of himself after I turned him down, shadowing me like an obsessed collector at a baseball card convention. That was enough of a story for them to swallow hook, line, and sinker.

I wasn't due at work that day, so I thought about looking for Tracey, then Kat, then Dan. Then I'd take a good long nap in the afternoon.

Tracey was easy–she was at work, as usual, keeping the locals fat and happy. But this morning, she took one look at me and almost dropped her coffeepot. I was still in the crummy tee-shirt and shorts I'd worn the night before and barefoot, besides. I smiled, waved, and ducked out the door to go home and get decent.

I thought about showering, but had a too-vivid mental vision of Ian strolling into the bathroom as I emerged from the stall. Not to mention a squeamish feeling in the pit of my stomach when I thought of Kat in her bath as I'd found her. Instead, I quickly spot-cleaned myself, flicked a brush through my hair and a brush across my teeth and bounded out the door as quickly as possible. There was no black truck in the lot and no sign of Ian. I mumbled a silent prayer and headed back to Dana's.

Once there, I made myself calm down and order a cup of coffee.

"Hey honey," Tracey said. "You okay?"

I nodded.

She leaned on her elbows in front of me. "Either you had too many or not enough. What's up?"

"We need to talk."

She shook her head. "Not here."

"Agreed, not here. Where, when?"

She tossed her head over to a newspaper reader in the corner. *Sonofabitch. Dan Gowan.*

She jerked her thumb in his direction. "And not where *he's* around, either."

"Agreed."

"This afternoon, four o'clock. We'll go to Pizzzazzz. Pick me up after work?"

"You got it." I finished my coffee and left some change on the counter.

I slipped through the back parking lot to the bungalow and crossed myself when I saw there was no truck, black or otherwise, parked in the lot and no sedan, brown or otherwise, either.

Unlocking my door, I grabbed my bag, went out the front, and coaxed the Mir into taking me back to Kat's. No black truck there, either. I didn't expect the brown sedan.

Knocking on Kat's jalousie door, I was greeted by a muffled, "Go away," a moan, and a rustle of fabric, like sheeting, inside the apartment.

"It's me, Stacey."

Footsteps thumped across the floor. After a brief scrabble at the latch, Kat opened the door a smidge and I quickly slipped inside. For a skinny dancer, she had a very heavy footfall–more like a horse than a prima ballerina.

The dim light inside the apartment didn't show off Kat to any advantage. If anything, she looked more sallow and more bruised than when I found her. She also looked completely, utterly spent and exhausted.

"Why aren't you in the hospital?" I asked.

"Treated and released." She smiled wanly. "The beating of a stripper isn't quite enough to make the evening news around here."

I fumbled in the cabinets as she slumped back down on the couch and found some teabags and a pot under the stove. I started to fill the pot with water from the kitchen faucet but Kat stopped me with a gesture.

"Thanks, Stacey, but I'd rather have a beer, if you don't mind." She pointed. "They're in the fridge. Help yourself."

I was kicking myself in the butt for not bringing over any Hennessy for a quick swig as well.

I turned off the water, put the teabags and pot away, found a bottle opener, and uncapped some ice cold tallboys fresh out of Kat's fridge.

I sat down next to her on the couch, we toasted to "Better Days Ahead," and took a long, deep drink. She crossed her legs and I saw the reason for the heavy footfalls–unusually large feet for such a slender girl. I wondered if she was a size twelve. I thought about the heavy-stomping outside the bungalow this morning. I knew whom I saw, but it reminded me to be careful when looking and judging who's who and what's what. Kat's abundance of feet made up for her lack of boobs and I thought about guys with foot fetishes really liking Kat and tipping her well. I hoped so, at least.

"Kat," I started, "I saw Dan Gowan yesterday and he's going to look into what happened to Loretta."

"Who's Dan Gowan?"

"He's a cop I kind of know."

"Oh, Jeez, Stacey–the cops?"

"Well, what the hell could I do with the information you gave me? Investigate it myself?"

"You weren't supposed to know I was the one who gave it to you."

"Well, hon, you slipped that note in the dollar bill that you put on the bar for me, so it was pretty easy to figure out. Besides, you wrote 'anemone' not 'anonymous'."

"Shit–that was a dead giveaway. I never could spell worth a damn. Ian saw me do it then."

"Is he the one who beat you up?"

"Yeah, him and his flunkies."

"You're lucky you weren't killed!"

"I was told it was a lesson in minding my own business."

I nodded quickly and steered away from *that* subject. "What about medical care? What'd the doc say?"

"I told him I got drunk at work and fell off the stage, so he gave me some Percocet and told me to take a couple days off. Cheers!" she said as she hoisted her bottle and popped a small white pill, chasing it with a long swallow from the tallboy. "Hurts like hell, but I don't give a shit."

She pulled her cheesy worn bathrobe around herself and settled into the couch. "Okay, so what's this Dan guy gonna do?"

I told her about our visit to Loretta's the day before

and finding the few minute blood spatters. I also told her I told Dan about her.

"*Shit*–what's he gonna do now?"

"Hopefully, he'll keep an eye on you. He seemed concerned."

"Yeah, that's all I need, a cop escort. Jeez. Damn."

"Hey, I'm sorry, but..."

"Yeah, look Stacey, it's not your fault. Maybe I shouldn't have said anything. Besides, Dan's just a man. I'll handle him."

"Ummm, whatever," I said. It was far more likely *he* would handle her. "Besides, you look like you could use a couple days off and a little looking after. I'm off today, anything I can get you–like at the store or anything?"

Kat hesitated then nodded. I got paper and pen out of my bag and helped her put together a list.

"If you don't give a shit that you hurt like hell, try to get the place in order a little bit and when I get back I'll make us something to eat."

Kat nodded, "Yeah, I could use something to do. Will you be gone long?"

"About an hour or so."

"See you then."

"Okay." I headed out to the parking lot and saw the black truck parked right next to my white Mir. I got to the car, turned around if I had forgotten something inside and headed back to Kat's.

Kat opened the door for me.

"Just put something on and come with me," I told her. You've got company."

Kat looked out, saw the black truck and nodded. She quickly threw on some thong panties and a skimpy little sundress. She stepped into a well-worn flimsy pair of cheap rubber flip-flops sold at drugstores. Shrugging into a thin shawl, she picked up her little bag and came with me out the door.

Together, we went to the Mir, arm in arm like good buddies going shopping or out to lunch. I looked in the direction of the black truck defiantly, daring that bastard to try something in broad daylight.

There was no one in the truck and, after opening the door for Kat and handing her in, I took a hard, cold look around. A brown sedan was parked down at the corner, but I couldn't make out if anyone was sitting inside. If it was Gowan, my tough-girl pose was wasted.

We went to the local supermarket and Kat waited in the Mir, listening to the radio while I stocked up on a few things for her humble abode. I left her my cellphone, just in case anybody tried any funny stuff, but we were fine. I had a few bucks put by, so we took a quickie trip to the mall where we picked up some fresh shower stuff and a new bathrobe for her. The look of gratitude in Kat's eyes was heart-rending.

As we got back into the car, she started sobbing.

"I feel so–" she hiccupped, searching for a word. "So–violated."

Thunder rumbled in the distance then, all at once, the rain dumped on us as if out of a bucket. *Welcome to Florida*, I thought and waited for the squall to pass both inside and out, then took off in the Mir.

"Maybe it's not such a good idea for you to go back to your place. You got anyplace else you can go?" I asked.

She shook her head. "What's the use, anyway? They'll find me. At work, at home. They want me, they know where to look."

"That Ian guy," I said, "you ever go with him?"

"Once, and he got rough, so I didn't want to go with him anymore."

"Is he giving you a hard time?"

"Not really, just whenever he wants some."

"How did you meet him?"

"Geoffrey's."

"Really?" We pulled into the apartment parking lot. The black truck was gone.

We unpacked Kat's stuff in her mini-kitchen, about the same size as mine, but set up differently. We just chatted girl-stuff. She was from the Midwest and came down here with a boyfriend. He took off for home one day and left her flat broke. She had to earn a living and thought cocktail waitressing might be the way to go. She was thin, pretty and, aside from the feet, quite graceful. She knew she didn't have the smarts or experience to bartend, but she could sling drinks, so she got hooked up at Geoffrey's when she'd met Ian one night in a bar elsewhere. He hooked her up so he could have her and thought if he did her a favor she'd do one for him. She did.

"So, what happened?"

"Originally, it was pretty easy. I just slung drinks and got paid a C and tips. The money was pretty good and until I got with Ian that one night, I was having fun.

"After Ian, there were several guys they wanted me to be 'nice' to. I didn't really give a shit, after all, what's a blow job between friends?"

I shuddered and tried to keep it to myself.

Kat continued, "We'd all go to this guy's house to party. It had a big pool, and a chick who served sandwiches. The guys would play cards and I'd be outside working a tan 'til somebody called me to come inside. We'd have a drink and then go to town. Then back out for more of the same."

"Did this happen a lot?"

"Not really–just every now and then and sometimes, the cards were good to the men, so I'd just sit by the pool by myself drinking. Then there was a boat party. We did the same thing, but on the boat. There were more girls, not just me. We'd go out for days. Sometimes, even hit an island and if a guy liked me maybe he'd take me shopping and buy me some stuff." All of this was stated flatly, as if she was talking about someone else. Or, if the conversation was really about her, it was more like one of those out-of-body experiences than reality.

I didn't want to seem nosy, but I just had to ask, "Why aren't you at Geoffrey's now?"

"Well," she started, "nobody stays at Geoffrey's if Dianna doesn't like her."

Aha. The Dragon Lady reared her ugly head once again. I decided to do a little fishing.

"Who the hell is Dianna?"

"You don't know?" Kat asked. A second later, I knew I'd hooked the big one. "She's the former Mrs. Vinny and she wants back in bad. Only thing is, Vinny likes cards and horses more than women. He can't be bothered to pay the price for a wife, but he'll throw all his money after poker and the track. Dianna will do anything to get with Vinny–anything."

So, that was it. I heard a "snick" as a hasp in my head fastened and everything fell into place. I, suddenly, felt like I was suffocating in Kat's small dim apartment and needed the fresh open air outside. I thought of the wholesome, fresh-faced girls I had worked with at Geoffrey's and how one of them didn't come back from their boat trip. Or, rather, she did come back, but in a way most unbecoming of a lady. I swallowed and decided to ask one last question.

"I thought she had a thing for Geoffrey."

Kat laughed. "Geoffrey? Yeah, right. Geoffrey likes boys. But don't let that get around. I think he's bi and will play with anyone."

"Are you all set?" I asked, trying not to look as if I was in a hurry to leave, but I was.

"Yeah, set. I'm pretty tired, anyway. Think I'll turn in for a while."

"Good idea, Kat. I'll check in on you tomorrow before work."

"That would be nice. I'm taking the rest of the week off."

I wanted to find out more about the boat trips, but thought it best not to push her too hard at this time. There would be plenty of time to probe her while she was healing and maybe I'd get some answers to help put this all to rest.

Packing my jumbled thoughts into the Mir, I couldn't wait to meet Tracey and bump heads together on all this. I headed home to the stately, shady silence of the large mango tree in our courtyard.

Tigger slippers underbed, I took a long, deeply satisfying nap and woke up at two. There was just enough time to shower and air dry before picking up Tracey. Remembering Kat's dingy digs, I tidied up the place before I left and headed out to pick up Tracey at Dana's.

Tracey was waiting for me outside. I asked if she wanted to go home and change first and she agreed. That small detail was attended to with great dispatch as I waited for her in the parking lot. Thankfully, there were no black trucks or brown sedans to be seen. We then wheeled off to Pizzzazzz and did some world-class shoe shopping. I still had to see Gowan, but we were hungry, so we found a little salad place up the beach and tucked into a couple of gourmet salads and cool drinks. A virgin for Tracey, experienced for me, with cute little umbrellas on top and lots of fruit as a side garnish.

After a few sips of our drinks, I said to Tracey, "I didn't know there was a Mrs. Vinny."

Tracey's eyes doubled in size as she almost spit out the sip she held in her straw, but admirably, sucked it down without so much as a hiccup. The eyes narrowed.

"Really?"

"Yeah–her name's Dianna and when we were together the other night I went on and on about this Dragon Lady and you didn't say 'boo!'"

"What's to say? Okay, you know who she is now.

Why does that matter?"

"Why does that *matter*? This bitch smeared me, called me a thief, and had me run out of Geoffrey's on a rail. I felt like I was set up. Why didn't you tell me who she was after all the talking we did the other night?" I felt frustrated and angry but Tracey didn't blink an eye.

"Finished?" Tracey asked coolly. I nodded. "Feeling better?" I nodded again. "Stop nodding, it makes you look stupid.

"Okay," she took a deep breath, and then let it out. "Look, I didn't set you up. You came in all fresh-faced and out of nowhere and wanted to know where to get a job. I told you. I even told you to be careful. You took it. You're a big girl. You got screwed. You left. Nobody held a gun to your head to go back and get in deeper. Why the hell did you, anyway, especially after what I told you?"

She had a point. I fiddled the straw in my empty glass, desperately wanting another drink. "Curiosity? Greed? Lust for excitement? Or maybe, I thought Geoffrey was really cute after I unlocked him from the freezer. Maybe that bartender got to me. I don't know, it seemed like something to do at the time."

"God save us from people who need something to do all the time." Tracey slapped a bill on the table. "I'm ready to go, whenever you are." Her shoes were in my car, so I had her.

"I'm not ready to go yet." I signaled the waitress for another drink. "Make it strong," I told her.

"You're driving."

"Yeah, I am." I replied. When the drink arrived, I took a long deep pull from it. Watching me, Tracey scowled and shook her head.

"Okay, I'll clue you in, since you're determined to be such a Sherlock Holmes–and you don't even like cops, or detectives."

I rolled my eyes skyward. *Here it comes*, I thought.

But when it came, it wasn't quite what I expected.

"Mrs. Vinny, aka Dianna, aka Dragon Lady at Geoffrey's, is another victim of Vinny's–just like me, just like you, just like all the other little girls in that big bastard's circle of friends. The only difference is that she doesn't know it and we do. I got out, you were never really in, but you found a way and now you want out. The little girls have no idea what they're into and this sicko bitch wants to get in *deeper*."

"Yeah, what's up with that?"

"Vinny put a lot of crazy shit into her head when they were married. Gave her a lot of stuff, took her places, but when she wanted to be her own person, out the door she went. If Vinny has you, he owns you. So, she wants to have her cake and eat it. She wants to have Vinny but she wants her own life. So, she helps with the girls at Geoffrey's and is an easy piece for Vinny, whenever he's in the market and he doesn't have to soil the merchandise. So, now, he's got a big mama bear in place to look after his interests at the bar. Get it?"

"Got it. But what did she have against me?"

"Who the hell do you think maybe locked Geoffrey in the freezer?" Tracey arched an eyebrow. "Who let him out? You did. In spite of your down-home southern corn-pone ways, you're smarter than the average bear, and people can sense this about you." It was her turn to roll her eyes skyward.

We paid up and left. Once in the Mir, we apologized to each other and had a good cry. I was into something I didn't know how to get out of, and people were getting hurt, maybe killed. It was definitely a nasty set up and there had to be a way out.

"Find Dan Gowan," she told me. That was all she would say on the subject.

"What about you?" I asked. She looked out the window and didn't reply. We rode home in silence until I dropped her at her door. She nodded a quick thanks, hopped out of the Mir, and briskly walked to her front door, Pizzzazzz bags in tow. She didn't look back.

I sat in the Mir for several minutes, feeling that things had taken a certain turn for the worse. There were no black trucks anywhere to be found, however, so I headed home.

The soft glow of Tiki torches lit the courtyard and people sat around the central table quietly polishing off the remains of a common dinner. I liked living here, I thought. You come and go as you please, you partake of what you choose and then everyone leaves you alone to live your life with minimal interference. I waved to Dhani and Edmund as I passed through, my own Pizzzazzz bags tucked under my arm, and entered the sanctuary of my bungalow. I knew I needed to find Gowan, but I also had work in the morning. I didn't think I'd be going to Dana's, so I dropped my bags and popped over to the Asian Mom & Pop store on the corner for some coffee, creamer, and a bag of those cheap little white powdered doughnuts for breakfast.

I put the stuff away and tried on my new shoes again. They looked great on in the store, and felt deliciously comfy prancing around with Tracey that afternoon, but after giving them the once-over at home, I decided they were nothing special after all, and I would return them in the morning. Maybe the fight with Tracey put a bad vibe on the shoes, I don't know. But back they'd go and I'd be better for it. Every shoe has a feel–some pairs are so lucky, you could get acquitted for murder when wearing them. Others were amazing, giving you confidence and almost super powers to quickly vanquish any other female foes in a room. Others, still, had that good old down-home feel that you just belonged in them and would keep them forever. There were shoes that made you feel so hot you sizzled as you walked. These new shoes were none of the above. I tucked them in their tissue paper and then carefully back in the box. I hated returning things, but after today, I wouldn't mind so much as I'd mind having to find Gowan and try to explain this whole mess to him.

I sat on my sofa-slash-bed and turned on TV. I found something on the animal station and watched as gently grazing deer-like things were cut down with ferocity by the kings–actually, queens–of the jungle, young lionesses. It was strange, watching this macabre dance. I'd watched enough of these shows to easily pick out which animal would be cut from the herd and gunned down, so-to-speak. I felt a strange kinship with the prey more than predator, and finally turned the TV off in disgust.

I thought about the women I knew and who was whom, or, rather, who was what: Tracey? Deer-like thing. Dianna? Lioness, definitely. The girls at Geoffrey's? Kat? Deer-like things. Loretta, an old lioness who, perhaps, got taken out in a fight for supremacy. Who knew? And what about the men who circled around the women, the true predators of this jungle?

I popped a beer and flipped the switch to the radio. Even music didn't soothe the savage beast tonight. I was restless with the prospect of having to do something I didn't want to do, but feared the consequences if I wimped out.

I called Gowan and set up a meeting for the next morning at the Egg and You early enough to get my ass in to work on time. I was in no mood for the company of a DJ on the radio, so I found some sad, soulful jazz on the radio, had a couple beers and a couple shots, closed the windows and cried myself to sleep to the dulcet tones of a mellow sax.

Chapter Twenty-One

Thursday morning, I woke up strangely relaxed, refreshed, and surprisingly un-hungover, given the amount I'd drunk the night before. I showered and dressed for my meeting with Dan Gowan; tailored khaki slacks, cork wedgie shoes, a white shirt, and a navy jacket. I put my hair into a ponytail, twirled it up-style and fastened it with a tortoiseshell barrette, applied a smidge of lipstick and mascara and was out the door before the rest of the Compound began to stir. I tucked a slick cordovan briefcase under my arm in place of a handbag and hoped I looked somewhat professional, as I felt I had some tricky business to transact and, after all, clothes make the game.

My cellphone rang. I took the call and the low, throaty voice on the other end informed me Saturday morning's run was cancelled. I was shaky about that. Did they know something was up? But I strengthened my resolve to carry out my plan.

Checking on Kat, as promised, I found her to be fine and not quite awake yet, so I promised to return a little later. I jumped back into the Mir and headed off to the Egg and You.

Gowan was there before I was, naturally. It's a power ploy to arrive first, just as it's a power ploy to arrive late. He was first, I was on time, and we knew who was in charge. I expected that. He gave me an approving glance as I slid across from him into the same corner booth we had previously. It was a good feeling to pass muster, so I figured the clothes worked. We both ordered this time, and while I was more than ready to pick up my end of the bill, I had a sneaking suspicion he was buying today, so I ordered good: a muffin, ham and eggs with potatoes, a side of rye toast, and lots of coffee. I had two cups of coffee before we even started talking. With sugar.

"Slow down, girl. You're going to give me sugar shock," Gowan said.

I smiled apologetically and spooned more sugar into my cup while the waitress sailed by with her ever-full coffeepot ready to pour more for me. Gowan held his up also, and she filled it with a little flourish.

"The lady's out-drinking you, sir!" she said with a wink.

"Slow and steady wins the race," he replied, and we all laughed as the waitress headed off to her next stop.

I took a deep breath, laced with sugar and the sweet taste of muffin and began my tale. Gowan was a good listener. He asked intelligent questions and nodded in all the right places. At one point, I thought he was going to take my hand, but I tightened it around the coffee mug and told him about the phone call that morning cancelling Vinny's that Saturday morning for a run and they'd "be in touch."

Gowan countered with the fact that the forensics team had found a quantity of blood in Loretta's apartment, thanks to special lighting that, when applied, showed bloodstains easily, even if cleaned up. Also, the tiny dots of blood on the wall were back-splatters, which are caused when a weapon is removed from a wound instead of the initial stabbing into it. There was more investigation to be done in the field, but he doubted anything would come of it. Loretta was done and gone. Her husband didn't really seem to want a big deal made of the case. There was no body to exhume and no autopsy to be revised and, except on some basic evidence and a hunch that an ice pick might have been driven through the lady's ear, nothing indicated that a stroke had *not* occurred to take her life. It was unlikely that anyone would be caught in conjunction with the killing. On the plus side, however, this would bring the focus on certain persons "of interest" who would be closely watched now and he hoped they would yield something in the future. I hoped so, too.

I explained I had promised to check in on Kat and then get to work. He nodded, let me go, and said he'd take care of the bill and would call me. I wrote my cellphone number down on a paper napkin and told him the best time to call was between six and seven. I'd hoped that would narrow my window of expectation for a callback and retain a little bit of control over my life.

I dropped by Kat's and found she was a bit better. In fact, she was sitting outside, on a chaise next to the apartment's meager bean-shaped pool, reading a novel and getting some sun. A white lace beach cover-up concealed most of her bruises while letting in some much-needed sun. A big-brimmed white straw sun hat and large white-framed sunglasses hid most of her face. She stretched languorously, like a cat–or a dancer–and I seated myself beside her on one of the lawn chairs by the pool. Her big feet were gracefully positioned *en pointe* at the end of the chaise lounge.

"Feeling better?" I asked.

"Yeah," she replied dreamily, "I love this Percocet."

"Yeah, well, don't get too attached, everything ends sometime."

"Yeah, but not today…" she rolled over onto her side and propped herself up on an elbow cocking her head to face me. "So, how are *you*?"

"Me? Oh, me… I'm fine, just fine. Couldn't be better."

She smiled. "You're all dressed up."

"Business in Fort Lauderdale, you know," I yammered. It must've been a result of listening to too much DJ patter on the radio. Either that, or this was my morning to talk.

Kat waved to an empty chaise beside her. "Got time? I've got more books inside–help yourself."

I figured I could keep her company for about a half hour until I had to go home and change for work, so I selected a spy thriller from her collection. In spite of the casual attitude toward general housekeeping evidenced in Kat's apartment, the books were meticulously shelved and well cared for.

She glanced at my selection and grinned. "That's a good one! You'll love the airplane chase."

I smiled at her. "Thanks."

"We had quite a chat yesterday. Sorry I got so unglued."

"No apologies necessary. I'm just wondering…"

"Yes?" she said quietly, her eyes softening towards me.

"How did you get from point A at Vinny's, to point B, the Booby Bar?"

"Oh, that…" she drifted off someplace in her own memories. For a moment, I thought she wasn't going to provide an answer.

Then she spoke softly and evenly.

"Dianna–you know her? Black hair, black eyes, black disposition–she got tired of me. She gave me lousy tables at Geoffrey's, so the money was shit and I didn't go to parties anymore. The last boat party I was invited to, I skipped because I was sick and when I went back to work– no job. I figured taking off my top was no worse than what I was doing, anyway, and if I wanted any action on the side, it would be up to me, not Vinny and his crew. So, I was better off without them."

"Yeah, but how are you with that?"

"I'm okay with it. I get paid good, I eat regular, I drink as I please, and now and then I get a boyfriend. It's enough."

What was enough for some people would be a hardscrabble existence for another, and I wondered where, indeed, this poor creature had come from. Where were her dreams? Where was the little girl who someplace wanted to be a beautiful ballerina and tucked paper dancers under her pink pillow at night to help the dream come true? Had all this come down to some cheap flimsy dresses and black platform patent-leather stripper shoes? I sighed and wondered what someone might think about my life and tucked into the novel to escape for a while.

About ten minutes later, I heard soft snoring and saw Kat with her book, open and facedown on her chest, peacefully sleeping. I kissed her forehead and bid her good rest and headed home. She snuggled deeper into the chaise lounge. I took the spy thriller with me. I'd return it next time. I pointed the Mir home and arrived safe and sound—no black trucks in evidence.

I had just enough time to change and dash to work. No time to check on Tracey. Then again, maybe a little time and a little distance was for the best.

I entered the cool closeness of Sparky's to have Little Ricky greet me with, "This is your lucky day!"

I headed toward my sinks and register, trying to ignore him and hoping he was speaking to someone else.

"I said," he said getting right in my face, "this is your lucky day! Didn't you hear me?"

"Oh, yeah, Ricky," I said casually over my shoulder while filling a sink and noticed the water was already hot. I turned off the faucet. "I heard you—I just didn't think you were speaking to me, that's all."

"Know why today is lucky–just–for–you?" he asked, dragging out every word along the way.

"Okay, I'll bite. Why is it lucky for me today?" I knew there was no way out.

"Because, my beautiful lady, I have decided to *forgive* you for the other night!"

Oh, joy. This truly was my lucky day.

"And... I'm giving you a one-day special–today only–to make it up to me!"

I rolled my eyes. Why would I *want* to? "Ricky..." I started, "about the other night..."

"Say no more!" he enthused. "I've decided to forgive you! It never happened! Tonight we're going out! Together!"

"Yeah, I remember the last time we went out," thinking of Loretta's soiree.

"No, no, no–nothing like that! We're going dinner, drinks, dancing, the works," and with that he grabbed me in his arms and started twirling me around the bar.

"Look, I've even done your sinks! And the ice! Now count your bank." And he gave me a playful little slap on the derrière. Oh, brother. But the sinks were freshly watered and hot, there was ice in the bin, and the bar fruit–lemons, limes, oranges, pineapple–was cut. All I really had to do was count my bank and wipe down the bottles.

As I started wiping down my speed rack, Ricky snuck up behind me, playfully kissed the nape of my neck–I still had my hair twirled up–and took the bar rag from my hands.

"There, there, sweetheart, leave that to me!" He quickly peeled the bottles out of the rack, wiped everything down, slammed the bottles back into the speed rack with a flourish and a casual toss of the bar rag right the hamper behind the bar.

"What's up with you?" I asked him. "You're in way too good of a mood."

"I'm getting my kid!"

"Whaaa...?" Visions of little tykes accompanying me on a date with this dude flashed through my brain and it was all I could do to hold back a shudder of disgust at the thought. I modified the "whaaa" to a "When?" with some grace and mightily hoped "when" would be no time soon.

"Next week! And I can't wait to introduce him to my future ex-wife. You!"

Oh, God. The picture became crystal clear: he wanted a mommy for his kiddie and he was, unfortunately, looking straight at me. I knew it was no dice, but I didn't want this to play out too soon, he was being way too nice to me and after all the shit I'd been taking from him, I wanted to take advantage of the situation a little bit now.

"Look, Ricky, if you want me to do you a favor and babysit sometime…" I said, figuring maybe I could swap a dead shift with him for the priceless privilege of tending his brat from another issue.

"No, no, no, not at all. It's about togetherness and family and fun! He's a pretty good kid. You might even like him! My ex-wife, the bitch, is finally getting married to this guy and she needs me to take our son while she's on her honeymoon with the dude. I'm gonna have him for a whole month!"

On the whole, I like kids about at much as I like drunks: they're surly, rude, uncontrollable and completely unmanageable unless you learn to deal with them on their own terms. Somehow, you have to worm, without wheedling–they can spot that in a sec–your way by making it seem like it's all their idea. That's way too much work and something I'm not at all prepared for. Dealing with a dying mother was easier.

I looked up at the ceiling and asked, "Why me?"

Ricky overheard me. He bounded to my corner of the bar, invading my space. "Because you, baby, are the best! Look, in order to get my kid I had to tell the ex-wife, the bitch, I met somebody who's a real good influence on me so I don't drink like a fish anymore. We're gonna go places and do things together and if this works out okay, maybe I'll get him for a month every summer and maybe even for Christmas, or Thanksgiving."

I secretly wondered to myself if his wife had

another name besides "the ex-wife, the bitch", and it made me smile in a very goofy way.

Of course, Ricky picked up on my smile all wrong, thought I was smitten with the idea and he continued unabated.

"So, all I need is for you to be a good egg and play along with me okay? Maybe–and I know we like each other a little bit... maybe we'll wind up liking each other a little more!"

I couldn't wait to see how it turned out. Customers entered the bar, so I focused my attention on them. Ricky acted disgustingly devoted to me for the remainder of the shift, and I was only able to peel him off me by agreeing to go out with him that evening.

"Thanks! You're a doll! Pick you up at eight and don't be late!" he said with a short hug. It was all I could do not to groan.

"I'll meet you–right here–eight thirty!" I called after him.

"It's a date!" he called back, doing a dipsy doodle on twinkle toes as he pranced out of the bar like a demented ballerina.

It looked stupid to me, and I wondered what the hell he was on. Maybe he'd get some for me. That might be a fun evening. At least we'd both be Twinkies instead of just one of us.

I had a little time to relax before my heavy date–and heavy it would be, since I'd have to break Ricky's heart and decline his generous offer, knowing I wouldn't accept it as a precious gift. Maybe he'd listen, after dinner–Dutch treat at Sparky's. I had to work with him after all, so I needed to think about a way to let him down gently. I thought and thought and finally came up with a fishy story that *might* work if I played it right. I remembered how intimately my brother Ed was acquainted with the Florida penal system, in more than he was out, so my chances were pretty good he was, once again, enjoying their hospitality. I'd explain that as his only family, Ed truly *needed* me, his ever-lovin' sister, to get out there and provide family support every chance I got. How would it look taking his kid to an "outing" at a prison? I bet his ex wouldn't cotton to the idea, and sonny-boy would be back in mommy's arms, pronto.

The sex part, the dating part, was easy. I just would tell him I'm waiting for the results of my AIDS test before I feel comfortable about bedding him. That usually cools 'em down right quick.

Feeling safe with my stories, I armed myself to go out. I fished the khaki-wedgie shoes I was going to return to Pizzzazzz, figuring they'd be good for mini golfing, bad dates or blind dates. I paired them with jeans, a khaki safari shirt two sizes too big, and retained the ponytail. All I needed was a pith helmet that said "Me Bwana, you game" and bang-bang, he'd go away.

I entered Sparky's and spotted Ricky at a corner booth in the back watching a Seinfeld rerun. He waved me over and motioned me to sit down next to him. I sat. He howled over every little thing this Seinfeld character said and I sat there feeling like a stupe because, for some reason, I wasn't getting it. Then he'd explain it to me and howl some more. I didn't even crack a grin.

I needed a drink. Nabbing one of the gals on the floor, I signaled her for a beer. She nodded and gave me a look of abject pity at my situation. I worked here; I didn't shit in my own nest.

Ricky got another drink and we watched another Seinfeld rerun. This was, obviously, the Seinfeld Channel. The only thing worse would be a follow up of *Friends* where everyone sits on a couch and just yammers away about nothing, or a rehash of other inane sitcoms. Why does TV have to be blaring in every entertainment establishment and restaurant in America? You can't even go to the dentist or the dry cleaners without some blow-dried bloviate telling you how to get the most out of your love life–whether or not you have, or even *want* one, for that matter. All over America, little kids are being fed dinner over this shit, everywhere they go–except at fast food restaurants. Maybe that's why they're so popular–no TV. It gives the parents a chance to actually talk to their kids, sometimes.

The thought brought me down to the real world. I had to focus on the moment for the right chance to tell Ricky how I felt and what was going to–actually *not* going to–happen.

After the second Seinfeld rerun, Ricky signaled for the check. The gal brought it and he paid it with a flourish, obviously over tipping the gal and giving me a big hug and a wet, sloppy smooch.

"Are ya hungry?" He leered at me.

"Ummm, yes, okay. Aren't we going to eat here?"

"You like Chinese?"

"Sure, that's fine."

We have one little Chinese joint at the beach and, since I knew Ricky didn't drive, I figured that's where we were going. It's kind of dumpy and they use too much curry in their food. I haven't had it myself, but I've smelled it when Dhani brought it home and it's way too much curry, believe me. However, anything beat another Seinfeld rerun, even if a free drink on Ricky was included.

I hadn't realized it in Sparky's, but as soon as the fresh air hit Ricky in the face, he was bombed. Totally, disgustingly blathered. Drunk as a lord. Inebriated. Stinking skunk drunk. In his cups–and I wasn't letting him near mine, either. Not in *any* state, but especially in this state. I was glad I didn't smoke, because he would have blown up if I lit a match. I was surprised the cars on Atlantic Boulevard weren't erupting in flames as we breezed across the intersection. I wouldn't have served him if he were my customer. Then again, maybe yeah, I would have, knowing I'd probably get a blockbuster tip at the end of this super king-sized bout of drinking.

I poured him into the Chinese restaurant and he flopped onto a bright red ripped vinyl waiting station in front of the cashier. Lucky bamboo woven in intricate plaiting decorated the cashier's desk while *Wheel of Fortune* was playing on the TV mounted on the wall, which was lavishly papered in gold trompe l'oile. He looked at the TV with all of his eyes (there seemed to be about six, the way he was zoning in on the set), as he tried to keep his balance. He tried to guess the phrase. He didn't. He got pissed. He stood up and cussed out the poor little Chinese girl who was at the cash register. He cussed out the Chinese guy in the white chef shirt and pants with the coolie braid down his back. He cussed out the customers waiting for takeout. Of all things and beyond the pale, as far as I was concerned, he cussed out Vanna White, claiming her to be a worse bitch than his ex-wife, the bitch, and how he wasn't eating at a restaurant that had this kind of shitty TV that pisses off such valued patrons, as him. I *like* Vanna White.

I asked him if he wanted to get something to go. He blearily replied he just wanted to leave and, after his little tantrum, I didn't object. I didn't feel he was quite safe walking home alone, nor was anybody he'd meet along the way, for that matter, so I offered to see him to his door.

We got to his place, I saw him in, he invited me in and I tried to decline. He was getting insistent and noisy, so I thought if I could get him in and sit him down, that would be that. He'd topple over and go straight into a drunken snooze. A mean drunk is a nightmare, but a pissed off mean drunk is nobody to wrangle with. Just get 'em quiet and sit 'em down and the rest, like passing out, takes care of itself.

He did exactly as I'd predicted. He sat down, toppled over, and seemingly fell asleep. As I went to let myself out the door, he mumbled his apologies.

"It's okay, Ricky. It's been an exciting day for you, getting your kid back and all."

"Are you still hungry?" he asked.

I thought maybe he had sandwich fixings in the fridge. "Yeah, a little."

"Well, *here*," he said and started unfastening his pants.

I gave him a disgusted look, said I wasn't *that* hungry and slammed the door as I left. I headed back to the little Chinese dive and apologized profusely, got a mouthful of teeth from the little Chinese girl and reassurances from the coolie who happened to be the chef that this had happened before. He asked why a nice girl like me was hanging together with a nut like him. I explained we were just co-workers and I was trying to be nice. They smiled, nodded, maybe understood more of what I said than they let on, and gave me a free Coke with my sparerib dinner.

I went home and greedily ate the ribs and rice just as the cheetah I was watching on the television animal program tore apart its prey. I pretended the ribs were Ricky's.

Tigger slippers underbed, I tucked in and tossed and turned all night.

Chapter Twenty-Two

The next morning, I was still pissed off when I woke up. I kicked a Tigger slipper that got in my way when I folded up the sofa bed and dropped the whole damned thing on my toe. It raised a helluva bruiser on my big toenail. *Shit*, I thought, now the toenail will turn black and fall out; how the hell am I gonna show off those cute little tootsie sandals? And me with a hot date with Gregg tonight, I hoped.

I showered then donned a comfy terrycloth romper and squishy overlarge flip-flops. I exited the bungalow and made my way to the corner super-drugstore. I scored a bottle of cheap Purple Passion nail polish to even out my discolored toenail and match up the rest of the toes for my "new" look.

As a rule, I don't like highly colored toenails. I guess it reminded me of my mom, carefully painting each little toenail a perfect hot Passion Pink or Chinese Crimson whenever she thought my dad might come home. I believed she chose these more for the names than the colors. Dad rarely came, but every Friday night my mom would religiously groom herself head to toe. About halfway through the pampering process, she would realize he wasn't going to call and wasn't coming home. So, she'd ask me to fetch us a couple of beers and *hey-what-the-hell*, we'd have girls' night in and she would paint my toenails to match hers. The beer made me silly and I remember laughing a lot. My dad hadn't left for good, then, but he wasn't home for supper every night, either, so it was usually just mom and me.

Now and again, when my dad did show up, I was given a peck on the cheek, a swat on the ass and told to skedaddle, which usually amounted to my going to my "secret" place, a dug out hole under the trailer where I could hear the grunts and moans of their "lovemaking" or, more often a "Fuck You Fight" above me. Then Dad would take off again.

Sometimes, I'd go down to the town library, where I could hang out until nine o'clock, relatively undisturbed. But more often than not, I'd run into big brother Ed who'd usually press me into service doing some of his dirty work or running his errands. It was best for me if Dad *didn't* come home, so I wasn't sorry on Friday nights if he didn't show.

I hadn't painted my toenails in anything bolder than Bare Ballerina since my mom died.

The good thing was, I wasn't pissed off anymore. I was morose. TV music videos didn't help. I flipped off the TV, flipped it the bird, and got ready for work.

Carefully dressing so as to not smudge the newly applied toenail polish, I stepped once again into the squishy flip-flops and started the slow, painful trek to Sparky's, toting a pair of sneakers for behind the bar.

I walked up Atlantic Boulevard with a distinct sense of dread. I didn't want to face little Ricky behind the bar for a full day of work. It was a relatively dry sunny day, so my hair didn't frizz.

My dad once said some things will tend to piss you off if you sit around and think about them, so you get moving and don't think. I don't know if that was to get me out of the way during his homecomings or a bit of good down-home dad-type advice. I picked up the pace and decided I could show up a little late for once and took a brisk walk along Ocean Avenue for a couple blocks then back again. The sea breeze dried my pedicure in a hurry and the walk helped the pain in my stubbed toe, so by the time I got to work I was ready to put on sneakers and get down to business.

I entered the cool, dimly lit cavern that was Sparky's. The pall of dread I felt lifted immediately when I saw Mike behind the bar instead of Little Ricky. I'd hoped Little Ricky would call in "dead" after the night he had last night but, no, he was just "sick," meaning hung over, and Mike was pinch-hitting. Mike was clearly sick of working doubles after working nights, but he didn't take it out on me. He was mad at Ricky for calling in all the time, for which I didn't blame him. But Mike's pretty mellow and made the most of it by keeping the regulars and the tourists happy, so I wound up with a fun shift and heavy pockets.

At six-thirty, I flipped Mike a wink, blew him a kiss, and started to head out as Tish, my evening relief checked in. Some of the regulars nicknamed her "Tush", to her distinct displeasure, because of her ample, but well-contoured derriere, however, a well-placed dollop of Tabasco in the offending customer's shot discouraged the practice quickly. She cornered me and begged a favor for me cover her shift tomorrow, Saturday night. I said sure, since I didn't work Saturday during the daytime. Sparky's had a pretty good steady rock and roll trio on Saturday night who packed the bar, so it would be a great money night for me.

Besides, Saturday nights you don't have to clock in until seven and my date was tonight and I didn't have a run tomorrow. Being in the bar business means you get to do a lot of favors. I felt accepted at last, as this was the first time anyone had asked me for anything. Tish and I shook hands on the deal.

As if on cue, my cellphone rang just as I walked out the door. I took the call, watching the first stars of twilight in the sinking indigo hour as I walked toward the beach.

"Hi gorgeous." It was Gregg.

"Hi gorgeous, yourself."

"You free?"

"No, but I'm easy."

He laughed. "Half an hour?"

"Make it an hour," I wanted to soak my feet, but didn't tell him.

"Yeah, cool, make me wait," he said.

"I'm worth waiting for."

"That you are, sweet heart." He said sweetheart in two words, instead of running it all together, which I really liked. I hate when guys start calling you pussycat, honey, babe or sweetie and get all lovey-dovey on you when you've just had a roll or two in the hay. It isn't anything much yet. Tell me I have a sweet heart, that's fine with me. I smiled to myself thoughtfully as I closed the flip phone. This was looking like we had an understanding.

I spent a few moments gazing out at the ocean and near-empty expanse of sand, the palm fronds gently whispered their secrets to one another as a few late-afternoon beach goers straggled off the sand. I watched as they loaded chairs, towels, and each other into their cars to go back to their safe little hotel rooms and happy little lives, utterly oblivious to the underbelly of the darker side of the city.

I thought about my first days here and how quickly I'd made a life after leaving home. There was Tracey, the job at Sparky's, some nice coworkers—never mind Little Ricky—who I preferred not to know any better than I already did, but there's always one in a crowd. The guys at the Compound were cool and a little something had started to blossom with Gregg. I decided it would be best to forget Geoffrey, his club Geoffrey's and the dead Lorikeet at the beach. It faded in my mind as day faded to evening. I hummed happily on the way home.

By the time I hit the Compound, I barely limped, even though I was on my feet all day, but I still thought a nice hot foot soak would do me good.

Everyone must have had other plans, because the chirp of neighborhood crickets instead of catcalls from my fellow inmates of the asylum called the Compound greeted me. Even the Captain was elsewhere.

Tucking the day's take into a hidey-hole I'd made in the wall under the window-shaker air conditioner, I settled down for a good hot foot soak. I popped a cold one and headed to the inner-sanctum of my mini-shower to complete my feminine ablutions.

I emerged, fluffed, powdered, and perfumed, but with a toe that still hurt like hell. I prayed I wouldn't trip over myself and land in a compromising position with Gregg I couldn't get out of before dinner. I was starving.

Of course, I did stumble into Gregg when he entered the bungalow, but he gently steadied me, drew me into his arms and kissed me. Softly, then growing stronger and more urgent. We settled in on the couch and before I knew it, he was loving my toes and my fingers and my arms and legs and everyplace else there are names for and others best left unmentioned. I forgot about the pain in my toe and went into orbit, focusing on the pleasures of the moment. The hunger pangs were forgotten as well.

Afterwards, we ordered in pizza and spend the rest of the evening munching, drinking, cuddling, loving and watching nothing in particular on TV. Gregg had pulled the sofa bed out sometime in the midst of passion, so it seemed as if we had one great big play bed to have fun on. There were enough shows and music videos playing keep us amused in-between. Never mind what. Use your imagination.

Chapter Twenty-Three

We woke up early the next morning; cotton-mouthed, slightly fuzzy yet mightily happy. As I lay next to Gregg before the first blush of morning lovemaking, I decided it was early enough and high time enough for him to meet Tracey at Dana's. Besides, he might enjoy a steaming hot cup of coffee and a scrumptious warm blueberry muffin straight out of the oven. I knew I sure would and my capability for breakfast at the bungalow was limited to beer and cheese. I hardly thought *that* suitable after so much enjoyment the night before. Besides, Tracey could scope out the new light-of-my-life and give me her opinion. I hoped it would be good.

We showered–but please, not together–there just wasn't enough room, much as we might have enjoyed it. I loaned Gregg one of my extra-large tee shirts and he had a pair of flip-flops in the car. That's a Keys boy for you. Have flip-flops, will travel. I wondered if it had been planned then decided not, he would have had a spare tee shirt tucked away, too.

We trudged off to Dana's. My poor toe was better, but not at its best and it gave a sudden twinge of pain, which hit me as I hopped off the curb on Atlantic Boulevard and dodged an oncoming Buick driven by an old blue-haired lady I would have sworn was aiming for us.

We got to Dana's. Louie was working the counter and he looked pissed. Louie is about five-and-a-half feet tall and about five feet wide, so running between the grill in the back *and* the counter in the front wasn't his favorite thing. He didn't bathe as often as he should, I suspected, but when dining in a local establishment, I take a "don't ask don't tell" attitude and try to accentuate the positive, like the muffins. We sat down and ordered. Louie poured our coffee then trundled off to the kitchen to take care of Gregg's eggs.

I was enough of a regular to open my mouth, so I called out to Louie, "Where's Tracey?"

Louie shrugged, "No show. Beats me."

"Did she call you?"

"No show. No call. Like I said." Louie grunted as he cracked some eggs on the hot griddle. I heard the sizzle and inhaled the warm, comforting aroma of eggs frying.

Louie looked peeved, so I stared into my coffee cup with a vaguely uncomfortable feeling. Gregg put his hand on mine and looked over to me.

"Stace–you okay?"

I nodded, then shrugged. "Not really. I don't understand it. She's always here." I took a half-hearted sip of my coffee.

"You know where she lives, right?"

I nodded.

"Okay, so after breakfast, we'll go over and check on her. She's sick, maybe."

I nodded. "Yeah, and she doesn't have a phone."

"There. See? I'm sure everything's fine."

Louie, sweating profusely, set the eggs and a muffin down in front of Gregg and a muffin in front of me.

"Eat hearty," he grunted, then filled the counter patrons' coffee cups. He headed back to the kitchen and out the back door.

We ate quickly, paid up and headed out. I ducked in the back to catch Louie having a smoke and leaning against the back of the building.

"We're going to check on Tracey." Gregg looked over to Louie. "What's the number here? I'll call you."

"Doesn't matter, they come and they go." Louie

shook his head. "If she wants to come back, she'll come back. If not, we'll just get someone else."

I nodded and gulped. People in South Florida are so disposable, it seems. One leaves and two others show up to take their place. In two weeks, it's like they never existed.

Giving Gregg quick directions to Tracey's, we arrived and everything was quiet.

Nothing seemed amiss at Tracey's front door. It looked closed, but a slight breeze blew and it gave, just a bit. The door was not latched shut.

I gently leaned against the door and pushed it open a crack. "Traceyyy?" I called, softly. I pushed open the door and hoped I wasn't disturbing her.

It was dead quiet inside.

Gregg, standing almost on top of me, silently motioned me out of the way and fully opened the door, taking the forefront entering Tracey's tidy little apartment.

Everything was in place.

"Maybe she went to the store. Or the doctor." Gregg said.

I noticed the unmade bed.

Tracey's handbag was hanging on one of her kitchenette chairs.

"Hardly likely," I said, and pointed at the purse. I looked around and got an empty, lightheaded feeling. I felt Tracey was gone and not because she wanted to leave. I stood in the middle of Tracey's clean little apartment, feeling utterly impotent. Something was desperately, terribly wrong. The tea things were out, the stove was on, and the pot was starting to burn.

Gregg turned off the kettle.

"Kat," I whispered softly, to myself.

"Kat?" Gregg said. "The one from the other week?"

I nodded.

"What's going on?"

We sat on Tracey's couch. Gregg, who is about six

feet tall, looked very out-of-place in these girly-girl digs. His large feet, in flip-flops, seemed almost the size of the cute little flip-flop rug in front of Tracey's door.

I told Gregg about Vinny, the cellphone, how I met Loretta, the dead Lorikeet on the beach, and Kat's latest escapade. I mentioned Tracey and I thought Vinny might be selling girls from Geoffrey's somewhere out in the middle of nowhere–namely, the ocean.

He whistled long, low and slow. "Let's go check on Kat."

"Don't you have to work today?"

"Not 'til tonight. There's time yet."

I agreed, not wanting to do this alone, and nodded for him to come with me as we went to Kat's place, just a couple of blocks away.

Kat's place was trashed. I wasn't able to tell if it was from the mess that happened before, or if Kat had a casual attitude about housekeeping. Gregg picked up the shards of a broken lamp and held them in his hand, looking at me questioningly.

"She's gone, too."

There was no blood in the bathroom, the kitchen, or anywhere else in the apartment, so I assumed between then and now Kat had her own private little war with the mess and won. This was new.

"Where would they go?" Gregg asked.

"We have to find a big black truck, that'll tell us."

"Who drives a big black truck?"

"I don't know, I think maybe this guy Ian. But whenever I see that damn truck, there's trouble not far behind."

In novels, sometimes the heroine has everything click neatly into place for her. With me, it wasn't a soft clicking sound as stuff snapped into place. It was more like a large, dizzying blow on the head. I wanted to smack myself for not seeing this sooner and opening my mouth to those nearest and dearest to me. After all, I had been told there would be no supermarket-shopping run today for Vinny.

"I think the truck might be at the marina. I've seen it there before," I said.

Gregg nodded.

We left Kat's as quietly as possible. Gregg looked somewhat ashen and I'm sure I looked no better. I was happy I was wearing the squishy flip-flops again because I was sure there would be a lot of running around today, and I had to be to work by seven that evening.

My Purple Passion toenails were a still bit jarring to me, though, as I looked down at my feet as we walked out to Gregg's car. I found the thought, in the middle of all this upheaval, funny and giggled. Gregg looked at me like I was weird. Guess I was weirded out.

Gregg asked where the marina was and I gave him directions behind Dana's. We pulled up and Louie was still smoking against the back of the building, looking more relaxed now that the morning rush had subsided.

Gregg approached Louie and put his hand on his shoulder. "Hey, buddy,"

Louie looked up sullenly at Gregg. "I know you?" He'd evidently forgotten we had breakfast there together earlier that morning.

"No, you don't know me, but you've seen this lady a time or two and we think her friend Tracey, who works for you, might be in trouble."

"Tracey don't work for me, I don't own this place."

"Okay, mac, whatever. But what we want to know is did you see a boat with some girls leave the marina this morning?"

"What's it worth?"

I pulled out a twenty, as Gregg reached for his wallet. "No, hon," I said to Gregg, "I'll get this." I ripped the twenty in half, a trick I learned from Ed, and handed

Louie half the bill.

"I didn't see nothin'," Louie said.

I held of my half of the bill and snatched the other half out of Louie's hand quickly. I figured I could tape it together later and it'd be as good as new.

We turned our backs on Louie and headed back to Gregg's car.

"Look, this is my deal, okay?" I said. "You've got to get to work."

Gregg gave me a sidelong glance and started the car. "Yep, it's your deal, babe. I've got to go to work, and I will once we get this straightened out a little for you. Where next?"

I thought for a minute and gave him directions to Stinger's. If anybody knew anything, it would be old Charlie behind the bar. Stinger's was open and Charlie was wiping down glasses and polishing bottles when we walked in.

"Hey, Charlie," I said. "I need a favor."

"Can I fix you up with a beer first?"

I thought about it, and shook my head no. "Maybe later. I need to know who owns a big boat called the Golden Girl and if you maybe saw this boat go out with a party this morning?" I laid one half of the ripped twenty-dollar bill on the rail.

Charlie picked up the half a bill, thoughtfully turned it over in his hands and laid it back on the bar.

"Can't say as I do. Not this morning, anyway."

"Last night?"

"Nope. But your friends, Edmund and Dhani, might have seen something. They came in early this morning after a night fishing run. I'm sure they're home sleeping, dead as doornails, because they were out all night and didn't catch a damn thing. Came in at seven this morning for an eye-opener. Maybe they'll tell you something." He pushed the ripped half-bill back towards me and I picked it up.

I laid a fin on the rail for Charlie and turned to Gregg.

"Home?" he said as we left Stinger's. I nodded.

The Compound was silent. Even the big old mango tree was still and the palm trees whispered no more.

"I don't have a good feeling about this, Stacey," Gregg said, "maybe you'd be better staying at my place today."

I shook my head no. "I have to work tonight, something is terribly wrong, and I can't just hole up at your place until it passes. This is a situation, hon, not a hurricane."

He smiled down softly at me.

"What?" I asked him.

"I like when you call me hon," he said. "Okay, let's see if Edmund or Dhani saw anything, and we'll figure out what to do from there."

He started walking over to the bungalow. "But first, I'm checking your place."

The door was still locked and the place looked the same as I'd left it.

"Wait a minute," I said, unlocking the bungalow and going to the window-shaker air conditioner. I grabbed the money out of the hidey-hole and tucked it in my purse.

"Now I know I'm your boyfriend, sweet heart." Gregg said, "I know where you keep your stash."

I gave him a quick kiss that said yes and said "Later, hon," and we headed to Dhani's, figuring he'd be easiest to wake up.

Dhani woke up slowly, and answered our banging on his door with less than a cheery good morning.

"What the hell…" he said blearily, as he peered out at us. "Do you know what time it is?" Our sheepish looks must have mollified him as he opened the door, turned and beckoned us inside.

We perched on his couch and he flopped into his

armchair. Half sitting up, he asked if we wanted a beer. I did, Gregg didn't. Padding to the kitchen, Dhani returned with two beers and a glass of water for Gregg.

We popped our beers, hoisted a good swig, and Gregg put his glass down on the coffee table without taking a sip.

"So, this is the boyfriend?" Dhani asked.

I shrugged. "This isn't about that."

"No?" Dhani said playfully, giving me a long, lascivious wink.

I paled. Dhani took notice, took a sip of beer and sat up in his chair.

"Okay, then what?" Dhani asked.

"Charlie at Stinger's told me you guys went fishing last night."

Dhani thought we were playing. "So, you're mad because we didn't invite you? We thought you guys were busy."

Gregg and I looked at each other, and Gregg took the lead, "No, we're wondering if you saw a big yacht party go out this morning."

"Big boat party? This morning?" Dhani thoughtfully sipped at his beer. "As a matter of fact, I did." He took another pull on the beer. "Stacey, you know the boat. It almost knocked us over when we went fishing that day."

I shot back, "The Golden Girl, right?"

"That's the one."

"Yeah, I remember. Holy shit! Dhani, we've got to find that boat!" I started to tell him why, my tongue tripping over the words in my urgency to get them out.

"Whoa, slow down, there girl." He spoke to me as a horse whisperer would to a skittish colt. "We're not going anywhere until we figure this out. It's a big ocean."

Yes, it was. And it was more than possible Tracey and Kat were out there somewhere and God knows how many other unfortunate women pressed into service as Geoffrey and Vinny's "party girls."

Gregg asked, "You know the boat, Stacey?"

I nodded. "I just didn't remember until now." I looked at both Gregg and Dhani, stricken. "We've got to get to that boat!"

"Okay, there's other ways of finding a boat than combing the ocean." Dhani said. "There's radar, there's radios, there are sailing plans, there's the Harbor Master…"

"Then let's start with the Harbor Master. Do you know him, Dhani?" Gregg asked.

"Not as well as Edmund."

I was out the door and across the courtyard to get Edmund out of bed immediately, leaving Gregg in my wake. We were back in five minutes, Edmund, shirtless and hung over stumped behind me. He looked like a dancing bear after a wild night on the town. He trudged into Dhani's apartment.

"What's this all about, anyway? Hell, get me out of bed. This the boyfriend?" Edmund said, glancing towards Gregg.

I shrugged, and Gregg and Dhani filled him in briefly.

"All right, let me grab a shower and a shirt." Edmund said.

"Just grab the shirt, and never mind the shower, hon," I said to Edmund. Gregg looked at me archly. "It's just a figure of speech," I said to Gregg, who shrugged.

Edmund lumbered downstairs as quickly as he could. For a man of his size and girth, he moved fast when he wanted to. He was back in two minutes and we were all outside.

"The Minnow's still hitched," Edmund said, "we'll take my car."

We piled into Edmund's car, Edmund and Dhani in the front, Gregg and I in back, and headed towards the marina.

We pulled up to the dock, the black truck was parked there, empty. The small yacht on which I had seen Brian Stone, the Cold-As-Ice bartender at Geoffrey's and Ian, on the deck talking, was still in its slip, floating quietly as the water of the Intracoastal lapped up along its sides.

"Back up!" I hissed to Edmund.

"What?" Edmund turned his head around to the back seat where Gregg and I sat and asked, "Why?"

"That black truck is trouble and we want to keep away from them if anyone's home on that boat."

Edmund backed up just as Ian came out of the cabin in time to see us pull away.

"We won't have much time," I said.

Edmund pulled up to the Harbor Master's shed and went inside. Dhani got behind the wheel and started backing the Minnow onto the launch.

"What're you doing?" Gregg asked.

"We've got to find that boat!" I said, more urgently than before.

"Not on your own! Aren't those dangerous people?"

"Of course they are, but we've got to find them! Just find them! If we can get them in sight until help arrives…" I let the thought hang in the air.

"And that would be… how, Stacey?" Gregg asked.

I fished in my bag. "Here, call Dan Gowan, Pompano Police," I said, handing Gregg Gowan's card. "Tell him you're a friend of mine."

"A friend? How do you know this cop?"

"Look, it's a long story. Hell, tell him you're my boyfriend," I said. Gregg smiled, just a touch, and I continued, "Tell him where we are, where we're going and what we're doing, he'll take care of the rest."

"…and I sit here and wait."

"Don't you have to go to work?"

"Hell with it," he said, and flipped open his

cellphone to leave a message for his job.

"Look," I was determined to find that boat. "Someone's got to wait for Gowan. It can't be me, don't you understand? My *friends* are on that boat."

Dhani piped up, "I'll wait for the cop. You two go with Edmund."

"You going to be okay?" I asked Dhani.

"Sure." He shrugged. "I'll be with the cop. How do I get in touch with him?"

Gregg handed Dhani the card. "You got your phone, Stacey?" Gregg asked me. I nodded. "Give it to Dhani."

"Give him yours, Gregg. I've got Vinny's and Geoffrey's number on mine." Also Gregg's and Sparky's, I thought.

Dhani pulled a flip phone out of his pocket and asked for my number.

Gregg hesitated for a second, and then gave it to him.

"So Dhani can call us, too," I said.

Edmund came out of the Harbor Master's shed, "We've got a fix on them. Harbor Master radioed them about some weather, I think they're headed to Bimini."

"There's weather?" I asked, rethinking my position in the Minnow on this chase.

Edmund grinned. "No, but it'll cost you fifty bucks when we get back. I paid the Harbor Master to say there's weather, and this is Florida. There's always weather." Edmund chuckled to himself.

"Never mind, here's your fifty." I pulled my stash from my pocket and handed a bill to Edmund.

Gregg whistled, "How much you got there, darlin'?"

"Enough," I snapped back.

"You're loaded!" Dhani said.

"It's my inheritance," I snapped again, lying. With the money I'd gotten from Vinny and Sparky's, I had a horse roll on me. And I was going for a dangerous trip on a boat? I threw the roll at Dhani who quickly pocketed my stash. "I want this when I get back. Now, let's unhitch this boat!"

We jumped out of the car and unhitched the Minnow. Edmund handed Gregg and I aboard off the dock. We got busy untying lines and loosening hasps. Dhani sat behind the wheel of Edmund's car, backing the Minnow into the water and off the trailer then pulled the trailer away from the launch.

In the second it took for the boat to come off the trailer, with Dhani pulling the trailer onto the sand and gravel parking lot, the large black truck drove up fast and smacked Edmund's car on the driver's side rear quarter panel. I couldn't see Dhani behind the wheel. The black truck backed up and, with a spray of rough sand and gravel from the marina lot, T-boned Edmund's car again. Square on the driver's side door. Dhani scrambled out the passenger door.

"Dhani! My car!" Edmund shouted and handed the wheel of the Minnow to Gregg. "Hold her steady."

Edmund popped out of the boat and hustled over to where the truck was wedged against his car. I'd never seen such a big guy move so fast. Edmund moved up next to the driver's side door and, keeping low, snatched open the truck door and pulled Ian out of the truck. Edmund stood the smaller man up and landed a roundhouse punch, which left Ian reeling in the parking lot. With no driver, the truck loosed itself from Edmund's car and rumbled off slowly. It finally smashed headlong into a telephone pole. The pole shook and snapped about a third of the way up and toppled towards Ian, who just started to get back on his feet. Edmund leapt aside as the crossbars and transformer box landed on Ian. There was a blinding flash and a smell like bacon frying. I saw Ian's astonished face for a second wreathed in blue-white flame, before looking away.

Edmund hustled back to the Minnow. "Now I can't leave. Dhani's got to call the cops. Can you handle this, Gregg?" Gregg nodded.

Sirens screamed in the background. Dhani ran up to us, rubbing a sprained wrist and shouting, "The Harbor Master must've called 9-1-1. Get out of here!"

I nodded and pulled the lanyard to start the motor. The Minnow's little outboard sputtered to life.

"Charts are in the locker!" Edmund hollered, as we pulled away from the launching ramp, barely audible above the Minnow's rackety engine. "Beer's still in the cooler!" That was clear.

I nodded and waved as Gregg headed forward, up the Intracoastal to the Hillsboro Inlet. The boat was small enough so we could get through without bridge openings, and we made pretty good time. Remembering my last outing, I raised the Bimini canvas top to give us some shade.

Gregg looked down at me fastening the last hasp of the top and reached his hand out to help me up. We stood together at the helm, the vast expanse of the Atlantic Ocean before us.

"This could be romantic," he said, "under different circumstances."

I lowered my eyes and gave him a hooded look. "Thanks. I'll make it official when we get back."

He nodded. "Get me the charts, sweet heart?"

"Sure, hon."

"It's just a figure of speech," he jibed.

"Not where you're concerned," I jibed back, shoving the charts at him.

"Take the wheel," he said. "You know how, right?"

"Yeppers," I said, remembering long lazy days at the fish camps, going out every now and then with one of the guides on a date. It would start off just fine; he, me and the boat. Then we'd fish a bit and pretty soon he'd go fishing for something else. One time I left a guy stuck smack in the middle of Lake Okeechobee with nothing but a life jacket when he tried to get fresher than I'd intended.

It didn't take Gregg long to view the charts against the Harbor Master's coordinates and get a fix on the Golden Girl.

I kept watch behind us, wondering when, or if, I would see the police or the Coast Guard. The police would be busy with the crime scene we'd fled and who knew if the Coast Guard would be notified of our absence, if ever. I mightily hoped we'd be reported.

Gregg's cellphone rang and he picked it out of his pocket, hit the answer button and said, "Hon, would you go get us a beer? I think we could both use a cold one after that," referring to the incident with Ian.

I nodded in agreement and went aft to grab a couple of cool brews from the cooler. Lite Brewski–ugh. Not my favorite, but would be cold and wet and more than welcome. I turned to go up and heard Gregg's voice on the cell call.

"She's with me. It's cool. We're under control."

My ears pricked up. I'd heard that before. This wasn't about any difficult cellphone customer. Gregg continued, "We're coming to you."

I froze in my tracks. Shit. The sonofabitch was a ringer. Vinny probably planted him to keep tabs on me, among other things. Suddenly, it was clear. What an idiot I'd been. I thought of last night and this morning. My stomach heaved. I wanted to scrub myself with a steel brush loaded with some good brown lye soap.

"Hon?" Gregg called. "I've never known you to be so slow about getting beers. Come on now, girl, get your pretty ass up here."

Still frozen, caught between rage and revulsion, I listened to the sound of Gregg's voice. There were way too many "Hons" and not enough sugar behind them to make me want to budge. But I didn't want him to know I'd heard him, so I kept my mouth shut, acted cool, and emerged from below, cold beers in hand.

"They cold?" he asked.

I nodded. He took one from me, popped it open and had a long, slow swallow. "Cold enough. Come here, hon." He held his arm out to me in a welcoming gesture.

I shook my head, "I got to pee."

"Now? Go do it off the end, hon. I'll slow down."

Off the end? He had to be joking. Anyways, we were too far from shore if I jumped overboard and swam for it. I headed aft and carefully positioned myself portside stern, hanging my butt off the back of the boat as if I were preparing to pee. Gregg gunned the boat.

I held on tight and didn't let the sudden jouncing motion over a wave toss me into the water.

"You bastard!" I yelled, barely audible over the noise of the Minnow's outboard and the crashing of the little boat over some waves.

"What's that hon?" Gregg said, and throttled up again.

My beer sloshed out of the can directly onto my tee shirt, right between my boobs. Gregg looked back at me from the wheel, grinning. His eyes weren't smiling, though; suddenly, they were sharp, watchful, and as cold as a cobra's. I felt a surge of fear; then anger welled up in me hotly. I wasn't giving him the satisfaction of playing his game. I kept quiet and suppressed a shudder. I held fast to the boat.

"You bastard!" I shouted at him, balling my fists. "I heard you!"

He gave me a long slow look and motioned me to come forward. I shook my head and he gunned the boat some more. I hoped the Minnow's old balky outboard would expire from such ruthless handling. But he was a Keys kid and knew just how far he could push an old boat.

The Minnow did not break down.

"What's the matter, hon?"

"Don't you 'hon' me, you bastard! Where are they?"

"Just ahead, hon," he motioned to the broad expanse of ocean towards a little speck of white on the horizon, "they're waiting for you."

I couldn't help myself and yelled, "You bastard!" It was all I could think of to say as the rage and hurt surged through me. I sat down and sulked in the stern of the Minnow. Then I felt a wave of gratitude. He probably wasn't going to kill me if he hadn't by now.

"Why?" I yelled, as he stood at the wheel, judging the crests of the waves for the roughest path through the ocean. "Why?" I yelled again.

He throttled down and turned back to look at me, "Why? It's all about the *money*, honey," giving me a slow smile and turning back to the wheel. "I get a nice chunk of change delivering you in one piece."

"And if I'm not in one piece?"

"It's payday when your body washes up on shore, hon."

"How did they get to you?" I yelled. "Was it all a lie?"

Gregg shrugged, "Maybe, maybe not. I don't know." He shook his head.

I had just been betrayed big time and I couldn't believe my questions, either. I chose that moment to just shut up. I knew if I sat around and thought about it I'd get good and pissed and I knew that would be no solution. I couldn't get pissed and I couldn't get moving. I had to keep cool.

I went forward and stood next to him. "How did they get to you?"

"I got to *you*, darlin'. Do you think you got your cellphone at my place by accident?"

I shook my head, "I could have gone anyplace. You're not the only cellphone store in the mall."

"But you didn't. Besides, if you did, they would've broke that phone and sent you to me. It just happened right the first time. But they would have found a way. They always do."

So, now it's 'darlin'? What happened to 'hon'?"

"Just a figure of speech, darlin'."

We trolled along at a more leisurely pace and, to passersby, we looked like a happy couple enjoying a day on the water. We passed an elderly couple in a sailboat. I thought about jumping up and down, frantically screaming for help. But Gregg must have read my mind, as he grabbed my elbow and twisted hard. I grimaced.

"Uh-uh, pretty lady. Just make nice and wave and make a pleasant smile to that old couple over there." He twisted harder and the pain shot up my arm.

I bared my teeth at him, not bothering to keep the hate and loathing out of my eyes. The couple waved brightly at us and tacked starboard, towards home and away from the Minnow.

"Smart girl, real smart." Gregg let go.

I seethed and rubbed my elbow. Gregg just grinned. I wondered if, as a kid, he got pleasure out of torturing stray kittens and other small animals. The random thought made me hate him even more.

"Darlin', sometime in the future, you might remember if something seems too good to be true, it probably is."

"Really?" I said archly. "You weren't that good. I've had better who didn't have to try so hard."

Gregg's grin became strained. He grabbed me by the waist and pinched much too hard. I stiffened and pulled away.

"Where you goin', girly-girl?"

"Can't go far, can I?"

He had to keep at least one hand on the wheel and shrugged, "Nope. Guess not." He let me resume my spot at the stern of the Minnow. His decidedly unpleasant look told me I'd scored a direct hit on his ego.

"You've got sand in you for sure," he said.

"It was all a lie." I looked down at my feet, ashamed I'd been such a sucker.

"Nope. I'm really from the Keys." Gregg added, "and I did like you, somewhat."

"But Tracey and Kat…" I drifted off.

"They're out there. On that boat. There's others there, too. It should be a nice party for you."

He pointed toward the Golden Girl, getting larger and identifiable as the yacht I'd seen that day coming in from my fishing trip with Edmund and Dhani, so long ago.

Gregg was in up to his teeth and I was pissed at myself for being so foolish. I thought of Tracey and Kat, the dead Lorikeet on the beach and Loretta. The former two, probably locked up in a cold, dark stateroom, the latter two wound up dead, in a cold morgue. To these guys, it didn't matter. It was just business, hon, all about the money. I thought about the blood money from Vinny in my stash and was almost sick. I thought about my fate. But just like my Daddy said: it was time for moving, not thinking, so I steeled myself and moved forward towards Gregg. I used my best come-hither look as we pulled up to the port side of the yacht. If I'd had a knife I would've filleted him like a Big-mouth Bass. The analogy of fish to man was enough to make me smile. We stood together under the Bimini top on the Minnow.

Gregg kept his face deliberately pleasant and bland. "That's more like it, pretty girl." He beckoned to me, "Come on darlin', time to party."

"Sure," I said sweetly, as I shoved my body as hard as I could against him sideways, knocking him away from the wheel and knocking the Minnow into the hard

357 • Tough Luck Lane

fiberglass side of the Golden Girl's hull. There was a loud thud and a crunch, but there wasn't much damage.

I went for a girls' last, best defense–kneeing him in the cojones, but he managed to grab my knee and twisted it upward and hard to one side. I stumbled and fell backward onto the floor mid-Minnow, butt side up. I yelped, kicked out and connected with my target, but it was too late. Gregg winced, but he wasn't incapacitated as I'd hoped. He dodged another kick and grabbed my foot, zoning in on the sore stubbed toe and twisted it hard. I yelped again and struggled like a beached tarpon.

Hearing the thud and the crunch, a face peered over the side of the yacht and saw us in the Minnow. I recognized Geoffrey. Vinny peered over the side as well, grinning like a caudillo presiding over a cockfight.

"Hey, stupid," Geoffrey called to Gregg. "Don't bruise the merchandise there."

Gregg let go and I stumbled to my feet, breathing hard. Gregg grinned at me like a towheaded farm boy fresh off a roll in the hay. I spat in Gregg's face.

I saw a large shark-gaffing hook descend over the side of the yacht as Gregg's grin vanished. The next second, I saw stars. A tent load of fireworks exploded in my skull as Gregg caught me on the jaw with a roundhouse swipe. I'd never been knocked out before, not even by Ed. It only lasts a few minutes, but it feels like eternity. And it hurt like hell.

Chapter Twenty-Four

I shook the cobwebs out of my head and woke up to see my wrists tied above my head and my ankles tied together below. I flipped around in the bottom of the Minnow, knowing how fish feel when they're caught.

"Hello, the boat!" Gregg called.

"She's a handful, isn't she?" Geoffrey called back. The large gaff was lowered down to Gregg. "You didn't mess her up too much, did you? I told you to watch it."

"Nothing a little lipstick and makeup won't cure," Gregg grabbed the gaff.

Vinny called down, "You'd better be right. Easy, now, just hang her on the hook."

Gregg slipped the gaff between my legs and positioned it on the rope. He sliced himself on the barb and swore loudly. I grinned at him and tried to squirm out of the way.

"Heave ho!" he yelled. I twisted in his grasp. "I wouldn't do that, hon," he added. "That barbed hook's sharp and it's rusty," showing me a bloody thumb.

"I hope it rots and falls off, you fucker," I spat at him.

Two crewmen flanked Geoffrey and threw some lines down to Gregg. "Hold her steady, we've got this one."

Gregg watched them haul me up the side of the yacht. "Bye-bye baby." He called and blew me a kiss.

"Fuck you!" I yelled. "Cocksucker!"

Geoffrey smiled. "I like 'em feisty. She'll be a lot of fun. Here, mac, this is to you!" He threw down a fat envelope similar to the many I'd collected over the past few weeks and it landed with a plop in the middle of the Minnow. Tucking the envelope in his shirt, Gregg cast off without a backward glance as he revved the engine and roared into the distance. The Minnow was nothing but a bobbling blot on the ocean's rolling swells.

"Dickweed!" I yelled, watching the Minnow recede in the distance as I was hauled onboard upside-down. I doubt if he heard me.

I held perfectly still, not wanting to fall off the gaff and drown. The crew hauled up the slack lines faster than I was being pulled aboard.

Finally, they had me over the side and stood me up. I was face to face with Geoffrey, a smirk on his weasel-like face. His right hand blithely stroked his cheesy little moustache and with mock-tenderness, he went to touch my face. I pulled my face back.

"Shit," I spat at him.

My hands and ankles bound together, two crewmen stood next to me, holding me up, one on each side. I tried brushing them off like the cockroaches they were, but they held fast and grabbed me under the arms, my feet barely touched the ground.

Geoffrey deliberately turned his back on me and, with a dismissive wave of his right arm, instructed the men to put me below, "…with the others."

I struggled as much as possible to get out of their grip, but they upended me and carried me through the salon and down the stairs, casually tossing me into one of the staterooms.

The room was dim. Sunlight filtered through a small, tightly latched porthole just above a small table. My eyes adjusted to the light and I saw I wasn't alone. Someone was lying on the bed. The stateroom was basically all a big, round bed, with teak drawers custom built into the walls. There was a teak door, which I presumed led to the head. Pretty fancy. While this probably wasn't the master suite, it was certainly roomy enough for my companion and me.

The form on the bed groaned and rolled. I hobbled close to get a look at my roommate. It was Tracey.

She looked up at me, her eyes glassy and vague. Someone had worked her over pretty good; her face was bruised and swollen. She was clad in only bra and panties and reeked of cheap booze. "Stacey? Is that you?" she whispered blearily.

I hopped the two feet to the bed and tried to sit down. It was difficult to maneuver, with my hands bound behind me and my ankles tied together but I managed.

"Yes, Tracey, it's me–oh, my God."

The yacht rolled.

"Can you untie me? Please?" I asked, holding my hands backward as far as my shoulders would allow.

Tracey flopped back on the bed. "I'm so tired," she mumbled.

"Tracey! Tracey! Wake up!"

Tracey groaned again and rolled away from me. I struggled to get up and hopped over to where I could look her in the face.

"Tracey! Look! Wake the fuck up! I think help's coming, but you've got to help me get untied!"

"Can't," she mumbled, "so tired… spinny…sleep." Tracey tried to roll again, but came up against the headboard. She cracked her eyes a little and her gaze tried to settle on me, but she was having a very hard time focusing.

"Tracey! Come on!" I bounced up and down on the bed, trying to get a response out of her. "Untie me!"

She struggled up to a half-seated position, bent from the waist up and tried to look levelly at me. I half-giggled, because, suddenly, she looked very much like the Captain getting up from his chaise. I clamped my jaw down on another giggle and forced as much urgency into my voice as I could.

"Tracey! I'm serious!"

"You don't sound seros. Wharry laffin' at?" Tracey grinned.

"Tracey! Get it together! Just untie my hands and I'll help get you fixed up!"

"Can't," Tracey sighed. "Sleep," Tracey flopped back down.

"Untie me! Get your ass up and help me! Then I'll help you."

"A'ight. A 'ight. Gimme sec." With a groan, Tracey forced herself upright. The effort almost jounced me off the bed.

"Whoa! If I hit the floor, I'll never get up! C'mon, girl! The ropes! Untie them!"

I scootched over to where she could reach my hands. She fumbled with the ropes enough to get them loose and I worked my hands free. I bent down to untie my ankles and she flopped back on the bed.

"Thass 'nuff," she mumbled.

I stood back up and bent over her. "You smell like a liquor store. What did they do to you?"

"Dunno," Tracey said. "Made me drink. Drink 'til I was pie-eyed. Then drink some more. When I wouldn't, they hit me."

I lifted one of her eyelids up, wide open and took a look. She had the out of focus look of someone on a bender. Her lips were dry and caked with blood.

Running some cool water at the small sink in the head, I wet down a washcloth and drew a glass of water. I went in the medicine chest and found a package Ipecac. It was expired, but what the hell, I dumped some in the glass anyway.

Bringing the wet washcloth and glass of water with Ipecac to Tracey, I swabbed her face and tried to force some water into her. She took a little and spit it back up.

"More!" I said, holding the glass to her lips.

"No more," she mumbled and rolled back over.

I moved swiftly to the other side of the bed and rolled her on her side.

"Sit up!" I snapped. Putting the half-empty glass down on a recessed nook in the beds' headboard, I grabbed her by the shoulders and sat her up. She felt like a Raggedy Ann doll, all floppy limbs.

"Ow!" she cried, "whasha doon?"

"Sit the fuck up." I tried to sound brisk and motherly, brooking no nonsense.

"*Shut* the fuck up!" Tracey shot back mushily.

"No. Drink this," I said and handed her the glass.

She barely took it, but looked at it, brought it up to her nose, and handed it back to me.

"Vokka."

"Yes, that's right. The best on the boat. Drink."

She looked at me blearily, skeptically, then took the glass.

"Firsty," she said and greedily drank it down. "More," she said and handed the glass back to me.

I said a silent prayer of relief. "You got it, babe. As much as you want." I sped to the head to get more water, plain this time, and plenty of it.

I looked around for an ice bucket or pitcher, but was shit out of luck. Tracey drank down three glasses of water. I ran for more then felt the engines rumble under my feet as the yacht started to move.

"Tracey, we're moving again."

"Yeah, we are." I handed her another glass of water, but she waved it away. "No more."

"Yeah, more. Drink."

She drank. I got more water. The yacht lurched in the waves.

"Frow up," Tracey said as she finished her sixth tumbler of water. "I'm gonna frow up." And she made good her promise on the bed's rose-patterned silk sheets.

"Oops!" she said and tried to stumble to her feet. "Gotta use baffroom."

I helped stand her up and half-walked, half-dragged her the three feet to the head. We went through this happy dance about three or four times. Finally her eyes started to clear.

"Enough! Stacey! Enough." And I knew it was.

"Stay right there," I said, rather stupidly.

"Where'm I gonna go?" she laughed weakly.

I balled up the puke-stained bed sheets thinking they must've cost a stinking mint and now they were just a stinking mess. I threw the filthy sheets in the corner with no regard for housekeeping.

"You finished being sick, Tracey?"

"Think so." She tried to unsteadily stand up in the head.

"Just a minute, hon." She looked up at me from her pitiful position on the floor. I went around and helped her stand up and make it to the bed.

"No sheets?"

"You took care of that, Tracey. They're a real mess."

Tracey smiled, good and slow through the bruises and swelling of her face. "Good."

"Yeah, good. Now sit down here and I'm going to find you something to wear," and I started pulling the beautiful custom teak drawer system apart, tossing the place until I found a tee shirt and shorts with the ship's logo on them.

"Here, put these on," I said and found a matching pair for myself. "We've got to change costume anyway."

Tracey looked up. The ceiling was mirrored. She saw herself for what was probably the first time and wailed, "My face! Look at my *face*!"

"Yeah, I know, I saw you first. Let me take a look."

She leveled a skeptically questioning glance at me. "So?"

"Nothin' that won't heal, hon. No cuts. Smile." Tracey complied painfully. "No teeth missing. What happened?"

"They wanted to know where they could find you. I didn't know."

"Well, they found me, all right, and you, too."

Other than a few minor, but ugly, bruises and some rope-burns on my wrists and ankles, I was in pretty good shape. My toe still hurt, but I was able to ignore it.

"Shoes?" Tracey asked.

"We're on a boat, hon. Barefoot's no big deal."

She shrugged. "Now what?"

"Can you stand up on your own?"

She shrugged.

"Try."

She tried, and fell back on the bed.

"Try again."

She tried again and shakily kept upright. She looked like a very small, very shaky, newborn giraffe who just fell six feet from mommy's womb to be born.

"Steady on, Tigger." I held her steady as she got her bearings. She put her arms out to steady herself and gauge her balance.

"Okay, I'm standing. Now what?"

"We find a way out."

She snorted. "Good luck."

I tried the door to the stateroom and it swung open easily.

"Dumb fucks," I muttered, and got a feeble smile out of Tracey.

I looked left and right and the corridor was clear. I motioned to Tracey to come forward and we tiptoed out of the room.

"I sure feel sorry for their maid," she said.

"Shush," I whispered.

There was a door down the corridor that led to a narrow companionway around the staterooms.

"We should be okay, they can't see us from up there," Tracey said, and pointed upwards. "I used to clean these for a living, remember?"

I nodded and motioned her to hush. I tried to decide on a direction and, getting my bearings, pointed aft. Tracey nodded and we crept around the deck towards the back of the yacht. We kept out of sight of anyone in the salon or on the afterdeck.

There was a clear, empty side on the deck with no windows, so I hunkered down and motioned Tracey to do the same. She shrugged and complied quietly, and we sat with our knees tucked under our chins, watching the water pass us by.

"I think we're starboard," Tracey whispered. "On the right side of the boat."

"Thanks," I said drily. "How do you feel?"

"Woozy."

"You gonna throw up?" I asked, and Tracey shook her head no. "Do you know anything about what's going on here?"

Tracey focused her eyes out on the horizon. The glazed, trancelike look faded from her eyes. She looked more like herself. She glanced sideways at me and smiled wanly. "I think they're gonna sell us."

I nodded impatiently. "That much I figured out, Trace. Do you know where? Who to?"

Tracey shook her head again, "I think it happens in the middle of the ocean. Soon."

I motioned her to crawl forward with me. "Who else is here?"

"I don't know who, but I'm pretty sure there are other girls onboard."

I softly whispered Geoffrey and Vinny were

onboard and that Gregg had betrayed me.

"I'm sorry," Tracey said. I shrugged as if it were not important. It wasn't.

Footsteps sounded above us. We flattened ourselves back against the side of the boat, tucking in our legs.

"Do you think they know we're out of there?"

Tracey shrugged. "Probably not. They'd be raising hell if they thought we were roaming around, loose."

I half-stood and crept forward again. We passed the door into the corridor of the boat and continued forward. Another porthole. I ducked beneath it and Tracey took the other side. We snuck a peek and saw Dianna, the ex-Mrs. Vinny, seated at a glass-topped table in a much larger stateroom, watching over several girls. She was dressed in something slinky and black. Her legs were casually crossed, revealing some cheap-looking, chunky black platform sandals. Two of the girls were sitting on the bed, a deck of cards between them, cocktail glasses in hand. Another girl, bone thin, was lying on the bed. It looked like Kat, but I couldn't be certain. She looked in about the same shape as Tracey when I found her, perhaps a bit worse. Dianna looked up and out the porthole. I ducked aside, barely in time, and Tracey snuck a peep through her side of the porthole.

"She's standing up. I think she heard you," Tracey said, ducking back and whispering to me.

We waited an uneasily long moment, and then took another cautious glance inside. Dianna was taking a hard look around the room and, seeing everything was in order with her charges, walked up to the porthole we flanked and looked left, right, then out over the water. She turned on her heel and walked out the door to the inside passage.

"Quick!" Tracey said, "There's one more door forward."

I shook my head and stood in her way. "No, we stay put."

"She's going to find us missing, anyway. We just can't leave them there."

"I know," I said, "but if she comes back…"

"We're in deep shit, anyway, Stacey," Tracey said. "Come on."

I crept forward and found the door. We carefully opened it and slid inside, but for all our care, the door betrayed us. The yacht rolled to one side on a particularly large swell, causing the door to slam shut with a sound like a pistol shot.

"Gotta move now!" I said as we raced toward the stateroom Dianna had left. There was no one in the passage. We opened the door and motioned the girls out. Fortunately, they had the presence of mind to realize this was a rescue mission and they came quickly, obeyed our signals to be quiet, and Tracey herded them out to the starboard deck. I was stuck in the stateroom with Kat.

Bony arms and legs draped themselves around me as I struggled to get her up. I hobbled her out to the corridor, but that was as far as we got.

Dianna stormed up the passage, her brittle features pale with rage.

"You!" she screamed at me, pointing a long red fingernail in my direction. "Stop!"

"No way lady! Fuck off!" I yelled back at her and stumbled along with the bedraggled Kat, half holding, half dragging her forward in the corridor, hoping to reach the door.

Dianna couldn't run fast enough in her platform sandals to catch us. She tripped over her slinky black skirt in the passage and fell, headlong, on the deck.

Kat, in worse shape than Tracey, instantly sobered up once she got a whiff of fresh air. She was banged up pretty good, but like Tracey, nothing that wouldn't heal in time.

"Forward! Forward!" Tracey yelled. "We've got to

get up and out!"

I thought maybe she knew where a lifeboat was stashed or something that would get us off this scow.

I glanced down at Dianna, on the deck, struggling to get up.

"Hey, lady," I yelled at Dianna, "anyone ever tell you you've got lousy taste in shoes?"

Dianna sputtered with fury and ripped the platforms off her feet. As she clumsily struggled to her feet, she fixed me with a red-eyed glare of raw hatred.

"Why you…" she started after me and Kat. "I'll fucking kill you!" she screamed.

Then Geoffrey appeared at the aft end of the corridor. His eyes widened then went small with disgust. "You dumb pussy, you could fuck up a wet dream," he cursed at Dianna as he pulled an automatic from inside his jacket.

"Fuck you!" Dianna screamed at Geoffrey. "You don't know shit, cocksucker! You should have tied them both up, you moron!"

"You goddamn uppity bitch," Geoffrey screamed. "You think you're running the show? You work for me, I run the show! Me!"

"Oh, shit, he's got a gun," I said, and started bundling the girls up on deck. "Go! Go!" I urged, and even Kat picked up the pace on her own. I wedged my body tight against the passage wall, and waited as the yacht rolled yet again.

"Bullshit!" Dianna screamed back. "You work for Vinny! He runs the show and I help him run it."

"Fuck you!" Geoffrey screeched.

Dianna wobbled in the hall and turned to face Geoffrey. Her eyes bulged as she saw the gun. "You stupid prick!" she screeched.

"Get out of the way, bitch!" Geoffrey screamed. Dianna ran towards me.

I turned and ran the few feet remaining in the passage.

A shot roared through the corridor of the boat below and a single, strangling scream ended in a pained gurgle. Something wet and sticky hit my back and the backs of my legs, but I hustled my butt up on deck myself. I turned to see Geoffrey leveling his automatic at me while Dianna slithered to the floor, an astonished, pained look on her face. Geoffrey dropped his gun down by his side and watched his boss's ex-wife expire in a pool of her own blood in the passage.

I skittered up through a hatch and found Kat, the girls, and Tracey had already emerged on deck, face to face with Vinny and the captain on the bridge. Tracey looked at the captain with sheer loathing. I mouthed a silent "*Oh...*"

Geoffrey popped out of the hole from which we emerged, brandishing his gun. The yacht lurched forward, tossing Geoffrey below. Clearly, Geoffrey had never gained his sea legs.

"Dumb shit," Vinny bellowed, motioning a couple crewmen towards Geoffrey. "Couldn't pick I winner in a one-horse race."

I gathered Tracey, myself, Kat, and the other ladies together and herded everyone toward the amidships rail. I heard the whine of propellers long before I spotted the bright red Coast Guard Search and Rescue helicopter. There was only one way out.

"Geronimo!" I yelled, facing the twenty-foot drop into the ocean, then stopped dead in my tracks as a gunshot cracked in the broad daylight and a bullet whizzed by my head like a very hot, nasty bee.

The helicopter hovered above the boat. "Stop your engines and put down your weapons," a harsh, metallic voice boomed overhead. Another shot rang out and the helicopter lifted itself high and out of gunshot range. I could see the captain on the bridge prepare to shut down the engines, but Vinny yanked him back and took the wheel himself. The crewmen were running all over the place, waving their hands in surrender.

Vinny gunned the boat as Geoffrey, freshly emerged from the hatch, unloaded his automatic at the helicopter, his face beet-red as he screamed obscenities between shots.

A police cutter pulled up alongside to port and threw lines to prepare to board the boat.

Geoffrey loaded another clip into his gun and prepared to fire at the cutter, but the helicopter's speaker blared again, "This is your final warning. Stop your engines and put down your weapons." Watching Geoffrey as he pointed his gun at a boat bristling with armed men and high-caliber weapons, I reflected that Dianna's assessment of Geoffrey was correct. He was, undoubtedly, a fucking idiot.

The loudspeaker from the boat bleated, "This is the Broward Sheriff's Office, prepare to be boarded! Stop your engines! Put down your weapons!"

Vinny pulled a gun from his jacket and blasted out the window of the flying bridge. Apparently, this business was not top-heavy with geniuses.

A burst of 50-millimeter rounds smashed into the bridge and took off the top of it with a mighty explosion. Pieces of the captain, Vinny, and the wheel went flying off the starboard side into the water.

Several small rubber boats were circling the yacht out of range, but coming ever closer. I was hoping for jumping proximity to one of those suckers.

Geoffrey had crawled around from the deck and crept towards amidships. He leveled his handgun at the bunch of us. "Drop your weapon!" the helicopter's loudspeaker blared. The crew had already jumped ship and the yacht was floundering without a steady hand to steer her.

Deciding it was time to go, I motioned the girls to scatter and jump. Geoffrey tried to get a bead on any one of us and could not. He fired. He missed. We jumped. The chopper lowered and let go another 50-millimeter burst at the yacht. Several of them caught Geoffrey and the deck of the yacht looked like a slaughterhouse.

We swam like hell for those little rubber boats. I had Tracey with me and the others seemed to be helping Kat. The little rubber boats edged closer to us and the BSO cutter edged away from the yacht. Another whooshing burst of 50-millimeter rounds hit the yacht, striking the fuel tank.

We clambered aboard the small rubber boats. They backed off in a hurry, circling around the Coast Guard cutter.

At that moment, the yacht was engulfed in a house-sized fireball and was sucked down by the sea in about thirty seconds, or so it seemed. Shit seemed to fall from the sky long after the yacht had sunk, but I knew it was a trick of perception. The shit fell first, then the yacht sunk. It was that simple.

Dazedly, I looked over at Tracey, leaning against the side of the inflatable boat. There were three other inflatables bobbing in the water and a maelstrom of churning water and debris where the yacht used to be. I looked over at the other boats and saw the other girls and Kat. I waved. The girls waved back exuberantly. Kat threw me an ironic salute.

The Golden Girl's crew was being handed up a rope ladder onto the cutter and the BSO cops took them into custody, carefully handcuffing each one to another. As they were all cuffed together, someone else put a rough gray blanket around my shoulders. It felt soft as feather down to me. A steaming hot mug of coffee was handed to me, and I wondered how the hell they managed all that comfort in a little rubber boat. I took the coffee gratefully and shrugged.

Tracey was enjoying similar comforts and we watched all the action around us.

The bright red helicopter waggled at us and flew off. The inflatables made for the cutter. My entrée onto the cutter was much more graceful than my entrance onto the yacht, even though I was hauled up in a sling made of crisscrossed canvas straps. If it had been a plastic sand bucket, I couldn't have cared less. Tracey, Kat, and the rest were hauled up in similar fashion and given a most gracious welcome aboard.

We sat on the deck of the cutter, huddled in our blankets as more steaming coffee was poured. Perhaps the caffeine was supposed to keep us alert. The hot steaming cup felt wonderful in my hands. I looked over my cup at Tracey and smiled. She burped and covered her mouth with a sheepish grin. I grinned back.

"You could use a drink," she said to me.

"Booze?" I said with a shudder. "This is just fine," I replied. I lifted my coffee up to her and we toasted each other.

Dan Gowan came over to us just as the last of the rubber boats was deflated and stowed on the cutter. The CG crew was lining up for coffee and grub. They seemed to disdain the policemen and kept to themselves.

"You guys hungry?" Gowan asked. We shook our heads. "I'll need to take your statements," he said. We nodded assent.

He nodded back and walked off, leaving us alone to watch the sunset together as the cutter headed west, to port, to home. When we got into port, the Harbor Master was waiting for us with softer blankets and more hot coffee. The mess from Ian had been cleaned up and phone and power crews were repairing the damage. Dhani and Edmund drove up in Dhani's big black truck. Kat and the other girls, whose names were Debbie, Dee, and Delores, I later learned, also waitresses at Geoffrey's, were huddled together keeping a careful watch over Kat.

Gowan took over the Harbor Master's office as each of us filed in and gave our statements. At the end, it was just me, Tracey, and Kat. Debbie, Dee, and Delores opted for elsewhere and I couldn't blame them.

Dhani and Edmund waited outside. As I emerged, Edmund threw a beach towel over my shoulders.

"You're a mess!" he said, "Get rid of that shirt when we get back. Outside, okay?"

I remembered why my shirt was a mess and nodded. Edmund gallantly handed us into the back of Dhani's truck bed and we headed the few blocks back to the Compound.

Chapter Twenty-Five

It was as if nothing had changed, but everything was different, somehow. I stripped to my bra and panties and hastily disposed of the borrowed yacht shirt and shorts in the same garbage can where I had trashed my Geoffrey's uniform. Tracey and Kat did the same with their clothes as Dhani and Edmund hosed out the inside of Dhani's truck bed.

I had plenty of clothes (and shoes!) for all of us, and we took turns in the shower and ransacking the closet. The bras and panties were history as well and we discreetly wrapped them in a plastic bag and gave them a decent burial in the garbage can.

I popped a beer, Kat did the same, and Tracey scrounged in my mini-fridge and came up with a Coke for herself. We were freshly showered and perfumed to emerge into the company of the Compound. The Captain reclined on the chaise, nursing a beer and asked me if I'd break out some of the "good stuff." I said maybe later and headed to the table in the center of the courtyard to sit with the girls, Edmund and Dhani.

The Minnow was home and looked broken-hearted. I later learned they nabbed Gregg and The Minnow just offshore outside of Hillsboro Inlet. I was sad, but not sorry.

"So," started Dhani, very matter-of-factly, "how was your day?" and we all roared.

Proceeding to enjoy one hell of a good buzz, Edmund called from his apartment, "I don't suppose you're in the mood for fresh fish tonight, ladies?" then trundled out of his bungalow with three of the biggest, juiciest porterhouse steaks this side of Kansas City.

"So, that's for us, what're you going to have?" the skinny Kat asked. Edmund shrugged and brought out two more steaks. We feasted and hung out until dawn broke.

As the purple hour was emerging, Tracey excused herself to go get ready for work. She was sure she was going to be "in the shit" with Lou, as she put it. Kat, who lived a couple blocks over, elected to walk with her, and planned on sleeping until noon next Tuesday.

I hung with Edmund and Dhani who had to be at work by seven.

"So, now what, Stacey?" Dhani asked me.

I shrugged. "Guess I'll go to work myself. I'm probably in the shit, too. I was supposed to cover last night."

Dhani rolled his eyes skyward and headed home to get ready to face his day.

"Want coffee?" he asked. I shook my head no and went to my bungalow to lie down for a few hours, to rest if not sleep, before I had to go in, with Tigger slippers safely underbed.

I woke up around ten, and headed to Dana's to check on Tracey. She was there, and very sparky for someone who'd just been up until dawn, never mind the day before the morning after. With a wink and a click, she got out a fresh cup of coffee for me and set down a warm muffin.

"How're ya doon, chicky-dee?" she asked.

"I'm okay, thanks–how are you?"

"I'm okay," she said and I believed her. Only the faintest purple was showing under her makeup and that could have been from a bad night's sleep to an untrained eye.

"How's Kat?"

"She's taking a couple days off, I think she'll be fine," Tracey said.

I finished my muffin and coffee and headed to Sparky's. Little Ricky was there, Big Rick, too.

"Hey, Lucy!" Little Rick said in a very phony Hispanic accent. "You got some 'splainin' to do!"

"Quit stealing my lines," I quipped at him, "Morning, Sir." I nodded to the boss.

"We heard what happened last night, are you okay?" Big Rick said, and put out his hand for a shake.

"Oh, no! Not again!" I pulled back.

"She's on to me, fellow," Big Rick said to Little Ricky. "Now what am I going to do?"

We laughed. "I'm not in deep doo-doo with you two?"

"Well, not with me," Big Rick said, "this nice guy here covered for you last night."

I looked at Little Ricky who was nodding and grinning at me like a monkey with a drum.

"Yeah, but that doesn't mean I owe you," I admonished Little Ricky and said a prayer to the Gods for him.

Little Ricky just shrugged and started filling the sinks.

Walking home after work, I passed by Pizzzazzz and Dana's, long closed. I looked out over the water of the Intracoastal and saw the small boat where Cold-As-Ice and Ian had been standing, watching me what seemed an age ago. Cold-As-Ice was on deck, mopping, and gave me a very level, very cold stare.

As I turned my back on him, I almost tripped on Dan Gowan in the shadows.

"Geoffrey's is closed, you know," he said.

"I didn't know. I work at Sparky's," I replied.

"We need to talk," he said.

"And maybe someday we will," I replied and headed home to my bungalow in the Compound.

About Lois Crockett

A self-styled "native Floridian by marriage", Lois Crockett was born in New York City and crossed the Hudson River in her baby carriage to grow up in suburban northern New Jersey. A Jersey Girl with a tropical twist, she is living happily ever after with her husband, John, a musician and their calico cat Weeble in south Florida.

Crockett's varied career has included bartending, a broadcasting career encompassing news casting/journalism, radio and club DJ and engineering for radio stations and nightclubs, high-level administrative positions even a Vice-Presidency or two.

Tough Luck Lane is Crockett's debut novel and she writes for those who love a good story with action, danger and even a body here and there.

www.ingramcontent.com/pod-product-compliance
Lightning Source LLC
Chambersburg PA
CBHW060928030726
47503CB00003B/511

* 9 7 8 1 6 2 5 2 6 5 2 3 4 *